P9-CNI-098

such a pretty face

Books by Cathy Lamb

JULIA'S CHOCOLATES

THE LAST TIME I WAS ME

HENRY'S SISTERS

SUCH A PRETTY FACE

Published by Kensington Publishing Corporation

such a pretty face

CATHY LAMB

KENSINGTON BOOKS
www.kensingtonbooks.com

KENSINGTON BOOKS are published by

Kensington Publishing Corp.
119 West 40th Street
New York, NY 10018

Copyright © 2010 by Cathy Lamb

All rights reserved. No part of this book may be reproduced in any form or by any means without the prior written consent of the Publisher, excepting brief quotes used in reviews.

All Kensington titles, imprints, and distributed lines are available at special quantity discounts for bulk purchases for sales promotion, premiums, fund-raising, educational, or institutional use.

Special book excerpts or customized printings can also be created to fit specific needs. For details, write or phone the office of the Kensington Special Sales Manager: Kensington Publishing Corp., 119 West 40th Street, New York, NY 10018. Attn. Special Sales Department. Phone: 1-800-221-2647.

Kensington and the K logo Reg. U.S. Pat. & TM Off.

ISBN-13: 978-0-7582-2955-7
ISBN-10: 0-7582-2955-0

First Kensington Trade Paperback Printing: August 2010
10 9 8 7 6 5 4 3 2

Printed in the United States of America

For Janelle

Prologue

∽

Ashville, Oregon—1980

I know when it started.

It was June 14th, two days after my tenth birthday. An eerie red-gold haze enshrouded the moon. Frothing gray and black clouds drifted across it, as if they were trying to hide its evilness, but couldn't quite overpower that glowing white light.

I noticed the moon as we sped toward the river, our car careening back and forth over the yellow lines as she chanted and I clung to my terrified sister.

The rain drizzled down through the darkness, stopped, then pounded the top of the car, as if millions of tiny black cannonballs had been released from the bag of the devil himself.

"Momma, stop!" I cried as she barreled through a red light.

But she couldn't hear me, not with the other voices clamoring in her head. She whispered, she raged, she yelled at her hallucinations. "Get out of here, Punk. This isn't about you. I'm not getting tied down to that chair again! You won't put your tentacles and ropes on me!"

I tried the other name. "Helen! Can you hear me, Helen?" She didn't respond, smashing her floppy yellow hat down on her head with both hands.

I realized, almost ill with panic, that the voices had won. It had been a long, soul-crushing battle, but I tried to save us anyhow. There was nothing else left to do. "There's no chair! I'll tell

Punk to leave and take the tentacles and ropes with him. I'll get him for you!"

"Punk is bad; he's chasing us with his red eyes and he won't let us go. I'll save you, girl kid!"

We swerved again, snaking all over the road, barely missing a truck.

"I scared, Stevie, I scared," my sister whimpered, her little face tucked into my neck. She smelled of soap and lemon shampoo, her fingers sticky from an orange Popsicle.

I was scared, too—so scared my brain felt as if it were rattling in my head, my knees knocking together. "It's okay, Sunshine. Grandma and Grandpa will be here soon."

But I knew it wasn't going to be soon enough.

I knew that.

We whipped around a corner and skidded onto a one-lane, wood bridge. Helen slammed on the brakes; the car fishtailed, and we crashed into the rail. She scrambled out, swearing at the "spying, bad Punk," then wrenched open our door and tried to yank us out of the car. Sunshine clutched me, screaming, as I gripped the seat, trying to save us both, my charm bracelet cutting into my skin. When Helen grabbed my heels and my hands lost their white-knuckled grip, I grabbed the door handle, then the door.

But she was strong—the voices made her stronger—and my fingers were pried away, one by one, Sunshine clinging to my waist as she shook with fear. Helen half dragged, half carried us to the rail as the boiling clouds parted and that strange moon mocked us in the distance, the only witness to our dance with death.

She had wrapped tin foil around the waist of her black dress, and it ripped as we fought her, as we scratched and shrieked. She was wearing her best black heels, and they tapped on the wood of the bridge, the black line up her nylons perfectly straight, which was so unusual, so surreal, it scared me more than anything else.

"Now you've made Command Center mad!" Helen yelled, wrestling us over to the rail. "Don't destroy the communications!"

We pleaded, we tried to run, and she punched both of us in the face, shooting us backward onto the bridge. "Shut up, girl kid! Shut up, Trash Heap!" She had never done that to us before, and it stunned me into silence, into obedience, for one shattered moment. "They're spying on us! They can see *everything!*"

Dizziness sent my mind into a whirl and I wrapped my arms around Sunshine, who was gasping with fright and bleeding. Helen ripped us apart, and I knew that what was left of my momma, if there was anything gentle and kind left in her, was way, way back, at the end of a labyrinth of tunnels in her troubled mind, crisscrossing the lines of insanity.

Her arms banded across my chest and waist as heavy raindrops hit me, the wind lifting my skirt up. I didn't recognize the raw, terrified scream that tore from my throat as I squeezed her neck and bony shoulders with my arms, my tears mixing with the rain, her floppy yellow hat flying off into the wind.

"No, Momma, don't," I begged. "Please, Momma! Stop!"

"Leave us alone, Punk," she commanded the moon. "You can't read my mind anymore. You're done. It's all done. Take Command Center with you down to hell."

She heaved my struggling body up on the rail and briefly held me close, rocking me like a baby, then kissed me on the lips. I saw Sunshine fight to stand up, blood streaming from her head. She tugged on our mother's arms, kicked her shins. "I hate you! I hate you! Let go of Stevie! Let go of sister!"

Her words flew into the churning sky, swirled around the moon, and then they were gone, making no impact on our mother.

"I am saving you," Helen yelled at me, the stormy wind whipping her blond hair around her face. "I am saving you from *them*." Then she dropped her head back and said, her voice edgy and guttural, "Save yourself. Do not save *it*. Don't save that Trash Heap." She shoved me over the rail of the bridge, then yanked my clinging hands from around her neck, our fingertips the last to touch before I tumbled and somersaulted into the rushing river.

It was freezing cold and pitch black, the water wrapping me up tight as I plunged through the silent darkness. My feet never hit, and I paddled to the top, choking, sputtering, knowing Sunshine would soon join me.

I have to save her. I have to save Sunshine.

I fought against the water as the current swirled me away, waves splashing against my face, surrounding my body like a wet vice, my head still reeling from pain. I twisted in the river's grasp and saw Sunshine, her pink dress billowing out like a bell as she was thrown over the rail into the murkiness of the river. Her cry, high and thin, echoed under the bridge.

I swam toward her, my arms pinwheeling as hard as I could, but I was panicking, gasping for breath, the water dragging me away, my black hair covering my face.

Between the shifting shadows I saw Helen standing on the rail of the bridge, arms outstretched, head back. The red-gold haze parted and the moonlight illuminated her slim form. I couldn't hear her, but I knew she was singing and I knew what song it was.

In a remote corner of my mind I noted her outfit again as she teetered on the rail. She was wearing her black cocktail dress, her best black heels, and her pearls. She got dressed up to kill us, I thought, as another wave swamped me. *She got dressed up to kill us.*

She curved her body, palms together over her head, then dove into the choppy water. I never saw her come up again. They did, however, find her best black heels later. Downriver.

I saw the pink dress but not for very long, as another current came, perhaps the sister current to mine, and swept Sunshine away. I heard her terror, I heard her sobbing my name, I hollered back at her, told her I was coming, I promised I would save her—but in the inky blackness, fighting off the chill of the water and the swirling waves, *I lost her.*

I heard her death in the rigid silence as soon my ragged voice was the only one left in that tragic, shattered night.

I have not saved her.

I have not saved my sister.

She is gone because of me.

Under that moon with the eerie red-gold haze and those frothing clouds, that's where it all began.

I started inhaling food the next day. Mountains of it.

It continued for more than two decades.

And the song my momma was singing?

It was "Amazing Grace."

My momma, after throwing her two daughters off a bridge, was singing "Amazing Grace."

1

Portland, Oregon—2005

I am going to plant a garden this summer.

With the exception of two pink cherry trees, one white cherry tree, and one pink tulip tree, all huge, I have a barren, dry backyard and I'm tired of looking at it. I almost see it as a metaphor for my whole life, and I think if I can fix this, I can fix my life. Simplistic, silly, I know, but I can't get past it.

So I'm going to garden even if my hands shake as if there are live circuits inside of them and a floppy yellow hat dances ominously through my mind.

I'm going to build upraised beds, a whole bunch of them, and fill them with tomatoes, squash, zucchini, radishes, lettuce, carrots, peas, and beans. But not corn.

I'm not emotionally able to do corn yet—too many memories—but I am going to plant marigolds around the borders, and pink and purple petunias, rose bushes and clematis and grapevines.

I'm going to stick two small crosses at the back fence, but not for who you think. I'm going to build a grape arbor with a deck beneath it, and then I'm going to add a table so I can paint there, as I used to, before my memories took that away. I'm also going to build three trellises for climbing roses over a rock pathway, one arch for me, Grandma, and Grandpa, which will lead to another garden, with cracked china plates in a mosaic pattern in the middle of a concrete circle, for Sunshine.

This may sound way too ambitious.

It is. But I see this as my last chance to get control of my mind before it blows.

I can wield any type of saw out there, and I have to do this, even if it takes me years. That I can even think in terms of a future, is a miracle.

Why? Because two and a half years ago, when I was thirty-two years old, I had a heart attack.

I used to be the size of a small, depressed cow.

The heart attack led to my stomach strangling operation, and I lost 170 pounds. Now I am less than half myself, in more ways than one.

My name is Stevie Barrett.

This is a story of why I was the way I was and how I am now me.

I am going to plant a garden.

Not even the glass walls muffled the screaming and shouting.

I leaned back in my swivel chair, away from my computer, and peeked into the conference room as the words "You are a cold, frigid snowwoman" echoed out after the words "I would rather remove my toes with pliers than sleep with you one more time!"

Two seconds later, high-pitched shrieking mixed with a baritone shout. "Living with you is like living with Antarctica. . . . I can't stand seeing your pinched-up, wrinkly prune face. . . . Move out of my house; you have poisoned it with your venom long enough. . . . You and your yellow teeth can shove it. . . . It's not your house; I'll burn it before you get it. . . . You are a mean, dickheaded prick with a small prick!"

Then there was a crash, which was a drinking glass hitting the glass walls of the conference room. I was quite surprised it didn't shatter. I sprinted into the conference room as my boss, and the owner of this law firm, Cherie Poitras, grabbed her client around the waist, a woman dressed to the nines in high heels and a cream suit. The woman had actually crawled up on the conference table and lunged for her husband. Cherie and I wrestled her off, but not before the husband's attorney put him in a headlock to keep him from strangling his soon-to-be ex-wife.

Even in a headlock, the husband, a local politician who stressed the sanctity of marriage and traditional values, struggled to get at his wife, his arms and legs flailing around and about like a trapped octopus.

I work as a legal assistant at Poitras and Associates. I work for Cherie Poitras directly and sometimes another attorney. I work with clients and witnesses, do a ton of legal research, write up documents, organize mountains of paperwork, summarize depositions, etc.

Sounds boring, but it's often exciting.

Cherie Poitras is five feet nine inches tall and wears cheetah patterned/striped/shiny four-inch heels and therefore towers over most of the male attorneys in town. She's very private, but from what I know she had a lousy childhood, grew up in Trillium River here in Oregon, and adopted four kids who had been abused. She loves a good fight, thrives off the law, and runs her firm like an honest, compassionate pit bull who must win every legal case no matter how hard she must bite. She is single, not surprisingly. How many men could handle Cherie? Not many.

Simply put: They're not enough for her.

We have a classy sign in the entrance of our elegant entry with gold lettering. It says, "WELCOME TO POITRAS AND ASSOCIATES. WE'LL KICK SOME ASS FOR YOU.

Anyhow, we handle a ton of different legal work. Personal injury. Environmental. Insurance. And we also handle many of the city's most spectacular divorces.

People spewing obscenities at each other, throwing things, and storming out is normal for our firm. We had one divorcing wife grab a knife out of her purse, stomp *across* the conference table, and try to stab her ex-husband. We had a shooting, husband at wife. He missed because Cherie tackled the husband. We've had fistfights between attorneys. Pencils and legal pads have been thrown, as has, one time, a small dog (dog wasn't happy), a designer purse (blackened an eye), and a shoe (it was a Manolo Blahnik).

You want to see ugly? Become a divorce attorney.

"Hello, Stevie. Good of you to come help," Cherie called out, her voice melodious, mellow, as she dragged her wriggling, livid client off the table. I grabbed the client around the waist, too, but she was strong and rage made her a madwoman with super-human strength.

"Come on, Mrs. Leod, let's go, please, let's take a break," I said. My black curls fell out of the bun I'd had them in as her hand swooped over the back of my head. "How about some coffee with fresh vanilla cream?"

"I am not going to take a break!" she screamed. "I don't want fresh vanilla cream. I am going to put my hands around his chicken neck and squeeze until his tongue falls out!"

I remember seeing Mrs. Leod on television, standing beside her husband, chin up, the feminine moral authority, talking about "the alarming erosion of family values in our state."

"If I have to run through all of our money, Frank, with legal fees, I'll do it," Mrs. Leod yelled. "In fact, if you don't back off I think I'll hold myself a press conference and tell them about the account in the Bahamas and your little dalliances into leather and whips—"

"Shut up, you stupid, prudish, witchly woman. . . ."

They continued shouting at each other, full throttle, full blast. We got her off the conference table, and I fell to the ground, on top of Mrs. Leod, but that did not stop her impressive tirade. Cherie and her short, leopard-print skirt fell on top of me. "She's a slippery little thing, isn't she?" Cherie panted. "Get her legs. I'll get her shoulders."

I gave Cherie an exasperated look. Why did I have to get her legs? They were more dangerous than the shoulders. A knee caught me in the gut and I said, "Ooof."

"I'll buy you perfume and pretty lotions, Stevie. Now, hop to it."

"Fine," I huffed. We both chuckled, couldn't help it.

The husband's face was becoming a darker red, stuck in his

headlock, but he was fighting like a furious four-legged octopus. I knew his attorney, Scott Bills. Scott had been in the army reserves for decades. If he had wanted to snap Mr. Leod's neck, he could have, but neck snapping wasn't on the agenda that day.

"Hello, Stevie," he said to me, calm and friendly.

"Hello, Scott," I said, trying to grab at Mrs. Leod's legs, which were flailing around, kicking me, one heel flying off into the glass wall. Cherie was on the top half of the woman, who had well and truly lost her mind.

"Don't think I won't tell everyone about your secret credit cards and precisely how you used them in Vegas!" Mrs. Leod said. "You big-nippled pervert!"

The woman was a psychiatrist. What would she make of herself, I wondered.

"If I could get it at home, I wouldn't get it there," Mr. Leod said, voice hoarse from the headlock. "And talk about big nipples! I could land a plane on yours."

Now that set our tiny she-devil off.

"How's Jae?" I asked Scott of his wife. The she-devil hit me in the chin with a knee. "Now, Mrs. Leod . . . take it easy."

Mrs. Leod was not in the mood to take it easy. "Do you know why I don't want to have sex with you? It's the size of your dick. It's so small it couldn't make a banana slug come."

"Maybe it's because you're dry as a desert," Mr. Leod said, sinking lower in Scott's arms, his breathing labored. "It's like having sex with sand!"

"You can't turn me on, sandman! Sweaty, sticky hands aren't sexy, Frank—not sexy. And you would know what it's like to have sex with sand, wouldn't you, because of the Maui trip you went on when you were supposed to be visiting your mother, the old fart!"

"Jae's doing pretty good, Stevie," Scott said, as if we were at a dinner party. "I'm taking her and the kids down to Long Shore this weekend. There's a kite festival."

"That sounds fun. The weather is supposed to be beautiful." I dodged a flying foot.

"Screw you!" Mrs. Leod said, arching in her fury. "Screw you forever!"

"I don't want to screw you," Mr. Leod squeaked out, his face now an even deeper red. "You are a sick sorceress."

A sorceress? Now that was clever. Me and Cherie exchanged another look.

"Hey, when is your annual dinner, Cherie?" Scott asked.

Cherie had a dinner every year, complete with a barbeque and a band to raise money for foster kids.

"October." She shoved Mrs. Leod's swinging arms back down as the woman spit out bad words through clenched teeth. "You and Jae better be there. And you, too, Stevie."

"Wouldn't miss it." Scott's octopus client was struggling but losing steam, because he was having a problem sucking in enough air, his arms flailing. "Can I say, Stevie, without getting slapped with a harassment suit, that you are simply gorgeous?"

I couldn't help but smile, even though Mrs. Leod's knee caught me in the chest.

"I hate you, you happiness-sucking prune!"

"I hate you, too. Your evil spell over me is gone. Vannnisshh-hheed!"

A spell? Cherie winked at me. It was so witchly here today.

"Thank you, Scott," I said. "I appreciate it. I'm trying. Walking every day."

"Doesn't she look fantastic?" Cherie gushed, her perfectly polished nails holding Mrs. Leod down. "Gorgeous. Stevie, you are an inspiration to all of us."

"You won't get a dime of my inheritance," Mrs. Leod hissed, her voice not quite as shrieky. I lay across her legs. "I curse you!"

"I earned that inheritance being married to you," Mr. Leod said, in a whisper voice, his face flushed. That headlock was good! Not too much, not too little!

"Let me up!" Mrs. Leod yelled. "I will not tolerate this for one second loooonger!"

"Release me," Mr. Leod hissed out, his neck in truly a bad position. "Reeeeleeasse me."

"Not unless you promise you won't try to decapitate your husband," Cherie said, tone so mild, sweet even.

"I'll release you, Frank," Scott said. "But I can't have you mangling your wife. It's impolite."

"This is none of your business!" Mrs. Leod shot out. "We demand that you let us go at once!"

"Stay out of this, Scott," Mr. Leod said, his voice tiny.

"This is *my* business," Cherie said. "No killings in Poitras and Associates. It's a rule we have here. The blood makes a mess, and I won't have anyone staining these new wood floors."

"I don't think I'm an inspiration," I said to Cherie and Scott, still holding onto Mrs. Leod's kicking legs. "My stomach has been squeezed into something the size of an egg. Gorging is now impossible no matter how much I want to shovel in chocolate cake. Buying clothes has also been a problem." I exhaled. Mrs. Leod finally relaxed her murderous self a bit.

"I'm sure," Scott agreed. "Every month you're skinnier."

Mr. Leod had finally collapsed, so Scott let him sink down to the floor.

"Easy does it," he said to his client. The client fell straight back. Scott made sure he was breathing, then said, "Jae said the same thing when we ran into you downtown last week. She said, 'Stevie Barrett looks terrific.' "

"I've told her not to lose one more pound. Not a pound. This is enough," Cherie said. "Now, everyone, take a breath, relax. Deep breath in, deep breath out, breathe in, out . . . We're not going to talk any further unless you two promise not to try to kill each other."

Mrs. Leod was trying to catch her breath, still lying splat on the floor. "I want him dead. I want him to be a corpse."

"Over my dead body," her husband wheezed. "Over my dead body, you wicked warlock woman."

"You are the spawn of the devil," she said.

"You *are* the devil." He coughed, inhaled. Our octopus had had enough.

"Remember, no killing in Poitras and Associates," Cherie said cheerfully.

I eyed Scott from the floor, where I still held Mrs. Leod. "Lovely to see you."

"And you, Stevie."

"Do tell Jae I said hello."

"I'll do that. Have a great day, you two."

"See ya, Scott," Cherie said, then smiled.

We hauled Mrs. Leod up and out the door. She tried to jam herself in the door frame, legs and arms splayed out, but we wrangled her away and down the hall. She still managed to call out, "I hope your pecker dissolves, I do, you ball-less wonder!"

"She's sure clever," I said to Cherie.

"Absolutely. Have to admire the vocabulary."

"Good-bye, sand pit!" Mr. Leod called, his voice scratchy. "You barren wasteland!"

Scott would remove his octo-client from our law offices when Cherie's office door slammed shut.

They would meet again another day, if neither had gutted the other. Mr. and Mrs. Leod were still living in the same mansion in the hills, so who knew.

We left Mrs. Leod in Cherie's office to cool off. She kicked the door. Three times. We had a temper-tantrum-throwing kid.

"Nothing like an acrimonious divorce to get the blood pumping, is there, Stevie?" Cherie smiled at me. We'd gone rafting last year for our firm's party and paintball shooting another time to "relieve the stress of warring spouses."

I smiled back. She is the best boss ever. *Ever.* And she loves a good fight.

"Nothing like it," I agreed.

When I got back to my desk and my computer, I noticed that my hands were shaking. They'd started shaking after I'd lost about thirty pounds and have gotten progressively worse these last six months. There is nothing medically wrong, we've checked that out.

It is, as they say, all in my head.

As the weight came off, the shaking started, the memories unearthed themselves, the visions grew, and the nightmares throttled my sleep. One problem solved, another problem stalking me.

The vision of myself in the mirror was truly the most alarming. Why? Because *she* was there.

She scared me to death.

I live in a one thousand square foot house built in 1940. I painted it emerald green with white trim and a burgundy-colored door. It has a huge backyard with a good-sized deck under a trellis. Because of my trees, and the neighbor's trees, it's quite private. My house is on a quiet street fifteen minutes from Portland, with a white picket fence that I built myself. That's Portland, Oregon, not Portland, Maine.

My home also has a detached garage, green with white trim. I have an obsession in my garage. It's rather an embarrassing, colorful obsession, but that is a story for later.

I bought this one-story, peaked-roof house about eighteen months ago after living in a dingy studio in a sketchy part of town for about a year after The Escape and all the new guilt. The studio came complete with occasional gunfire, domestic disturbances, and exciting carjackings. I was robbed once; all they took was my jean jacket and my pink robe. I have no idea why they wanted a pink robe. I think they took it to punish me for not having anything better.

During those dark months I tried to recover emotionally and physically from the heart attack, my operation, and a couple of other heart wrenching things I don't want to speak about.

This house, here in a funky, older, classy-hippie neighborhood called Newport Village, three blocks from a street of eclectic stores and coffee shops, was in foreclosure. To buy it I sold my car for a clunker truck I named The Mobster, because the previous owner probably could have been in the Mob, only without the dashing facial features.

I also sold my TV and a ton of stuff online, including some fat clothes, and used my savings from the divorce settlement for the down payment.

My house was in a pretty poor state of disrepair, like me, although the structure was intact, sort of like me. The first thing I did was put my hope chest in the attic. All the women in my family line have hope chests where they hide their secrets and preserve their treasures. When the woman dies, they're handed down to the next generation. Opening the chest would unleash too many emotional ghosts, so I've left it shut since I closed it with trembling hands twenty-four years ago.

The second thing I did was replace the two toilets. I would have had the EPA at my house if I hadn't.

The third thing I did? I took a sledgehammer, after talking to a contractor so I didn't bash any wires or pipes, and I smashed three walls down inside the house. The first wall I smashed out was between the kitchen and dining room. Another was between the kitchen and family room, the third between the family room and a bedroom. I am not embarrassed to say that I swung that sledgehammer again and again, and swore, and yelled and cried, the drywall dust and wood splinters covering me.

Have you ever smashed a wall down? You should try it. There's something so . . . *fulfilling* about bashing something, especially if every time that sledgehammer hits the wall you think of something, or someone, deep in your memories who hurt you or set afire an anger in your stomach you thought would burn you straight through.

I pounded the heck out of those walls.

By the time I was done destroying those walls, I could breathe a little better and my house seemed three times bigger.

Funny that.

A contractor cleaned things up and I had myself a home.

After battling only two hours of insomnia, I dreamed.

I dreamed of the cornfield by the Schoolhouse House. It was golden and warm, and I was running through it, Sunshine behind me. The corn formed a path and we followed it. Our stream flowed through it and we jumped over it, pink and green fish swishing below. The sky was blue, and a willow tree on the property rose in the distance, a tree house built on its strong limbs. We climbed the steps on the trunk and entered the tree house, with its yellow curtains and pink and yellow furniture. At a table there were two teddy bears in chairs, chatting, and we sat down to have a tea party.

I ate three white-and-pink-striped cupcakes, and then a door opened and Helen stomped in. She was hollering and wearing a bat with red eyes on her head. She ripped the heads off the talking teddy bears, then threw Sunshine out the window. Finally, she turned to me and said, "You're next," and she sat on my stomach. In my dream I struggled for air. I kicked, I fought, but her expression didn't change. It was blank.

I woke up tangled in my sheets and sweating, and peered through the window at the dirt outside my house.

I cannot plant corn. I wrapped my arms around myself and rocked back and forth, feeling the air constrict in my lungs, my body tightening.

I cannot plant corn.

"Pssst. *Pssst!*"

I stopped on the steps of our office building in downtown Portland.

"Stevie! Right here!" My head swiveled around, stiffly, as I had apparently pulled myself into a pretzel while I slept, at least that's how it felt.

"Are you blind?" the voice asked, sarcastic, disbelieving.

Aha. I knew that voice. I saw her head poke out around a pillar.

"Peekaboo, Zena Loo!" I called. "Why are you hiding?"

She made a face at me, rolled her eyes, *sooo* impatient.

I laughed when I saw her. It was glaringly apparent why Zena was hiding like a skunk in a log.

Zena, an overgrown Tinkerbell at a size 4, with a voguely cut wedge of black hair, was not dressed in appropriate professional attire for work as a legal assistant at Poitras and Associates. Tinkerbell was wearing a tiny black, slinky dress, plunging in front to show full cleavage, with four-inch black heels; a variety of chains, including one with a skull on it; and a black leather dog collar type of necklace with spikes. On her wrists were matching black leather dog collar bracelets.

She was also wearing something that resembled a plastic black snake winding up her leg.

"By golly gee, I don't think you're ready for work, Zena. Nice snake, though."

"Funny," Zena snapped. "Perhaps you'd enjoy taking the snake home to play with?"

"Do you have a leash to go with that dog collar?"

"You're a frickin' barrel of laughs, Stevie." Zena is twenty-five but has lived through enough to be eighty. Her mother died of a drug overdose, and her father was in jail for aggravated assault and drug dealing. Her brother and she were split up when she was seventeen and he was twelve. At eighteen, she went to court and got full custody. They lived together from then on out. The brother, Shane, is a huge science nerd. He won the state, then national competition for his experiments with genes and DNA and something I still can't understand, then received a full-ride scholarship to Stanford where he is majoring in biology and minoring in French. He adores Zena and calls her every day.

"You haven't been to bed yet, have you?" I asked my snake friend.

She made an impatient clicking sound with her tongue. "If I had, would I be hiding behind a pillar waiting for you? Haven't you ever been out dancing all night and then you check your watch and go, oh, shit, I have to be at work in fifteen minutes?" She tapped her heel.

"No. Never. Remember, I was huge until a little while ago."

Zena rolled her eyes. "Yeah, I remember. Can't forget that."

I didn't take offense. Zena was probably the only person in my life besides my cousins who didn't treat me any different pre- and post-fat. She was sarcastic before and sarcastic after.

Zena tossed back her head. "Help me get dressed. I don't want to give all the male attorneys and Caroline a boner when I walk in."

"Do I have to?" I whined, knowing I would. I had done it many times in the past.

"Yes. No boners. Give me your coat."

"Nope. No can do. This is my favorite."

She tugged, I tugged back, she tugged harder, and I let her win. I mean, she was wearing a plastic snake!

She stuck her arms through the sleeves and flipped up the collar. The coat came down to midthigh on her.

"Give me your scarf."

I sighed, pulled off my blue sparkly scarf. If I didn't, she'd take it, strangling me if she had to. She tied it at her waist.

"Voilà! You have a dress," I drawled.

She took off her chains and the skull and the metallic earrings that hung to her shoulders and shoved them in her purse. She took off the black dog collar, the black leather bracelets on her wrists with spikes, and the snake. Then she reached under my coat, pulled on the black straps of her dress and gave it a yank. She got an extra six inches of material at the bottom. She took out a comb to brush her hair, swiped on lipstick, popped in breath mints, and said, "Thanks, Stevie. Here we go."

I was disgusted. She took my dreary corduroy coat and my sparkly scarf and transformed them into chic style. "I think I hate you today, Zena. No one who has been out partying all night should look that good. It should be illegal. You should be arrested."

What was funny about Zena is that though she danced into the wee hours, she did not "do men." No boyfriends, no lovers. She wasn't into women, either. As she explained it, "When I meet a man I'm dumb enough to fall in love with, that's when I'll do him. Until then, no. They just fuck with your brains."

The elevator swooshed up and I glanced in the mirrored walls, then quickly away. My blue eyes appeared tired, my black curls messy. I still had a hard time recognizing myself without that extra 170 pounds. I still moved as if I were heavy, giving myself extra space I didn't need. I automatically cringed at the thought of airline seats and seat belt extensions, movie theatre seats, and chairs in general. And then I'd remember.

Zena linked an arm around me and smiled. Her smile is huge and takes up half her face. "I love you, Stevie."

Damn.

I wiped at my tears. Zena is such a cool friend, and I am falling apart.

"Your mascara is smeared, Stevie. You're a mess," she said. She whipped out a tissue and cleaned up my face.

Yes, indeed. I am a mess.

"Steve, my office." Crystal Chen stood next to me, her sharp red talons slashing through the air. She flipped her stick straight black hair behind her. "Now."

I hated the way she instantly made me feel so nervous.

"Hello, Crystal," Zena drawled. "How's the stick up your ass?"

I coughed.

Crystal narrowed her eyes. "Shut up, you skinny pole with a head."

Zena said, "That's a good one. Creative. Accurate. Bet you've been up nights thinking of that one."

Crystal flushed. "At least I'm not up nights with a cigarette in my hand staring out my grimy apartment window. Steve, now." She turned away.

"Excuse me," Zena said, quite loud, when Crystal was half-way down the hallway. "I don't smoke, I dance, and prunes *will* help constipation, Crystal, don't you worry. You'll feel better in no time. Your colon is probably bursting with defecation."

Crystal checked for other attorneys, saw none, then flipped Zena off.

Zena laughed.

Crystal and Zena don't care for each other much.

Poitras and Associates is located in the second tallest building in Portland on the next to the top floor. We have spectacular views of the city, the hills west of Portland, the river, and the whole east side. We have about thirty attorneys, of all ages, colors, and cultures. Half are women. Our attorneys cost between $200 and $600 an hour. The lower end is for the newbies who are worked about fifteen hours a day, six days a week, slobbering with stress into their cereal each morning.

Crystal has been with the firm for six months and brought The Case That Will Rip Your Heart Out with her. I have no idea what Cherie was thinking when she hired her. None. She's the only attorney I don't want around me.

"Are you coming, Steve? Follow me," Crystal said.

I traipsed behind Crystal into her office, much as a young girl in trouble would, my head sort of down, shoulders slumped. She has a view of Mt. Hood, the river, and a bunch of Portland's bridges.

She sat down behind her huge desk, did not invite me to sit down, crossed her arms, then crossed her legs, her black four-inch heel swinging back and forth, and glared at me. Crystal wears $1,000 suits. This one was gray.

"I need to talk to you about the Atherton case, Steve."

She did not call me Stevie. I had corrected her several times, but she didn't listen. Re: I'm a nonperson.

"I will smash them to bits," she muttered.

The Atherton case is The Case That Will Rip Your Heart Out. I hated that case. A boy, Danny Atherton, had a congenital heart defect and had been hospitalized for surgery at Harborshore Hospital. Now, all heart operations are serious, I get that, but this one was routine. Very routine. The doctors were going to fix it; the kid would be in and out, and back to playing baseball and reading about dragons, which he loved doing.

The operation did not have the intended results. In fact, Danny now spent most of his time lying in a hospital bed, unable to eat, drink, or pee on his own.

This fact was not in dispute: Danny was on a heart–lung bypass machine during the operation. His parents and their attorneys were asserting that the breathing tube attached to the ventilator was not inserted correctly by the anesthesiologist, which deprived Danny of oxygen.

The hospital was claiming that this type of operation could have adverse results, it certainly wasn't because the boy was deprived of oxygen, the parents signed off on the procedure with the pages and pages of teeny tiny print, they had done their best, they're doctors, not God, didn't Mr. and Mrs. Atherton know that, stupid people, and no, they owed the boy nothing. Too bad, kid. Too bad for your parents. Not our problem.

Unfortunately, we were not defending Danny, his life reduced to mush, who was fed through a tube and couldn't even *think* about playing baseball. We were not trying to get money for the Athertons to care for Danny, who had three other sons and a maxed-out insurance plan.

Nope. We were defending the hospital. Aggressively. Mercilessly. Without morals or ethics, as far as I was concerned.

"We must win the Atherton case, Steve. Win. Win. Win." Crystal pounded a fist against her desk with each word. "The family wants ten million dollars." She laughed. "For a kid. They say they need nurses around the clock. Hell, the mother's at home. She's a housewife. Broom, mop, laundry, that sort of thing. Eww. She doesn't have time to take care of her own kid? She's a hard-core *housewife*. Come on!"

Crystal spat that word out as if she was spitting out: Slimy vermin. Lazy loser. Bottom-dwelling infected crab.

I didn't say anything.

"How much does it take to take care of a kid? They think they're gonna win the lottery. I already met Mom. She's fat. Frumpy. Dumb hairstyle, probably hasn't changed it since high school. Dad's a plumber. A plumber! They want money for life, *for life,* for this kid. Stupid."

"But isn't he going to need care for the rest of his life? He needs nurses, caregivers, he won't be able to work, his mother won't be able to go back to being a teacher, they have enormous medical expenses—"

She glowered at me, then slammed a pile of documents on her desk. "That's not our problem. It's not the hospital's problem. They're not responsible for every kid who was born with a problem with their heart. Don't you get that, Steve?"

"Uhhh . . ."

"Uhhh." Crystal mocked me.

I rolled my lips in. I was so uncomfortable around Crystal. I knew it was me, it was my lack of self-esteem, I got it. But she was awful. Zena called her a walking sexually transmitted disease, which I would never repeat aloud, because it's rude to say that Crystal is an STD. Quite rude. So I won't say, "Crystal reminds me, too, of an STD."

"I need people on my team who are with me on this case. Are you with me, or not?"

I didn't say anything. Didn't matter. She was suddenly swearing at her cell phone, which had rung. She silenced it.

"Where is the deposition of Dr. Shintoleva?" she spat out, suddenly angry.

"I'll get it for you and bring it in," I said.

"Right away. I also need the deposition of that nurse. You know. The blonde who seems to hate me?"

Everyone hates Crystal. I nodded. "I'll get that to you as soon as possible as well."

"Sooner than possible, Steve, sooner than possible. We're going to screw this greedy, plumber family with the housewife momma who was head of the PTA."

She shook her head and put her skinny ankles back up on her desk so her soles were facing me. "Are you up to this, Steve?"

"Yes, I'm up to it but, Crystal . . ."

"What? What is it?"

I squared my shoulders. "Shouldn't we settle this case? If it goes to trial—"

"If it goes to trial, and it won't, but if it does, we'll win. Sure, people are going to feel for the poor kid, but it's not the hospital's fault."

Not the hospital's fault? I had read what had happened in there, and I did not believe the hospital's claim of a lack of culpability. I thought they were lying. The boy's current condition was in line with an operation going haywire because of a lack of oxygen.

"You can go, Steve."

I turned to leave, feeling sick. I did not want to be a part of this.

"One more thing," she snapped, standing up, suddenly agitated. "Now remember what I told you a couple of months ago. Any piece of paperwork you see that you don't understand, hand to me. There might be one letter, from a Dr. Dornshire to Charles Winston, who is, as you know, the president of the hospital. I want that e-mail."

"Why don't you ask Dr. Dornshire for it?"

"Dr. Dornshire no longer works for the hospital."

"He doesn't?" Dr. Dornshire was a doctor who apparently had entered the surgical room at the end part of Danny's operation.

"Dr. Dornshire is now in his own medical clinic in Africa attending to starving or beat-up or depressed kids or something like that. Yuck. I could not stand being around all those poor people and the snakes and bugs and lions. Too hot, too. Anyhow, we can't reach him. We tried. Can't find him. He's in the jungles, gone."

There was something not right here.

"If you see the letter, hand it over pronto. You don't even need to read it. Got that, Steve?"

"Got it."

The vast majority of our cases are legitimate cases. Who we are defending needs defending for valid reasons. Or, you can at least make an argument that they should not be forced to pay the amount they're being sued for. However, not this time.

"Good. Not too complicated, is it? You fully understand?"

"Yes." I wished I didn't sound so meek. I turned to leave.

"You can go now. I have important people to talk to right this second." She waved her hand in front of her. Off you go, shoo fly, shoo.

Zena saw my face when I returned to our shared cubicle, and called down toward Crystal's office, "Have you found the stick, Crystal? Keep searching! You might have to bend over!"

Crystal slammed her door.

Zena laughed.

*   *   *

Zena has a job at Poitras and Associates for life. Lawyers are always stopping by our cubicle and asking her for help, sometimes with white, pasty, panicked expressions on their faces.

"Zena, I forgot to file those papers on the Hubernach case. . . ." Inhale, exhale. Pant, pant. "Any chance you did?"

Zena would nod and say, "It's gonna cost you, you brainless wonder. Fifty-dollar coffee card."

Or, "Zena, the federal case, the water thing, I didn't call, oh, my God!" Hands to head, sweat dripping off nose. "I'm dead. Any chance that you—"

Zena would nod and say, "I did it, you lame-duck loser. Fifty-dollar coffee card."

Zena bought us coffee every day. She had piles of cards.

But her photographic memory was what stunned everyone. "Zena, remember the Thompson case in eastern Oregon four years ago? What was the name of the neighbor we deposed after the lady with the fluffy red hair?"

Zena would know who it was, first and last name.

Or, "Zena, remember that pollution case? What was the name of the attorney who was handling the small claim with that business in Grants Pass and who was his client?"

She knew the name of the attorney, she knew the firm he worked for and the location, she remembered the claim and client.

She is one wild gal, mouthy and opinionated, and Cherie thinks she's great. Secretly, outside of the office, those two are fast friends. That's why Zena doesn't usually work for Cherie directly.

"I'm going to get a huge pile of sticks and dump them on Crystal's desk," Zena said. "Then I'll use the copy machine to take a picture of my butt and put that picture on top of the sticks. I think she'll get it, don't you, Stevie?"

I nodded. She'd get it.

Zena's so darn funny.

2

Ashville, Oregon

Helen's face ended up in my birthday cake.
As incidences with her went, it was rather mild.

The lights were off, candles were lit and, singing as the ex-Broadway star she had been, Helen brought the cake in from the kitchen. Sunshine, next to me, held my hand. She had given me a charm bracelet with a clover, cross, flower, dog, cat, house, and heart, "because I wuv you."

I heard the girls around me catch their breaths because Helen was so beautiful. She was wearing a red, silky dress over her slim figure, her golden hair swept up in a chignon, and her pearls. The only thing out of place was her boots.

"Happy birthday to you . . ."

Her black rubber gardening boots, which she always wore, were wrapped with chicken wire to "catch the voices" that spoke to her. "They're so damn loud," she'd told me. "I have to turn them down. They're screaming at me on microphones. And they're spying on me. Do you see them spying?"

Grandma and Grandpa watched Helen like hawks. She had insisted that she be the one who brought me my cake, in a treasure chest shape and filled with gumdrops. The day before the party she had a meltdown and told them she knew they were part of the "plot" to keep her from the cake.

"You're spies. I know you are. Cake spies. Turn that Lerblomerbing off," she'd commanded, pointing at the TV. "That's how they get to me."

Grandma turned the TV off, flicked her long white curls over her shoulder, and continued baking my cake in her cowboy boots, pausing only to help Helen readjust the tin foil crown she'd made herself.

"Happy birthday to you . . ." Helen's voice soared and dipped.

Helen had sung so beautifully in high school that people from all over the state came to see our town's musicals. She single-handedly funded the drama program, basketball, band, choir, track, volleyball, cross-country, cheerleading, soccer, and various clubs at school.

She had gone to an Ivy League college on full scholarship, then had spent four years on the stage in New York City, singing to packed houses in musicals that always had to extend their runs. As Grandma told it to me, Helen came back home when she walked onstage wearing her blue fuzzy pajamas. She had refused to get into her Egyptian costume. Her singing was incredible until Momma took her pajamas off onstage and sang naked.

Some would say the performance became better after that, but the newspaper reporters spoke of a "total nervous breakdown" and "the loss of one of America's most promising singers," and, less articulately, "She is outrageously crazy."

The promising singer, who was pregnant at the time with me, ended up in a straitjacket that night. Weeks later, Grandma and Grandpa were able to take her home from the hospital with a nasty label attached to her: schizophrenia.

"Happy birthday, dear girl. . . ."

Helen put the chocolate treasure chest right in front of me, the candles flickering. She sang full throttle, raucous, clear, with a long trill at the end, then burst into a Broadway song that had all my girlfriends giggling, but my smile froze on my face. Helen was on new medications but they sure weren't helping, as usual, and now I was worried.

She did a little tap dance and finished with great fanfare, and my girlfriends clapped. Grandma and Grandpa came right in close to us. It was the prelude to disaster, and they knew it.

I took a breath to blow out my candles and make a wish. My wish was that Helen would leave the room and go to bed and not embarrass me.

I was unable to blow out my candles because Helen's head was suddenly in my treasure chest cake and I was staring down at her chignon. I heard the gasps of the girls, half of them related to me, and the groan from my grandparents as they moved in to save the situation.

I should have been surprised. I mean, really, how often is your mother's head in your birthday cake? She was, by the way, singing another Broadway song through the cake and ice cream. I believe it was from *My Fair Lady*.

But I was used to using humor to excuse Helen. It was my only coping mechanism—all I had left. I blew out the two remaining flaming candles, licked my fingers, then tapped her on the shoulder. "Momma, how does the cake taste?"

"Shhh," she said, her voice muffled by icing. "They're listening to us. I can hear them. They're by the gumdrops."

"Who wants ice cream?" I asked the girls, their mouths hanging open in shock, their eyes wide.

My best friend, and also a distant cousin, Lornie Rose, burst into tears and reached for my hand.

"It's your favorite flavor, Lornie Rose," I reassured her. "Chocolate chocolate mint!"

I didn't burst into tears until I was in bed that night, Sunshine's body curled up to mine, the light of the moon glinting on my charm bracelet.

I hated myself for hating Helen.

3

Portland, Oregon

That night I dreamed I was inside a cake with Helen. She shoved icing down my throat until I couldn't breathe. The river came and washed me away. From the top of the cake she stood with Sunshine, then threw her up to the moon, which was reddish gold. Sunshine got stuck on the moon for a minute, teetered off, headfirst, into the river, then down the jaws of a fish shaped like a cornstalk.

I couldn't find the fish, couldn't find her.

Helen whispered to me while I choked on the icing, "It's all your fault, Stevie. That's why she died. You killed her."

I get up at six o'clock every morning and walk for an hour and a half. I rarely sleep past six anyhow, might as well get something done. Plus, I find that walking helps calm my nerves after another night full of horrendous nightmares involving gingerbread men, a left hand held out at a weird angle, a rushing river with claws, and catatonic behavior.

I used to be a window person.

I saw almost everything through glass.

Dusty, dirty, sometimes clean, but always through that pane of glass. The outdoors and me avoided one another, simply because I couldn't walk very far, or long, without panting or worrying my heart would explode.

Now I'm not a window person.

Every time I walk, I can't get over that I can walk in the first place.

Sounds strange?

It isn't.

Walking, when you're morbidly obese and can't even see your shoes, hurts. It hurts your bones, your joints, and your lungs feel as if they're being blown out. Plus, you can't breathe. The fear of a heart attack is quite real. You might be pushing your body right over the edge into Coronary Land. You could die in the middle of the sidewalk, teetering on your stomach. You could die on a neighbor's front lawn by a gnome.

I had had to start out slow. I could walk for only five minutes the first few times out after my bariatric surgery, when I could get out of bed in the first place. I tried to increase my minutes each week. At first I walked three days a week, then four. After a few months, I walked six days a week, thinking one day off to rest would be good, but that didn't work. I never felt alive on that seventh day. My body learned to exercise, and it would not wake up until I did it.

So I walk every day, an hour and a half, and on my walks I study other people's gardens. Some people's yards are flat and boring. One well-trimmed tree, perfect grass, a couple of bushes, done. Others are messy, or half done, skateboards and scooters in front. Some houses have potted and hanging flowers, which are so pretty.

Then there are the gardens that make you stop and stare and gawk and feel gobs of envy. The ones where the flowers are piled up, happy bursts of color, with a decorative walk, maybe some outdoor art, the borders in layers, short plants and flowers first, then the medium sized, finally the flowering trees. Maybe there's a fountain or a pond, a gazebo in the backyard.

That's what I want to create. That kind of garden.

A Garden of Eden sort of garden, lush and ripe and blooming, the type that Adam and Eve could be found gallivanting around naked in.

I want Adam, but only if he's hot, funny, and doesn't blame

me for everything bad that happens in the world when, in fact, he could have and should have protected Eve from that apple in the first place, and he certainly shouldn't have told God that Eve had messed things up big-time, that she was to blame, she started all the evil, bad woman, not him. What a wimp.

Come to think of it, I don't want Adam in my garden at all. I'll take Eve if she promises to help me build my raised beds and never walks around naked.

Or Noah, the ark builder. I could take him. He could build a mini-ark and I could fill it with flowers and vegetables.

But not corn. No corn in the ark.

At the end of my walk I had to leap over a three-foot-high, pokey green hedge owned by my neighbor, Nancy Bull, and hide myself facedown in the dirt like a bug.

I do not want him to see me.

Ducking was instinctive. Immature. And almost, but not quite, funny.

My neighbor, Jake Stockton—what a romantic name, doesn't it set a beat in your breast?—was leaving for work. He lives six houses down from me and moved in about seven months ago. I know he travels, sometimes for weeks at a time—not that I am stalking him at all. That would be weird. Not that I am spying on his house, either. That would be creepy. Nor am I keeping an eye out for gorgeous Jake at all times. That would be obsessive.

I don't know where he travels to. Whenever he sees me, and I cannot make a leap into an escape, he waves. Now and then he stops to chat, but I scuttle off, quick as I can, as a paralytically shy mouse would, because I can feel my vocal chords stiffening in fear. Plus, when he first moved in, I hadn't had my second operation, so loose skin was hanging off me like uninflated parachutes.

If there is a more gorgeous man on the planet, I have not seen him. Jake's almost as tall as my grandpa and built in the same oxen form. He has blondish hair; is probably a little older than forty; and has huge, kind, green, mushy, yummy eyes and a jaw that could break a board in half. He is not pretty. In fact, I think he's spent a lot of time out in the sun, because he has that tanned, weathered cragginess. He has a smile that reaches into my heart, wraps itself around me, and makes me hope.

I avoid him *at all costs*.

I stuck my head up when I knew he and his truck had zoomed off to work. I spit dirt and, I think, a small spider from my mouth and leveraged myself up, flicking dirt off my front.

Yes, I avoid Jake at all costs because I envision him naked and smiling and cannot speak in his manly presence and therefore come off as imbecilic and fluffy in the intelligence department.

But, my, he makes my heart flutter.

"One day you're going to have to talk to him, you know, like a real woman."

I about jumped out of my skin, then relaxed when I saw Nancy and her rake. She has blond hair, is on her third husband ("Upgrade your husband now and then," she'd told me. "Look for improved models."), and is a gardening maniac.

"I know, I know," I panted. "But not today."

"Gee whiz. How about tomorrow?" She rolled her eyes. "How about the next day?"

"No, can't do it. No, no, no."

"I've seen him talking to you. He looks at you like he likes you, and there you go leaping over hedges, landing on your face in the dirt."

"He doesn't like me." That was infinitely silly.

She thumped her rake. "Yes, he does. Get some guts, you flying wonder woman, and go talk to him."

"No, no, no." Whew. "No guts."

"Wuss."

"Manaical gardener," I shot back, spitting out more dirt.

She thumped her rake at me. Twice.

He brought his full-sized female blow-up dolls to my little green house with the white picket fence. Lance, my cousin, had to make two trips back and forth to his car to bring in, with much pomp and circumstance, "the ladies."

"This one is Tiger Momma," he announced proudly, pointing at the bikini-clad blow-up woman that he propped up right beside me on my red couch. He took two steps back and grinned, chest puffed out with pride. "And this one—" he turned and grabbed another doll. "This one is *my woman*, Veronica! I'm going to get ten thousand of these made up."

Veronica was wearing ... nothing. Veronica was naked. Poofed out in all the right places.

I swallowed hard. I am not a prude. This, however, was a tiny bit too much.

I glanced across my living room at Lance's sister—my cousin, Polly—who was perched on the church pew I'd decorated with red tasseled pillows.

Polly is tall and leggy and rangy, very thin, excessively high strung, and has super curly auburn hair hanging halfway down her back. She was rocking back and forth in nervous agitation, fluffing her hands in front of her face, as if to cool herself, her expression pained.

"Please tell me you won't advertise these in the newspaper." She rocked and fanned, rocked and fanned. "Don't go on TV again. We have the same last name, Lance. Everyone will know. Oh, ohhh!" She fanned. "Ohhh." She groaned. "Ohhh!" She inhaled in and out of her cupped hands.

I was so worried about Polly, and not because she was having trouble breathing.

Lance pushed Veronica onto the couch, too. She started to slip off and I grabbed her, accidentally, by the boob.

"Advertising is the name of the game, Polly Wants a Cracker, name of the game," Lance said, bumping his fists together. "Advertising and marketing."

"But I don't appreciate your advertising," she protested. What Polly was wearing could best be described as "ethnic." A cotton shirt from Mexico with embroidered animals across the bodice. A wraparound, orange and red cotton, Texan-style skirt with fringe and a golden East Indian scarf with tiny mirrors around her shoulders. Cowboy boots, dangling earrings. This was in direct contrast to what she wore on the air as Portland's most popular news anchor. "I feel sorry for the dolls. Can you imagine what these poor girls are going to have to go through? It's embarrassing. I can hardly breathe when I think of it."

"I think Veronica's having a hot flash," I drawled.

Lance turned on me. Lance is an interesting man and I love him dearly. He's a former professional football player, two years older than Polly and me. He's six foot six inches tall, has piercing gray eyes, broad shoulders, and slim hips. Women go crazy for him, and yet he can barely speak around them, barely utter a consonant. He is pathologically shy around them. Plus, he's *very* emotional. "She is not having a hot flash. She's flushed. She's healthy, rosy cheeked."

"She's a plastic doll, Lance," I said. "She's not healthy or unhealthy. She is . . . there. She is an 'it,' not a person."

Lance's face became flushed, like his doll. "I know she's not a person, Stevie. I know it. I get it." He spread his arms wide and reminded me of a giant eagle. "Is it too much to ask that my sister and my cousin support my new business?"

I cleared my throat as he victoriously grabbed another doll and started pumping her up with a small red machine. Feet filled first, then the shapely, slender, impossibly long legs. I did not need to see the upper half inflate.

"So. Another business?" I asked.

"Yep. Make fun of me all you want, but this one's gonna go flying. I can feel it. *Feel it.* My left ankle is twitching. *Twitching!*"

I would not doubt that he would make millions, especially if his left ankle was twitching. Lance uses his left ankle for answers to everything in his life. He has never formed a company without the blessing and twitching of his left ankle and has made millions. It started with some computer software he developed when he was in college. He sold it for a gazillion dollars. He was twenty. He morphed into a real estate mogul, which made him a fortune, as he bought at the exact right time during his pro career ("My ankle was almost thumping during those deals, almost thumping!"). He provided venture capital to two new start-up, online socializing sites, and they both took off like rockets toward Uranus.

He's a modern-day Midas.

"I think your dolls are gonna be felt by a lot of weirdo, middle-aged freaks who can't get a date to save their flabby butts," Polly whimpered. Rock, rock, rock. She brought a brown sack up to her mouth and breathed. "And everyone will know that my brother is a blow-up-doll dealer."

I muffled my laugh, shook my head.

"Those men should be arrested," Polly went on, her mouth still forming O's as she tried to capture oxygen. "They should be arrested and tried in court and sent to jail. If they want a freaky relationship, they should find it with their cellmate."

Polly might end up having a "mate" in her life soon. I shivered. I was going to have to force her to deal with her problem.

"Treat my dolls with respect." Lance kept blowing up his doll. She had blond hair and huge eyes. "This is going to go national. International. I'm going to sell to the Russians and Alabamians and the French peoples and the Africans and the Delawarians. I'm selling to everybody."

"Fine. I respect Miss Bongo Boobs. My respect is sky high! Sky high!" Polly waved her hands high in the air.

I propped Tiger Momma up and told her, "You need to sue this man. Make him pay. He's not your pimp."

Tiger Momma kept that weird grin on her face. She freaked me out.

"This is a business opportunity. An investment in the future internationally." You would never know Lance is a multimillionaire by looking at him. He's got the weathered face of a mountain man, a head of brown hair, and a short, scruffy beard. He wears flip-flops, jeans, and sweatshirts. He does have a modern, woodsy, Oregon sort of home with incredible views of the coast range, and a boat, and a Porsche, but nothing else showy.

He stopped pumping and asked, "Do you think they have conventions and stuff for this kind of business?"

"Lemme see." I pretended to stare into space. For someone who had made so much money already, sometimes Lance came off as shockingly naive. "Maybe the United Blow-Up Dolls Convention. I think that was on Jupiter last year. The Squish Me

Conference is in Vegas in July. I think there's even a Puffy Girls Union. You should know that the Blow-Up Dolls Girls have filed a union grievance against heavy men. They don't want their boobs smashed. It makes them feel deflated."

"That's not funny, Stevie," Lance said. "Why are you girls making fun of my new business? You've both hurt me. Right here." He thumped his heart. "You've hurt my beater."

Polly eyed one of the dolls on the ground, then grabbed her and hissed, right in her face, "Run! Run for your freedom, your dignity, your very soul. Run!" She threw the doll up in the air, and Lance protested in outrage, catching the doll with one hand.

He pushed the doll onto the couch by me. I was now surrounded by a bunch of blow-up dolls, as if they were people.

"This isn't funny, Polly. My feelings are hurt again!"

Anyone else and I would have discarded that. With Lance, by golly, he's telling the truth. I saw a sheen glistening over those gray, deep-set eyes.

"I think the dolls are . . ." He waited eagerly for my opinion. "I think . . . they seem real. As if they're smart and they would have interests and hobbies and that they . . . that they would want, uh, desire to be . . . uhhh . . . fondled."

Lance beamed. "That's right. You got it! Now I want you two to be investors in my business." He stood tall, huge chest out, chin up. "It'll be a family business. A *family* business! Great salaries for the employees, great benefits. I'm thinking health insurance, dental, ortho, eye, time off for the ladies poppin' out babies, time off for the new fathers, time off when Grandma gets sick. You know. The best of the best companies to work at. You two are gettin' in on the ground floor. You can be vice presidents, if you want!"

"I want to be an investor," Polly squeaked, "about as much as I'd want to wake up in the morning with a blow-up plastic woman in my bed playing with my hair."

"Come on, I want us to do this together!" Lance pleaded. "It's a great venture! It's a business! You'll make a fortune. I'll *give you* part ownership. Four dollars each and you're a part owner of Lance's Lucky Ladies."

I gagged. Blow-up naked girls? For yucky men? No. Not me.

I elbowed one of the naked dolls. She was kind of pretty in a plasticky way.

"Thank you, Lance," I told him, squeezing his hand under the mound of girls. "I appreciate the opportunity, the thought. That you even asked me, it makes me feel . . ." I struggled for the right word.

"Warm inside?" he asked, eyes hopeful. "Cared for? Loved? Flattered? That's how I would feel." He squeezed back. "You girls and I . . ." He paused to gather himself. "I feel so close to both of you. You're my kin. My sister and my cousin." He pounded his heart. "But you're the sister of my soul, Stevie." Pound pound. "The sister of my soul."

I started feeling emotional again.

"I want to do something with you both where we can see each other every day. Where we can communicate as only family members can, with confidence and love and trust and love and laughter and love. . . ."

I sniffled. I didn't want to work for Lance in any of his companies. It would be taking advantage of him, and I don't want to mix our family relationship with business. It would feel wrong in my bones to do so, but Lance was so sweet.

"Oh, no, Stevie!" Lance's face twisted. "You're not going to cry, are you?"

"No, I'm not." But my voice was already ragged. "I'm not going to cry." I sniffed again. I tried to hold it in, I did, but there was no fooling Lance.

He burst into tears, holding his big head in his hands. "Oh, Stevie, Stevie!" he cried. "Stevie!"

I wiped my face. I was a mess.

Lance reached across the blow-up girls and held me close. We squished Tarzan Sister between the two of us.

"Come on, Polly! Everybody together!" Lance said, voice breaking.

Polly was having trouble with her breathing—stress does that to her—but she came over anyhow and hugged us and Tarzan Sister.

"Tarzan Sister does feel awfully sexy, Lance," I said, choking back my tears. "I'll admit that."

"Yes, squishy in all the right places," Polly said, trying to be reassuring. "Sexy. Cuddly."

Lance smiled. "She's a warm, giving woman, Tarzan Sister is." He wiped his tears. "She'll be very popular."

I am almost broke.

Cherie pays me well, and my house payment is a little high but manageable, but I have medical debt. Huge medical debt.

After my deductible, my insurance paid for most of my bariatric surgery to strangle up my stomach so I would feel full ultra-quick, lose weight, and not die of another heart attack. They did not, however, pay for my second operation, which was needed to cut off the massive, hanging folds of skin that were no longer propped up by 170 pounds of fat. They said it was "cosmetic." All that skin was causing heat rashes, irritation, and pains in my back, shoulders, and stomach.

In addition, I was frightening naked. It looked like my entire body had been stretched and pulled by invisible hands until I resembled a white, mushy Gumby doll.

I didn't even try to fight the insurance company. I had my boobs lifted and enhanced and my extra skin whacked off. The doctor, who had actually been through the surgery himself, agreed I could pay him monthly.

I double up my payments because I hate debt, and therefore I am almost broke.

Was it worth it to get this second operation?

You bet.

I don't regret it for a second. Sometimes I sneak a peek at my boobs and I giggle. They're upright and they're full, but they're not the mammoth jugs I used to have that killed my spine and thunked around on their own like bouncing bowling balls. My stomach is actually flat. I am not wearing wings under my arms and fat globules on my legs. My butt is not drooping to my knees.

People do not gasp, giggle, snicker, or make stabbingly hurtful remarks when I walk by, like, "She is disgusting" and "I can't even look at her."

But now I have to pay for it.

I sent out my résumé by mail and Internet, hoping for a weekend job in retail, a café or a local business open on weekends.

There's a restaurant that needs someone to dress as a chicken and stand on a corner with a sign advertising the company's meal specials.

I laugh.

I would never dress as a chicken.

That would hit way too close to home.

I searched further.

I watched the news Monday night after work. I had had the fifth of my allotted small meals. I could not eat more than fifteen bites without feeling full, so I had to eat five times a day. I wanted to eat more, piles more, which is how I've handled my vast emotional issues my whole life, but I couldn't shove it down, I knew that, or I would get dumping syndrome. Dumping syndrome is what people who have had bariatric surgery can get if they're not careful. Here's how I would describe dumping syndrome: Envision someone putting a spear in your stomach and twisting it around. Add panic, breathlessness, profuse sweat, cold chills, diarrhea, and a sense of delusion. Lots of fun.

I avoid it at all cost.

It's the only thing that prevents me from eating my pain away.

Polly smiled serenely out from the TV, proper yet beautiful in a pink suit and white silk undershirt with the slightest bit of lace. Her curls were pulled back conservatively, only a few artfully escaping, her nails polished. It is amazing what the spray-on, pancake makeup that people on TV wear can cover up.

She receives regular offers of marriage.

I've been to the newsroom right before she's on the air. She is running around, a paper bag clutched in her hand, snapping orders, asking machine gun, rapid-fire questions, and making moaning sounds.

She collapses in her anchor chair minutes before the camera rolls, yanks her papers toward her, hands shaking, yelling directions, and as soon as the producer points at her, camera on, live shot, three, two, one, she settles right down, smiles peacefully, cheekily, and calmly delivers Portland's best newscast.

The second it's over, she's pulling a bag out from under her bottom and breathing into it. Sometimes her co-anchor, Grant Joshi, has to hold it for her, propping her up with one arm. This is not an act. Polly sags after each newscast as if all the air has been sucked out of her with a vacuum.

When Polly can breathe again, she gets up, thanks Grant politely, and heads back to her office where she resumes working at a frantic pace, bellowing orders, but breathing without the aid of a sack. Grant and Polly are close friends. Polly is also close friends with his partner, Kel, but that is hush-hush. The station prefers to egg on rumors that Polly and Grant are "lovers."

She and Grant delivered the news seamlessly, professionally, yet with warmth. They chattered together now and then. The chatter should have sounded shallow, but somehow it didn't. The newscast was perfect. Right before the commercial, I saw Polly's hand reach below the desk. No one else probably would have taken note, but I knew she was reaching for her brown paper bag so she would not hyperventilate.

I felt sick for her.

And I felt this terrible sense of dread.

She had lost control.

Again.

"Look what I did," Zena whispered to me the next week at work, flipping that wedge of hair back. "You're hot now, Stevie. So, so hot. A woman of the night."

I kicked my rolling chair toward Zena's computer.

She grinned and hit a button with an exaggerated flourish on her keyboard.

I felt my heart stop.

My breath seemed to choke on itself as my body ting-ting-tinged.

Oh no, oh no, oh no!

I stared at Zena, stricken. "You didn't," I rasped out, holding my throat.

"I did." She stood up, wriggled her skinny hips, clad in a red wraparound skirt that I believe was a cotton scarf she wore around her neck the day before. She cackled, "Ha! Hooo ha!"

I wanted to disappear. To hide. There was my face, on the computer screen, under the beaming banner, "Make a Super Date!"

I grabbed the edge of Zena's desk and held on for dear life as my world tilted in a nauseating way. *You didn't.*

"I sure did!" Zena chortled. "You're out there, woman, *you're out there*. Ready for action. Ready to get laid."

Zena had put my profile on an *Internet dating service*.

Without my permission.

The world tilted and retilted again. "I don't want to date. I don't want any action. I don't want to get laid." No, all that scared the tar out of me.

In my "Date Me!" photo I was smiling, my curly black hair tumbling down my back, my blue eyes tilted up, the dimple in my left cheek like a smile. It wasn't a bad picture of me—I had taken far worse—but all I saw was this: frumpy. Definitely geeky. *Totally exposed.*

I remember when Zena took that photo. I was laughing at a story she told me about the night before. She had gone to a costume party dressed up as a volcano that a nerdy, brilliant tech friend of hers built. In the middle of the party, she stepped out of the volcano, dressed only in a black leotard, tights, and a hat with attached paper flames, pushed a button, and the volcano exploded, with smoke, a firework, and ketchup. She had won first place and been rewarded with a bottle of tequila.

Picture snapped.

"You know, Stevie, you have one of the kindest, sweetest faces I have ever seen. You're a damn freakin' Pollyanna. I mean, that dimple! And the way your eyes light up when you're smiling. And you got fat lips. All guys get hard for fat lips. It's facial porn to them. Facial porn."

"Please tell me this is a joke," I finally stuttered, fumbling with the collar of my black work jacket. Blah and boring, identical to my black pants. Bought used and cheap. But I don't want to call attention to myself anyhow. And I'm broke. Those are my excuses. "Please tell me I am not on the Internet for men to ogle and reject. . . ."

"Yep, you are, freakin' Pollyanna. I paid you up and everything. Six glorious, glorious months of dating."

I gasped. "What is that?" I pointed to a column.

"Those are your interests! See? You enjoy hiking on mountains and doing outdoor activities, for example, rafting and kayaking down Oregon's rivers. You're an outdoor adventurist! You lust over Class IV rapids and fast cars! You're always in a quest for speed and danger and living on the edge of reason!"

I squeaked. "I do not!"

"You like to work hard and play hard and you're interested in—"

She abruptly stopped talking and covered the screen with her hand, then frantically tried to scroll down.

"What did that say?" I pulled her hand off the screen. She put her other hand on it, and I pulled that away, too. I screeched and she screeched back as we wrestled in the law offices of Poitras and Associates. Then I gasped. "You said I'm interested in *erotica?* Erotica!"

She cleared her throat. "Well! You want to seem seductive, Stevie. You know, daring in the bedroom in a sexy way. . . . A woman who knows herself, embraces a slippery toy or two, maybe a costume . . . willing to try a chocolate handcuff . . . no cages."

"Erotica?" I semishouted that word, then hushed right up. Don't ever yell "erotica" in a law firm. It distracts the attorneys. They think it's a legal term. "I don't even know what that is. I can guess at it, but no, I don't want to do it. I wouldn't know how to do it. Oh, my goodness." I buried my head in my hands, hearing my grandma's voice. She always said, "Oh, my goodness," too.

"Moving on!" Zena declared. "See here, Stevie, before you vomit like a sick cow. I wrote that you're searching for a man between the ages of thirty and forty-five who is ready to commit, who likes to camp and travel to Italy. You also want a man who is romantic and will take you to nice dinners. . . . You're not into star signs or witchcraft, at least we got that right. You won't be casting spells on anyone and boiling their balls."

I groaned. "I don't want to do Internet dating. I can find my own dates. I sure don't want to boil anyone's balls."

"Where? Here? You can't date a lawyer. That's out of the question. Lawyers are all shits. All of them. *Shits*."

She did not bother to lower her voice when she announced, "Lawyers are all shits. All of them. *Shits*."

"Dare to date, Stevie. Don't be a puss."

"I'm not ready to date." Heck, no. The only person I wanted to date was Jake, but he would never ask. I could only dream pathetically. "I'm not a puss." Was I? Was I a wuss? "I'm not a puss or a wuss." I said that too loud and cowered down a bit.

"You're going to get ready," Zena said. She is half drill sergeant, half brainiac. One time she threw a stapler at the head of a young, snobby male lawyer from another firm who whispered a suggestive, smarmy comment to her outside the firm's bathroom. "Lock, stock, barrel, and a push-up bra. You've got a stupendous rack now, and you need to show those girls off to their best advantage. Pull 'em up, push 'em out."

"I like my boobs tucked in." I so did. I was still hiding from my new body. I was not ready for it, didn't know what to do with it, and did not want attention.

"Yoo-hoo! You already have an interested gentleman. His name is Zack (Shorty) Holcomb and he likes midnight walks on the beach, massage, traveling to Central America, and piloting small airplanes. He says he wants a woman between eighteen and thirty-five who is financially independent, chases the high life, doesn't have to be attached at the hip, is cool on fast cars, and likes camping in the mountains, skiing, running, nature, and adventures."

"He's . . ." Zena paused, staring at the screen. She flicked her earring. It was long, wiry, and almost touched her shoulder. In her other ear she wore an earring, half as long, frog shaped. "Interesting. Especially if you lust for men with two chins who resemble donkeys. But let's see who he is. All men lie, you know. It's in their DNA. They're all deceptive, sneaky, vague, untrustworthy. That's why I never fall in love. I don't believe in it. Love is simply passion unchecked. People don't get it. They're lustful and want a naked romp and a leg twister so they think they're in love. Give me a break." She clicked to another Web site, punched in some sort of pass code, and then typed in the name Zack Holcomb. Zena's uncle is a private investigator, so she has access to his skills and tricks. She can look up anyone and get the scoop. "Let's check this lecher out."

This was a bad, bad day. "If you think he's a lecher and all men are disgusting, why do you want me to date?"

For a second Zena contemplated me, cat-like brown eyes zooming right in like a target. "Because, Stevie. Now and then, when the moon is full and bluish, when the galaxy is all calm and peaceful and serenity rules and even the falling stars are falling gracefully, and the wind creates a beautiful song, that's when you find one outstanding man. Kind. Loyal. Funny and smart, great in bed but not kinky. A lover in his head and in his body. A man who doesn't think as a dick-obsessed monkey with a brain the size of a testicle, but one who is thoughtful and can hold his emotions in one hand and hug you close with the other. A man who is a hunky, manly man but who can talk to you like your best girlfriend, because that's what he wants to be for you. Your best friend."

Zena could get so poetic sometimes, so melodic, it cut right through the sarcasm. It was always a shocker.

She pointed at me with both hands. "That's what I want for you because I love you, Sister Stevie. Now, let's get shakin' here."

I sniffled. I blinked hard. I've known Zena for years. Every-time she tells me she loves me, I cry. I patted my touched heart.

"You're such a baby, Stevie," Zena whispered, then she winked, her frog swinging at me. She typed in two more pass-words. "This will take a second. Damn, these computers are so slow. They've got condoms stuck in their hard drives. Maybe you'll need a condom soon, too, Stevie. We can only hope. I hear they have condoms with stars on them now. Glittery, too. They have glow in the dark, that's frickin' hilarious. A glowing penis prancing about."

I rolled my eyes. I could almost—almost—give sex up com-pletely. I didn't even like it that well. Nothing makes a woman more vulnerable than sex, and the criticism that comes with it when you're not "good enough" is devastating. I should know. I am bad in bed, that's what I've been told.

But I couldn't help think of Jake Stockton. He could bring up some passion in me for sex again. Maybe I wouldn't be bad with him in bed.

Maybe. But maybe not.

The computer screen flicked alive, and there we had it.

Double Chin's mug shot.

He was a doozer.

Long history of arrests for drugs, DUI, identity theft, bur-glary. A court case for delivering drugs in and out of Central America was pending. Bankruptcy. Owed child support for four kids and alimony for three wives.

"Well," I said. "Now we know why he wants adventure, likes Central America, camping outside, piloting small air-planes, fast cars, and needs a woman with money. At least he was honest about his interests."

"Too bad neither of us does drugs. We could probably get a discount. Maybe he has coupons or something," Zena said.

"Take me off the Web site. I beg you. I do not want to date and I do not want to do erotica or slippery toys. I do not want chocolate handcuffs in my bed. I only want a pillow." I heard the clacking of high heels.

"That would be Crystal," Zena singsonged. "Hey, Crystal. How are you today?"

"Shut up, Zena."

"Aww. Now that hurts my feelings."

"You don't have feelings. Why aren't you wearing one of your skull necklaces?"

"Oh, gee!" Zena pointed a finger up in the air. It was her middle finger. "I lost them when I was picking up sticks for you to shove up your butt."

"Zena, you should spend more time working. Without a college degree, let alone a law degree, you don't want to lose your job. You could end up driving a bus or something."

Something flashed across Zena's face. Fleeting, but I saw it: Raw pain. Crystal had smashed a nerve.

I stood up. "Good-bye, Crystal."

"Don't dismiss me, Steve. Sit down and work. I need the Compton file in ten seconds. On my deck. Clip clop."

I have no idea why Crystal used the "clip clop" expression. None.

"Clip clop," Zena said. "I hope you get the clap."

Crystal glowered, then left on her towering heels.

A few days later at work I heard Crystal yell on full throttle. "Arrrgggh! Dammit, Zena!"

I peeked in Crystal's office. Her desk was covered with sticks with a copy machine picture of Zena's butt on top of them.

Zena is so darn funny.

We had more excitement at Poitras and Associates.

Seems that a local married businessman was a bigamist.

He had two wives; neither knew about the other. The wives were in Oregon and Washington and were uncannily similar. Both were doctors, both were slim blondes, both had two children with him, both were office holders in their elite clubs, and both were snobby and cold.

Both were beyond head bangingly angry.

We represented the Oregon wife.

Her first words to Cherie: "I want his penis on a platter."

I took another face-plant on my walk on Saturday to avoid Jake. He likes to run and varies his route. If he didn't, I'd hide out behind someone's house so I could watch him and that body on a routine basis with my binoculars—not that I would stalk him. That would be creepy. I saw him coming and darted into an alleyway I used often, then hid behind these giant green recycling bins we have in Oregon. I heard him breathing past. When I thought he was gone, I came back out in time to see him in the distance. My, he had a nice bottom.

I could never converse for long with that man with the nice bottom—too scary—but I could not deny that perfect shape, those strong hips, those grippable shoulders. But I am not obsessed with him. That would be freaky.

She snickered. I saw it. Her hand covered her mouth pretty quick, but it was there.

"What?" I hastily put the red dress back on the rack.

"Oh, nothing." Eileen turned her face away, pretending to be interested in other dresses.

I felt my throat get all tight. Silly to get a tight throat over a dress. But it was so *stunning*. It had a draped V-neckline, spaghetti straps, and a ruffle at the bottom. I had seen it and instantly sucked in my breath. If only I had the nerve to wear that red dress!

I felt the material again, my breath still caught.

She giggled.

"What? You don't like the dress?"

"Well . . ."

"Say it." I sighed. I hated that I sighed. It sounded so petulant and childish. Why do I become petulant and childish around Eileen?

"If you really want to know. . . ." She smiled with a slight shake of her head, her real and mongo-sized diamond earrings flashing. "It's not your style. That's for someone . . . younger, very thin. Sexy. Hey! You don't have to look all hurt, Stevie, you asked for my opinion."

I took one last peek at the red dress, then idly flicked the hangers, one after another, pausing here and there at other dresses. All of them paled in comparison to that spectacular red dress.

She giggled, hand over mouth.

Eileen Yorkson and I have known each other since seventh grade. We were chubby then and got fatter together. Almost all of our time was spent eating, cooking, baking, eating more. We were eating partners. She ate because she had a terrible relationship with her mother and then the mother walked out when she was fifteen and Eileen refused to "ever, ever speak to her again, that loathsome bitch," though her mother begged her. I ate because I was trying to numb my insidious grief.

To say that my operation has had an effect on our relationship would be like saying an earthquake, ranked as a nine on the Richter scale, shook things up a wee bit.

Eileen still weighed more than 300 pounds.

She reminded me every time I saw her that I had not lost the weight on my own.

I picked up a purplish-colored dress. It shimmered and shone.

"You're not serious," Eileen laughed, ripping the dress from my hand and slamming it back on the rack. "Try this on." She pulled out a large bluish green shirt with white flowered buttons. Even if I was still heavy I wouldn't have worn it. People would think I was a daisy patch.

"I don't think that's my style—" I said, softly, so as not to start yet another argument.

"Not your style!" Eileen exclaimed, perfectly made-up eyes open wide. She threw her shoulders back. She's about two inches taller than me and wears $500 heels, so she towers over me. "Yes, it is. You love flowers!"

"Ummm . . . well . . ."

"You can't wear anything tight, Stevie," Eileen said, "because of your *chest*." She eyed my chest, as if it had somehow leaped up, wriggled around, and affronted her that second. "That *chest!* You can cover up some of that excess fake boob with this shirt."

"Uhhh . . ." I crossed my arms in front of my chest. My chest wasn't that big. I was a 34C, not exactly bopping about uncontrolled.

"Take it." She shoved it into my arms. "This one, too." She handed me a shirt with swirly designs that resembled amoebas. "Come on over to this section." She dragged me to the Women's Section, for large women.

What do you say to your friend who still weighs more than 300 pounds: "Eileen, I don't fit here anymore? I know we used to shop here together, but now I can't." Wasn't that insensitive? Wasn't it calling attention to her weight? But wasn't it obvious?

She must have read my mind. She patted her short brown hair. She used gel to make it stick up on top. "You think you don't belong in this section, but you do. You so do. Maybe not the pants." She shook her head in pity. "I feel so sorry for you, Stevie, for all you've been through. You're a little grayish, today, honey. Are you okay?"

"Yes, I'm fine."

"And you look exhausted."

"Thanks."

"Oh, don't get all sensitive on me. I'm honest, you know that."

Why do people think they can tell someone, "You look so tired!" and get away with it with a smile? It's the same as saying to someone, "You look terrible."

"I know you have a problem with my being honest, Stevie, but you have to hear it sometimes. Better from me, someone who cares about you, than from someone else."

"Eileen—"

"Eileen what?" she mocked, her face flushing. "Eileen, I'm too good for this section now? I want something that remakes me into a teenager? Come on, Stevie, it's time someone told you that you're trying to dress too young. Remember Mrs. Tomissan in school? Heather's mom?"

I remembered.

"Slutty. She was slutty. She was trying to be young again. I think she was trying for sexy, but it didn't work. So don't be a Mrs. Tomissan."

I felt hot and stupid. "I'm not trying to be her—"

"Good. What about this shirt?"

She pulled out a patterned, long-sleeved blouse. It looked like a puzzle squished together by ghouls. "I don't think—"

"It'll be flattering on you. Add some color to your face. You know, you can't wear blah *all* the time."

She piled a few more shirts on my arms. I hated all of them but said nothing because I am spineless. "This one will slim down those shoulders of yours, get rid of that football player look." She smiled at me, then went back to her shopping.

Eileen Yorkson is wealthy. Her father owns an investment company and she works as the "manager." She's paid more than $250,000 a year. I hear about that often. She is "invaluable" to the company, she tells me. She has an expensive home in the hills of Portland, shops obsessively, and dumps tons of money, which she uses as an excuse to treat the salesgirls as one would treat contagious cholera.

I sighed again. This time, the sigh was for me and my patheticness.

"Can I help you, ladies?" a saleswoman asked. She was in her fifties, stylishly dressed with a gentle, kind face.

"Yes, thank you." I smiled back, tentative, insecure. Shopping scared me to death. I had no clue what to buy or even the remotest hint of what would be right on me. I had been buying used clothes for almost two years, after buying only tent-sized clothing, changing them out as the weight dropped off.

"Let me see what you have there," the saleswoman said. She examined the shirts that Eileen had pulled off the rack in my arms and held them up.

"This will be perfect with your coloring," she told Eileen, smiling, friendly.

"They're not for me," Eileen snapped.

"Oh, I'm sorry, a gift then?"

"No, not a gift." Eileen's voice dripped derision. "These clothes are for her."

The saleswoman held up the shirts again, huge, billowy. "Oh, no." She laughed. "Not for her. These are way too big. Honey, this isn't your section. You're in the wrong one. Let me help you."

"We're in the right one," Eileen huffed.

"Not at all. She's way too thin for this section. Are you a size 10, dear?"

I smiled back at her smile. A size 10! I had dreamed of being a 10! "I'm not sure."

"I'm Phyllis. Come with me." She turned and I followed, as if I were following the Pied Piper of clothing. I almost expected her to whip out a flute.

Eileen's hand yanked me back, and she hissed, "Remember Mrs. Tomissan, the slut. Do you want to be a Mrs. Tomissan?"

"No, I don't, but neither do I want to wear clothes that don't fit, Eileen." It was as if I'd told her she was uglier than Frankenstein. Her face grew mottled, her eyes narrowing into slits. Lately I had noticed how mean her eyes are. I glanced away.

"Here we are." Phyllis beckoned us over with a wide grin, then threw out her arms. "Right here. This is your section."

If horns had blasted, followed by a sweet trill of violins, and a ba-bong-bong on a huge drum, I would not have been surprised. I'd entered paradise. I admired the mannequins. The racks. All filled with finery and fluff and skirts with ruffles and pants with pizzazz and—

"I would look okay wearing these clothes?" I had to confirm it. *Had to.*

"Absolutely!" She tilted her head, quizzically. "Oh, I understand. You've recently lost weight, haven't you?"

Eileen giggled. "She took the shortcut out. Bought into society's twisted vision about how a woman has to be thin to be valuable, threw out her life savings, didn't have a penny to her name, then saved all her money *a second time* to have another operation to cut off the loose skin and risked her life, all so she could be thin—"

"Yes, I have lost weight."

The saleswoman studied Eileen for a second and then her mouth opened, a slight bit, and she nodded, as if to herself. She understood the situation, I knew it. She smiled at me. "Congratulations!"

Eileen snorted again. "Ask her how much weight she's lost, why don't you?"

"It's none of my business," Phyllis said, a slight edge to her voice.

"She's lost 170 pounds," Eileen said, as if I'd committed the crime of kidnapping. "She took the cheater's way out, if you know what I mean."

Phyllis stared at Eileen for long seconds, then, as if in dismissal, she turned toward me, a hand under my elbow, her back to Eileen. "Now, dear, what can I help you find?"

"Everything."

"A makeover then?" She was delighted. I couldn't blame her. She was probably on commission.

"Yes, you could say that." I could feel Eileen's seething anger.

"Rather a start-over," Eileen said, her diamond bracelets flashing. "She has no fashion sense and—"

"Let's go on over here and pull some jeans off the rack, shall we?" Phyllis grabbed my arm. As we were walking away, she said to Eileen, who started to follow, "There's a chair by the dressing room where you can rest. We'll meet you there in a minute."

She hustled me off. I didn't even dare sneak a peek back, I was so shocked. Someone had handled Eileen. Not me, but someone else, and she was off my back.

I almost skipped. I could hear the flute music trilling, tra-la-la. Phyllis and I dumped one outfit after another into our arms.

"Too tight," Eileen barked as I came out of the dressing room to show her and Phyllis the jeans I was wearing.

"Perfect fit," Phyllis said at the same time. "You look fantastic!" Eileen glowered at her.

"Do I?" Did I? There were violins and a cello!

"If you want every part of your butt to be outlined for men's consumption, you do," Eileen said. "Take my word for it. Those are too tight."

Phyllis turned to Eileen. "This is the style. It's the way women wear them now—"

"Not me."

"Well, of course not," Phyllis blurted out. I knew she regretted the words as soon as they were out of her mouth. "I'm sorry—"

"Forget it," Eileen snapped, crossing her arms, after thumping her $1,000 purse on the floor. "I get it."

There was a silence, and then, "All right." Phyllis turned back to me and smiled.

I was stunned. Usually when Eileen was offended, people stumbled all over themselves trying to apologize. Her anger was a living thing, intimidating, controlling. They would say they were sorry once, twice, three times. She never budged, only glowered. I should know.

This woman, this Phyllis, moved on. She said she was sorry, Eileen didn't accept it, and she let it go.

Whoa.

"Now, take off the shirt you're wearing and put on the red shirt with the criss-cross bodice we picked out. It'll be beautiful."

I skedaddled back into the dressing room. I hadn't worn red since I was a kid, even though it was absolutely my most favorite color. I stripped off the dowdy blue T-shirt I had on and slipped on the clingy red shirt with a scooped neckline. I didn't turn around until I had adjusted the neckline.

My mouth dropped when I saw myself in the mirror, the flute music now a full blast orchestra.

I loved it! The shirt clung to my curves and the material felt so gentle, so . . . so sexy!

I fluffed my hair out. Dowdy. Maybe I'd get it cut, too.

I braced myself for Eileen's reaction but couldn't wait to show Phyllis.

Their reactions were as I imagined.

Phyllis said, "That is fabulous, absolutely fabulous!"

Eileen let out a shriek-groan and said, "Slutty Mrs. Tomisson! Here she comes!"

Tra-la-la!

In the end I bought jeans, skirts, slacks, six dressy shirts in all colors and styles, two belts, and two jackets—one was denim, the other khaki corduroy. I had not dared to buy the red dress. I couldn't. Too daring. Where would I wear it, anyhow?

Eileen and I were both silent for the first ten minutes as I drove her home.

"Stevie," she sighed.

I braced myself.

"Can I be honest with you, honey?" She reached out and squeezed my hand. "We're best friends, right? We've always been there for each other."

I knew what was coming. I wanted to tell her to be quiet, not to ruin the glow I had.

"You've spent a fortune."

"I needed clothes, Eileen. All of my clothes hang off of me." I'd gotten paid last Friday. After I paid my mortgage, bills, and medical loan, I would have $15 for food for two weeks, plus what was in my pantry. How many ways could I eat spaghetti?

And you know what, *I didn't care!*

Spaghetti, here I come!

Eileen smiled at the pathetic person that I was. "Those clothes aren't flattering, Stevie. I'm sorry to tell you that, I am. Phyllis is on commission and you bought whatever she told you. You could have bought them for a fraction at Goodwill. You don't make enough. You've lost some weight, now you think you can wear anything. It's not true, I'm sorry."

"I don't want to be a frump anymore, Eileen," I said weakly.

"You don't want to be a frump anymore? What? You're saying I'm a frump? That's what you're saying, isn't it?"

"I didn't mean—"

"You didn't mean what? That I'm fat and dull compared to you? I get it, Stevie, you're better than me now. Thinner. Prettier.

And I'm still obese. Did you need to point that out? You can wear jeans, you can wear red, you need a belt. I'm sick of this. You're going to dump me, aren't you, because you're thin and I'm not. I see it coming."

"I am not going to do that. . . ." It was weak, I knew it. But I wouldn't drop her for her weight. I would drop her for her mouth.

Eileen went on and on, and I stopped protesting, stopped apologizing, shut down.

Why did I stay friends with her? Obligation? Guilt? Loyalty? Do I feel sorry for her? Is it okay to dump a friend? If it is, how do you do that?

My delight over the clothes was dimmed to almost nothing by the time I dropped Eileen off. Maybe she was right. Maybe the clothes were too clingy, too young, too too.

By the time I arrived home I was so relieved to see my emerald green house with the burgundy door and white picket fence I almost cried.

I put the bags in the back of my closet and pulled on my sweats and a T-shirt.

That night I flipped through a stack of gardening books and magazines by my nightstand, then worked on the sketches for my garden before turning out my light when I couldn't keep my eyes open any longer. I knew what to do with most of the garden, but I had a corner filled with weeds that was stumping me.

As usual, as soon as I snuggled down, sighed, and told myself to go to sleep, I was wide awake.

Insomnia is a plague. It tiptoes after you and then when it's dark it snaps its jaws over your sleep and flings it around, teeth clamped down hard.

I watched the clock.

I started worrying about work, money, my medical debt, and what would I do if I lost my job, had no money, couldn't pay my medical debt, and ended up living in a shed? Sheds are cold! What would I do if something happened to Polly, Lance, or

Aunt Janet? What if I lost my mind and started collecting cats? What if I had another heart attack on my walk, lost control of my bowels, and Jake found me in a mess?

I gave up after an hour. My hands shook as I turned on the light and studied my gardening magazines again. I drank milk. Finally, about two in the morning, I fell asleep. I woke up after I saw Sunshine riding a horse away from me. She was headed for the bridge. She turned her head, panicked, screamed my name, but I couldn't catch her because my feet were stuck in red paint. I saw my grandparents' faces across a field of corn. They were melting. All their features seeping to the ground, only their white hair left and their cowboy hats, then Sunshine melted, too, and I was alone. The horse kept galloping across the bridge, then jumped over it and turned into a black, frothing cloud.

I sat straight up in bed, struggling to breathe.

Sunshine wanted something, I knew that. I have tried not to think about her very much these last decades, or about my grandparents, because it hurts so much I think I'll die of the pain of it, but in the last eighteen months, Sunshine keeps coming back, again and again, and I don't understand what she's trying to tell me. I wiped my face with trembling hands. The tears are coming more and more since I lost all this weight.

I briefly toyed with the idea that I was losing my mind, that I would soon be wearing a floppy yellow hat, but I shut that thought down. I got up, went to the bathroom, and drank a glass of water. My eyes automatically went to the mirror, and I shuddered.

She was there.

4

~~~

Portland, Oregon

"Thank you for your orders. It will be a pleasure to serve you and your guests this evening, Mr. Barrett," the waiter said, deferential. He was suited up in black and white.

"Thank you," Lance said. "Thank you so much."

Lance is a grateful person. He says he is so grateful he lived through his childhood and so grateful that he doesn't have to see Herbert every day that each day is a gift that must be enjoyed, "with love and friendship."

Lance also has very expensive tastes in dining and insists on treating me and Polly to dinner all the time. We were at the Portland Que, one of the fanciest restaurants in Portland, the type of restaurant where the food arrives on your plate as if it is art. Edible art.

"You're welcome, Mr. Barrett," the waiter said. He nodded and smiled at me and Polly. We smiled back. The candles flickered over the white tablecloth and shiny silverware.

Lance was a regular customer, so the owner, *under no circumstances,* was going to protest that Lance had brought two of his blow-up dolls with their plasticky smiles to dinner and placed them in chairs around our table.

Fiona Butterfly was lovely in her purple bathing suit with gold butterflies flitting across it.

Katerina was also splendid. She was a naked doll, so, for

modesty's sake, Lance had draped her with a gold sari. Already two people had made comments and Lance had handed out his Lucky Ladies business card. One man almost slobbered over Fiona Butterfly. His wife yanked him away.

"I think we should talk about your parents' fortieth wedding anniversary party," I said as I slipped a spoonful of strawberry sorbet into my mouth, which was supposed to "clean my palate."

"Even thinking about talking about Mom and Dad's fortieth makes me want to blow in a sack," Polly said, breathing hard, her mouth in an O. "I don't want to go. I don't want to plan it. I don't want to think about it. I don't want to be a part of this crime."

"But we have to, Polly," I said. "It's coming up."

"Dad should plan it," Lance said, his face darkening. "Nothing we do is going to be right."

"That's true. He'll hate the whole thing." Polly put her white cloth napkin over her face and breathed deep. "All will be wrong. All done poorly. Putridly. Such a disappointment his kids are to him—it's his wife's fault, her family is crazy."

I felt my usual pangs of pain.

"He wants us to do it so he can tell the state of Oregon what a fantastic dad he is. See here, Portland, my kids gave me my anniversary party."

I finished my sorbet and put my spoon down. My hands were starting to shake. See what the mention of one boorish, testicle-trouncing man can do to sane people?

"I'm going to bring my blow-up girls to the party," Lance announced.

"You're kidding," I said.

"Oh, stop," Polly wheezed. "Let me get my hyperventilation under control before you throw something jack-crazy at me. I'm picturing all these naked blow-up dolls with cushy boobs sitting at the head table with Mom and Dad."

"I'm going to do it. Good advertising." He reached out a hand and patted Katerina. She almost fell off the chair. I caught her by the hip and propped her back up, ignoring the pointed stares of the three well-dressed, snobby women behind me.

"Plus I need the comfort they give me," Lance said. "Good comfort."

"Are the invitations ready to go?" I asked. The party was months out, but Herbert wanted everything shipshape.

Polly didn't answer.

"That was your job, Polly Wants a Cracker," Lance said, real gentle and sweet.

Polly balled up the napkin in her hands and rocked back and forth. Her hair was up in a ponytail, the auburn curls cascading down in red and gold. She was wearing an overly large, white T-shirt; a flowing red, cottony shirt down to her knees; and jeans. She was trying to cover up. I felt sick for her.

"You did do the invitations, didn't you?" I asked.

Polly whimpered and breathed into her napkin.

The waiter came by and discreetly took my and Lance's sorbet cups, but not Polly's. She hadn't eaten hers.

"The invitations aren't ready, are they, honey?" Lance asked.

Polly whimpered again.

"You haven't even started them, have you?" I asked.

She threw her napkin down.

There was an electric silence, and then I said, "I'm going to take that as a no."

Polly threw both hands in the air, shook them, stomped her feet under the table, and said, in a pitchy voice, "I don't think they should have the party. There's nothing to celebrate, and I don't want to be a part of this lie. I hate that Mom married Dad. I hate that she's still married to him. I see this as forty years of Mom being stuck with Dad. She probably would have had more freedom in prison with a girlfriend named Maude. And a penchant for handcuffs."

No one moved except for Fiona Butterfly, who fell off her chair. Our waiter scurried on over and put her right back up, then patted her on the shoulder.

"Poor Mom," Lance said. "Oh, oh, oh. Poor Mom."

"Poor Mom? Yes, poor Mom, but I've got ticked off issues, too," Polly said, wriggling, agitated. "I'm mad that I spent my whole childhood trying to protect her from Dad, watching Dad attack her, belittle her, mock her, and she didn't do anything. That wasn't exactly a healthy environment for us to grow up in. He wouldn't let her drive, wouldn't let the mail be delivered to the house, buttoned her up tight with those staid blouses, and she put up with it because she's weak. *Weak!* For our sakes, she should have left him so we would be protected, but she couldn't summon up the strength to do it." She threw her napkin in the air. "She was *weak!*"

"Polly," Lance said, broken. "Mom's an alcoholic. I know she doesn't drink now, but she did then, and it rattled her poor mind to mush. Dad's abuse controlled her. She was like a bunny in the jaws of a tiger. In everything he said to her, in every action, he showed her that he thought she was stupid, incapable, incompetent, uneducated, beneath him. She listened to that for years and years, poor Mom. Decades. She was freakin' brainwashed and she didn't have anyone to turn to, no parents, no sister—" His voice cracked and he picked up Fiona Butterfly and put her on his lap. For good comfort.

"I know, I know," Polly moaned. "She's a wreck." She twisted her hands. "I'm a wreck."

"I'm a wreck, too," I said. "I've got visions, nightmares, flashbacks, and they keep getting worse."

"And I can't talk to women," Lance said. "I can't even open my mouth around them because Dad told me so many times I'd be a terrible husband, that I was weak, ineffectual, unmanly, dumb, and wouldn't amount to anything but a stupid jock. I've only had two girlfriends in my life and they both broke up with me because I couldn't speak around them. I'm a disgrace to myself."

The waiters came with our salads. The lettuce was artfully arranged, like a 3D painting, dressing drizzled on the lettuce and then curlicued on the plate. The croutons formed a straight line. The blow-up girls did not get salads.

Polly fanned her face to get more air. She had been complaining about heart palpitations lately.

We were silent for a minute, then Lance reached out his huge hand and covered both of hers, Fiona Butterfly leaning with him.

"You do know that you're coming close to totally crashing, don't you, honey?" Lance asked.

"No, I'm not." Polly shifted in her seat.

"Polly, you are." I reached my hand out and put it over Lance's. Polly not being well made me feel so sick. "You can't live like this. You can't continue to carry a bag tucked under your bra, you hyperventilate, you can't breathe, you never sleep, you're not eating. You're so stickly thin."

"I'm fine, Stevie, back off. You, too, Lance," she snapped. "But I love you."

"You're way too thin," Lance said, his voice hoarse. Fiona Butterfly wobbled in his lap. "I worry about you all the time, and sometimes I get so worried I have to go and lie down and knit. I knit for two hours straight on Sunday from the worry. I made you a hat, Stevie."

"Thank you, Lance." Yes, Lance knits. Learned it from some other guy named Timor on his pro football team. Timor actually owns a giant knitting store now with an order catalog and everything. Lance is "in love" with his designs. Every year he makes me and Polly at least two matching hats and scarves. He's quite talented. We wear them all the time in winter.

"Well, quit worrying, you overgrown wimp. I'm fine. I'm fine."

The waiter came with three types of bread and two types of butter. The blow-up girls did not seem hungry.

"Now, this lady." He picked Fiona Butterfly up. "This lady's got curves. You need 'em. You need 'em here"—he pointed to the doll's boobs—"and here." He pointed helpfully to the doll's ass, spinning her so Polly got a close-up view of said ass. "You need more of that, honey. More bottom."

"I don't need more bottom," she said. She dropped her head in her hands.

"Women should have meat on their bones, curves. They feel better with curves, too. Without curves, there's nothing to grip in bed," Lance said. "Not that I know much in that department . . . not much at all. . . ."

Fiona Butterfly tipped toward me, and I pushed her back up. I ignored the pointed stares of the snobby women again.

"I'm not going to talk about this," Polly said, panting a bit. She put her hand on her heart. She does that to calm herself down. Then she said, "It's okay, heart, calm down. Everything's okay."

Me and Lance didn't say anything, awash in our miserable worry, so Polly said, "Tell us about your rock party, Lance."

"Well, dang, Polly, I don't want to talk about it, I want to talk about you and getting yourself some boob fat and bottom fat and—"

"Lance!" she said.

"Okay, fine." He hugged Fiona Butterfly close, then put her back in her seat. "You two are coming to Lance's Lucky Ladies Hard Rock Party the night after the anniversary party, right? It's out at the McMannis Brothers' property. I rented the whole place. It's gonna be a rock concert. I got a band that plays eighties music and everything. Oregon beer, Oregon berries, Oregon chefs. Everybody has to come dressed up as their favorite eighties rocker or they can't get in the door. It's gonna be awesome." He put a hand on Katerina's shoulder. Katerina knocked over his water glass. In seconds, two waiters were there mopping it up. More water appeared immediately.

"The ladies are gonna be the stars, but if you two don't come—" He paused, cleared his throat. "If you two don't come . . ." He got all teary-eyed. "The party will be ruined for me. *Ruined*. All for nothing. Please tell me you'll be there."

"I'll be there, Lance," I said. "For sure."

"Me, too. Lance, I wouldn't miss it," Polly said.

"Promise me," he said.

"Lance, my legs would have to be detached from my body before I would miss your rock party for the ladies," I said.

Polly breathed into her white napkin again, the candlelight casting a shadow on her face. "Me, too, brother. I'm already planning what head-banging rocker I'm going to dress as."

Lance's face got all red, and he blinked rapidly. "I love you two." He sniffed, wiped his eyes. "You're always there for me, always have been. Even when we were young and Dad was so mean, so mean, so mean, hurting my feelings, my soul, the deepest part of myself. It's always been us three, us three till the end."

Oh, we are such babies. At the same time, me and Lance and Polly all burst into tears.

It sent our waiters scurrying right on over, panicky. "May we help you? What is it? Is it the dressing? The breads? How about some more wine?"

Being in a family is like living inside a tornado. Sometimes you're spun around, sometimes you're spit outside the tornado all by yourself, and sometimes you're able to join hands with someone inside of it and wait the whole darn thing out.

Me, Lance, and Polly held hands. Fiona Butterfly fell on her head. Katerina fell backwards. The waiters picked them right back up, then brought our meals, which were not food but art disguised as food.

Neither Fiona Butterfly nor Katerina seemed hungry.

When I bought my house I knew two things: One, I didn't have much money, and two, I would have to do almost everything myself.

My thought?

Big breath, and then, from out of nowhere I heard myself say, *I can do it.*

Joseph, my uncle's kind, compassionate long-time landscaper and handyman, had taught me how to use every saw and tool under the sun, and I'd spent hours with him, as had Lance and Polly. We could build about anything, except an ark. (We would need Noah for that.)

I ripped up the 1970s brown and yellow linoleum and moldy carpets and replaced them with old-growth timber salvaged from a turn-of-the-century home that had been torn down (free). I tore out the brown cabinets in the kitchen and hauled in an antique, slightly dented armoire to hold pots, pans, griddles, etc. It had so much personality I named it Tally ($12). I cleaned up another armoire (Tally II) with no doors to work as a pantry ($40). I then put in floor-to-ceiling open shelving, painted bright white on one full wall to hold my mismatched collection of dishes, colorful glasses, and linens.

I love old, interesting furniture that looks like it could speak in four languages and tell secrets. My kitchen island is a mechanics work table complete with tons of drawers that I bought at a country antique sale ($52). I repainted it green and spray painted the knobs gold. I heard through a neighbor that a friend was taking out her huge butcher block island counter for a new kitchen. I brought my saw, walked off with the block, and fastened it onto the mechanics work table.

I stripped the old cabinets in my bathroom and repainted them green, had a plumber install a claw-foot tub I got from a hotel that was being demolished ($25), then slapped up silver corrugated metal. (Free from a construction site. Manager said he'd pay me to take it.) It's modern wallpaper, I think.

I use a barn door I bought for $1 at a country garage sale for my kitchen table. I painted it blue, and sawhorses (also free) act as a base. A one-hundred-year-old church pew in my living room sits across a red couch I had hauled in from a flea market sale (no fleas, $12).

On both sides of my fireplace I built white bookshelves. I didn't know what to put in them at first. I had the same problems with filling my bookshelves as I did with choosing paint colors and furniture for my house.

Why the mental freeze? Because I had lived with Eddie, who smashed anything creative I wanted to do with searing anger and incessant ridicule, and before that with Herbert, who smashed everything in me altogether. So, with very little money, I would go to Goodwill and Value Village and garage sales and have conversations with myself as I stared at things.

What do I like?

What do I not like?

What do I want in my house?

Do I like blue glass? Do I like antique perfume bottles? What colors make me smile? Does everything I buy have to have a use or can I buy it for the pretty aspect alone?

Who am I?

Who am I?

Fixing up my home can be compared to fixing up myself. It was a constant experiment.

Ploddingly, over months, I filled my shelves with all kinds of things I learned I love: very old books, shells, lots of clocks, colored glass, blue jars, and small paintings and embroiderings. I attached a piece of wood to form a mantel over the fireplace and painted the cheesy fake rock wall white.

I found three chandeliers at garage sales, and from each chandelier I have hung crystals, pink Christmas tree balls, or colored, fake jewels. I repainted the pink, aqua, and greenish walls in my home in rich mocha and café au lait colors, with one sage wall and one brick red wall thrown in. I decorated one wall with intricately painted trays and another wall with china plates.

My house is the first thing that is completely my own. The light flows in abundance, the colors are earthy, soothing, and because of the vanilla and cinnamon potpourri, it smells good. Most important, *he's* never going to be here, nor are his huge TVs, his toy car collection, or his beer bottles.

No one appreciates their home, and their own safe, peaceful place, filled with the things that make them *them,* more than someone who has lived in chaos, bone-gnawing loneliness, and emotional upheaval for years. The kind of emotional upheaval that is so confusing, mind-twisting, and manipulative that you don't know which way is up anymore, let alone which way is out. As in: *Out the door.* That feeling of utter gratefulness for a home that exudes safety, for those of us who have lived through our own personal night terrors, never goes away. At least, that's what I think.

I painted my bedroom ceiling blue with lots of white stars, including the Big and Little Dippers and other constellations. I call it the Starlight Starbright ceiling. It's what I stare at when my insomnia is chasing me down like a rabid leopard.

Sunshine came to me in my dreams. She was sitting on the chair in my room, her legs swinging back and forth. She was smiling at me, talking, but I couldn't hear what she was saying. She was holding playing cards in one hand and wildflowers in the other.

Suddenly, two words came through and I heard what she said.

"Schoolhouse House."

Schoolhouse House.

I swallowed hard, scrunched my eyes closed, then opened them again. She was gone.

She was gone.

I *knew* she was gone. I had been grieving, or shutting out my grief, and my anger, for more than two decades.

So here's a question: Does grief end?

Does the effect of trauma ever end?

Does your mind insist on going over and over your sad, crushing memories because you haven't dealt with them or because they were simply horrific? Does it make a difference?

Was I losing my mind?

I had a lot of time to stare at my Starlight Starbright ceiling that night. Would I ever go back to Ashville? No, I couldn't. It would tear me apart like a blender on puree.

I cringed when I heard Herbert's voice over the telephone.

"How is the anniversary party planning going? I haven't had a report." No hello, how are you, how are things at your house, how's your job, how do you feel? Never. After I'd lost 100 pounds he'd said, "At least you now have a modicum of control in your life, Stevie. *Control.* You're controlling yourself. Control will get you somewhere. It will get you out of your rut. You'll have a life you can be proud of. You'll get something done for once, be productive."

When I lost 150 pounds he said, "Better. *Much* better. More presentable. Not such an embarrassment." He'd actually nodded at me as if he'd given me a glorious compliment.

"Are you there, Stevie?" he barked.

Herbert did not mince words.

"Yes, Herbert, we must have cut out there for a minute. The phone line was interrupted; it's a bit windy today—"

"Yes, yes. Tell me about my anniversary celebration."

We hate the celebration, I wanted to say. Me, Lance, and Polly think it's a terrible idea to celebrate forty years of indentured servitude on the part of Aunt Janet, and we think you're dysentery. "The party planning is going well, Herbert. Every-thing will be in order."

"Good. We're counting on you, Stevie, to do this right. To do it well. To have everything ready, oversee the work your cousins are doing on my behalf. The invitations are going out?"

"Uhhh . . ."

"Do not say 'uhhh,' young woman. Are the invitations out?"

"They're going out very shortly—"

"I haven't spoken with Polly for days, but I understand that you are now in charge of the invitations. Good for you, too, Ste-vie, to have a part in this celebration, not just the kids. Polly works very hard. She has a career, Stevie, a *career*. She is focused and motivated and driven. That's how you get somewhere, that's how you do it, that's how you become someone. You climb up the ladder, not down. Anyone in your way, go through them or yank them down, Stevie. Polly's making something of herself, and I know her success must be hard for you, but you are who you are." He sighed.

From the moment I lived with him, Herbert compared the three of us to one another. I heard all the time about Lance's athleticism, Polly's outstanding grades and top abilities in track and piano, etc. All aimed at telling me, in one way or another, that I was deficient. Not enough. I didn't fit in, wasn't good enough.

He harassed Lance and Polly about my high test scores. How come I was so much smarter? Were they stupid?

Why? I think it was for control. He didn't want us getting close to each other. He wanted the conflict, the dissent. It made him feel powerful.

It made us feel like we were nothing. *Nothing.*

"Remember, for the invitations you are to use the photos that I initially sent Polly, the one of our wedding, and a photo of us now, with the accompanying date and time of my anniversary celebration."

He ranted on and on after that, until he ran out of steam. This took a while. Herbert is short, stocky, with a hook for a nose and a shock of white hair.

"Dinner on Sunday night, seven o'clock, Stevie. The whole family will be there, and I will expect you to be in attendance as well."

See how he does that? Continually points out I'm not quite a member of the family. It is deliberate. "I'll come and sit with your family for dinner."

"I'm glad you've dropped the weight, Stevie. I was worried about the photos for my campaign Web site and my anniversary celebration with your size being such an issue, but it's not much of an issue now."

"Thanks, Herbert. I would have hated to ruin the photos with my body." I felt my anger trip.

"Obesity is a sign of weakness. Weakness does not run in the Barrett family." He cleared his throat. "Except with Janet. She was not born a Barrett, though, like you, so I have had to train her in our values, strengths, and traditions."

I conked my head on the table. I hated talking to Herbert, I well and truly did.

"I'll try to control my weakness," I said, trying to smash down my anger.

"Excellent. Now, I'll let you in on a family secret," Herbert boomed out.

I shuddered. I did not want to know any of Herbert's secrets.

"I'm having some trouble with your aunt Janet."

"What's wrong?"

"She's getting uppity."

I gagged. "Uppity?"

"Yes, I think it's a midlife problem that she's indulging in. Janet has led a very sheltered life with me as the protector and provider, the head of the home, and now she wants—" He cleared his throat.

"She wants what?" I thought of Aunt Janet. A woman swamped by her marriage and the unkindness that had been a relentless, erosive force for decades. Mousey brown hair, blouses buttoned to her neck, plain skirts swirling around a thin figure.

"She wants to spread her wings, flap a little. That terrible friend of hers, Virginia Ross, she's the one pushing Janet to do more, says that Janet needs to develop herself, become herself, find out who she is through travel and reading and the arts, that sort of psychobabble baloney. She's a raving, loony, nonthinking, bleeding heart liberal, Virginia is, and I have done everything possible to keep those two apart. I have even forbidden Janet to see her, but she has defied me. *Defied me!* The woman lives across the street, and Janet will actually sneak over there to visit her when I'm at work. The woman divorced years ago; she travels the world with a group of women, or even *on her own,* and then tells Janet how wonderful it is to travel, as if Janet could handle traveling. The woman is filthy rich, and for some inexplicable reason, she and Janet have become friends."

"But doesn't Aunt Janet need a friend, Herbert?" She needed many friends. And a life.

"Janet is a simple woman, Stevie. You and she have much in common."

I rolled my eyes.

"She is most comfortable at home, keeping her home in order. She enjoys her role as wife and mother and does not need more from the outside world. She knows her job is to serve the family and be my helpmate. She gets her security and her esteem from her role as my wife. It's an important role."

"How do you know that?" I asked, surprised I did. I blinked at my own self.

Herbert stopped mid-rant. "How do I know what?"

"How do you know she enjoys her role as wife and mother?"

He sputtered. "Because I've been married to her for forty years. I know my wife. Inside and out. She's not a complicated person."

"Maybe she's more complicated than you think." Sheesh. Had I said that, too?

"What on earth do you mean by that, Stevie?" he scoffed.

"I mean, Herbert, that maybe Aunt Janet isn't happy."

There was a stunned silence.

"Of course she's happy," he snapped. The notion that his wife might not be happy was clearly not something he'd thought about. Was she even a person? Nah. She was a helpmate. Did she have thoughts and dreams? No. She was A Wife.

"She's suffered on and off from severe depression your entire married life. I remember her leaving for weeks at a time when we were growing up."

"That's because she was drinking."

"Have you ever wondered why she was drinking?" Was I still asking questions?

Another stunned silence, then, "Because of her weakness!"

"Maybe she was drinking because she was lonely. Because she felt alone and lonely and you didn't make her feel loved or important." I slapped my hand to my forehead.

"Nonsense. You're sounding exactly like that Virginia across the street. Janet was weak, that's why she drank. I have strengthened her and we have put that chapter of our lives behind us. I only need to remind her of her drinking years now and then and admonish her so she does not cause more problems for me."

"Aunt Janet hasn't had a drink in years, Herbert, but that doesn't mean she's happy."

"You're being ridiculous."

"Am I?" Was I? No, I wasn't.

"Yes, you are. And, if this Virginia Ross would stop putting thoughts into Janet's head, we could go back to normal."

"Does Aunt Janet want normal still? Is normal good enough for her?"

"Young lady, I did not call you to be questioned. I certainly did not call to talk to you about my marriage. How dare you even offer an opinion. Plan my anniversary celebration, get the invitations out, and send me a report immediately." He hung up.

The thought of planning a "celebration" of Herbert and Aunt Janet's marriage made me feel sick.

I had to meet this Virginia person, though. That was a given.

Maybe she wanted another friend.

I don't remember many of the details of the first five years after I came to live with Herbert, Aunt Janet, Lance, and Polly. I was eleven and I was traumatized.

What I do remember is a family meeting Herbert called the

third day I was there. Aunt Janet was keening on the couch over the loss of her parents. Lance and Polly sat by her, quietly crying, until Herbert accused Lance of being a "sissy," Polly a "crybaby," and Janet "a damn mental case—are you turning into your sister?"

"With Stevie living with us from now on, there's bound to be questions. You all are not to tell anyone, *anyone,* what happened to Helen and Sunshine," he roared. "No one. You are to tell everyone that Stevie's parents died in a car crash and that I, out of kindness and generosity, have agreed to give her a roof over her head. Snap out of it, Janet! For God's sake, pull yourself together, woman!"

I shrunk into an even tighter ball on the couch by Lance.

"If you tell anyone our family secret," he thundered, "you will leave my home. Janet, you will be committed, unwillingly, if I have to, to a hospital. Lance, I will shuttle you off to reform school. Polly and Stevie, you will go to a home for wayward girls. These are not places you want to be. You will have to fight off violent people, blacks and Mexicans and immigrants, every time you turn around. You will have to work all day under exhausting conditions. You will be punished there for the slightest infraction. This is our family secret. Never," he thundered again. "Never talk about this embarrassment, this humiliation, this shame!"

"What are we supposed to be ashamed about?" I whispered. We were probably supposed to be ashamed that I hadn't saved Sunshine. I already felt so much guilt about that I could barely function.

Herbert gawked at me, shocked that anyone had even offered up a question in the middle of his tirade. "You are supposed to be ashamed, Stevie, that your mother was a psycho and murdered your sister and tried to murder you! She was a murderer! Your mother was a murderer! That's why you should be ashamed, Stevie."

I started to feel dizzy and sick and angry, too, and I wanted to eat.

"Now you listen to me, young woman. Your name is Stevie

Barrett from now on. We're hiding the sordid realities of your life. Never, *never,* tell anyone your other name. That name can link us to that scandal through the newspapers, and I won't have it! Your other name is gone, dead. That life is gone. Dead. Dead! You are Stevie Barrett. Your name is Stevie Barrett!"

I saw him through a haze of devastation, the room starting to spin. I didn't like that name. I wanted my name.

"Your name is Stevie Barrett! Say it!"

I shook my head, my curls swaying against my cheeks.

"Your name is Stevie Barrett!" He stuck his face three inches from mine and shook my shoulders, hard, my head flopping back and forth. Aunt Janet leaped to my defense; Lance tried to pry his fingers off, as did Polly. He shoved Lance to the floor, "you sissy," then lifted Polly, "you crybaby," and Aunt Janet, "you mental case," and threw them to the couch. Aunt Janet's head smashed into the wall.

"You say it right this minute, young woman, or you'll go to your room with no food." Uncle Herbert's breath was foul, enveloping me.

"No."

He shook me again, pain splitting up my back and neck.

"Say your new name!" He was purple with rage.

"No."

"You will not win, I will win! I will win, Stevie Barrett!"

That night, he won a slew of vomit down his suit and tie from me.

I was locked in my room, only allowed out for school, despite Aunt Janet's defense on my behalf, for which she was slapped. Each night Herbert came upstairs and shook me. "Say your name is Stevie Barrett! Say it! You're your sick mother, aren't you, in younger form . . . argumentative, stubborn, difficult, emotional! Say your new name!"

After three months, exhausted, grief stricken, scared to death of Uncle Herbert, who shook me so hard my neck constantly hurt, I gave in.

"What is your name?" he roared, slamming his hands on the wall above my head, as usual. "What is it?"

"Stevie Barrett," I whispered, feeling this broken horror invade my heart.

"Say it again," he shouted. "Say, 'My name is Stevie Barrett!'"

I paused, and again he shook me until I thought my head would fling off.

"My name is Stevie Barrett," I whispered, the sobs coming up in my throat.

"Say it louder!"

"My name is Stevie Barrett," I said, the sobs rocking my body.

"Louder!"

I didn't say it louder, I couldn't, the sobs making mincemeat out of my words.

He stood back. "I am the head of this household. I have taken you in as my duty. You will not defy me again. You will do what I say, when I say. Do you understand me? *Do you understand me?*"

I did.

I understood.

I understood I wanted to die.

If you could line up the family secrets in this country, word by word, undoubtedly the words would wrap themselves at least twice around the entire galaxy. Most families have them. But here's what I know now: Family secrets rot and destroy. They become living, breathing, black, infected, seeping messes.

We had a seeping mess on our hands in that house that stretched into our adulthood. Me, Lance, Polly, and Aunt Janet rarely mentioned what had happened on that bridge, that night, under that eerie red-gold haze.

I almost died that night on the bridge, physically and emotionally, and then this secret, clinging to our family like mildew, darn well did me in. There was no one to talk to, no one to heal with, and no one to cry with, so the darkness was able to wrap me up tight. I shut down and out in that mausoleum/home.

I hardly spoke at all, but I did eat.

In Herbert's cold, controlled, dark mansion, in the midst of a sweeping expanse of lawn trimmed to almost psychotic perfection, groomed trees, and bushes whacked into submission, I ate my grief.

On my walk the next morning through the rain, I noticed Jake's truck leaving his house. He always drove the other way down the street, the opposite way I was walking, so I let myself daydream about how gorgeous he was. Shoulders like a tractor, huge smile and white teeth, lanky build, lanky walk. My breath caught thinking about him, a flutter in my breasts.

He pulled out of his drive, started to turn in the opposite direction as usual, stopped, and then, *and then,* he drove straight toward me.

What?

What?

This was breaking the expected rules!

I glanced around for a hedge to jump over, a trash can to leap into, a wheelbarrow to crouch behind. Rain was dripping off my rain hat, I had no makeup on, my rain pants were soaked, and I resembled a drowned muskrat. He came closer and closer, and I tried not to stare at his truck, tried to walk, as if I was a normal person, not half in love with a neighbor I wanted to stalk but didn't because it was creepy.

"Hi."

Oh. My. Goodness. There he was, leaning out of his truck, blond and friendly.

I tried to speak. *Speak, throat! Speak!*

"How are you?"

Speak, throat! Speak!

"It's a little wet today, isn't it, Stevie?"

Ha. Whenever he said my name I thought of sex. Then I thought of him naked. In his truck, naked with sex. I coughed. *Please speak, throat! Please speak!*

"Yes, it's wet." Ahhh, brilliant. I was so brilliant.

"Want a ride back to your house?" He grinned. I could get lost in that grin. It was open and gentle, not scary.

"Well, it's wet." Ahhh, more brilliance! Once again, I stunned myself.

His green eyes looked a mite confused, but he didn't stop smiling. "Yes, it's wet. Do you want a ride?"

Did I want to ride *him?* Naked? In the truck? Yes, I did. If I wasn't bad in bed and if I didn't have a scar in an anchor shape across my front, I would leap with joy to ride him. I was a boat, without the boat. A graphic image of naked Jake filled my rattled brain, rattling it more.

"A ride?" Where did he want to ride to? "You mean because it's wet?" My. I could strangle myself. I could reach up with my own bare hands, wrap them around my neck, and squeeze. . . .

"Yes, hop in. I'll drive you back to your house."

I wanted to hop on him. But I couldn't. I couldn't move. Is it sexist to be this overcome with passion whilst gazing upon a man? Was I reducing him to a sex object, not a person? Did it matter?

"No?" he asked.

"No. Yes. No." Please, my hands, do your work on my neck. "Yes."

"Okay, then." And then, Jake, huge Jake, with shoulders the size of a tractor, got out of his truck, smiled at me, the drowned muskrat, and waited.

Move, feet. *Move!* My feet shuffled along, and I walked around to the passenger side of his blue truck, my head down. If our gazes caught, would he know that I was thinking of him naked? If yes, would that sicken him?

He opened the door for me.

"I'm wet," I said, before climbing into the truck. My brain was fuzzy, filled with Jake heat.

"I can see that." He was so close to me, so close, and he smelled like soap and mint and musky aftershave.

"I'll get your seat wet."

"Stevie," he said, his voice quieter, "I don't care at all."

"You don't care?"

"I do care," he said, his voice still quiet. "But I don't care about my truck getting wet."

I took a deep breath, peered inside that truck, then at him, and I saw that he had hazel flecks in his green eyes and they were rimmed by dark green, and I swear I saw gentleness in them, and humor, and I smiled. I did. I smiled at him.

And in that rain we smiled at each other.

"Please?" he said.

And then, more brilliance, I said, "Please."

He nodded, a mite confused once again and I don't know why I said these next two words, but I did.

"You're welcome," I said. "I mean, thank you, I mean. Yes. You're welcome." Oh, I could die. I got up on the seat and he leaned in and said, "You're welcome, too," and sort of chuckled, and closed the door.

And while he walked around to his side, his lips still smiling, I said to myself: Strangle your neck before you make a fool of yourself.

I have an obsession in my garage.

A garage is not a bad place to hide an obsession.

It's rather dark, you don't invite friends over to hang out in it unless you're a beer-slugging guy, no one wants to peer inside at your rakes, and you can lock the door and keep people away.

My obsession is not something I relish showing to other people, as it is a close-up examination of the inside of my brain, which, it seems to me, is a labyrinth of near-boiling emotions, my tenuous hold on sanity, sticky memories, swirling hopes, and eerie creative rants. I envision sometimes a man followed by a mob of cameramen and an uncontrollable crowd gathering in front of my garage doors. They're laughing, voyeuristic, nauseatingly nosy. The goof points to the doors and shouts, "Who wants to see those doors open?" The crowd roars.

He shouts again, taunting them. "Who wants to see those doors open?" The crowd roars even louder.

I am off hiding behind my pink cherry tree, cowering, begging them not to open it, gnawing at my nails and slobbering in fear.

The doors open. There's a loaded silence, and then . . . laughter. Gut-wrenching, rocking-back-and-forth, leaning-on-each-other-for-support kind of laughter as my obsession is revealed.

So what's in there?

Chairs.

Chairs piled up, chairs hanging, chairs at odd angles. Chairs in pieces. Chair legs stacked in a corner, and chair seats propped against a wall. In the center of this mess are my heavy work tables, a reciprocating saw, a band saw, a jigsaw, a scroll saw for my detail work, clamps, a lathe, wood glues and gorilla glue for problem joints, wood pegs, and battered furniture that I take apart. There are chisels, hammers, screwdrivers, and other tools scattered about.

Odd, isn't it?

I rebuild and repaint battered chairs. That is my obsession.

I scour garage sales here and in other cities and towns for old wood chairs, benches, and rocking chairs. I am especially fond of antique school chairs and the chairs and desks that are attached together for students. I do not do high chairs. Too painful.

I haul them home, strip them down, and clean them up, or I build them completely from scratch with odd angles, swirls, and waving designs.

When the chair is, what I consider, naked, I sit down and talk to it. Thankfully, I still realize this is crazy. I am hoping I always realize this is crazy, but my genetics may not favor that end result.

I ask this type of question: What makes you cry? What was the worst thing that happened to you in your childhood? What have you become? What did you hope you would become? How has life surpassed your expectations? What are you disappointed about? How do you see yourself? How do you think others see you? Who's right on that? What do you feel guilty about? What's your worst flaw? What makes you laugh? What do you daydream about?

Pretty soon I get an idea of the chair's personality, its desires and quirks, that sort of weird thing. That's when I name the chair, as if it's a person, based on its physical characteristics. I've had a Priscilla, Big Dwayne, Happy Flower, Mr. Stud, Russel, Yao, Enrique, Dr. Maya, Queen Clementine, Blaire, Bear, and Pole Swinger. At night, I think, I plan, I twist and turn that baby in my head. With my insomnia, I have plenty of time.

If thoughts of a woman in a yellow floppy hat, a bridge, churning clouds, drowning, or an impish face with an upturned nose and freckles intrude, I force myself to think harder about that chair.

For example, Tammy Q, a wood chair that came to me black and peeling, was lonely—starkly, utterly lonely—and alone. She never felt truly connected to anyone. She was always the one who didn't fit in. So, I decided the chair should embrace that part of herself, the not-fitting-in part. I painted the whole thing purple, then took off the old, squarish seat and used a jigsaw to cut a piece of wood into a jellyfish shape and painted it neon pink. To the back I added green wings with rainbow feathers and painted the legs black and white checked.

If you know you're never going to fit in, why continue to try, right?

Queen Clementine's mother died in the seventies of mental illness. To deal with the love she never received, I made the chair huge. I took off the old legs with a band saw, then cut legs four feet high and reattached the seat and back. I used a scroll saw to inlay a flower design, then painted the whole thing in a tie-dye pattern with a red heart in the center.

Maya Lopez, the rocking chair, missed her sister. So, I took out the spindles, put in a full back, and painted red poppies with green stems and yellow centers in a swooping design. I went to the craft store and bought fake red poppies and attached them around the legs and handles. I painted the base black.

Obviously, I have a lot of personal problems I address in my chairs.

How many have I transformed? How many chairs now have green wings or yellow spotted tails or claw feet or stripes or cheetah prints or seem as if they've sprouted from *Alice in Wonderland* or some futuristic world? How many sport giant teacups or pink crows or Picasso-style angles? How many are sprayed gold or silver or are superbig or miniature?

I'm afraid to count.

I am so, so ridiculous.

But I can't help myself. When I'm with my chairs, I am not with the world.

When I rejoined the world, that night, on my deck, I thought about Jake. What kind of chair would I make for him? A throne. A throne shaped like a giant heart with hearts all over that chair.

He had been so kind when he drove me home while I dripped on his seat.

"What are your plans for today?" he asked.

Ahhh. He has such a low, gravelly voice. I basked in that voice, so nervous I could barely process what he said. *Speak, throat!*

"Are you going to work?"

Low and gravelly and sexy. *Speak!*

Naked Jake.

He looked at me expectantly, that smile hovering around the corners of that mouth, *that mouth!* What could that mouth do? I bet he had a girlfriend. I knew he wasn't married. Nancy had told me. "You work downtown, don't you?"

Speak, utter something!

"Yes," I said, my throat constricting while I dripped.

"I'm working down there for a while, too."

I nodded.

"We should ride in together sometime." He smiled.

Ride in together? In the same truck? Me and The Mobster and Jake?

I inhaled too loud. It sounded like a cannon going off.

"I mean, not if you don't want to," he said, hurried. "If you're not comfortable with it. . . ."

Oh, I was uncomfortably comfortable with it, I was . . . I inhaled again, and another cannon went off. Naked, warm Jake.

He pulled in front of my house. "You have a nice home. I could see it used in a kids' book."

And then I displayed my wisdom and brilliance once again. "You're welcome," I said.

And then he, with another smile reaching ear to ear, said, "Thank you."

"I mean," I flustered, "thank you for driving me home. That was nice of you." I had been struck by lightning in the brain, that was a given.

"You're welcome."

"I like your truck. It's very big."

"Thank you," he said, his eyes twinkling.

"It's a nice, uh, powerful, truck."

He grinned.

"I'm sorry I'm wet."

He chuckled.

"Usually I'm not. Usually I'm dry. I don't drip like this."

He laughed and then said, low and soft, "Well, Stevie, you're welcome in my truck, wet or dry."

"Right. And you . . ." I coughed because my throat was still constricting me as a boa would around my neck. "You can come in my truck anytime, too."

"I would definitely like to do that."

"You can come in my truck and I'll drive."

"Or I'll drive. I like to drive." He chuckled again. Such a nice chuckle.

"Yes. You can drive, or I'll drive. I don't like to drive so much, I'd rather be driven." And then I blushed, because he laughed, that musical, manly laugh of his, and I quick as a lick scuttled right out of that truck before I sputtered out anything else flamingly stupid, then leaned back in and said, "Thank you for letting me ride your truck."

I heard his laughter as I ran into my house, truly *dying* of embarrassment, then slammed the door and huddled into a blushing ball. I am so ridiculous. I am.

Naked, warm, cuddly Jake.

5

Ashville, Oregon

My earliest memory is being snatched in the middle of the night from my bed by my momma.

"You can't have her!" Momma yelled to the star-filled sky as she ran out of our Schoolhouse House with me in her arms, my pink princess nightgown flowing behind me as I screamed in terror. "You can't have her! Get away from us!"

She sprinted by our barn and cornfield as if the devil himself were on her heels, then down a hill. She jumped into our shallow stream, with both feet, and sat down with me on her lap, as the water flowed over us. "Don't let go! Don't let go!"

I clutched at her shoulders, petrified, her blond hair swirling all around. I thought someone was after me, after us. Maybe it was a monster! Maybe it was a bad guy with an ax!

She splashed around in the water with both hands, then started kicking it with the sparkly pink heels she wore, as if she was trying to smash something in it. I screamed and clung to her as a white phantom raced toward us. Soon the devil was behind the phantom, in black. I could see them up on the hill by the house charging down toward us.

Momma was right! They *were* after us! "They're coming! They're coming, Momma!"

She splashed more water, soaking us both as I shook and continued my high-pitched wail.

Momma shouted, low and deep, in a voice that wasn't her own, "Hide! Hide! Get under the bridge!"

I didn't know what she meant by this because there was no bridge. "Run, Momma! Let's run!" I struggled to get off her lap, but she held me fast and wouldn't let go.

The phantom and the devil were closing in on us, and who knew what they would do to us then!

"They're taking over the world! We have to get out of here! They've been watching us!"

I felt hot water leak between my legs as I lost control of my bladder. Momma felt it, too, because she whispered, "They're burning us! They're burning my legs!"

The phantom and the devil got closer and closer, and I heard them calling my name. "Stevie, honey! Stevie, it's okay, honey! We're coming! Hang on, sweetie!" I had no idea how they knew my name, which scared me more, and I screamed again, as loud as I could.

I tried to get out of the stream, to pull Momma out, to run run run, because we were surely going to get murdered, but she wouldn't have any of that. She pulled me down into the stream, and we rolled through the water. I sputtered and shook and choked on the water, Momma's body over mine, and suddenly Grandma and Grandpa were there, and I was in Grandma's arms, Grandpa trying to haul Momma out of the stream, too.

Momma cried, "Watch out! I'm gonna kill them, kill them! They're trying to poison me! Listen to that poison."

Even after Grandma hugged me close and I realized that she was the phantom running from the house in her white night-gown and Grandpa was the devil in his black robe and cowboy boots, I could not stop screaming. Grandma called my name again and again, pleaded with me, then finally ran to the house with me in her arms. I tried to stop, but I couldn't. Even my own ears hurt from my screams.

I turned around and watched Momma, still in the water. She slugged Grandpa in the face once, the second time he ducked, the third time he grabbed her wrists, yelling her name. Grandpa was a huge man, almost six foot six, with a chest like a bull, and white hair that went past his collar, but he was the gentlest man I've ever met.

"You won't get me! I have my rights!" Momma said, so tiny and helpless next to his strength. "I am a legal alien of the United States of America, and the government does not own me! You hear me, the government doesn't own me! You can't have my body!"

I reached out my hands for her, wanting to help her, lost and panicked and confused, as Grandma hurried me back to the house. By the time we got there, the Ashville police were there. "Help Albert," Grandma said to them, breathless. "He's down by the stream."

The two policemen, both friends of Grandma and Grandpa, ran on down to the stream. Grandma took off my soaking pink princess nightgown, wrapped me in a blanket, then held me close, rocking me back and forth in the kitchen of our Schoolhouse House as my teeth chattered, my knees knocked, and I dissolved into hiccupping sobs.

I didn't see my momma for a long time after that. Grandma told me that Momma had gone off to get some rest. "She has to sleep for a while, and see a few doctors. She has a sickness in her head, honey. It's not going to go away, and we're trying to help her."

Grandpa hugged me to his huge chest, his cowboy hat shading his blue eyes. "Now, you come on outside with me and let's go tease the chickens."

Grandma made chocolate and pinwheel cookies and pink cupcakes with me; Grandpa and I made omelets and pastas. I ate to assuage my fear and my loneliness. Relatives and friends descended with platters of fried chicken, salad, desserts of all sorts, whipped and baked and smothered in icing, and I ate with them because their laughter and chatter helped me to forget that my momma wasn't home and had rolled with me in the middle of the night under the stars in a stream.

I saw Grandma crying when she swung on the porch swing with Grandpa late at night. Grandpa started bringing Grandma flowers every day, and Grandma made Grandpa his favorite dinners every night. Grandpa said, "Glory, give me a glorious hug," all the time, and they slow danced outside on the deck, their cowboy boots toe to toe. They were so tired their faces were sagging, like sugar cookie dough.

I learned that my momma did not want my hugs when Grandpa brought Momma home weeks later.

I saw her getting out of Grandpa's truck when Grandma and I were cutting out gingerbread men on the cutting board in our white and yellow kitchen. I dropped the cookie cutter and ran to the car. I ignored Grandpa's call to be careful with Momma and wrapped my arms around her tight.

I grinned into her face as she stared down at me. She did not hug me. She did not kiss me. She did not respond. Nothing. She studied me, tilting her head this way and that, but her eyes, as blue as mine, were blank.

She was wearing a blue dress I'd never seen and flat blue shoes. She was not wearing her necklaces, scarves, tin foil hats (the tin foil, she believed, kept the voices away), beige trench coat, bikini, or cat pajamas.

"I missed you, Momma."

She blinked. She shook her head. She blinked again.

I finally let go and took a step back, my stomach clenching with pain. I could feel the hot tears bubbling on up. *My momma does not want to hug me.*

"Do you want to say hi to Stevie, Helen?" Grandpa asked, touching her arm.

Momma rolled her lips together, three times, I remember that. I watched her mouth, waiting for her to smile, to say hello, say she missed me, normal things a momma might say to her daughter. "No. No, I don't want to say hi."

No, she does not want to say hi to me.

I leaned into Grandpa, crushed.

"Helen," Grandpa said. "Stevie's missed you."

She rolled her lips in and out again, then cocked her head and leaned in close.

"I don't know that girl kid. She looks like the place with all the singing." That's what Momma called New York—"the place with all the singing." She poked the dimple in my cheek. "I've seen that before. That dent. Bye, girl kid."

I felt my body start to shake.

"I think they're watching you," she hissed. "Watch out. They have eyes everywhere." She pointed to her eyes. "Eyes everywhere."

Grandpa gave me a squeeze on the shoulder and a wink, and said, "Helen, no one is watching us. Remember, we're out on the farm. There's Bessie the cow, and see the chickens? The lambs are over there near the pigs."

My momma peered around. "It's in the fence post. That's how they spy on us. And I don't like the barky animals. Big or small. No barkies."

I watched my grandpa's face drop, then he smiled at me again, but I knew he was making himself smile.

I tried to take Momma's hand, but she snatched it away and made a growling sound in her throat.

My momma is not happy to see me. She does not want to hold my hand.

I put my hands in the pockets of my dress and stared at the ground. Grandpa reached in my pocket and squeezed my hand. I squeezed back.

I peered up at my momma. She was staring at me, unblinking. What do you do with a staring, unblinking, blank Momma?

"Helen," Grandma said, smiling, hustling toward us with her yellow apron. "I'm so glad you're home, honey." She reached out her arms and wrapped them around my momma.

My momma did not respond. She did not move. For some reason, it didn't make Grandma cry as it did me. I quickly wiped my tears away.

"Come on in, sweetie. How are you feeling?"

It did not take us long to figure out how Momma was feeling.

"They're still watching us!" She made a fist and smashed three of the gingerbread men that me and Grandma made for her. *Bang bang bang.* "You can't take my mind away from me."

She smashed another one. *Bang.* "I'm not going to be tied down to that chair! No tying!"

I bent down to look around the kitchen, under the table. The people were watching us? They're going to tie us down? Where? When?

I heard a cry slip out of Grandma's mouth, like a hurt bird, before she covered it. Tears formed in Grandpa's eyes.

"It's okay, Momma," I said. Almost four now, and I wanted to help. "It's gingerbread men. We're going to eat them. They're good. Here. You wanna eat one?" I held one out, then I bit the head off. "Yummy!"

She snatched it from my hand, lightning quick, and threw it against the wall, then grabbed another one and threw that, too. "Die! You will not get my brain waves again! Die! And I'm not wearing the white jacket! I won't wear it! No more shots, either! No more cups with candies in it that make me sick and dizzy and sleepy!"

After she grabbed the bowl with the batter in it and heaved it across the room and through the window, Grandma and Grandpa grabbed her. She fought both of them, her blond hair flying out of her bun, her blue dress ripping on the right sleeve as she tried to hit Grandpa, who ducked. She swung at Grandma, but Grandpa moved fast and took the hit in the chest.

She fought against Grandpa, who held her wrists loosely so as not to hurt her. When she head butted him in the chest, he did little to stop it. When she tried to kick his legs, he moved them as best he could, all the while talking to her gently, softly. "Sweetie, it's Daddy. I'm here. I'll protect you. Now, don't you worry. . . ."

"Oh, no! I will not be on that bed with the jump rope straps. You are not drilling a hole in my head, you are not. I am a singer and you are not going to drill the hole. They're trying to poison me. I can hear them." She turned to me. "Girl kid, don't you hear that poison from the voices?"

"I don't think so," I said, unsure, scared.

"No, sweetie, Stevie doesn't hear the voices," Grandma soothed.

"We don't hear the voices, and we're going to help you turn them off."

Momma shook her head, her shoulders slumping. "You can't. You can't turn them off. They're here to stay. They told me that. They're never going to leave me. It's me against them. It's a battle. Bad battle. I lose. They win."

"Oh, my goodness, yes, honey, they'll go away," Grandma soothed.

"No. They're attached to me." She sagged against Grandpa. She looked so small next to him. "Leeches. Black leeches sucking my brain. Suck, suck, they're sucking Helen. Helen's going away and they're eating her up. She'll be gone soon. Only a leech left then. It's a bad battle."

Grandma and Grandpa kept talking to her, their voices like honey or warm marshmallows, but they couldn't hide their tears from me.

They both helped Momma to her room, up the stairs, a beautiful room, next to mine, with a pitched roof and a pink flowered bedspread.

While they were doing that, I picked up the pieces of the gingerbread men and women and girls and boys and I tried to put them back together. I used the icing for glue and put their heads on their shoulders, patched up their arms, and got their legs back on the right places. I used all the icing to fix them up.

When I was done, I couldn't eat any of them. I sat at the table and didn't move.

Soon the voice of a male opera singer filled our home and my momma quieted down. Whenever she heard that voice it calmed her, although sometimes it made her cry. I didn't know why.

I didn't know why my momma acted that way.

I didn't know what she would do tomorrow.

I didn't get what was true and what was imaginary.

But what I did know was that my momma didn't want my hugs.

It was after that incident that I started calling my momma by her given name, Helen, unless I was speaking directly to her. I think I did it because it separated me from her, and it separated her role as Momma from me. If Helen didn't hug me, that was one thing. If *Momma* didn't hug me, well, that hurt like holy heck.

So she became Helen in my head.

It is amazing what young children will do to save themselves.

6

Portland, Oregon

I could never go back to Ashville. Too many memories.
That night, in my dreams, I saw Sunshine.

She was in front of the Schoolhouse House. She was painting.
Helen was beside her.

Sunshine lifted her brush and started painting the air in front
of her. She drew cornstalks. Helen tipped the floppy yellow hat
back on her head, picked up her brush, and painted over all the
cornstalks. She painted them red. Blood red. The blood started
dripping down the cornstalks. Sunshine turned to blood and the
cornstalks exploded, and even in my dream I felt so guilty for
not saving Sunshine.

I woke clawing at my blankets.

I was losing my mind, wasn't I?

I couldn't swallow. I couldn't move. Paralyzed with fear, I
watched the darkness turn, from black, to dark blue, to robin's
egg blue, to pink and yellow and orange.

Had it started? Was I to become Helen, the woman with the
floppy yellow hat?

"I've set up a lunch date for you," Zena told me. She gave me
a piece of paper with the name of a restaurant and a time. "Be
there."

"No, oh, no." I argued. I threw a pencil at her, she threw it back. I told her that I would never let her borrow my clothes again when she'd been out all night partying. "For example, this morning, Zena, when I had to give you my gray jacket so you could slip it over your leather wifebeater shirt."

She took a bite of doughnut. Why is it that skinny people can eat doughnuts?

"I'll let you borrow my wifebeater shirt tomorrow," she said. "And my skull necklace."

"I think I'll pass, but gee, thanks."

Crystal summoned me to her office as she whizzed by on black heels so high she was straight up on her toes. "Let's go, Steve, move it."

I followed her as an obedient mouse would, but Zena said to Crystal, "Have you won the award for Portland's Most Obnoxious Attorney yet? Oh, yes, that's right. You won last year! Can't win two years in a row!"

Crystal said, "Shut up, ant head."

"Clever. You've been up all night again, thinking." Zena tapped her head. "Thunk, thunk, thunk!"

When I got back to my desk Zena was gone. I went to the date because it started in fifteen minutes.

"Tell me about you," he said, leaning toward me across the café's table.

Rog Rakue had almost no resemblance to his photos on the Date Me! Internet dating site. He was at least fifteen years older, had a growth on the side of his face with hairs popping out of it like spikes, almost no hair, and a stomach that clearly had been stuffed with bowling balls.

Now, I am not one to talk about bowling ball stomachs, I realize this, but I also believe that it might be a wee bit important to be honest about one's appearance.

"Well, I—"

His cell phone rang. "Hang on, sweetie." He picked it up and said, "Hey, dude. Yeah, I got a minute." He listened. He talked. On and on. He ended with, "Na, I wasn't busy, no problem. Catch ya later."

He flipped the phone shut, but not off, and leaned his stomach into the table. "Where were we?"

I smiled tightly. Waited. *I am an idiot. I do not want to date, yet I am on a date.*

His face cleared with understanding. "Oh, yeah, let me tell you about myself. I'm an entrepreneur."

"Really?" Entrepreneur usually means unemployed/criminal.

"Yep. I've started four different businesses. I always got something in the pot, always got something cookin' up, always got the fires in the iron, you know what I mean? You can't ever let things get too hot. You always have to have something on the back burner. Ya never know when the oven will explode and ya gotta find something else."

I nodded at all his kitchen references.

"My business now is smokin'. Can't tell you what it is, puttin' the deal together now, but it'll make me a fortune. I'll be richer than damn Midas." His cell phone rang. He picked it up. "Hey, hey! Antoine! Yep. I'll cut you in, but you gotta be quick. My house. Four o'clock today. Oh, yeah, everybody wants in and I'm doin' you a favor . . . sure thing. . . ."

He flicked his phone shut. "Where were we, doll?"

"You. Your business." Honestly, men can be compared to wind-up dolls. You ask them about themselves and they'll go on forever.

"Yeah, my business is incredible." He scratched his pit. "I have a lucky touch, you know? Everything I touch is successful, everything I go into, I dunno. It gets huge so fast. I know when the trends are coming, where they're going, when to get out. I got the touch or something." His phone rang again. He rolled his eyes at me. "Can't stop 'em . . . Hang on, sweetie." He reached across the table and squeezed my hand.

I pulled my hand away and wiped the sweat off. I examined my salad. It held no appeal for me.

Before the operation, I wasn't picky about who I ate with. I would hide how much I ate by bringing a small sack lunch to work, hiding snacks and treats in my desk drawers, and sneaking out once a day to scarf down a half gallon of ice cream or ten cookies, but I could sit down and eat with anyone.

Since the operation, for some inexplicable reason, I can't.

I have to like the person I'm around in order to eat.

Which is why I couldn't eat the salad in front of me.

Rog kept yakking on the phone. His lips reminded me of two slugs, twisted together at the ends, which forced me to ask myself, *Why are you still sitting with this rude vermin? Why don't you leave?*

Rog hung up the phone. "Sorry again. Where were we? Hey, babe, can you get me another one of these?" He picked up his vodka tonic and signaled the waitress, then wiped his nose with two fingers.

He launched again into his own résumé. He was in love with himself, in love with his ambitions and accomplishments, in love with the sound of his own voice. After ten minutes of nonstop talking he said, "Tell me about you, sweets. Damn." He picked up his cell phone, rolled his eyes as if to convey, "I'm such an important person, I can't get people to stop calling me," and yakked off again.

Leave, I told myself. *Out you go.*

Rog hung up the phone. "Do you have any siblings? I got a brother. He's a teacher. Middle school, social studies. Lives up in Seattle. He makes nothin'. No money. He's got the benefits, but he's makin' $45,000 a year. Nothin'. Pennies. Yeah, he and his wife have a cute house. She's a teacher, too. They got four kids. They coach their kids' teams. They're so damn strapped. Always going out on their old boat or campin' or hikin'. They don't got two quarters to squeeze together and four kids to put through college. They hardly got enough money to go to the movies. I tell him all the time, 'Toby, you ain't cuttin' it, you ain't gettin' anywhere, you gotta be someone. You gotta make something of your life. You gotta be the man. I can get you making $100,000 a year, no problem.' But he wants to be in a classroom with brats all day."

He smothered a burp, then another, fist to mouth. The hairs sticking out from his growth wiggled at me.

Hello, Stevie? Is your butt stuck to the chair with glue?

"I haven't seen him in about three years. Every time I call to get together he's too busy with work and the wife and the kids. His wife's a hot little thing; don't know why she got together with my brother. I told her that, too, joshing around. Should have been me. She got ticked at that one, told me to shove it, but I think she knows the truth of what I'm saying. She got the short end of the stick. Married a teacher. Married the wrong brother. That ain't me, hon, that ain't me. I wanna own the theaters that play the movies, you know? That's part of my next deal. Real estate. Businesses. Burgeoning markets. Tell me about you, Stevie. Sexy Stevie." He winked at me.

"Well, I—"

His phone rang. "Hang on, Sexy Stevie."

Did he think that was a turn-on?

I got up, grabbed my purse. He put his hand over the mouthpiece. "Gotta go to the ladies' room and get your lipstick on? See ya in a sec, sweetie. I gotta tell you about my last business venture. You'll laugh your head off at the money I'm making."

"I'm not coming back." I squared my shoulders. In my other life, preoperation, I avoided conflict like I would avoid a pit filled with tarantulas.

"Hang on, Darrell." He put his hand over the mouthpiece. "What?"

"I said, I'm not coming back."

"Why?" He was genuinely perplexed. I laughed.

"You've got to be kidding. I've been here for almost forty-five minutes and all you've done is talk about yourself. You're a bragging, boring, boorish man. There. I've used three b's in a row to describe you. You're not the slightest bit interested in anyone but yourself. You talk on your cell phone on a date. Your photo on the Internet is at least fifteen years old and you have the class and manners of a Tyrannosaurus rex who hasn't eaten in a week. I feel sorry for your brother. He has a nice life except for you. No wonder he never wants to see you. No one wants to be with a person who tells them they're not good enough and criticizes their life. Good-bye."

His mouth hung open, his face slack with shock.

I left.

I felt guilty for being mean.

I felt he deserved it.

I did not even try to get to know the chair that night. I went home and painted it black. Tomorrow I would paint flames on the seat and up the arms. I'd put two worms on it, intertwined, on the T-shirt of a scrubby-faced, beer-bellied, spiky-haired loser.

I would name it "Internet Dating."

The next morning was Saturday, and I decided it was time to start cutting the wood for my raised beds and all the tomatoes, squash, zucchini, radishes, lettuce, carrots, peas, and beans I would plant when the rain stopped. Maybe peppers, too. But not corn.

As I was sawing, sawdust flying everywhere, I thought about Joseph, my uncle's handyman and landscaper, who had taught me everything I knew about woodworking.

We were not Joseph's only client. In fact, he had about forty men and women working for him. He started his own land-scaping company after he did two tours in Korea and two in Vietnam, retired, and ended a long, distinguished career in the army. Between a little Googling I did of him and his unit, and a couple of talks I had with his wife, Marguerite, it's pretty clear that Joseph was a highly trained special forces officer who did an awful lot of secret work in both countries.

Joseph taught us how to build birdhouses, trellises, arbors, wooden stools, bulletin boards, tables, shelving units, and one time a bed for Lance, because Lance was way too big for his own bed, and Herbert refused to buy him another. Lance worked on weekends to buy himself the mattress to go with it. Joseph paid for half.

He taught us how to use every saw on the planet, plus he carved one animal each for us every year as a present. Lance got a rooster, Polly a horse, I got a raccoon, and so on.

Herbert scoffed at them. "These blue-collar people and their handiwork. Silly. But all men need to be proud of something, I suppose, even if it's only a wood product."

I have hung up each one of my "wood products" on the wall of my second bedroom. Lance has his up in his headquarters under a banner that says, ONE PERSON CAN SAVE A LIFE, and Polly's are in her bedroom in her condo in the Pearl District.

I hammered and sawed, the sawdust sprinkled about, and soon, very soon, I would have my garden, thanks to Joseph, a man who saw three lost, lonely, mentally tangled kids and put out a hand to hold so we wouldn't drown in misery.

"My anniversary celebration will be the place to be in this town. *The place,*" Herbert announced, chest out, from the head of the table. "If you're not there, you're no one. And"—he paused grandly—"I've made a decision."

I caught Polly's and Lance's eyes across the table. The candlelight from a pair of perfectly placed candleholders flickered over the perfectly white tablecloth and perfectly proper wineglasses, except for Aunt Janet's glass, which was for water. It was tinted blue. Herbert insisted she use it so she would not forget "her weakness for alcohol and destructive behavior that seduces the unwary and unvigilant."

Polly's lips tightened. Lance's eyes rolled. Aunt Janet dropped her silverware down on her china plate at her end of the table and clenched her hands together.

I could barely breathe in this formal, stuffy room. Even the fire in the fireplace felt vaguely threatening, as if it would burn me down if it could, the windows almost completely covered in heavy, damask, mauve-colored curtains, with a chandelier, somehow ponderous and disapproving, hanging over the middle of the table.

The decor could best be described as: overwhelmingly suffocating.

Herbert waited until all eyes were trained on him, the showman, the star, the patriarch.

"I've called the press and the reporters," he said, so proud, so arrogant.

He let that sentence hang in the air.

"*Why?*" Aunt Janet finally said, her voice stricken. She reached for her blue glass with a trembling hand.

"I want my anniversary celebration to benefit all of Oregon. I want to make a statement to families everywhere and to stand up for what's right!"

"What are you talking about?" Lance said. "I thought we were having a party to note that you and Mom have been married for forty miserable years."

Herbert glowered at Lance, then repuffed his chest out. "We will use my anniversary celebration as the launch to the No on Gay Marriage campaign here in Oregon."

I thought I would vomit.

Aunt Janet's blue water glass clattered to the table and spilled. "You can't be serious," she whispered.

I dabbed up the water.

Polly said, "Oh, no. That's a terrible idea. Hideous, Dad. Come on. You're not even that creepy, are you? Well, yes, you are, but Mom isn't, so let's not launch that racist campaign here."

Lance said, "NO. No, that's mean, Dad, Mom doesn't want that!"

Herbert glared at Polly, told her to keep her liberal ideas to herself, and then dismissed us immediately with a wave of his hand. Who cared what his wife wanted? He didn't. "I am the president of this grass roots organization, and this is an excellent platform. Plus, it will help my state senate reelection campaign."

"No." Aunt Janet was appalled. "Our anniversary is not the place for this! It's a day for us, for the kids, for friends. The pastor will be there. . . ."

"Even more outstanding!" Herbert declared. "The renewal of our vows will demonstrate to all that marriage is a Christian-based partnership, blessed by the church, between a man and a woman. We'll rededicate our lives, our children standing around us, supporting us, all under an arch of virginal white roses. Virginal! A sign of reblooming. Rebirth. A new start for the state of Oregon."

I couldn't even speak. Not a word.

"It's a crucial time for me, crucial. May the good people of Oregon reelect me for another term in the senate."

Aunt Janet slumped in her chair. I was shocked to realize that I saw Aunt Janet slumping in her chair all the time now. How long had that been going on?

Herbert didn't even notice his wife's reaction as he continued pontificating. "We will uphold marriage, an institution that was created for children and family, companionship and friendship . . ." Blah, blah, blah.

"Mom," Lance said. "Are you okay?"

Aunt Janet was pale and I reached for her hand. "Aunt Janet?"

"You've upset her!" Lance accused, throwing down his napkin and glaring at his father. "You should be loving to your wife, respectful and kind. Can you do that, Dad?"

Herbert blinked twice as if to pull himself from his own reverie, his own wondrous speech. "What is it, Janet?" His voice was brusque, annoyed.

She shook her head and I noticed her eyes. In their depths I saw the usual hopelessness, dejection, defeat, but there was something else . . . anger. That was it. *Anger*.

"Herbert, I do not want the press at our anniversary party."

"Yes, you do, Janet. You're not thinking clearly."

"I am, I am thinking clearly," she said, her voice swelling. "I don't want them there. You know I don't want cameras. I don't want the attention on me."

"The attention on you!" Herbert scoffed, another wave of the hand. "Don't worry on that score, my dear. I'll be making a speech, and no eyes will be on you, I can assure you."

"Nice, Dad, that's so nice of you to put it that way for Mom," Polly said, putting a paper bag to her mouth, inhaling and exhaling. "You're so nice. So damn nice, you troll."

I noticed she didn't eat anything. I didn't, either. Lance had shoveled his food around his plate. We couldn't eat around Herbert.

"Let's be realistic," Herbert clipped after telling Polly to shut her mouth. "Please. Use your thinker." He thumped his head with a finger. "Use your thinker, Janet."

"I am being realistic," Aunt Janet said. "I didn't even want to do this party in the first place, I'm only doing it—"

She put her hands over her face and tilted her head to the ceiling.

"You're only doing it, why?" Herbert drawled, sarcasm lacing every word.

"I'm only doing it, I agreed to it, because for months, every day, every damn day, you were hammering at me to agree to it. I couldn't take it anymore, couldn't take *you*." She fisted her hands and slammed them on the table.

I jumped I was so surprised.

A little smile tilted Polly's mouth, and I knew what she was thinking: About time you stood up for yourself, Mom.

"I couldn't take it." Aunt Janet hit the table again, both fists. "Couldn't take living in this house with your constant haranguing, your badgering, your bullying—" She slammed the table again.

"Janet, control!" Herbert rapped out. "Control! We've talked about you getting hold of your emotions before this. You must control yourself, especially in front of the children! Set an example, woman! For God's sake!"

"Don't talk to Mom like that, Dad," Lance said, so angry his own fists were balled up. "She's your wife. You should speak to her with respect and love and gentleness. How many times do I have to tell you that—"

"Stay out of this, Lance! You don't know what's going on here at all. No one does except for me and Janet. I will speak as I wish to speak to her. We're husband and wife, and she knows her role. Janet, you are excused from the table to go and lie down and rest. I'll be up shortly and I will reexplain things to you."

"No." She shook her head, many times, too many times, but she was stressed. "We won't discuss it. I don't want to discuss it. I am telling you I don't want the press there. I won't come, I won't stay at that . . . that . . . *party* if they're there. I will not be a part of a political statement, a statement against gay people, especially not on my anniversary!"

"You will!" he bellowed, standing up, throwing his white napkin down on the table. "You will do as I tell you to do as my wife!"

I stood up. "Herbert! Stop yelling at her! It's her anniversary, did you forget? It's supposed to be for *you two*. Not you and your political ambitions, your ballot measure in November, and all your anti-gay friends!"

"Sit down this instant, Stevie! I will not have you interfering in my marriage, or in this family!"

That hurt. It shouldn't have. I shouldn't have let it, but it did.

"This is her family!" Lance and Polly said together.

"Sit down!" he bellowed again, his face reddening.

"Why should I sit down?" I said, not sitting. Before my operation I did not stand up to Herbert. It felt good to be standing now. "Why should I sit down? Because I'm not a part of this family? *I already know that.* I've known that since the first day I came to this house. I knew you didn't want me here, that I was a burden to you, trouble, a stupid, fat girl that you had to take care of because she was the daughter of your wife's sister. Sanctimonious you. Self-righteous you. Taking in an orphan. I get it, Herbert, I do. I have never fit in, and you've never let me forget it."

Herbert's eyelid started to twitch.

"You fit in with me," Lance said, his voice cracking, tears popping up. "You always have, Stevie girl. You've always been my sister, not my cousin." He pounded his heart. "You're my sister in my heart."

"And I have loved you, Stevie, each day—" Aunt Janet said.

"Me too, Stevie," Polly said, near tears. "I have always loved you. Sit down and shut up, Dad, you're a walking garbage disposal."

"Polly, you will silence yourself. Silence yourself! Don't you ever tell me to shut up or I will write you out of my will."

"I don't care, Dad. I don't want your money. Take me out of your will. Shove your money into any crack you care to."

That was true. Polly was about as thrifty as me. She believed that rainy days came and saved for them like the dickens. Lance was the same way. Generous, but he had his gold tucked away, too. Herbert had forbidden Aunt Janet to pay for almost anything for us after the age of fifteen so we had scrambled for babysitting jobs, tutoring jobs, and burger-flipping jobs from a very young age.

Herbert held up both hands, about two feet from Polly's face. "This is my home, you will obey—"

"This isn't your home, this is your house of terrors," Polly said. She reached up both her hands and smacked Herbert's hands, hard, with her own, then she whipped that paper bag to her face.

Herbert tipped up his chin, then coughed, sat down. He pulled at his lapels. "I didn't mean you don't fit in, Stevie."

"Yes, you did. Don't try to manipulate me, don't try to twist what you've been saying for years. Don't try to deny it or change things. I get it, I'm not stupid. What I don't understand is why you're making a political statement when your wife has told you she doesn't want you to so many times. She does not share your rabid attitude when it comes to gay marriage, anyhow."

"You're always trying to smash Mom down," Lance said. "Her feelings don't even count to you. She says she doesn't want the press there, so respect that wish."

"Who are you to tell me what to do?" Herbert said, his tone scathing. "You're not even married, Lance, not even married. You have no idea what marriage entails. You have no idea of the problems, the challenges and difficulties—"

"I would like to know!" Lance said. "I want to know more than anything!"

"Yes, there have been many challenges and difficulties for Mom in your marriage," Polly snapped, removing the bag from her face. "It's been a terrible time for her. The decades have flown by, filled with emotional torture. She can't speak her own mind, you're constantly putting her down, controlling her, she can't even think what she wants to think, she's never been able to become who she wanted to become—"

Aunt Janet, tiny and frumpy, leaned way back in her chair, hands on her face.

"Enough!" Herbert shouted. "Enough. I will not, *not,* have you four interfering with my decision again. Do you understand me? We will be making a statement about what a happy, successful, long-term, heterosexual marriage is at my anniversary party! We will be an example to the whole damn state. Janet, you will smile and be a gracious wife even if you have to come home and go to bed for three days afterward. You will not fall apart. You will exercise control. Control! Restraint! Control! You will pretend you are a model wife. Do you hear me? Do you hear me?"

Aunt Janet heard him. Her eyes teared up, she bit her lip, her hands shook, and she dropped her face, her *face,* right into her plate. Right straight into the steak and mashed potatoes.

We were all, at first, too stunned to move, even when Aunt Janet's sobs ricocheted off each wall in that formal, intimidating, ghastly dining room that Herbert had insisted they have because he was a leader in Oregon politics. A *leader.*

And there his wife sobbed, her face in her dinner.

7

Ashville, Oregon

My grandparents, I remember, did not care for Uncle Herbert at all.

One weekend, Herbert, Aunt Janet, Lance, and Polly all came from Portland to see us at our Schoolhouse House. Aunt Janet, Lance, and Polly always came for at least three weeks in summer, and then twice a year beyond that. This was one of their "twice a year" visits that Herbert allowed, and it was the visit that he attended, too.

I now know why he came: He wanted to see Helen.

I knew we were not looking forward to seeing Herbert because Grandpa, kind Grandpa, who treated everyone from Helen, to me, to Grandma, to his employees, and everyone in town with respect and care, said to Grandma, "So, old Hatchet Face is coming to visit."

And Grandma, who volunteered at church, constantly brought crates full of fruits and vegetables to people in our town who were on hard times, and ran the town as mayor with admirable leadership and compassion, said, "Please don't strike me down dead, Lord"—she raised her right hand up—"but I wish that Herbert would be eaten by a rabid coyote and dragged into the hills by his toes."

To which Grandpa rolled his huge shoulders and said, "Honey, the Lord isn't going to strike you down. Every time he deigns to see Herbert, I know he's rolling his eyes and saying to himself, 'I screwed up with that one. What was I thinking? I must have been drunk on the apples from the Garden of Eden. Drink makes a man do things he would never otherwise do. Shame on me. I screwed up.'"

Grandma pushed her white curls back and said, "When I see his pointy, scrunched face I want to use my mother's scissors to poke him in the privates and turn him into a hen!"

Grandpa said, "Honey, the other day I was studying the pigs' troughs and wondering if we could squish his dead body into one."

"I'll get the head, you get the feet," Grandma said, waving her hand. "Praise the Lord!"

"Praise the Lord, Glory, and give me a glorious hug."

My grandparents could not understand where they had gone wrong. Why had their beloved daughter Janet fallen for Herbert? True, Aunt Janet was rather homely (they didn't say that, it's what I thought then), and her light was completely smashed by Helen's brightness, and she had low self-esteem when she left the farm and went to college and met Herbert, but surely she could have done better.

It was a constant source of heartache to my grandparents that their beloved daughter was married to, and I quote from Grandma, "a putrid thug," and from Grandpa, "a eunuch."

Praise the Lord.

Grandma and Grandpa greeted Herbert politely enough— they faked it—with no mention of pig troughs or hens, then went to hug Aunt Janet, Lance, and Polly.

The problem was that Helen didn't know how to fake liking someone, nor did she understand that sometimes you have to be polite, and civil, to family members that you do, in your heart, wish were in someone else's family who lived in Siberia.

It was the middle of summer, and Helen came down to dinner in a sleeveless red satin dress with wildflowers peeking out of the neckline. She had Grandma put her hair up in a ball, and then she stuck little branches from trees and a fork through the ball. She was also wearing a purple bikini top over the dress and her black rubber boots, complete with the requisite chicken wire to catch the voices.

Halfway down the stairs she stopped and stared at Aunt Janet, Herbert, and the kids.

"Hello, dear Helen," Aunt Janet said, her voice gentle, weak, and wobbling. Her voice was always that way with Herbert around, as if she was afraid he was going to sling a sledgehammer at her. "It's wonderful to see you." She gave Helen a long hug, then wiped her eyes. Helen patted her nose.

"Nice boots," Lance said.

"Hi, Aunt Helen," Polly said. She was all done up, as usual. She was wearing a blue velvet dress and matching shoes. She resembled a doll. "Dad tells me girls should dress to please their fathers, then their husbands." She told me later, as adults, that she hated dressing as she did, but Herbert insisted on it.

That gave me the creeps.

Helen stared at all of them, one by one, then she lifted her chin, scratched the wall, and sniffed, twice. Her eyes focused on Herbert, standing uncomfortably in our foyer, shifting from one foot to the next. She walked down a few more steps, paused, and tilted her head. "Hmmm," she said. "Hmmm." She stopped to within two feet of Herbert, eyeing him up and down. "I remember this one now." She farted and said, "I think he's the short weasel fart."

I watched with astonishment as Herbert's face got red and blotchy.

"Helen," he said, quite seriously, although his voice quavered. "How are you?"

"I remember now." She growled like a dog. "Bark bark, there's a weasel fart!"

We all stared at my momma, transfixed.

"What do you remember, honey?" Grandma said.

Helen kept staring at Herbert, her gaze never leaving his eyes, although his eyes started to dart around nervously.

"Let's go into the dining room," Herbert said, coughing.

"I reeeeemeeeembbbbber," Helen dragged the word out. "Yeesss, I dooooo."

"What is it, sugar?" Grandpa said. I did not miss the smile tugging at his lips, his delight at seeing Hatchet Face Herbert twist and turn already making the evening worthwhile for him.

"I remember him," Helen said. She pointed her finger at Herbert. It was the middle finger, which she tilted up toward the ceiling. "I do. It was on a night with rain. It was in the place with all the singing."

Suddenly she dropped on her haunches, her face about one foot from Herbert's bottom. I heard Grandma's quick inhale, then I heard Grandpa's chuckle. Herbert turned about purple.

"Hmmm . . ." she said again, still staring.

Herbert put his hands over his buttocks. "Helen. Stand up," he said, as one would order a dog.

"No," she said, in almost a singsong voice. "I'll do it when the voices tell me to, not you."

"Helen," Herbert said again. "Stand. Stand!"

"Do not speak to my daughter in that tone," Grandpa rapped out, coming in close and making short Herbert look small and ineffectual.

Herbert flushed further.

"No. The voices haven't told me to stand, but I remember." She tilted her head again. "Short weasel fart."

"What?" Lance said. "What do you remember?"

Those words, from an eager child, seemed to knock a little something into Helen, and she stood up again. "I remember that this alien had a pee pee this size." She pulled a skinny stick out of her hair. "This size. It was small. I didn't want it." She turned to her mother. "I didn't want his pee pee. He wanted me to have it. I said no. Bad. I made him go home. I had to hit him, like this." She slapped herself across the face. Twice. Hard. "Like that. And he still didn't leave." Her cheeks got red, and then she launched into her own brand of poetry, of which she had immense talent. "He's mean. He's a stick. He's a slug with a tiny dick."

And then Helen turned and walked to the dining room table, sat down, and put a red napkin over her head, completely unaware of the chaos she had started.

* * *

Oh, the dinner that night was tense.

I could tell that Grandpa was about to spring a gasket.

Grandma was so mad she actually slammed down her mother's serving dishes.

Aunt Janet's head hardly lifted up at all. That's probably a good summation of Aunt Janet's total life with Herbert: Her head hardly lifted up at all.

This, after Herbert's heated, repeated, continual denials that he had ever shown Helen his pee pee.

Helen did not make the dinner much easier when, after grace had been said and the meals were before us, she got up, took another stick out of her hair, walked around the table, and stuck the stick right into the mashed potatoes on Herbert's plate.

"That's the size," she said. "Sticky. Pokey. Thin."

He stood up, furious. "Stop that, Helen! This instant!"

I thought my grandpa was gonna blow. He was out of his chair in a flash. For a giant of a man, he sure could move. "Do not *ever* speak to either of my daughters in that abusive manner, you runt."

I drew in my breath. Was *runt* a cuss word?

Herbert shrunk down in his seat and Helen went back to arranging her food in the shape of a bird. Once the bird shape was formed she tweeted at it.

Herbert again said, "I deny her accusations, Albert."

Lance said, "Please pass the salt."

Polly said, "What's for dessert?"

Then Helen took out three of the sticks in her hair and threw them down the table at Herbert, calling out, "Small pee pee. Very small."

Oh, Herbert was raging then, and red, and humiliated. That's when I knew for sure that there was total truth to this story of Helen's.

Aunt Janet glared at her husband. I didn't miss the tears. "You didn't, did you, Herbert? I remember you went to New York, several times, when Helen was still there."

"You're going to believe your sister, a raving schizophrenic, over your husband?" Herbert shouted. "She's crazy, she's absolutely crazy."

"All I can think of is those pig troughs," Grandma said to Grandpa, her voice tight, pained, angry. "I think if we slice and dice him, we can squish him in. He's a little man."

"I'm thinking they'll be big enough, too," Grandpa said, slamming down his napkin. The crystal glasses shook. He got up again. "Get out of my house, Herbert."

Lance said, "Please pass the salt."

Polly said, her voice quavering, "What's for dessert?"

And Helen tilted her head up to the ceiling and her face cleared, everything miraculously, inexplicably clearing at that millisecond, as if she had a picture in her mind's eye, in rainbow Technicolor. "I threw a wineglass at his head. I threw a wineglass at the head of that short man with the small pee pee who's wriggling over there on his bottom. He wouldn't stop showing me his pee pee, but I said, Stop stop stop. Gross. It was gross, Momma. He shoved me against a wall. Bang. My head hit the wall and he grabbed these." She held her boobs up, then turned her eyes again slowly back to Herbert. "Him. I threw a wineglass with a blue swirl at his head right there." She pointed to the right side of her forehead, then she slowly, deliberately, pointed her finger straight at Herbert's scar on the right side of his forehead.

I heard Aunt Janet gasp and Grandpa roar, and then I saw Grandma crawl *across the table,* her cowboy boots knocking over the carrots in her mother's serving platter, and she leaped right at Herbert, knocking him straight to the ground, and hit him, by golly, with a clenched first, right over that scar.

At the end of the table, Helen tweeted at her bird, then took the fork out of her hair. "I miss that wineglass. Where is that wineglass?" She cocked her head at me. "Do you know, girl kid?"

Grandpa did not pull Grandma off of Herbert, but when she was done, he dragged Herbert up and out the door by his collar, Herbert's heels scraping the floor. Aunt Janet was making high-pitched noises and Grandma, *Grandma,* was swearing. I remember I had to ask Lance what "fucking bastard" and "lecherous damn asshole" meant.

I heard Herbert's Cadillac spin around in our driveway as he left. It took about five minutes for Grandpa to come back into the house and drop his cowboy boots to the floor. When he did he found his wife comforting his crying daughter, Janet, his other daughter ripping up a napkin and putting the pieces on her head, and me, Lance, and Polly wide-eyed.

"I got the salt," Lance said.

"Are we having dessert?" Polly asked meekly.

The next month was one of the best of my childhood. Lance and Polly and I played on the farm the entire time.

Aunt Janet did a lot of crying. I heard her tell Grandma and Grandpa she couldn't leave Herbert because he would take the kids from her, use something against her that she had done. I didn't know what that could be. I heard the name "Victor" and "wanted to marry me." It was yet another secret. "I'll never see them again, I know it. I can't risk it. . . . He'll say I'm a slut, an adulteress. . . ."

I didn't know what that meant.

"He'll say I'm a drunk. . . ."

I wasn't clear on that one, either.

"He'll say I'm unfit and mentally ill, because I had to go and get help with the drinking. . . . He had his attorney write me a letter. . . ."

No understanding there, either. Aunt Janet needed help to drink?

Lance told me his father didn't think much of him. "He wishes I was better. More *better*. At everything. I don't do anything right, you know, Stevie. Nothing." He said this matter-of-factly. He believed it as truth.

Polly told me her father never said anything nice to her, but she kept trying as hard as she could to make him pay her some attention. "He always says, 'Don't get fat as your mother has,' but I don't think Mom's fat at all, but I try not to eat much, but he keeps saying it to me. Do you think I'm fat, Stevie? When my hair is messy do you think I look like a stray dog? Do you think my lips are too fat? Dad does. He tells me to roll them in tight so men don't think I'm cheap and easy." She rolled her lips in so hardly any lip showed. "Do you think I'm cheap? What does cheap and easy mean on a girl?"

Lance asked, "Do you think all kids are dirty? Dad says they are. Do I look dirty to you? He says I won't make a good husband because I'm dirty and sweaty and I won't amount to anything. Does that mean I'll grow up to be a burglar or something?"

Polly said, "If other girls get better grades than me, does that mean I'm stupid? That's what Dad says. He says I'm too sexy. Do you know what sexy means? Is it bad?"

Lance said, "Sometimes I think I hate my dad."

"I know I hate him," Polly whispered. "I know I hate him."

Both of them said they wanted to live with me forever.

I wanted that, too. With Lance and Polly I wasn't embarrassed about Helen, even when she started having long-drawn-out, disjointed conversations with Command Center, which as far as I could determine as a kid was a mean voice in her head. I wasn't embarrassed when Helen leaned against the wall, eyes closed as she hummed. I wasn't embarrassed when she dressed up in a ski outfit, complete with mittens and hat, even though it was eighty-five degrees out, and attached a rope to the back of her pants as a tail and started speaking into it. They were family, after all. Helen was *their* aunt, so why should I be embarrassed?

I loved that summer. I never wanted it to end. We played all day and spent hours with "The Family," which consisted of an enormous number of relatives.

It ended when Herbert drove up in his Cadillac. He stayed right near the door of that car and honked the horn. Lance, Polly, and Aunt Janet scampered on out . . . and that was it.

They were gone.

8

Portland, Oregon

"Aren't you going to eat that?" Eileen asked me, peering at my salad.

"I am eating it," I said, forking another tomato into my mouth. The restaurant was one of those chic, fancy places. Eileen knows that I am barely making it financially, but we still come to this expensive café often.

I could say no.

I do say no.

And she says, "Stevie, I'll see you there at twelve o'clock." And hangs up.

I could not show up.

I always do.

Before the operation, we would treat each other, every other time, even though I asked if we could meet in other, less expensive places, which she declined. Since my operation, half the time she leaves the check to me. Half the time we go Dutch. I don't mind spending the money as much as I mind allowing myself to be taken advantage of.

"This chicken cacciatore is delicious," she says, smacking her lips. She was wearing a bright red shirt, snug on the top so about five inches of cleavage showed. She was wearing red lipstick to match and large diamond hoops in her ears, on her neck, and both wrists.

"Oh, good. This salad is delicious, too." Before my operation, I had wanted to eat a salad about as much as I wanted to dine on grass, so a whole new world of salads has opened up for me. My salad was called a Luau Bikini Salad.

Truly delicious. I couldn't even believe it was a salad.

Eileen snickered. "Come on, Stevie, you can be honest with me. You don't want to eat that salad. You're eating it so you can stay on your diet."

"It's yummy—"

She held up her fork in front of my face, waved it, as in, "Don't go there with me."

I sighed inwardly.

"Stevie Barrett, I feel sorry for you. You can't eat anything good anymore, because you feel that being thin is more important than really living, enjoying life."

I did not bother to remind her that my heart attack could well have taken the word *living* right out of my life.

Change the subject, I told myself. "How's work?" I then listened as she ranted about the firm's customers. "They need to know how their money is doing all the time! Wait for the quarterly financial statements!" The office staff in her father's investment firm were so incompetent—a stockbroker had screwed up, a partner was a screwup, and three women stockbrokers couldn't find their bras if Eileen wrapped them around their faces.

"How do you like your new furniture?" I asked.

She liked it. Except the interior designer for the furniture store who had come to her house was "one of those skinny girls, the ones you and I can't stand, who was rude to me. I called her boss and gave the boss a piece of my mind. She kept suggesting durable material. Well, I knew what she was talking about. The furniture should be durable for the size of my butt. When I called her on it, she got all defensive and said she recommends durable material to all her clients. She wanted me to get blues and yellows, I like mauve and green. I could tell she didn't approve of my choice, tried to sway me away from those colors . . ." She went on and on, ordered a pop from the waitress, more bread, more butter. "Don't forget it this time. Be quick about it."

"How is your father?"

Oh, he was fabulous, but her stepmother, the woman who had been married to her father for fifteen years, was "an awful witch. . . . I can't stand her . . . always fund-raising for sick kids, asking me to join her, as if I would have the time. . . . The woman never lets me see my father. . . ."

"Don't you and your father have lunch once a week and dinner once a week and work together?" I asked.

Yes, they did, but the witch was always trying to control her father. She hated going to Easter at their house—it was such a chore. The stepmother had three grown children and nine grandchildren, and Eileen *could not stand* children, and the woman's children always smiled at her, and the parents made their kids say hello, and the kids had asked her why she was fat, and their parents shushed them but the damage was done. "They don't want me in that family, which is fine. I don't want to be in their family. They're loud, stupid, uneducated, obnoxious, low-class . . ."

The waitress took away our plates. Eileen ordered a piece of seven-layer chocolate cake, and the waitress brought it. At no time did Eileen thank the waitress, who kept refilling her glass with lemonade. In fact, she never acknowledged her efforts. I thanked her. Eileen snapped at her.

She tucked into her chocolate cake. Five bites disappeared down her mouth, then she put a piece of the chocolate cake on her fork. "Try that. It's delicious."

"No, thank you."

She glared at me. "You can have a bite of cake, Stevie. It won't make you fat again."

No, it wouldn't. But I didn't want any cake. Since my operation, I can't eat sugar as well as I used to. Same with chocolate. It's a bizarre thing. Plus it can cause the dreaded dumping syndrome.

"I don't want any cake right now, but thank you."

She was furious, I knew it. I could tell in the frozen silence and the stabbing of the cake by her fork. It was a milder form of the fury she aimed at me when I was on a gurney at the hospital, where she had come uninvited, had thundered at me not to do the operation, was I insane, what the hell was wrong with me, I was risking my life to be thin, how stupid is that, you think you'll be happy when you're thin, you won't be, Stevie Barrett!

I had had a heart attack. I had almost died, and she didn't want me to get the operation.

"So you're going to make me feel guilty?"

"I'm not making you feel guilty, Eileen. I don't want any cake."

"Can I be honest with you, Stevie?"

She studied me with wide-open, sad eyes, and I braced myself.

"You're going to make yourself sick, sicker than you've already been. I'm so worried about you."

"Don't worry about me—"

"You're obsessed, you know. People who were obsessed with eating still have obsessions after bariatric surgery, they just turn them somewhere else. A lot of people become alcoholics or shopaholics. You're an exerciseaholic."

"No, I'm not. I walk—"

"You walk every day, Stevie. *Every day.*"

This sounded as if she was saying, "You stick a syringe up your arm filled with powdered pot and heroin, every day. *Every day.*"

"I love to walk."

"You need a shrink." She put another bite of cake on her fork and held it toward me. "Take one bite. It's delicious. You can't fill yourself up with vegetables. Yuck. Splurge."

"No, thanks, Eileen." She tried again, the bite of cake six inches from my mouth. I leaned back and put a hand up. She was disgusted with me.

"I didn't want to say this. . . ." A cake crumb was stuck in the corner of her mouth.

She trailed off.

"It hurts me to say this."

She had another bite of cake. More got stuck.

I put down my fork. I wanted to shout, "If you don't want to say it, don't."

"You're extremely sensitive, though, Stevie, so I'm afraid to say it."

"I'm not sensitive, and if you think it's going to be something that hurts me, keep it to yourself."

She laughed. Ate another bite of cake. Cake crumbs settled on her shirt.

"Yes, you are sensitive. You get uptight so easily."

"No, I don't—"

"See? You're doing it right now. You get on the defensive."

I leaned back in the booth and watched her. I was hurt. I was irritated. I was bracing myself for whatever it was she was going to say. And part of me was wondering, "Why on earth am I even here?"

She went back to shoveling cake in her mouth. "One bite and I'll leave you alone." That fork came flying toward me, and that finally pissed me off.

"No, Eileen," I said, throwing my napkin on the table. "I told you I don't want any cake! Are you deaf? What do you not understand about no?"

Her hand froze, then she slammed it to the table, the bite of cake falling off the fork. "You ungrateful, rude—" She spit out chocolate crumbs, then shut her mouth tight. "You think you're better than me, don't you? You've changed since your operation—"

"I would hope that I've changed," I sputtered. "That was the point. I wanted to change. I wanted my body to change, my thinking to change, my whole life to change. I didn't want to be myself anymore."

"You didn't want to be Stevie?"

"Yes. No. Sort of. Part of Stevie, not the other part." I was confused, rattled.

"I don't even understand you anymore. You're not even the Stevie I knew."

"Yes, I am—"

"You," she spit out. "*You* are all you talk about."

"I've hardly said anything this entire lunch—"

"When you can apologize for this conversation, then we'll talk. Not before."

"What am I supposed to apologize for?"

She heaved herself out of the booth, crumbs flying. "You're never going to understand, are you, Stevie? You don't have the capacity to. You're not able to. And look at you!" She glared at me, all her diamonds sparkling. "The way you dress now. Think about what you've said and done."

She grabbed her purse and left. One waiter jumped out of her way. She snarled at a child in the aisle and slammed the door.

I glanced down at my clothes. I was wearing a red T-shirt and a blue skirt.

I paid the bill when the waitress brought it by and gave her a huge tip.

My hand shook when I signed it.

Over the next week, I was still upset, and ticked off, about my lunch with Eileen, and since I couldn't eat my way into a food frenzy, I spent a lot of time with my obsession.

I had a chair with a full back, and I asked it questions: Do you think you're running out of time to be who you want to be? Do you feel that you're late to your own life? Do you count the seconds until you leave work? What other job would be more fulfilling? Do you take time to think about you, or do you only think about everyone else? If you had the time to do one trip, where would you go? You could die tomorrow, so why don't you plan that trip?

I decided I needed a time chair.

I sawed in half an old clock I'd found at a garage sale. It was wood, painted beige, the numbers in black, and it had a loop at the top. It was like one of those old-fashioned timepieces men used to wear in the 1800s, only it was about a foot tall. I wanted to attach each half to the sides of a wood chair I had painted blue.

The chair had a full back, not slats, so it gave me a complete canvas, so to speak, to paint on. I painted curving clocks—one red, one blue, one green, one yellow. Each had an *Alice in Wonderland* type of design to it. Each clock had a face, eyes, a nose, a smile.

The red clock had purple polka dots, the blue clock had cheetah legs, the green one had stripes and duck feet, and the yellow one had pink flowers sprouting around its square face.

On the seat of the chair I wrote the words "Don't be late!" under a woman who was totally normal—curvy, in blue jeans and a red T-shirt with colorful bracelets up her arms—except her face was a clock. The clock had blond curls springing out from all sides.

I called it Mrs. Clock Chair.

I am a nut.

I know this.

But for some reason, transforming chairs calms my nerves, and the flashbacks are controlled.

When the chair was done, I would put it in my garage with all the other chairs. I am not a talented painter or woodworker, so none of these chairs are good. They are weird, unprofessional, silly. That's why I keep my garage doors locked up tight.

The doors are not the only thing in my life locked up tight.

"You need help, Polly," I said.

"I'm fine."

"You're not fine. You need help. You can't do it on your own."

"Yes, I can. I'm managing it, exactly as I learned before, and I don't need help."

I didn't say anything.

"I can hear what you're thinking, Stevie. Knock it off."

"I'm worried about you."

"Well, stop."

"I'll take you."

"No. That's a no, stop asking, stop bugging me, you're pissing me off."

"Good thing I love you so much, Polly, because you are a pain in the butt."

She sighed. "I love you, too, Stevie." Her eyes dropped to my butt. "By the way, your butt is very nice."

"Thank you."

"Not that I'm hitting on you," she said.

"I didn't think you were hitting on me, being my cousin and all," I drawled. "But if I swung that way and you weren't my first cousin, hey, baby, bring it on."

We both laughed

Then Polly wiped tears away with shaking hands.

"You need to go," I said, gentle.

"Shut up."

That feeling of dread—raw, real, unstoppable—bubbled up inside of me.

"Please, Polly."

"No." She patted her heart. "We'll be fine, right, heart?"

That night I showered, spread on vanilla-scented lotion, climbed into bed, and worried myself sick about Polly.

I had built my own bed, thanks to Joseph.

What would Jake think of it? I speculated on that. Speculated what he would look like naked. I had had to hide behind my neighbor's car the other day to avoid him. Mr. James had hobbled out on his walker and said, "Hiding from Jake, honey?" I denied it. He laughed and thumped his walker. "Don't worry, me and Nancy ain't said nothin' to Jake about it. He's a good man, though." Mr. James winked at me. "And you're a good woman. Good and good go together!"

When I moved in, I had only a mattress that I got from a friend of a neighbor. That's what I slept on for months. I would dream of what kind of bed I would build myself when I had the time and energy to do so.

I took the measurements of my incredibly small bedroom and made a bed out of oak that stretched from one wall to the next. I built the bed frame high, so I need a two-step ladder to climb in, then built a squarish, abnormally tall headrest and footrest that reach almost to the ceiling. I found a pink quilted bedspread with little white flowers, and a puffy white down comforter, both at Goodwill, then collected eight pillows for decoration in pinks, whites, and a little black. The Throne Bed, as I call it, takes up almost the whole room except for a comfy blue jean chair and a small TV on a white shelf I built.

The other bedroom is actually much bigger than mine, but I love sleeping in a small space. To me, it feels cozy and safe, co-coonish.

The caterpillar in the cocoon turned off her light, then stared at the Starlight Starbright ceiling for hours, afraid to sleep and step into the nightmares—afraid I wouldn't sleep, and my mind would snap.

Not relaxing, folks.

"So you believe, Mrs. Atherton," Crystal said, disbelief ringing around each word, "that your son went without oxygen for"—she fiddled with her papers for effect—"four minutes, at least, while under sedation at Harborshore Hospital? Is that correct?"

I sat on Crystal's right in the conference room. Across from us was Mr. and Mrs. Atherton, the parents of Danny, a boy who had gone from playing baseball and reading about dragons and loving music to resting on a hospital bed full time in their dining room, with a feeding tube and a bag for urine.

The Athertons were in their thirties and clearly exhausted, unbearably saddened, and angry all at the same time. Mr. Atherton was well built and muscled with bright green eyes, his wife plump with an attractive face. They sat across the table along with their attorneys, two young people in their late twenties named Sonja Woods and Dirk Evans.

The attorneys for the Athertons had been a standing joke for Crystal. They were three years out of law school, going up against her, the powerful and smart Ivy League–educated Crystal Chen, and Harborshore Hospital. They couldn't win. They wouldn't win.

As Crystal said, "We will bury them alive. We will smash them. When I am done those attorneys will wish they had become plumbers and were under a sink with Mr. Atherton handling a wrench with their cracks slopping out their pants."

"Yes, that's right," Mrs. Atherton said. "We believe, based on Danny's condition now, that he was without air for about four minutes."

"Mrs. Atherton, were you in the room when your son—" Crystal sifted through papers ostensibly grasping for their son's name. She well knew the boy's name was Danny. She lived and breathed the name of that child, investigating, searching for ways that the hospital could win this case, but she was trying to undermine the couple, intimidate them, smother them down, bury them in so much paperwork, threats, and hopelessness that they'd bow out and quit.

"Danny," Mr. Atherton said, his face reddening. "Our son's name is Danny."

"Yes . . . Dan," Crystal said, offhanded. "You weren't in the room, so how do you know that he did not have oxygen for four minutes?" She narrowed her eyes at Mrs. Atherton, then tilted her head. I actually saw her eyes taking in Maggie Atherton's hair and clothes. Maggie got the message. Crystal Chen did not think much of Maggie, her curling hair, the lack of makeup on her face, her plump figure under the blue blouse and beige pants, the dark circles under her eyes.

Maggie tilted her chin up. "No, I wasn't in the room."

"Are you a doctor?" Crystal asked.

"No."

"Do you have any medical training at all?"

"No."

Crystal pretended to be confused. "Then how could you possibly offer a medical opinion when you're clearly not qualified to do so?"

Her attorneys cut in. They fought with Crystal while Mrs. Atherton paled.

"Mrs. Atherton," Crystal drawled. "Isn't it true that you signed these papers"—she shuffled the papers again—"that the hospital gave you, indicating that you knew your son's heart operation could have a poor result, even death?"

"Yes, I did—"

"And you, too, Mr. Atherton? You signed the papers?"

"Yes. We had to sign the papers or the operation would not be performed and—"

"Thank you. I have the papers." Crystal put the copies of the papers that the Athertons had signed in the middle of the table. The couple barely glanced at them. They had seen the papers.

"As you can see, it says right here"—Crystal tapped the paper with her red-tipped nail—"that this operation can have poor results. . . ."

"Ms. Chen, you know as well as I do," Sonja Woods said, "that the fine print on anything from a medication prescription to a minor operation involving three stitches lists any and all possible medical problems that can incur. You can't swallow a basic pain medication without reading that you could instantly die—"

"I'm not talking about pain medication, I'm talking about a heart operation," Crystal interrupted. "These people"—she flicked her eyes to the couple, then smoothed out an invisible wrinkle on her designer suit—"signed off on the operation. They were told there could be medical consequences."

"There's nothing in there, Ms. . . . *Chen*"—Mr. Atherton deliberately paused before her name, as if he was trying to recall it, as Crystal had done with his boy—"that says we should expect the oxygen tube to be incorrectly placed in my son's mouth." Mr. Atherton's voice rose. "Where was the anesthesiologist? What happened to him? Why wasn't he watching?"

"Mr. Atherton, please." Crystal held up a hand. "Your son was born with a congenital heart defect. The doctors tried to save him, tried to help him. They're not God."

"No one asked them to be God," Mrs. Atherton cut in. "We asked them to do their jobs."

"Let's move on—"

"Let's not," Mr. Atherton said.

Dirk Evans, the other Atherton attorney, raised his eyebrows at Crystal. "This is why we're here, Crystal. As much as the hospital is trying to hide it, that breathing tube was incorrectly placed. That's why Danny is in the tragic condition he's in. The Athertons deserve compensation to care for Danny."

"You can't prove it." Crystal leaned back and smiled tightly. I saw her swinging her foot under the table, her expensive heel rocking back and forth. This was fun for her. Fun. Make 'em miserable. Put up a wall. Make the wall so unscaleable, so terrifying, they give up.

"Yes, we can," Sonja said, but I could see the doubt in her eyes.

"We'll prove it. We'll take you to court, in front of a jury and judge," Dirk added, but I could tell he wasn't a hundred percent confident. Crystal saw it, too.

"There's no way we're going to pay you ten million dollars."

"Why not?" Sonja said. She was young, but she was determined and passionate about this case. "That's how much it will cost, throughout Danny's life, for medical care. That's how much round-the-clock nurses will be, medications, oxygen. Mrs. Atherton won't be able to work. . . ." The list went on.

Crystal shook her head. She was so sorry she was dealing with imbecilic people. "We will never agree to this number. It's idiocy. Harborshore Hospital tried to help. They tried to save your son's life—"

"They almost killed him. Seconds more and he would have been dead," Mrs. Atherton said sadly. I did not miss the way her hands trembled, the pallor of her skin. Her husband linked an arm behind her chair.

"That's not true. Had they not done the operation, your son would not have lived. They saved your son's life."

"Saved his life, they did that indeed," Sonja said. "It's not in dispute that the operation saved Danny's life. But is it a life now worth living? The doctors failed."

The arguments went on and on, the numbers floated around and about, for about fifteen minutes. I could tell that Mr. Atherton was enraged, Mrs. Atherton crushed. Their attorneys—intelligent but, even in my eyes, inexperienced—were furious.

"I think we'll have to take this one to court," Crystal said. I knew she was bluffing. No one wanted this in court, especially not the hospital.

"Go ahead," Dirk said. "We'll wheel Danny in, in his wheelchair and we'll see how the jury feels about this."

"The jury will understand that the hospital did all they could—"

"All they could?" Mr. Atherton stood up, hands on the table, his voice choked. "All they could? They almost killed him. They almost killed my son and they won't admit, not for a second—"

"Yes, we're all sorry. Poor kid," Crystal said. "Too bad you parents can't be grateful, grateful to the hospital for what they tried to do, and it's come to this. We're done here. Steve?" She stood up. That was my cue. We left. I pretended not to hear Mrs. Atherton crying and Mr. Atherton swearing.

This was a horrid case, horrid.

"Was the breathing tube out of Danny's mouth for four minutes, Crystal?"

Crystal shuffled papers on her desk. The Athertons and their attorneys had left. I had ducked behind a file cabinet as they passed. Their pain made me feel as if I couldn't draw a breath. I could feel it in my own heart.

"Doesn't matter."

"What do you mean it doesn't matter?"

"It doesn't matter." She pushed her straight black hair behind her back. "It's irrelevant. A nonissue. Who cares? It's of no consequence."

"No consequence? It's of consequence because a child has been permanently disabled because of it."

"That's not our concern. Our concern is to get the hospital off the hook. To defend them. To continue this fight until the Athertons are too fried to go anywhere else with it, and it'll happen. They'll get sick of it. They'll realize they can't fight with the big guys. The big guys always, always win. Plus, their two attorneys, those young hotshots." She snorted. "I've checked them out. If Sonja's husband wasn't working as a nurse and Dirk's wife wasn't working as a kindergarten teacher, they would both be eating cat food right now, they're so broke. They've set up their 'legal offices' "—she made quotes with two fingers in the air—"in the garage of Sonja's ranch house. They've taken out second mortgages on their homes. They have nothing to their names except $40,000 in student loans. Each." She snorted again. "This is their only case and it's taking up all their time. They're using their own money to hire experts, court fees, and so on. They'll give up. They'll have to. Sonja and Dirk are going to bankrupt themselves. They're hoping they'll get thirty percent plus costs if they win a settlement, but what's thirty percent of nothing? Nothing."

"You think they'll drop the case?"

"Sure. We might hand over $50,000 to make the whole thing go away. Sonja and Dirk will get $15,000, the Athertons will get $35,000. Everybody will sign a confidential, 'Don't say a damn thing to the media' agreement, and that will be that."

"But where will the Athertons be then? That $35,000 isn't very much with their costs. I've seen the expense sheet."

"Again, Steve"—she stood up to glare at me, arms crossed in her "Must I deal with an imbecile" position—"we don't care. I don't care. You shouldn't care. We're attorneys, okay? It's not our job to care, and I certainly don't care about this."

She turned back to her desk and picked up her BlackBerry. "Damn," she muttered, then pierced me with those narrow eyes. "You can go now, Steve."

I nodded.

"Wait."

She fiddled with the edge of her suit jacket. "You haven't seen the letter from Dr. Dornshire yet?"

I shook my head.

"Keep searching. It's *none* of your business what's in that letter, but keep searching."

I left.

I had a stack of documents on the Atherton case, and I'd flipped through them searching for that letter simply because Crystal wanted it so badly and I couldn't figure out why.

What is in that letter?

Zena and I sat in Pioneer Courthouse Square for lunch, as usual. Pioneer Courthouse Square is in the middle of Portland. It's this huge bowl with brick steps, a fountain, and a statue of a man with an umbrella. There're concerts and cheer fests for our professional basketball team and sandcastle-building contests.

It's the place for businesswomen and panhandlers, mothers with strollers and homeless teenagers, executives and suburbanites coming in for some city lights and action.

Everybody has a different story, and if one person had had the unfortunate misfortune of landing in the same shoes as that homeless person right over there, their life would have been completely different.

Nobody wants to think of it that way, but it is the truth.

"Do you believe in reincarnation?" Zena asked me.

"I don't know. It's the ultimate in recycling, though, isn't it? Don't waste, reuse! Here's a soul, now stick it back out there."

"I think I was Cleopatra in another life," she said. "I have a thing for snakes. And I think I might have been a pirate. Probably the captain of the ship. I might have been a king in my past, too."

"That would be a problem." I handed her slices of pear. "This is the best pear in the world."

"Why would it be a problem?" She handed me cheese sticks.

"Because you'd have to have a queen and you're not gay."

"Maybe I was a manly man back then and chased women. Or maybe I was a king and let my wife run around with the knight out in back with the sexy thighs."

"Could be."

"In my next life I want to be a magician, magic and all, none of these fake tricks. What do you want to be?"

I thought about that. "I think I want to be an explorer. A world traveler. Someone who goes all over the world, meets new people, sees new things, and is brave and courageous. Exactly the opposite of how I am now—my world so small, seeing the same things, same people, every day, because I'm too scared to set fire to the walls of the box that surround me."

"You'd be good at that." She handed me a handful of raspberries and I took them.

"That's who I'd want to be. An adventurer." I nodded. Good choice.

We saw Crystal teetering on her high heels toward a Chinese food kiosk. She said something to the man and woman serving lunch. They handed her a plate. She nodded at them, and the woman came out and gave her a hug.

"Gee. Somebody wants to hug Crystal? That's a shocker," Zena drawled.

Crystal teetered off, butt swaying. Even walking she seemed ticked off.

"I think Crystal's stick is bugging her," Zena drawled.

"Have you had a boob job?"

I choked on my water, put the water glass down, and mopped up my face. "What?"

"Come on now, sweetie. Tell me the truth. Job or no job? Natural or popped up?"

Why had I even gone out on this dinner date? Why can't I say no? I cursed Zena silently. She had set this date up for me and cajoled me into going. "Come on, Stevie. Don't be a puss."

My date, Dave Berg, who also had almost zero resemblance to his photo on the Date Me! Internet site, raised his eyebrows, then brought his beer—his third, and we hadn't even had dinner yet—to his lips. His eyes dropped to my chest again.

"Why do you want to know?" I wished I hadn't answered. He didn't deserve an answer.

"Man. Those knockers are yours?"

I resisted the urge to wrap my arms around my chest.

"Yes. Whose else would they be? The waiter's? The chef here? Do you think they belong to the woman in purple over there?"

He laughed, wiped a hand across his beer-drippy mouth. "Nice, lady. Nice. You're funny, too, and you've got a rack and a half."

Now I didn't even hesitate. I crossed my arms to cover myself.

"Hey! You're oodling my noodle." He nodded toward my boobs. "You go, girl, squish 'em on up so I can get my teaser teased." He grinned, wet lips slimy. "The pecker's pecking!"

I realized my mistake. Crossing my arms had brought my boobs together, creating cleavage.

It's time for you to leave, I told myself.

"You're doing that to turn me on." The candles on the table flickered. I wondered if I could turn him off by tossing one of them at his face.

"No, I'm not."

"No? I doubt that. You know what you're doing. You chicks. You hens. You know how to turn a man on, don't you? Get him hard up, be demure, and then—" He growled under his breath. "You know how to rev him up with those innocent blue eyes, doncha, Stevie?"

"No, I don't—"

I think we're definitely done here.

"Oh, yeah, I love it. The protest. The sweet face. The curls." He reached over and tugged on one of my black curls. "You're Kinky Kareena and Sex Goddess Gail all wrapped up in one, aren't you?"

"I don't know why—"

His eyes dropped again. "Do that thing with your arms again, will you? Squish up those knockers so I can get a peek. An eyeful of an eyeful. A handful of a handful."

Your hands are shaking, that's a sign. Hello? Let's exit.

He leaned over the table and whispered to me, "I would like you to sit on my face, would that turn you on, boob momma? I want you to get naked with me and sit on my face until we're both going to explode, and then I want to handcuff you to the bed and have my way with that rack of yours and then I'll spread your legs out and I'll lick—"

He stopped talking when I picked up his plate of curlicue pasta and dumped the whole thing in his lap.

When he stared up at me in shock I pointed to my boobs. When he was staring at them, I reached down and grabbed his water glass and threw the ice water in his face.

I hate, hate, hate dating.

I grabbed my purse, spun on my heel, and started out the restaurant, chin up.

My chin was not quite high enough up, however, to not encounter the gaze of someone else.

That someone else was Jake—yes, my Jake, Jake of the big truck, who I had invited to come in my truck, so to speak.

He was with three other men, and I stopped short when I saw him, my mouth dropping. I did not miss the expression on his face. Surprise, yes, laughter, yes, and then . . . was it admiration? The jaws of the men around him were open, as if they were trying to catch tiny fairies flitting about.

I cleared my throat and brushed my hands over my skirt. "Jake."

He grinned at me. "Stevie, it's a pleasure to see you."

Oh, how I could barely breathe, my brain squishy. "It's a pleasure to see you, too." *Don't think about him naked!*

"Bad date?" He raised his eyebrows at me.

"Yes. A bad date." I was still mad about it, actually. Men are such jerks. Except for Jake, obviously. "But the bad date is over. . . ."

I saw Jake's three friends scrambling out of the booth, along with Jake, Jake's eyes fixed on something in back of me.

It was Dave Berg, who wanted me to sit on his face. I will be brief. Dave was upset with me. He had pasta hanging off his pants and his face was still wet. He wanted to know "who the hell I thought I was," and before I could answer, Jake was standing in front of me, his friends on either side, and I could hardly see Dave around his shoulders, the size of Mt. St. Helens.

"Back off," Jake said.

Dave growled and bad-mouthed, and then he shoved Jake, and that was it. Jake swung up a fist and powed Dave down to the floor, where he lay with pasta hanging off his pants, stunned into silence, the snake.

"Perhaps I could interest you in dinner one night?" Jake said. "If you can promise not to dump pasta on my lap. What do you say?"

I believe I nodded. *Don't think about him naked.*

"Yes, you're welcome," I said. "Thank you."

Jake winked at me. His friends grinned.

I thought of him naked.

* * *

As usual I watched Polly and her co-anchor, Grant Joshi, on the air that night after I'd thought of Jake naked for a long time.

Their newscast was flawless, flowing, clear, never an error. They segued from one story to another, smiled at the right time, eyes growing serious with the heartbreaking stuff, playful with something funny. One story, then another, a little chitchat in between as they brought in the weatherman and sports guy. Polly was beautiful, glamorous, but not too glamorous, her auburn curls tied back.

At the end of the newscast, I saw Polly reach under the desk a millisecond before the newscast ended.

I pictured her with that brown bag over her face and knew that much of her hyperventilating problem would be taken care of if she got the other problem taken care of.

Dealing with adults in denial is excruciating. You can't force them to get care, even if their own life is at stake. Talking won't do it, threats won't, tears and hysterics, nothing.

They have to want it themselves. They have to want to help themselves.

And until they've hit the bottom, until they're literally fighting for their lives, struggling around, gasping, scratching for an edge to grab to bring their noses above water, until they can actually touch death with their own fingertips, they'll refuse help.

And sometimes, even when death is dancing on those fingertips, they'll try to flick death off, as if death can be flicked, and they'll die.

They will die and their deaths will leave emotional wreckage, blistering grief, and overwhelming guilt to the survivors' lives forever.

I walked out on my porch after the newscast and shook out my hands, which were shaking like hummingbird wings.

A star shot through the night. That star was now dead after millions of years of brightness.

Please, Polly, save yourself.

I can't lose you, too.

9

Portland, Oregon

Herbert had never been interested in saving Polly. He had never been interested in saving anyone except himself and his business.

"Some men are good at business," he told me, about six months after I'd moved in. "And some men are leaders, innovators, visionaries in business."

Aunt Janet was off on another "vacation," which meant that Herbert had shuttled her off to a detox place because her alcoholism had "embarrassed" him again. How anyone could stay sober married to Herbert was a mystery to me, but I do know that Aunt Janet was always kind to us. She simply drank herself into a stupor each night starting at seven o'clock.

"I am a leader, an innovator, a visionary." He blew pipe smoke into the air, sighed, then his ferret eyes pierced me. "Your grandpa's business . . ." He sighed again. "I've had to take it over, and it's taken up a lot of my valuable time. I hope it doesn't go bankrupt."

I had no idea what he meant by all that sighing. As far as I knew, Grandpa had the best business of all. A whole bunch of people in town worked for him. I assumed that people were still working there. My numbed, grief-stricken young mind simply didn't go further than that.

"He was too soft-hearted. Not a true businessman. Sadly, he

didn't have the opportunity of the schooling I've had." Herbert leaned back in his chair and studied papers framed in black. "See that? Ivy League education. My family could afford those opportunities for me. As you know, we own timber, real estate, small ventures. Your grandpa was not as successful. As a businessman, he didn't have the acumen, the intellect, perhaps the mental toughness that you need to run a company. He certainly could have benefitted from my wisdom and advice, but he didn't ask. I have grown my family's company exponentially over the years. Business is second nature to me."

He cleared his throat. "He had other things on his mind, though, didn't he? Your mother . . ." He shook his head. "She was a handful."

I felt the anger that I harbored all the time, the anger that burned like boiling-hot rocks in my stomach, slide up my throat. I tried blocking all my raging thoughts of Helen out of my head. I still hated her, hated what she'd done, but that didn't mean that Herbert could say anything against her.

"I would have handled her differently, had that been my child. Your grandpa and grandma were too lenient with her, too permissive. She turned out the way she did because she was a spoiled child, did not know her role as a woman in our society, and thought she could run off and have her own career singing, in New York. She cracked under the strain. Her mind turned to mush." He tsk-tsked. "They never should have allowed her to go. She needed someone to control her, to give her limits and boundaries."

He put his feet on the desk so I was staring at the bottom of his shoes. Then he blew more pipe smoke into the air and squinted at me through it.

"I'll never forget how she wore chicken wire. And that foil. Your grandparents should have reigned her in or committed her to an institution until she agreed to behave appropriately. They should have told her, in no uncertain terms, that her behavior was unacceptable. Unacceptable. They didn't. It led to a tragedy, didn't it? And now here I am, raising you."

He sighed heavily.

"But I do my duty, meet my obligations. No one can accuse me of not doing so."

He sighed again, tapped his pipe.

"No, my family is well respected in this town. Thank God I had the foresight to change your name the minute you stepped in my front door. That incident with you and your sister was all over the news, and it could have wrecked my reputation. Remember, what happened is a secret. You're not to tell anyone. It would be mortifying if people found out. It would smear my family name. If I hear of you telling anyone, Stevie, I'll turn you out on the street, do you understand? You'll be out on the streets."

I nodded. I understood. "Could I go back to Ashville instead of the streets?"

He slammed his hand so hard on the desk it shook. "No," he yelled. "No, you cannot go back to Ashville. I have told you that many times."

I was scared, but I had to ask. "But why not?"

"Why? Because your grandparents said you were to live with your aunt Janet—" He cleared his throat. "With me. They knew I would take my burdens and do right by them."

"If I'm a burden, maybe I should go and live with one of my other aunts or uncles?"

"No, dammit! We will not speak of this again. Never. You are not returning to Ashville, and you are not going to any of your wacky, strange uncles or aunts. You are not allowed any contact with them."

"But—" I had asked many times if I could write letters to my cousins and aunts and uncles, but Herbert had forbidden it. I had asked if we could visit, but he had forbidden that, too. I had asked if I could call—no, I could not. I had been silenced into nothing and sent to my room.

"But one time I thought I saw Uncle Boynton and Aunt Cora leaving this house."

"That didn't happen. You're delusional."

"But last week when I got off the bus I saw Cousin Tyco's truck."

"You didn't see it. It's your wishful thinking."

"But I was sure I saw Great Aunt Telly leaving here when me and Aunt Janet got home from shopping a couple months ago. Mr. Chen, too."

"You have many emotional issues and you're confused. They did not come."

"But, I know I saw them!"

"They weren't here! I've told you that many times. You're wrong! *They did not come.*" His eyes skittered back and forth as he pounded the desk. "You're mine. I am legally your guardian, and let me tell you something, they don't want you."

"They don't?" I whispered. I was so traumatized by that statement, one more mammoth hurt piled upon my own devastation, I could hardly see. I tried to pull myself into a smaller ball. Why didn't they want me? Was it because I didn't save Sunshine and they blamed me for it? I had tried as hard as I could! Was it because of what Helen did? Did they think I was bad, too? Was it because I was getting fat? Was it because I was a burden, as Uncle Herbert said? Did they think I wasn't a good granddaughter and that's why Grandpa and Grandma died? Did they think I caused Helen to be as she was? Was it all my fault?

I tried to breathe through the searing, aching anguish. But what Herbert said might be true. My family back in Ashville hadn't called, hadn't written, hadn't come to Portland to visit. I just *thought* I saw them because I'd wanted to. They didn't want me. *They didn't love me.*

I probably could not express how bleakly alone, how devastated I felt at that moment, so I won't try. Let's compare it to drowning. Drowning in black grief within black grief.

"They don't need you around as a reminder of all that happened, Stevie. They all want to forget, so forget them."

Forget them? I could never forget them . . . but they had forgotten me or were trying to forget me. I reminded them of dead people they had loved. No wonder they didn't want to see me. I pulled my arms around my legs so tight, my face down.

"What happened is shameful. Your family is gone, and if you

were in Ashville they would feel compelled to take you in, all the time worrying that you had the same demented genes as your mother and would kill someone. Be a murderer. You don't think you'll turn out like her, do you?" He blew smoke, straight out at me. "A murderer?"

I didn't move. *Her?* Who was her? I lifted my head. "You mean my momma?"

"Yes, your mother. I hope you don't have schizophrenia. I'll watch you closely for signs and then I'll take a firm hand to you, Stevie. I won't allow you to have it. I'll be the parent your grandparents should have been with their daughter."

I thought of my grandparents. I could see them right in front of me. I could hear Grandpa calling Herbert Hatchet Face and Grandma talking about dumping him in a pig trough.

"Did your mother . . ." Herbert let the words hang in the air. "Did your mother . . ." He blew smoke again, and I could tell he was trying to act casual. "Did she ever mention me?"

I nodded, the black sorrow in my heart heavy and dull, seeming to drag on every beat.

"She did?" I did not miss the thin smile that pulled on the corners of his mouth. He took his feet off the desk and leaned forward. "What did she say? I know you saw that one incident where she lied about me being in New York, but hopefully, young woman, she told you the truth."

I squirmed.

"Come on, now, don't be embarrassed. Your mother, before she went entirely eccentric, had a certain allure, a sex—" His eyes got soft, snaky soft. "Well, I'm forgetting you're a child, but let's say your mother used to be a beautiful woman." He stared into space for a moment and licked his lower lip, his tongue darting in and out. "She was a beautiful woman." He grunted, then shifted his private area a couple of times on the chair. "So tell me." Those snake eyes focused on me again, with a sneaky, eager smile. "What did she say about me?"

The sobs were coming up in me, I could feel them. Would they drown me? Did I care?

"Right now, Stevie, speak up! I'm the head of this house and

you are to obey me, without question. None of this gross le-
niency that you've grown up with, this cock-eyed, liberal, hippie, everyone-is-equal mentality."

I swallowed hard, the sobs now in my throat. I felt my insides
crying. "Are you sure?"

"Yes, I'm sure, although I think I can guess what she said." A
smile tugged again at the corners of his mouth and he coughed,
pulled on his trousers, wriggled his private area again in his
chair. "So. Out with it, Stevie. What did your mother say about
me?"

"Are you sure you want me to say it?" I asked, hesitant,
scared.

"Haven't you been listening to me, girl? Tell me the truth this
instant."

"Well, okay," I said. Soon I would be dead from crying anyhow. "She said . . ." I stopped. Would drowning in my sobs
hurt?

He rolled his eyes. "Speak, now, for God's sake, Stevie. We'll
keep it between us. We don't need to tell your aunt Janet. I don't
want to make your aunt feel any worse. Lord knows living
under your mother's shadow was hard enough. She doesn't need
to hear that her sister was an admirer of her husband, too."

I wasn't sure what he was talking about, but I decided to
speak up and tell the truth so I could leave and go drown privately. "My momma said you were short as snot. I'm sorry, but
that's what she said. Short as snot. She said you had the face of
a ferret. She'd screw her face up so she was a ferret and then
she'd claw the air every time before you came to our house."

His smiled disappeared.

"She said you kept calling her and calling her on the snocker-
phonola when she was in New York, that's what she sometimes
called the phone, and that your voice made her think of diarrhea."

He made a gurgling sound, deep in his throat.

My sobs were coming up again, swirling around, my whole
head aching. My tears would kill me, I figured. "She said that
she told Aunt Janet not to marry you. She begged her, and my

grandparents said the same thing, because all you wanted to do was control a woman like a dog. Helen barked when she called you a dog. *Bark, bark,* like that."

His pipe dropped from his mouth to the floor.

"She said you had a fart smell to you. Sorry to use the word *fart.* So when you came over my momma would always fart. That's what she remembered. She would say, 'Here comes the short weasel fart,' and she'd fart. Sorry again to use that word, Herbert. You can't help being short."

"This is absurd—" His face flushed.

"My grandparents didn't like you, either. They wanted to put you in the pig trough. Grandma wanted to use her mother's scissors on you, in the, you know, privates, so you would become a hen. Grandpa said you weren't a real man. Does that mean you're a fake man? I didn't get that."

He was furious. "That's enough, Stevie."

"You said you wanted me to tell you. My momma also said you had a small pee pee. Remember the sticks?"

"You can go now." He was darn near to frothing he was so mad.

"Okay. I'll go now." I got out of my seat and turned to leave. "My momma said you had Napoleon Syndrome, then she would get down on her knees and crawl around with a fake sword. What's that?"

He yelled, I ran.

I went upstairs, lay down, and waited for my tears to kill me.

When they didn't, I snuck downstairs and ate six cupcakes.

10

Portland, Oregon

The women clearly didn't care if they killed each other.
I had never seen such aggression, such flat-out, blatant, rip-roaring competition in my life. And all from women who were wearing fishnet tights and roller skates. This was the fifth roller derby bout I'd watched, and I know this: Women's roller derby competitions are not for the faint of heart.

Zena belonged to Portland's Break Your Neck Booties roller derby team. Her derby name was Badass Z Woman, and she was constantly trying to get me to join. "I know there's a she-devil in you, a knee breaker, a bottom booter, a savage Rollerblading demon."

I sucked in my breath. *I couldn't join the Break Your Neck Booties.* No way. They're all women, aged twenty-two to fifty. With the fishnets they wear short black skirts, red satin shirts, helmets, elbow pads, and kneepads. Their ferocious battles fried any preconceived notion that women are naturally gentle. These women played to win. They are rough. They are tough. They are deadly. They are Alpha Women.

I am only an Alpha Woman in my daydreams, but I secretly, in my wildest dreams and fantasies, want to belong to that group. But I can't. Too scared. Too out of shape. And I'm not vicious enough.

"Oh, my goodness, those women would mush me. Mush

me," I said. Off the track the team consists of two doctors, one a brain surgeon no less, a prosecuting attorney, a defense attorney, two full-time mothers with seven kids between them, a makeup artist, a tow truck driver, a minister, and Zena. "None of them would even be interested in viewing the mush I became."

"Then toughen up, you wimp!" Zena shouted, her arms in the air. I had caught her lurking outside the pillars of our office again last week. She had insisted on wearing the oversized red sweater I was wearing. The red sweater came almost to her knees. She pulled a rope—a rope—out of her desk and tied it around her waist three times and kept her black cowboy boots on. She was so chic that Caroline and the other male attorneys probably got boners.

"You can do this, Stevie," she pleaded.

"Oh, I can't. Didn't you break someone's arm last week?"

Zena smiled, proud. "Not intentionally. She was in my way. She scratched me later. See that?" I dutifully admired her very long scratch.

"You're an Amazon woman, Zena. A warrior."

She pleaded, I declined, but that didn't mean I couldn't watch the roller derby bouts and cheer my head off.

When Zena stepped off the track after a particularly bad crash with a competitor who was wearing a blue silky half top, a jean skirt, and red tights, she spit blood out of her mouth, checked her teeth with her fingers, wiped the blood off, and went speeding back onto the track with a roar—no kidding, she actually roared.

I wanted to be a Break Your Neck Booties gal.

I did.

I couldn't, though.

Could I?

I called cafés, coffee shops, restaurants, and asked if they had received my application.

Yes, they had.

One restaurant had 200 applications for a hostess position.

"Ma'am, I have people with doctorates applying for this position," the manager told me.

A café had 122 applications for two jobs as baristas. "We'll give you a call." He coughed. "Maybe." Coughed again. "Don't hold your breath."

A copy shop, a garage door repair service, and an automotive shop all had advertised for help. "I'm buried in résumés," one man said. "Buried."

I needed a second job.

I sure as heck wasn't going to take the chicken job.

On Monday morning I went for a walk through a light drizzle starting at six o'clock.

When I heard footsteps behind me, I whirled around quick. It was still dark and quiet.

"Hi, Stevie, it's me."

It was Jake, the he-man neighbor who put a flutter in my breast. *Don't think of him naked!*

"Hi." I thought of the pasta-dumping incident. "I want you to know that I don't usually do that, it was an aberration, with the pasta. I don't usually dump pasta on men, but you see my friend, Zena, set me up on that date, she put me on this Date Me Web site, I didn't even know I was up there, and then I went, and I didn't want to go, but the guy was so disgusting, and he made my skin crawl, and all I could see was that pasta and that ice water. . . ."

"So he wasn't your boyfriend?"

"Uh, no. That would be a no. I do not have a boyfriend. Do you?"

"No. I have never had a boyfriend," he said in all seriousness.

"I didn't mean to say that. . . ." My face got hot.

"It's okay, we'll just clear the air right from the start." He chuckled again. "Can I walk with you?"

I nodded, almost jiggled I was so pleased despite the naked thoughts. We made small talk for a while—the weather, Oregon in general, our neighborhood—and I was able to utter words in an appropriate, and not deranged, fashion.

"Stevie, I bought my house about seven months ago."

I nodded. I knew that. I knew the day he moved in because me and Nancy had gawked at him as he and some buddies moved furniture and technology stuff into his home that one would find in accordance with the male species.

"And I've waved at you, tried to chat with you, and . . . well, I think"—he paused delicately—"I think you're avoiding me."

I closed my eyes, then opened them again, lest I trip over a sidewalk crack, splat straight down on my face, and break my nose.

"Are you avoiding me?" He stopped walking. "Stevie, I sure would like to get to know you, but I don't want to push here, either. You have this beautiful, beautiful smile. . . ."

I did?

"And that dimple in your cheek . . ."

My dimple!

"And I like . . . I don't know how to say this, but I like how you live. I like the way your home is painted, and how you drive that truck that makes so much noise, how you walk all the time, and know how to use a saw. I've heard the sound from your garage. I think you're a kind person, and I thought it was hilarious when you dumped pasta in that guy's lap, but, well . . ." He brushed his blondish hair back with a hand, and it fell right back to where it was. "Have you been avoiding me, and if so, just say it, and I won't keep trying to say hello, or visit with you at all. I don't want to make you feel uncomfortable or uneasy around me. . . ."

I could lie. I could twist things, say I'd been busy, and so on, but so much of my life had already been a lie. Who I was, my own name, who my parents were, what had happened to me and Sunshine . . .

"Yes," I said, and my voice squeaked. "I have been avoiding you."

He wasn't smiling, and those green eyes were suddenly sad. "Can I ask why?"

I bent my head for a minute, juggling a hundred thoughts, trying to put them into some cohesive order. "I . . ."

"It has been somewhat amusing to watch you leap over hedges, dart into alleys, and hide behind recycling bins, but I think it would be best if we could alleviate some of your troubles and calisthenics. The other day I thought you landed pretty hard."

I dared to stare up into those eyes—sad, but laughing now, too, and I laughed.

"I have been rather kamikaze-ish with my escape moves, haven't I?" Oh, what to say, I was so embarrassed. "Jake, I'm sorry. I . . ." Say something, brain. "I have, uhhh . . ." Come on, mouth, be articulate. "I, uhhh . . ." All failed me. "I am still trying, uh, to find myself."

I peered up at him, waited for him to laugh, but he did not.

"I am not quite me yet, and I know that sounds truly insane, but there have been a few, uh, slight changes in my life the last few years, well, maybe there were herculean-sized changes and, well, I'm not altogether yet, and you . . ."

"And me?"

"Well, you seem altogether, like you know yourself, and you get yourself, you get Jake, if that makes the remotest amount of sense at all, and I am still trying to figure out who I am, who Stevie is. I know . . . I know I want to have a vegetable garden, with carrots, and I know that I like furniture with personality, colored glass, and walking, and I know I don't like a couple of people in my life, or my nightmares or a messy house, but me, who I am, I'm not sure of that yet and you—"

"Back to me?"

"Yes, well, you are . . . " I gazed at him head to toe and tried not to think: Naked Jake. "You are . . . well, very, handsome . . ." Why did I use that word? "And you seem very . . . man-like." Oh, dear. "And you are tall and broad up there on your shoulders." I am an idiot. "And you have a great smile and you seem so confident in your man-like attitude and it's . . ." I breathed in—oh, cease, my pounding heart. "And you're too much to take, I don't know what to say to you, I don't know why you even want to talk to me, I'm working on myself but I'm not quite there yet. You think I'm the strangest person you've ever met, don't you?"

We stood in the drizzly rain and didn't say anything for a while, but his eyes never left mine, although mine skittered from his.

"You are not the strangest person I have ever met, but quite possibly the most endearing. I don't know what to say about my man-like attitude—I'm stuck with it—but I do appreciate you telling me I'm handsome. Haven't heard that word in a while, but it's a pleasure to hear it—and I have an idea."

"You do?"

"Yes. Let's you and I, as friends, find out who you are."

"I don't think you want to do that. I am complex and odd and have many troubling issues you probably don't need in your life. I think we should go back to my jumping into alleys."

"Please, let's not. The next time I see you do that, I'm going to follow you in."

Now that sounded almost romantic, and I smiled and blushed. I knew he saw that blush.

His smile, warm and honest, came right back at me like a golden, flashing light. "How about if we find out who you are by going out to dinner soon?"

"You're kidding. You want to have dinner with me?"

"Yes, I do, Stevie, yes, I do."

I love rainy days in Oregon.

I darn near clicked my rain boots.

Mr. and Mrs. Leod were due at one o'clock.

This time Cherie asked me to sit at the conference table with them.

"For wrestling purposes," Cherie told me, and winked. "Holding Mrs. Leod last time took the two of us, and I got my nails done yesterday. It would be a shame if they chipped—aren't they pretty?"

I laughed. I had become a legal assistant after putting myself through two years of college. I broke three chairs in college classes, was beyond humiliated, had terrible health problems, and dropped out. I wished I'd finished college, but I do love working for Cherie even when I have to wrestle.

Today Cherie was wearing a black leather skirt, a black leather vest, and a purple lace top. She was also wearing boots to her knees. Not your typical attorney.

Scott Bills came in with Mr. Leod, who seemed slightly more subdued today, but nervous, antsy, his hands diving in and out of his pockets.

"Hello, Cherie." Scott shook Cherie's hand, then mine, military firm. "Hello, Stevie. Recovered from our last meeting?"

I laughed again. "Absolutely. And I've already warmed up my muscles for this match." I flexed.

At the exact moment that Mr. Leod settled in his seat, Mrs. Leod stormed through the foyer of our offices. She was wearing an elegantly cut charcoal brown suit with a lacy scarf tucked in, her hair and makeup magazine perfect.

It was the stormy expression on her face that gave us our first clue, and the fact that she had already used the F word twice. She screeched it, then attached Mr. Leod's name to it. The second clue was the box she was carrying in her hands.

"Here we go," Cherie said. "The tornado has arrived."

"Prepare for impact," Scott said.

"Shiiiitttt," Mr. Leod said.

I held my breath as Mrs. Leod charged into the conference room. I said, "Good morning, Mrs. Leod."

"To hell with your good morning," she shrieked. Then, before we could stop her, she leaped up on the conference table—she's a nimble thing—and held the box high up over her head. "Say good morning to Sam, Frank!"

What? Who was Sam?

Mr. Leod's primal roar echoed right around that room. Cherie reached for Mrs. Leod's legs, and Scott grabbed Mr. Leod.

"Put him down!" Mr. Leod shouted. "Put him down!"

"You son of a bitch! You sold my Jimmy Choos, all of them, online!"

"You deserved it! I will never forgive you for painting my boat pink!"

"That's because you cut my fur coat in half and hung it on our flagpole! Now say good-bye to Sam!" She held the box above her head, then tossed it up in the air.

"Nooooo!" Mr. Leod roared.

Mrs. Leod caught the box and half ran, half wobbled down the conference table on her four-inch heels as Mr. Leod writhed free from Scott and leaped up on the table.

"I feel the beginnings of a headache. . . ." Cheri murmured.

"Can we charge them extra for being a pain in the butt?" Scott asked.

"You can itemize it under PITB," I said. "You know, Pain In The Butt, but acronymic."

Scott nodded at me. "You are very clever, Stevie."

We watched as Mr. Leod grabbed Mrs. Leod from behind and lifted her up.

She struggled around as a worm on a hook would. "Let me go or this will be the end of Sam." She tried to throw the box in the air, but he blocked it. Then she turned around and kneed him. Mr. Leod doubled over.

"Up yours!" She brought her heel down on his foot.

"No, up yours, you cantankerous witch," he wheezed out, dropping to his knees, hands on crotch.

Then Mrs. Leod ripped open the box lid, put her hand inside, and grabbed something. She threw it straight up in the air.

Mr. Leod scrambled to his feet, pale with pain, leaped, and knocked over Mrs. Leod. He grabbed whatever it was flying through the air, landed, and the table cracked, right down the middle. Mr. Leod fell through with an "Oooof."

Mrs. Leod landed on Mr. Leod with an enraged "Dammit to hell! Don't you mess up my hair!"

And raised up high, in Mr. Leod's hand, was . . .

I peered close.

"What is that?" Cherie said.

"It's green," Scott said.

"Oh, my gosh," I said as it wiggled.

We all gathered round.

A lizard.

It was a lizard.

"Sam!" Mr. Leod said, tearfully, choked up.

Have you ever seen a man kiss a lizard? It is a sight to behold.

"Sam, are you all right?"

Lance's Lucky Ladies was starting to boom. King Midas and his twitchy left ankle. The daylight basement of his home was filled with boxes of both blown-up and deflated blow-up dolls and the accompanying packaging. There were more at the office/factory that he owned, where his new staff was working. The president of the company was a fifty-five-year-old, single mother with three sons in college who had previously been laid off. The vice-president was a sixty-two-year-old grandfather who had been "downsized."

"Here's what happens with the older guys and gals in corporate America," Lance told me. "They start making too much money, so the company lets them go. Companies think they want the young guys so they can pay them less. They think the young guys are hot, ambitious, driven. Big mistake. Huge. You lose the experience, the wisdom, the maturity, and the work ethic, and you lose the contacts the older guys and gals have with all the other old guys and gals out there who have all the money. So I got Lizbeth and Harold running my company, and we're skyrocketing. Plus, I trust them. I felt it in my left ankle."

Harold's wife was so grateful Lance hired Harold that she sewed him a quilt of his modern home, complete with the large pine trees in back and the view of the mountains.

Lance was so grateful he cried and hung it up in the entry of the factory.

"All my ladies here," Lance announced to me and Polly, spreading his arms wide, "are going to make a fortune."

"It's like standing in the middle of a freak show," I murmured to Polly. "All these unmoving, plastic faces. But no one talks.

No one moves. They all stare with these cheesy smiles on their faces."

"You feel that you're in a crowd, but not in a crowd," she said.

"These gals are going places, yeah, they are," Lance said. "They're travelling ladies. I got orders from Singapore, Russia—oh, yeah, a ton from Russia. Those guys and their dolls and vodka. Can't blame 'em needing dolls. It's cold there. The Italians want blondes. The French want Italians. The Americans want all colors and sizes. A bunch of dudes have contacted me and told me that the dolls are too skinny. One dude said, 'I want a woman with curves I can squeeze. Big ones. Big boobs, big thighs. Big. Send me big.'"

"Big, bouncy babes," Polly said. She seemed calmer. It was Sunday, so she wasn't working. She'd told me that she'd slept until four o'clock, went out for a ten-mile run, had a tuna sandwich, then came here. She was about the size of a toothpick with a head. "They're all freaky, although a stunning group of ladies in their own way. Can we go upstairs now before they come alive and bite me?"

Lance was surprised. "Why? We'll scoot 'em over and talk about the anniversary party from hell here."

"Are they listening?" I asked.

"No, they're not listening!" Lance said, in all seriousness. "They don't have real ears. Now, I still want you ladies to be part of my team." His eyes begged us. "Our family, the team. I'll send you on selling trips all over the world. You can go to Iceland. I'm getting huge business there because they probably don't go outside much, and I got orders from South Africa and the Middle East. Man, you ladies would have to dress up like giant penguins to get into those countries, but man. *Man!* I got a good business going there, too. You could go to Iran and sell dolls to the sheiks!"

"Thanks. If I wanted to end up in an Iranian prison after getting lashed with a plastic belt in the public square for wearing pants I would go on the double," I said.

"Me, too," Polly said. "Nothing better than sitting in an Iranian hellhole trying to make my brother a buck while rats scamper over my ankles and I'm told I have zero rights because I have a vagina."

Lance's face changed. It went from ebullient excitement to acute anxiety. "I would never send you two anywhere that would be dangerous."

"We know, Lance, we know," I said, trying to be soothing.

"I would never want anything bad to happen to either of you." He rubbed his forehead, scrunched his eyes shut.

"Lance," Polly said. "We were kidding you."

"If anything happened to you two . . ." Lance snuffled.

"Lance, honey, it's okay."

Lance snuffled again, groaned.

People sometimes have a hard time reconciling tearful, emotional Lance with the ex–pro football player with shoulders the size of an ox and the height of a sequoia. "Lance, it's okay. We're not going to an Iranian prison to hang out with a bunch of women who had the audacity to participate in a protest against a fraudulent election."

"I was fine, but then you two had to give me a terrible thought for my imagination and now I got it stuck in my head and it's bad." I put my arm around him. "I'm seeing both of you in those jail cells all beaten up, and it's wet in there and damp and dark and there's a bunch of men with long beards gawking at you in those sheiky white pajama things they wear, and you're sick, all because of my dolls!" He drew in a shuddery breath. He has a very vivid imagination. "I would have to hire that group I hired the other time to rescue you." He sighed. "They were so damn good."

He wasn't kidding. He has a couple of businesses in dangerous parts of the world, and three of his employees were kidnapped once in Honduras. He refused to pay the ransom and sent a team in to rescue them. All came out alive and well, but I later read blurbs in the newspaper about an "unexplained incident . . . bombs . . . Honduras . . . special teams . . . casualties . . . details sketchy."

"Lance, relax," I said. "I'm not ever going to sell your dolls, and neither is Polly. We would probably resort to selling earwax before we'd promote blow-up dolls with vacant stares, so stop crying, stop that imagination of yours, and sit down."

"You're never going to sell my dolls?"

"No!" Polly and I said together.

Lance wiped his tears away. "Okay. Now at least I don't have to be up nights worrying about you two girls in prison in Iran eating termites or snails."

"That's right. Now let's sit down and figure out this party."

We scooted the dolls here and there, and the three of us sat down.

"What do you think of Daisy? I love her eyes!" Lance said, taking a shaky breath. "There's Pam. A boring name, but take time to get to know her. So friendly. And Sage. She's already a hit. Red hair, curls. Good-sized rack."

Polly elbowed a doll off the couch.

"Now be careful with Titus. She's sensitive," Lance said. "Here, Stevie, you can put Buxom over here by your feet. . . . And add Bouncy Beatrice next to her. For company."

I laughed. I couldn't help it.

Polly laughed, too.

Then she threw Pam at me. I threw Sage at her. She flung Bouncy Beatrice back. I kicked Buxom over to her.

It didn't go over well with Lance, all these ladies going here and there, bopping about.

"Treat them with respect," he insisted. "Don't hurt their feelings with your disregard!"

"I regard them well." I giggled.

"Me, too," Polly said. "I regard that they have giant boobs, and I think you should rename your company Boob City."

"Or Vagina Rama."

"Or Penises and Plastics, Don't Go Spastic."

"Or Tittle my Tittles."

Lance did not appreciate our suggestions.

* * *

I woke up, choking, sweating, tangled in my sheets, my heart hammering.

I dreamed I was stuck in Helen's paintings. The tiny marks, the circles that swirled on forever, the twisted chairs she always drew, the ominous weather, the tilted barns, the animals that weren't quite animals . . . I was thrown from one painting to the next. The circles made me dizzy, the tiny marks jolted my body, and the chairs wrapped themselves around me, squeezing tight until I couldn't move.

I flipped off my sheets, pulled on my curtains, and stared up at the moon. No red-gold haze, thank heavens.

I sagged back on my stack of pillows. It was Helen who had left me with this legacy, this pervasive fear, these chilling nightmares.

Had she left me with something else, too? Something that would come later, something that was lurking, in the darkest recesses of my brain, that would squirm and grow and bust, until I was just like her? Had she left me with that? Wasn't I too old to get it now? *Probably.* But would it come for me in a different form later in my life? I hugged my pillow to my chest as my body shuddered.

I saw Sunshine's pixie face, and I sank back onto my pillows.

I could have saved her.

I should have saved her.

I didn't.

I closed my eyes as the tears came.

I never bother to hide my tears in the middle of the night.

No one can see them except me.

11

Ashville, Oregon

Painting made Helen growl.

Every summer Grandma bought me and Helen new paints, pastel crayons, colored pencils, and sketch books. I always ended up watching Helen. She had inherited her talent from her grandma, who had inherited her talent through the family line, via her aunt.

"I'm going to draw my mind . . . I'm going to draw what's in it so you'll understand where Punk is, girl kid," she'd tell me. "I'm not going to draw Command Center. He said no. He's bad."

The drawing of her mind? A mass of swirls, a collage of angry animals with sharp teeth, pieces of limbs, a dead cat, flowers that appeared to have their own demented minds, open doors with blackness behind them, a noose, a woman cowering in a corner.

"I'm going to draw this place, with all the spies." Our red barn became a blurry, curving building, every blade of grass in front of it twisting. Behind the barn, she'd drawn a shadow. "That's Punk," she told me. "Always watching me." For days or weeks she would work on the same picture, every crack in each board of the barn drawn with copious care, every hair of a horse or dog individually drawn, until they were living, thriving things on their own.

She would growl softly, as if she was stalking something.

Sometimes she'd add something truly sinister, perhaps a knife stuck in a fence post or the outline of a body. "That's Punk," she said, pointing at the body with red eyes. "But he's not dead yet. He wants to tear me to pieces."

"Punk," as far as I could tell, was the evil assistant to Command Center.

Helen drew chairs, too. White chairs, usually, the type you would find in a hospital. Or a mental ward. The chairs would be twisted, curving, alive, and she always drew a rope around them, handcuffs, chains, black claws. It was not unusual for there to be blood on the chair. Once there was a limp left hand, detached, hanging from the seat.

"Chairs are duwomberbangs," she told me. "Chairs twist and take your breath away and then they poke you and hurt and burn." The chair drawings drew out the worst growls, the scared growls, the sound an animal would make when cornered.

But when she drew our house, which used to be the town's school, so we called it the Schoolhouse House, she used only white or pastel colors. Our white Schoolhouse House wasn't twisted, it was drawn with the bell tower on top; the stained glass windows and two sets of French doors that Grandpa had installed; wildflowers; the sprawling addition that Grandpa had built with a family room, den, and bedrooms; and the huge back deck with potted flowers. The sign above our red front doors read ASHVILLE ELEMENTARY SCHOOL, 1925.

She worked with no growling, flowers lined the walkway, and a sunrise or sunset glowed in the background. She added tomatoes, corn, carrots, two different types of lettuce, peas, radishes, onions, and sunflowers in the garden. She drew the floppy yellow hat she always wore in the garden, which she'd found in the attic squished in a trunk. She thought the sun was sent by the government to burn her head and the yellow hat thwarted them.

Now and then when she was done, she would pick up the canvas she had been working on and balance it on her head under whatever hat she was wearing and walk around our barn and property, "to show them I'm the boss of the bad battle." Other times she would tear it up and put the pieces down her dress, "for protection." And sometimes she'd walk away and leave the drawings. "I won't have that drawing talking to me." That's when I took them for myself. I put them under my bed unless they were small enough for me to put them in my carved wooden hope chest that had been Grandma's great-grandmother's.

The drawings scared me, the growling scared me, but they were something Helen had done, and I wanted them. I wanted that piece of my momma.

If one has to live in chaos, Ashville, where we lived, was the place to be.

Although I have not returned since leaving there as a child, closing my eyes as we drove through town for the last time in a numbed, semiconscious state, I remember it as being charming and small with a downtown street where you could buy ice cream, go to Victoria's Cutting Station for a trim and style, and stop at the candy shop. It was about a ten-minute drive from our farm, tucked between rolling green hills and farmland in southern Oregon. We were related to at least a third of the town by blood, more by marriage, and most by friendship.

All of Ashville knew us, we knew them, and people were used to seeing Helen in various states of craziness. Everyone would know exactly where to find Grandma and Grandpa so they could come and get them if Helen escaped their watch.

Grandma was willed our farm from her parents, who got the land from her maternal grandparents, who got the land, and a crumbled-down barn and farmhouse, from her maternal great-grandparents, pioneers to Oregon. Grandma's mother donated the land for the schoolhouse, and when the schoolhouse was no longer big enough for all the kids as Ashville grew, a new school was built, in town, and the family got the schoolhouse and the land back.

Family history was that Grandma's pioneering ancestral family all came out together, about thirty of them. They were from the backwoods of West Virginia and they went west via Independence, Missouri. One relative committed suicide by jumping off a cliff because he saw visions of ghosts on the plains midway through. An uncle was of almost no help because he was "daft in the head" and "talked to himself as if he was the best company there was." There was also a cousin who got here, took a look around, and started collecting piles of sticks. That's all she did all day long. She piled up sticks.

They did not get much work out of Agatha, so the family considered her "lost." Apparently she lived to be 101. She gathered a lot of sticks.

Grandma's father died when she was sixteen, the fourth of six siblings, and Grandma's mother didn't blink an eye. She couldn't stand the man. But I don't think the rumor about her trying to kill him, circulated by a few of the senior members of the population, via cyanide is true.

Grandma's mother was normal except that she washed her hands all the time and, when they were clean, she refused to take off her white gloves, even at night, even while gardening.

Now, Grandma's aunt Charlotte clearly had bipolar disorder, which was documented by doctors and in a biography written by a renowned writer. Aunt Charlotte was a very famous artist, who would hardly sleep for months at a time and who'd produce the most mind-boggling, inspiring paintings of flowers and landscapes I have ever seen. The paintings were troubled, sad, and confusing. One day you would think you understood the painting, and the next day you'd see it totally differently. The paintings made you want to cry, as if they were tapping into your own tragic problems and the secrets that were killing you.

Charlotte smoked incessantly and guzzled whiskey while painting, and when all the paintings were done, she would lapse into an almost comatose depression. Her paintings are in museums all over the country. Grandma told me you could always figure out which ones were Aunt Charlotte's and which ones were fakes because Charlotte always drew a picture of a dead blue bird with a noose around its neck in the left-hand corner of the back of the canvas. She died alone in a shack in Wyoming, where she'd gone the week before.

But Grandma herself was completely with it, as was Grandpa,

the middle of five boys and a sister. Grandpa's family here in Ashville also had pioneer roots, via Alabama, although no one lost their mind on the way in on wagon trains.

One of Grandma's relatives shot one of Grandpa's relatives in a brawl over, you guessed it, a cow. He lived. Two sets of relatives were engaged and broke up. This caused one jilted bride to set a torch to her ex-fiancé's wagon. The other jilted groom owned an ice-cream saloon and barred his ex from entering it for ten years. In retaliation she didn't let him buy any of her mother's pies at the bakery her family owned. He was super mad about that.

There are long-standing, generation-long friendships and enemies between the families. Two cousins twice-removed lived next door to each other for forty years and never spoke. They fought over a woman. The woman ran off, literally, with the circus. The men never forgave each other.

Two women, one on Grandpa's side and one on Grandma's side, lived together their whole lives. They were teachers, and in summer they left town and travelled the world. They lived to be ninety-six, dying one month apart. They weren't gay. In fact, it was rumored they each took to their own romances every summer. There was suspicion that they weren't even travelling together in summer, but took off separately to find their man and their adventures. One new man a summer, got all their passions out, and came home and taught math to Ashville kids, their hair in buns, shoes flat and comfortable.

We have all types in "The Family." Millionaires, paupers, drunks, ministers, teachers, Marines, air force pilots, gamblers, doctors, nurses, business owners, artists, writers, executives. It's an eclectic lot. One thing we have in common? Each other. I grew up going to parties all over town and having mobs of people at our house, when Helen wasn't home.

That was a good thing, I think, because I was raised among people who were relatively sane, although Grandma had a cousin who dressed as a Revolutionary War general all the time and talked about the "hell-damned English and their poisoned tea." He was one of the millionaires. He bought and traded war memorabilia.

Grandma had another cousin who had agoraphobia and had to be taken care of her whole life, as did an aunt of hers who killed herself at fifty because she thought the end of the world was coming via an asteroid. A second cousin also had a slight hoarding problem. Okay, it was huge. She saved *everything,* but she was very nice.

Grandma and Grandpa met in kindergarten when Grandma threw a block at his head. It gushed blood. He had knocked down her block tower.

The kindergarten teacher, the sister of an ex-wife of a great uncle on Grandpa's side, sewed him up right there. Grandma held the thread and, she noted, "Your grandpa didn't shed a tear."

They were best friends from then on out. They got married right out of high school because Grandpa said, "I cannot resist you anymore, Glory. And I will not disrespect you by making love to you in our barn or my car or in some field. You deserve more, and I will give you more. So, you tell your momma to get a dress ready and let's say our vows. I love you, I'll love you forever, you love me, and that's that. Set a date, any day you want, as long as it's this weekend."

That weekend it was. The mob of family showed up, and except for one cousin pulling a gun, briefly, on another, everything went smoothly.

Grandpa founded a company that made all those machines that mass produce food, and it grew and grew, and they even sold nationally and internationally. Their only sadness? For some reason, my grandma could not get pregnant. It took her twenty-two years to get pregnant with my aunt Janet, a nervous, anxious sort, but together in the head, although a mouse compared to her sister Helen. When she was pregnant with my momma she had German measles and was deathly sick. The doctor feared Grandma would die. The Family came over all the time to care for her. Two brought incense, one brought herbal remedies, another brought her fortune-telling cards and said Helen would be born with a galaxy in her head.

My grandma said she spent the whole time praying for God's sweet intervention. "I prayed to Mary and Joseph as well, to cover my bases. I figured they could talk to their son."

Well, God's son intervened and Grandma's daughter lived. But there was one problem.

Helen was not together in the head. One could say there was a galaxy in there.

The girl who was not together in the head drove Grandma's gray car into the town fountain when I was six.

She zoomed down the hill and away she went. Me and Grandma dropped our paintbrushes and Grandma said, "Oh, Lordie, help me with that girl," and we hopped in the old pickup truck and sped after her.

We choked on Helen's dust as she took one curve after another too fast. I heard Grandma praying as we went. "Lord a mercy, Lord a mercy, help me. . . ." That was often Grandma's prayer during those years. She told me that God only needed to hear two words, "Help me," and he listened straight up.

Ashville had flowers hanging from every lamppost, the sidewalks were wide, and off the center of town we had a huge fountain inside a huge city park, complete with a meandering river, picnic tables, a covered area, a gazebo, and basketball courts. It was maintained by a mentally disabled man named Callender who called it "my park" and worked there every day.

I don't know how Helen made it down Main Street without hitting anybody. Maybe it was Grandma's increasingly louder prayers or the honking of her own horn, but we chased Helen, and Grandma's gray car, to the fountain. Helen smashed through the brick and plunged all the way in. Grandma said, "Mary, mother of God," and parked the pickup truck with a screech of her brakes. "Stay in the truck, Stevie," she ordered, and sprinted for the fountain, where a crowd was gathering.

I did not stay in the truck, scrambling right on out. I worried that my friend Natasha Golobev and her little brother, Vladimer, were in the fountain, under the wheels of the car. They loved playing in that fountain. Apparently, Grandma was worried, too, because she jumped into that fountain lickety split, put her face under the water, and swam, her cowboy boots sticking up. Keaton Seo, a cousin, and cousin Cane Michelles jumped in and did the same thing.

When they stood up they were soaking wet and panting. I think the thought of smashed kids got their hearts going. A crowd had formed, half of them family and friends, but they knew enough to let Grandma handle things with Helen.

"Stay away from me," Helen yelled out the crack of the window, her feathered hat from a New York performance falling over her face. "Stay away from me. I know what you want and you can't have it. I have my own brain and you're not going to shove it in a jar and watch me think! You're not opening my head!"

"Helen," Grandma said, her voice calm like the swish of the wind, though she must have been devastated. "Come on out, Helen. I've got everything under control and no one is here for your brain."

"No! I won't go when they're standing around waiting to take off with my brain. I'm not getting out of the car until you get rid of them." She pointed at all the people.

I saw Grandma take a deep breath and think, then push back her wet white hair.

You see, what I learned growing up with Helen is that you have to do a lot of thinking. How do you handle this person in this situation? How do you talk to her? What are the triggers for explosions? What will calm her down? What words should be avoided? How long does it take?

"Honey, these people aren't here to take your brain," Grandma said.

"Yes, they are! I can tell. I've been there and I know what they want. Shitheads." The water from the fountain was hitting the front of the car, and Helen screamed at it. "Turn that syrup off! Get rid of the syrup!" She took off one of the feathers from her hat and threw it into the water. "That'll stop them! That'll stop the shitheads."

I knew that was a bad word, but it did not appear that anyone took offense.

Grandma said to Helen, "These people are here to protect you, sweetie. You see?" She turned toward the crowd and did a little wave. Suddenly, the crowd waved at Helen. I waved, too.

"Hello, Helen. . . . Hi, Helen, it's Mrs. Gruback from Ashville Elementary. I was your second-grade teacher. . . . Hi, Helen, it's me, Darla, from high school. . . . Hello, Helen, it's Dr. Dix. . . . Hey, Helen, it's Tracy, your neighbor, remember me? Hi, Helen, it's Aunt Trudy, darling. . . . Hello, Helen, it's me, Uncle Mac. . . ." And on it went.

I could tell Helen was suspicious for a while as she peered out at all the people waving at her, calling her name, but then Geoff Gobinsky, a fifteen-year-old neighbor, held up his German shepherd, Twinkles, and waved Twinkles's paw at Helen. I saw her analyzing that situation, that dog.

"This doesn't appear to be enemy territory," Helen shouted out the window.

"It's not, sweetie," Grandma said. "These are all your friends." Grandma turned and indicated they were to wave again. Everyone waved. By this time Grandpa was climbing into the fountain with his cowboy boots, his cowboy hat on his head.

"Hi, sugar," he said.

Helen nodded at him, then took out one more feather and threw it in the water. "All right. I don't think these people want to take my brain and make it think. I'm coming out."

"Good, good, lovely," Grandma said.

Grandpa gallantly opened the door, put out his elbow, wet now from the fountain spray, and Helen took it quite graciously. Everyone clapped and waved.

Helen bowed, right in that fountain, right and left, right and left. It was her performance bow, I thought, from the time she spent in New York, so I braced myself.

She walked to the little ledge around the fountain, near a part she had demolished, stepped up and sang three songs, one right after another from *Annie Get Your Gun*, including the song "There's No Business Like Show Business."

At the end, we all applauded again. It was a much bigger crowd by then because Helen had the best voice and people came running to hear it.

Then she gave her finale. She sang "Amazing Grace." I can still hear her singing that song in my head, haunting, piercing.

Amazing grace, how sweet the sound that saved a wretch like me—I once was lost, but now I'm found, was blind but now I see . . .

It brought us all to tears, even me, but especially Grandpa.

A bunch of his cousins stood around us then, patting him on the back. Two of them had tears streaming down their faces, which they did not bother to hide, because they were manly enough not to worry about that stuff.

I cried, too. My momma was a wretch, and I wanted her to be saved so I could have a real mother who didn't worry about leeches on her brain.

Now, in any other town, driving a car into a fountain would be a pretty significant problem, but not in Ashville because of the relationships Grandma and Grandpa had with their relatives, long-term friends, hundreds of happy employees, and their happy employees' families.

Grandpa and Grandma, privately and through the company, had quietly funded the new library; bought land to extend the park; installed the fountain Helen had smashed through; installed the best playground equipment ever, complete with tunnels, slides, wobbly bridges, and swings; and donated money for the senior center and a home for the mentally handicapped. Grandpa's company funded the fireworks display every year, a huge town Christmas party, and a summer barbeque in the park.

Grandpa's company was one of the few in those days that hired, and promoted, women at the same rate as it did men. In addition, no one was forced into retirement. He had many people working for him in their seventies and eighties, hobbling around with canes and walkers. "They don't quit, sugar, and I'm glad of it. They've been with me since the start. Jefferson knows more about the company than I do and he's eighty-four. Mabel knows every single one of our clients and has more knowledge about them in her head than I do in my filing cabinets. Jan Wu has memorized each employee's personnel file. Their friends are there. I pay them and they're valued. Why quit?"

Grandpa ran a clean, honest, family-centered company where they closed down the week of Christmas and had spring break for family time and everybody got two weeks off in summer. There was, apparently, no turnover at Grandpa's company.

Unless you got fired, and Grandpa did fire people, including his own relatives if they weren't working hard enough. One man made the mistake of rubbing up against the body of the mother of a friend of mine, who was the head of a department. First time she warned him. The second time it happened she hit the man so hard she bruised his jaw, and when he fell back he caught the corner of a desk. He bled like a sieve. The idiot had wanted to know if she needed a little "woo-ha" at night since her husband had recently left her for a twenty-two-year-old. When he got off the floor, Grandpa fired him and, according to town lore, said, "Nice hit, Sandra. Next time follow up with a kick to the groin." He gave the woman a bonus for putting up with "too much baloney. This will not happen again. I apologize, Sandra."

But he and Grandma were people who believed in second chances.

They went to school with a man named Herman. Tough, tough home life. He went off the bad end, had problems with liquor and drugs and finally hit bottom when he got himself involved in a burglary. He went to jail. Grandpa visited a couple of times. The man found God in jail and came out a changed man. Grandpa hired him as a janitor. Grandpa said he was the best damn janitor ever. Grandpa paid for his degree in accounting and Herman worked his way up the ladder.

Now he's a vice president and says Grandpa saved his life.

"Without your grandpa, Stevie, I would be in a coffin, that's the truth. He believed in me until I could believe in myself."

There were also many people who were on the receiving end of their financial gifts, especially children. Grandma and Grandpa believed that not helping people was a sin and that turning your back on suffering was a "double sin with a huge dose of arrogance and selfishness thrown on top," according to Grandma.

My friend Rudolph had a cleft palate. They paid to get it fixed. A teenager, Helga Alena, got cancer. Grandpa and Grandma rented the family an apartment in Portland while she underwent treatment. She lived, grew up, went to college, then went to work for Grandpa. She, too, ended up a vice president.

One woman battled depression and was suicidal. She was from my grandma's side. Her hobby was sewing, so Grandma encouraged her to sew. The woman started a clothing business. She became famous, moved to New York, and sent Grandma four new outfits a year.

So after Grandma and Grandpa got Helen into the pickup, Tryler Torelli got his truck and his wrench, got the car out of the fountain, and towed it to Dwayne O'Holloway's shop, where he got things running again. Gen Shiner fixed up the brick that Helen had knocked out, and when the city turned off the fountain and drained it, a bunch of ladies went in and cleaned out the mess and skid marks.

No one made a big deal about it. No one pressed charges.

And life could have gone on and on, I suppose, for Grandma and Grandpa. Exhausting, frustrating, so disappointing, fraught with worry, grief, pain, but it could have gone on.

But Helen started to get violent.

And that's when things got worse. So much worse.

But I'm skipping ahead.

I miss my relatives in Ashville, but I don't think I could ever go back. It would hurt too much. My presence there might hurt them, too. Then they would have to remember what happened, as I do. Every. Single. Day.

12

Portland, Oregon

I will plant corn, I told myself.
I can do it.
  I will do it.
  I shuddered.
  I can't do it.
  Not ready yet. No.
  I held my hands as they automatically started to shake.
  I can do it.
  I breathed in.
  Deep.
  I wished my hands would stop shaking.

  Jake left a note, on my front door, asking if I would go out to dinner with him. He left an e-mail address and a phone number. He was going to be out of town for a while, but please, please call and let him know if that would work. He thought it would be best if we did not go out for pasta.

  I curled up on my red couch and pulled a pillow onto my lap. My toes wriggled. My stomach flip-flopped. My whole body felt warm and cuddly and liquid hot in that private area.

  My brain sizzled and descended into *absolute panic*.

* * *

The hospital had upped the amount they were willing to pay for the Atherton case.

"We're basically going to pay to make it go away," Crystal said, sneering. "We don't want it in the newspaper. Bad for the hospital. Hopefully the country hicks will have the sense to take the money and go back to their pitchforks and wagons and plumber cracks."

The whopping amount the hospital would agree to: $75,000. No admittance of wrongdoing.

Compared to the costs the Athertons were incurring for in-home care, and the medical bills outstanding and coming down the pike, it was comparable to offering to pay the Athertons grocery bills for a few months, but no pop.

Mr. and Mrs. Atherton rejected that amount through their attorneys. I can only imagine how insulted and ravingly pissed they must have felt. Mr. Atherton's comment came back to us through their attorneys: "We will never agree to that. It is our goal to change the policy at that hospital and ensure that not one more child has to live as ours does, half dead, half alive. If I can do that, then I will have done my job. I do not want any parents, or children, to go through what we've been through, and by God's grace I will fight the good fight."

"We'll still squish them and their good fight," Crystal said, her high heels clacking around her office floor, her skinny hips swaying. "The Athertons' attorneys are newbies. They haven't a clue how to win a case of this size."

I thought of Danny, in a hospital bed, half here, half not, and I stared at the boxes and boxes of papers, endless folders we'd already accumulated for this case. I'd seen Crystal going through them the other day, and as usual she seemed nervous, anxious. "Have you seen the Dornshire letter? Are you sure you haven't seen it, Steve? Positive? Think hard."

Why did she want the Dornshire letter so bad?

When she was out of the office, I thought I'd try to end that mystery. . . .

* * *

"I have a girlfriend who's nursing twins," Zena told me as we ate in Pioneer Courthouse Square. It had been raining, but now it was sunny. Earlier in the morning it had hailed. Typical Oregon weather. "She says she knows how a cow feels now."

"I would feel that way, too." I choked up about that, couldn't help it. She had two babies. That was so nice. I blinked hard.

"She says her boobs are twice as big as normal and she hates it. Can't run, can't exercise, she leaks all over the place, and when her husband touches her, milk squirts out. She was ticked off at him the other night in bed because he wasn't helping her with the twins and she only sleeps about four hours a night so she squirted him with her breast milk."

I laughed. "Good for her. That'll get him up and at 'em."

"It did. Hasn't done much for their sex life."

"She has twin babies. Why does she want to have sex?"

"She doesn't. It's her husband."

"Lemme guess. She's exhausted all the time. He thinks going to work for nine hours a day is hard work and comes home, wants dinner and sex for dessert. She, however, is entering her second shift and can't stand the man, and wants him to take his horn and go away."

"That'd be about it. She said to me the other day, 'Zena, I make milk in these jugs. I have a yeast infection so I'm making yeast. Blend those two together, add the salt from my tears, and I can almost make bread. Aren't I special?' Then she started crying. If you were bread, what kind would you be?"

"I want to be cinnamon, but I think I'm more blah whole grain bread."

"Nah, you're cinnamon."

"What are you?"

"I'm cheese garlic bread."

I nodded. "Yep, Zena, you are."

I handed her some grapes. She gave me a sprinkled donut. I handed it back. She ate it. How come skinny people can eat donuts?

* * *

"Janet, you will go with Stevie to the caterers on Tuesday to firm up our order for the party," Herbert intoned to his wife across the dining room table. He did not bother to see if she was listening, or even alive, and kept consuming the meatloaf he always insisted she make on the first Thursday of the month.

Lance stared straight ahead, the candlelight flickering, that ponderous chandelier still evil. He cannot stand to watch Herbert chew. Polly had her hands in her lap. I pushed the meatloaf around my plate as if it were a train.

"I can't, Herbert," Aunt Janet said, as the fire made a popping sound. "I already told you that I have two classes on Tuesday."

He scoffed, still didn't deign to look in his wife's eyes. "You are not to go. We have other things more important than your . . . classes."

"What classes?" Lance asked. Tonight he was wearing a shirt that had an imprint of his blow-up dolls on the front, with the words, "Buy Me," and the number for Lance's Lucky Ladies on the back.

Aunt Janet didn't say anything. I dropped my fork. I could tell she was trying not to cry.

"Oh, Momma," Polly said, leaning over and holding her hand.

Lance glared at his father.

Aunt Janet put her head up. "I am taking classes at Portland State University."

"You are?" Polly was shocked, yet totally delighted.

"That's great, Aunt Janet," I said. "Which classes?"

"Three classes. One on the works of Jane Austen, a Russian history class, and basic math."

"No, it is not great," Herbert snapped. "Aunt Janet's place is here at home, helping me and taking care of the household chores. A woman belongs in the home. She's sixty-two years old. Why does she need to finish her degree now?"

"Because she wants to, Dad," Lance said. "It's never too late!"

Herbert pounded a fist on the table. Even the evil chandelier shook.

"The woman has not been in school since she was twenty years old—"

"That's because she dropped out of school to put you through college, Wonder Man, then graduate school. She worked until the day before she had Lance," Polly put in. She didn't even bother to hide the paper bag in her hand. She put it up to her mouth and took deep, long breaths.

"Young lady, I will accept no back talk at my table," Herbert said, pointing his fork at Polly.

"She wasn't talking back, Dad," Lance said. He had tried so hard, all of our growing-up years, for Herbert's approval. It had never worked. "She's saying that Mom never got a chance to finish her business degree because of what she did for you."

Herbert laughed. Weren't we all amusing? So entertaining! "What your mother did for me?" He laughed again. Ho, ho, ho, how funny is that statement! "Your mother has led a privileged life. Perhaps you've missed this home that I bought for her, her expensive clothes."

We knew all about her plain, frumpy clothes. Aunt Janet dipped her head.

"This furniture, her car." Aunt Janet drove a Cadillac. New, every five years. But the car wasn't for Aunt Janet. Anyone who knew her in the slightest way would know that car didn't suit her. Herbert bought her the car to show off his money. See what I, a community pillar and leader, can buy for The Wife! The Helpmate!

"She hasn't worked a day in her life."

"She raised three kids," Polly said. "She took care of the house and she stayed married to you. An impossible feat, if you ask me. Mom's been married to Godzilla, frankly. Overly large teeth, clenched face, pointy claws, nasty . . ."

Polly and Herbert locked eyes.

"Herbert," I said, while Polly had to stand up, then bend over, bag plastered to her face. Isn't family life fun? "You don't own your wife—"

"I won't take any further argument. My wife needs to be home. Janet, you will miss your classes and go to the caterers on Tuesday, do you understand me?"

At the end of the table, Aunt Janet bent her head, studied her plate, and then I saw her shoulders square and she tilted her head back up. "No. I am going to my classes."

Yeeesss! Go, Aunt Janet!

"I've had enough of these fun and games, Janet. I said you could take your classes, waste my hard-earned money, but only if they did not interfere with my life here." Herbert suddenly stopped his lecture and his jaw got tight. "It's Virginia, isn't it. She's going to class down there, too, isn't she?"

Aunt Janet didn't say anything.

"She is, isn't she?" Herbert roared as he realized that his wife was meeting Virginia without his permission, and he leaped to his feet. "I have forbidden you to see her."

"Get control of yourself, Dad!" Lance said, standing square in front of him.

"You are not to see that crazy woman, Janet! She's a bad influence on you—a liberal, loud woman who has no understanding of her role—"

"Control, Dad, control!" Polly inhaled again, then pulled her bag away from her face. "You're the most narcissistic, critical, controlling person I've ever met in my life."

The silence was electrifying.

Aunt Janet burst into tears, then said, "Do you think so, sweetheart?"

I gaped at Aunt Janet. "Do you need to ask?"

"Mom, Dad is a miniature dictator. He and Napoleon would be best friends. They'd certainly see eye to eye. If you weren't here, I would never set foot in this house again, although every time I'm here I want to shake you upside down because you're still, *still*, taking loose crap from Dad."

"Get out, Polly," Herbert ordered Polly. "How dare you. I have done everything for you. I have been an outstanding father and mentor to you. You are where you are because of me, and this is how you pay me back—"

"I got where I am, Dad, because I worked for it." Polly threw her fork. It hit the wall. "I put myself through college, I found my own jobs. You didn't help at all, not one bit. In fact, you made me pay you back your medical insurance deductible when I went to the hospital in college! I was broke, I was sick, and you made me come up with $500, which you easily, easily had—"

I heard Aunt Janet gasp. "Oh, my God, Herbert, you didn't! You didn't!"

"That's neither here nor there—" he shouted, eyes shifting.

"He did," I said, quiet, but sure. "He made her pay him back. He's a millionaire but he made Polly come up with that money herself. We both worked extra hours to pay him back."

"Stevie, you get out of my house, too!" Herbert roared. "I liked you better when you were fat. You were more pleasant to be around. You didn't argue, you kept your head down, and you mostly did as you were told. Ever since you lost weight your attitude has been appalling. You think you know everything now. You think you can come in my home and tell me how it is. You have all these radical opinions and you have the temerity to voice them. I have been wanting to speak to you about it for months, privately, but now you've forced my hand!"

"Yes, let's address it as a family. Stevie is a better woman now," Aunt Janet said, chin up. "She sticks up for herself." She sat up straight. "She carries herself better. She smiles more. She laughs. She works hard and she walks and she has a job and the partners are always asking her to work late because she's so good at what she does." She nodded at me. "She's so valuable to the firm. She's wonderful."

My jaw dropped.

"I am going to take those classes, Herbert, and I am not going to the caterers on Tuesday. If you want to oversee the food, then you go. I don't care."

Polly said, "Woo-hoo, Mom!" Lance raised a fist in victory.

"You don't care? You don't care about the food for my anniversary party?" he hissed out, knuckles to the table, leaning forward to intimidate her.

"I don't care, Herbert."

"You don't care?" He pounded both fists, once, on the table.

"No. Not at all. I'm sick of this. I'm sick of you. I'm taking classes with Virginia. I'm going to Portland State. I am going to finish my degree and I'm going to get a job. Do you hear that, Herbert? I'm going to get a job and a life."

With that, she got up, kissed all of us on the forehead, except for Herbert, and left the room.

"Whoa," Lance breathed. "You should have been nicer to Mom, Dad. Now you're in trouble. The door is opening to a whole new, colorful world without Godzilla, and I'll betcha she's gonna choose that world, I'll betcha."

"Way to go, Mom," Polly said. She laughed, bag at her side. "Way to tell off Dad, the ultimate whack job, and keep it classy."

I thought of the expression on Aunt Janet's face. She seemed . . . confident, victorious, *proud of herself.*

And on Herbert's face?

Shock. Total and complete shock.

Lance called me at work the next day.

"Honey, I know you're busy and I feel bad I'm not doing more for this anniversary torture chamber that Dad's got going down, so I'll do the invitations. You're doing the food, getting the tents, the flowers, so I got 'em, no problem. I got a gal who's a graphic artist and she said she'd do the invitations for the anniversary torture chamber and for my eighties Hard Rock party the next night and send them out. I met her on the corner of Broadway and Market when she was painting a picture. She's very cool, although my left ankle didn't twitch."

"Hmmm. Well, it's not a business deal of yours, so maybe it's okay to work with her even though there was no twitch?"

"Unclear, very unclear, but I'll handle it. Trixie's very creative, and we talked about my invitations. They're going to be red and black with a white skull on the front and an electric guitar. She's going to use some silver stuff to make the guitar shiny, then there's going to be a pop-up in the middle—you know when you open up a kid's book sometimes there's pop-ups? Well, this is a pop-up of one of my blow-up dolls. I think it'll be Fiona Butterfly—she's warm and friendly. Then it'll say the date and time and to dress up as your favorite hard rocker."

"And you'll have her do your parents' invitations, too? I'll e-mail you the photos of them, the day of their wedding and the time. Herbert wants the invitations in white with the writing in gold. Thanks, Lance."

"No, Stevie, thank *you*. You're doing most of the work, I know that. And I'm going to take all of us on a cruise when this is all over!"

"Oh, no, no, you don't have to do that, Lance...." I knew he'd do it. He'd taken us all on cruises before and the three of us had had a great time.

"It's already done. I called my travel agent. Gotta run, Stevie. Love ya, honey."

Click.

Cherie got another interesting divorce case. She was representing a woman named Tabitha Ruhn.

Tabitha was livid, and then delighted, when she found out her husband was cheating on her. Livid because it enraged her that the balding, plumpish, dough-boy man had cheated, delighted because she had an excuse to clean him dry and could move on to a man younger and more virile. "I want a man with power in his pants," she told Cherie. "Power. But I sure as hell am not going to get married again. That would end my alimony, right?"

Tabitha's a computer whiz and tapped into not only Husband's e-mail at home but also two secret e-mail accounts he had set up. She made a big deal out of leaving town for a few days and noted that her husband quickly made arrangements for one of his girlfriends to meet at their charming, yellow Queen Anne house in the country.

Tabitha Ruhn was supposed to be hiking the Appalachian Trail. As Tabitha wears four-inch heels and never hikes, Husband should have gotten a clue. He did not, because he was following his floppy appendage and not his brain.

Tabitha was not in a tent on the trail, hunkered down in a sleeping bag kicking off raccoons. She was in a nearby bed-and-breakfast that specialized in blueberry pancakes after making sure that the multitude of cameras an investigator had inserted into the ceiling of their charming, yellow Queen Anne home were not malfunctioning as they filmed the lovebirds. She sat on top of a four-poster bed, eating blueberry pancakes and drinking coffee, while she alternately seethed in anger and cackled at the impressive amount of money that would soon be hers.

The two lovebirds giggled their way in, all alight in the danger and excitement of their affair. They went at it like rabbits, not forsaking fishnets, high heels, and a pink feathered hat that Husband wore, along with the pink silk dress his girlfriend had him slide into. His girlfriend, Chantal—exactly the name you would imagine your husband's girlfriend would have—had a thing for bondage, leather, a whip, and a little black policeman's hat.

It was a busy weekend for the three of them.

The lovebirds thrived in their role-playing! One time Husband dressed as King Tut and Chantal dressed as Cleopatra, and they both applied thick black eyeliner. They played a game they gigglingly referred to as Egypt Sex Scene. Cleopatra dominated and Tut willingly turned up his butt for a swat or two with Cleopatra's whip.

Another time Chantal brought in a human-sized cage and Husband crawled in. Chantal locked him in the cage until he promised to do all sorts of wild things to her including, but not limited to, tying her up on the kitchen table that Tabitha had purchased from Italy and nibbling on her bottom.

It was unfortunate that Tabitha felt it was necessary to put the lovebirds' video on YouTube.

That Husband was a judge and Chantal a prosecuting attorney made things a tad bit more complicated.

Husband, the judge, in our conference room, said he was going to "burn his wife to pieces in a mega-lawsuit before hell could get to her."

"Go ahead," Cherie said cheerily. She was wearing a purple

jacket, purple skirt to midthigh, and black boots that rose over her knees. "The resulting publicity will be fabulous for my firm. I'll have to hire three more people, poor me, as I did three months ago in another star-studded divorce case. How did Chantal's bottom taste?"

Husband threatened to sue for defamation. "Defamation!"

"Onward ho!" Cherie said. "You have defamed yourself, but if you want a jury and the good people of Portland to have more opportunities to watch the videos, you're welcome to it. How did it feel being in the cage? Did you feel dominated? Sexily out of control?"

Husband declared, so self-righteously, "That was illegal!"

And Cherie said, "Laws were made to be broken. How did it feel to play King Tut? Powerful? Dead?"

Husband huffed. "You will regret this, Cherie."

"Nah. I don't think so. I still have one more video. Tell me about where you got the Little Bo Peep costume? I loved it!"

Husband hissed, squirming. "You don't have another video."

"I do." Cherie swung her boot. "Chantal made a great wolf. I loved how she wore a wolf mask and nothing else but a tail! And you, Judge! Who knew that you would make such a fun Tarzan!" She made the call of Tarzan. It echoed through our offices. When Husband protested, she howled a second time.

The divorce was settled quite quickly, and Husband and Chantal had to move. Husband moved to Iowa, and Chantal moved to Missouri. Tabitha made out with six million, the house in Portland, and the condo in Maui. Not bad.

A bunch of us from Poitras and Associates went that night to watch Zena in her roller derby bout, then out for beers to celebrate. Zena almost lost a tooth, but they won! We cheered ourselves hoarse. Cherie yelled like Tarzan.

I kept studying garden books and magazines when my insomnia caught me in its jaws. I was planning how I would use my yard, where the raised beds would go, the walkways, the arbor and trellises, and so on. I was getting to know all the scientific names for plants instead of calling them water lily (*Nymphea dauberyana*), swordfern (*Macrothelypteris torresiana*), and sweet alyssum (*Lobularia maritima*).

In fact, I knew about thirty scientific plant names right off the top of my head.

Folks, when you memorize the scientific names of plants, you have gone over the edge gardening-wise, and yes, you are a gardening maniac.

Don't let anyone tell you differently.

Get your gloves on and accept it.

I listened to Herbert's voice on my answering machine after a twelve-hour day at the office. When I was done I had to go to bed and read my gardening magazines and draw pictures of flowers to calm down.

"My anniversary celebration is right around the corner, as you know, Stevie. For the sake of your aunt and the importance of this occasion to her, I am willing to put behind us the regrettable dinner at our house. I know you three are under some stress. You all have your own problems at the moment, and perhaps, I can admit, I was a little hard on your aunt. She needs to get out of the house, away from the laundry and household chores, and this is the way she's choosing to rebel from her natural and rightful place. It's a phase she's going through. She's asserting herself, and I know it will end. I am a patient man, indulgent, and she can go to her classes. It's a waste of my money, but I have agreed to pay for it. Her allowance will take a cut, however, to help cover the cost."

I had talked to Aunt Janet the other day on the phone and she loved her classes. "I'm learning so much, I think my brain was shut down and now it's opened up." She loved going downtown with Virginia. "Such an adventure!" Loved her teachers and all the people they were meeting. "I think I'm finally learning how to think."

"I'm having a midlife crisis, dear," she told me. "It's this fortieth anniversary party that I'm so, so dreading. I started to study my life, up close, you know, dear, and I was so unhappy with what I found."

"What did you find?"

"I found a mouse. A very unhappy, timid, scared little mouse who had used up decades of her life being unhappy, timid, and scared."

"I'm sorry, Aunt Janet," I whispered, my heart heavy.

"Me, too, dear. I'm way past the halfway point. I may have only twenty years left, maybe less. I started thinking about dying and I wondered how I'd feel on my death bed about the life I'm living and that . . ." She stopped, and I heard her crying. "That depressed me beyond all else. I do not want to die knowing that I was unhappy and, worse, knowing that I did nothing—nothing—to change my own life, to put happiness in it. So my midlife crisis involves changing me."

"Good for you."

"I need to find myself. I need to be more than I am. I need to dare and I need to get out of the house!"

"You've certainly done that. You're out of the house most days, aren't you?"

"I am, dear! And Virginia and I have started volunteering with a medical clinic here for the poor. Every day. Four hours a day. And sweetie, this has helped me with your mother. There are so many people in Portland who come in muttering to themselves, talking to voices, violent and angry and scared, and by helping them, I feel . . . I feel that I'm reaching out to your mother through them. Do you know what I mean?"

"I do, I so do, Aunt Janet."

"You always understand, dear Stevie." She paused, and I knew she was getting control of herself. "Every time I see you, sugar, you look more like your mother. She was so beautiful, sweetie, as you are. I'm so sorry for what you went through, Stevie, I am. And when you came to live with us, I'm so sorry . . ." Her voice caught. "I was not there for you. . . ."

"Aunt Janet, you've already apologized to me about this so many times, don't torture yourself, please, I understand. You had lost your sister, your parents, your niece, you were in this lousy marriage . . ."

"No excuses, none, sweetie," she said, her voice breaking. "I was weak. And I did not take care of you, the granddaughter of my parents, daughter of my dear sister, the way I should have. I was too caught up in my own grief, my own depression. My drinking."

"I have told you that I forgive you, because you asked me for forgiveness—"

"And you forgave me because you are a gracious and giving person. Your mother, Stevie"—She paused, gained control. "Your mother would have been so proud of you."

"Now you're making me cry, Aunt Janet." You see, I understood Aunt Janet. I was scared to death that I would never live, like her, never become who I wanted to be, although I didn't know quite yet who it was I wanted to become.

My uncle's commanding, irritating voice intruded.

"Stevie! Continue helping the kids with my anniversary celebration. I am handling the political side, so all you have to do is make a couple of calls to the caterers and florist and make sure those invitations get out on the list I gave you. Remember I will not swallow scallops. Remember no pepper on anything. And don't forget that we will not be having anything chocolate for dessert. Get back to me immediately with your report."

He hung up.

He was such an awful person.

The chicken job was still available, I noticed. Ten dollars an hour.

I sighed.

I absolutely could not apply for that.

I had a lot of emotional issues with chickens and I couldn't do it.

I could not.

I am not a chicken.

Am I?

On Saturday morning I went on my walk. I hadn't fallen asleep until about two in the morning and I woke up at six because in my dreams Sunshine was staring through my mirror, tears rolling down her flushed cheeks. On the other side of the mirror was me. She was screaming for me, hands outstretched. I tried to reach through the mirror for her hands, but a bridge arched up between us, and then water swamped the bridge and carried Sunshine off into a whirlpool. She turned purple because she had no air, then exploded, and the glass from the mirror lacerated my face.

I woke up shaking, exhausted, depressed, sweating.

I was exhausted from the shaking, depressed about the sweating. I wanted to pull the covers over my head but knew that wouldn't work, so I set out on my walk, hoping it would take away the shakes.

I trudged out the door, into a spring drizzle, but then stepped up my pace as my muscles woke up and my body leaped into a rhythm. Though the mirror dream was clawing on my mind, I tried to leave it in the tangle of sweaty sheets with every step I took.

I love watching the seasons change close up on my walks.

Before my operation I wasn't able to "do" seasons. Now I can. The blustery wind that blows my hair around, the rain that trickles down my face, the snow that sticks to my eyelashes, the sun that warms me, the darkness in the morning when I watch the sun inch up, my feet pounding out a familiar pattern. . . . The colors are so tasty to me, almost magical. The leaves change—greens, reds, yellow, brown, then there are no leaves, only the branches crisscrossing like millions of tree freeways. I stare up at trees, I crouch down to see little flowers blooming, I catch hail in my mittens, and I stop to watch birds and ladybugs and spiders on webs and a garter snake or two.

I pause when the geese fly overhead and I pet dogs on leashes and grin at cats that sidle up to greet me. When I walk through the park I embrace the silence, and when I walk through the woods I listen to the sounds of the forest, the crunch of pine needles, the rustling of little animals, the croak of a frog, the tweet of a bird.

I was a window person.

Now I'm a nature person.

I have missed out on so much for so long, months ago I vowed I would never miss a day of nature again in my life.

So I walk.

Every day.

And hope I can fend off a nervous breakdown.

"I'm lonely."

I gripped the phone in my hands and sat down in an Adirondack chair on my deck, the stars twinkling at me between my cherry trees.

"Lance, I'm sorry," I said.

"I know," he sniffled. "But I am. I want to get married, I want to have kids, a bunch of them. Maybe ten. But I've never met anyone I want to marry. Not one woman made my ankle twitch, ever. No twitching."

"One will make your ankle twitch, honey."

I so understood Lance. I knew he was lonely. I was, too, sometimes.

I thought losing weight would take some of my loneliness away, and it has somewhat. It has certainly taken away the massive isolation I felt from the rest of society, to whom I was invisible and judged to be "less than," but it certainly didn't magically alleviate my loneliness, or aloneness.

"I wonder if I'll be lonely my whole life," he mused.

I wanted to tell him differently, but I wanted to be honest, too. "I don't know, Lance. Sometimes, with me, and my loneliness, I've come to the conclusion that I have to get used to it. See it as someone who's with me, who comes and goes."

"You mean a lonely friend?"

"No, not a lonely friend, but . . . a person, a being, a thing."

"So accept loneliness."

"I don't know how else to handle it. I work, I talk to people, I walk, I see you and Polly and Aunt Janet, but there are moments when I'm stark lonely. Other moments when I think my loneliness will eat me alive. And sometimes it's vaguely there, hanging around, waiting to go away, maybe on a trip somewhere, and often I'm not lonely at all and feel happy to be alive. Does that make sense?"

"Yes, honey, it does."

"So I try to get busy, I work in my garden, I read and make things, and move through it."

"That's about all we can do, sweetie, move through it, right?"

"Yep. Move through loneliness and isolation and hope you can outrun it for a while."

He sniffled.

"It's nothing to be embarrassed about, Polly," I pleaded with her over the phone. "It isn't."

"It is. I'm a loser. I'm thirty-five years old and I have the same battle." I could hear her "soft-crying." Soft-crying, in my mind, means, "I can't have the full cry I deserve because I'm at work." And Polly was at work. She had an hour before she went on the air.

"Polly, we all have stuff we have to work on. Everybody. I read the other day that a majority of Americans have some sort of mental problem during their lifetimes."

"You think I have a mental problem?"

"Polly, you know what you have. It's catching up to you again. You need help. You need to push it back one more time."

"I am pushing it back."

I heard her talking to her heart. She whispered, "Calm down, my heart. It's okay."

"It's pushing back harder; it's winning. I can see it in your face."

"What's wrong with my face?"

I didn't say, "You're a slight shade of blue, your cheekbones are sticking way too far out, you're pale." I said, "You're gorgeous, but it's showing up again, and you know it."

"I'm winning. I know how to handle this. I was at group the other night, even."

"What did the people in the group say?"

Polly said something under her breath.

"What?"

She spoke again. I couldn't understand her.

"What?"

"They said I need to . . ." She cried again, her breath gaspy. "They said I need to go in for treatment again. But they're wrong. They're a bunch of skinny people. One has pink hair, one has a tattoo of Groucho Marx, one has a doctorate, one's a lawyer—they don't know. They're wrong. I know what to do. I'm stronger now, I'm better, I'm not a teenager. . . ."

"Go to the clinic, Polly. Let me take you there—"

"No. I have to go, Stevie. I love you."

The dial tone rang in my ear.

13

Portland, Oregon

It was date night with Jake, and I was petrified.
I called Zena.

"Help me," I wheezed.

She was over in forty-five minutes. "I am going to take you in hand, girlfriend—here I go—and why didn't you tell me you had a date?"

We went to a salon and she told the stylist, her friend Josi, how to cut my hair.

"You need to get rid of all this." Zena held up the frizzy ends of my black curls. "And you need to shape this mess." She pulled on my well-grown-out bangs. "And she needs lift back here so she doesn't have a pelt for hair and resemble a black beaver." She yanked up the middle of my hair.

I cowered while Zena and her stylist friend chatted, my hair flying to the floor. Honestly, I would not have been surprised if I had no hair left when they were done.

"Okay, now you can look. Unsqueeze your eyes, Stevie, there ya go. Be a Wonder Woman and glance at the mirror."

I did. I unsqueezed my eyes.

Zena smiled. "There. Much better. You don't resemble a toadstool at all anymore."

Josi smiled. "I know you've heard this a million times, Stevie, but you have hellaciously awesome blue eyes. They're amazing."

I waved my hands in front of my eyes to dry the tears.

I loved my hair!

Zena came home with me and made me try on three different outfits with the clothes I'd bought from Phyllis at the store. She told me to wear the jeans that, in her words, would "make his dick rise, so I call them dick-riser jeans," the red shirt with the crisscross bodice—"Your girls will leave him panting like a dog"—and earrings, a necklace, and bracelets with natural stones she was wearing that she took off and handed to me. "Phallic good luck symbols. Stevie, give me a minute." She put her hands over her face. "Emotions get to me sometimes...." She shuddered in a few breaths. "You, friend, are hot." She pulled my forehead to hers. "Don't be scared, Stevie. You are going to make his balls bounce together, and that's the highest compliment I can give you."

By the time Jake was on my front doorstep, I was shaking, and trying not to think of him naked or his balls bouncing together or any rising that might possibly be going on in his pants, although I doubted it. Was that objectifying him? Was I as bad as men are about women?

But still. You should have seen his chest!

Jake had on a jacket and button-down shirt and he smelled like aftershave and mint and the woods in the morning.

"You're beautiful, Stevie."

Now he said this in all sincerity as he towered over me, so I got choked up and made a waving motion with my hand for him to come into my house. He stepped in, and my small house instantly became even smaller, because he's so tall, and yet it also became instantly warmer, too, as if it were reaching out to hug him.

I saw my house through his eyes—all the colors, the funky furniture, the wine barrels that were now side tables, the church pew, the bookshelves full of pretty things I'd found used, my butcher block counter . . .

"It's you, that's for sure," he said, turning to me. "It's you. I like it. I like it a lot."

He stared right at me when he said, "I like it," and I knew I was melting on the inside, kidneys into bladder.

Could I do this? Could I go to dinner? Would I be able to articulate words like *bird,* or *hello,* or *thank you* or would I only stare and think lustful thoughts about this blondish-haired giant?

"I'm sure you've heard this from many people, Stevie, but your eyes are stunning."

I did not say, "They're my momma's eyes," but I thought it, and that put a damper on things a bit, but then I said, "Thank you, yours are, too," which I couldn't believe dropped out of my mouth, but he seemed pleased, so I showed him the house. He loved all my furniture and wanted to know where I got certain things and was very admiring that I had made others, for example, the blue table made from a barn door and a mirror frame I'd decorated with long tree branches.

I showed him the second bedroom, with Joseph's wood carvings, and whisked by my bedroom, but he stepped on in.

"That's the most incredible bed I've ever seen," he said, awed. "Where did you get it?"

"I built it."

"*You built it?* It's . . ." He ran his hand over the wood. "It's incredible. Original. I've never seen anything like it. . . ."

I bit my lower lip, holding my smile to a minimum, though I was so flattered that the man with the possibly bouncing balls admired my bed.

Jake wanted to see my woodworking materials, but I steered him away from that, lickety quick. No need to share my obsessions yet.

He opened the door to his truck and I climbed in. He put on, of all things, piano music. "My mother made me take piano lessons my whole life. All I wanted to do was play sports, which

I did. She agreed to it, but said I had to take piano, too, so I would be a well-rounded person, so I did, and now I love hearing it."

"Do you still play?" I'd like to play with him.

He grinned at me. "Sure do."

"I'd like to hear you play sometime." I'd like you to play with me.

We drove around the block twice, chatting, then stopped in front of his house. "This is the restaurant I'm taking you to."

I froze. Oh, no. Had I given him the wrong impression? My stomach dropped. Did he think I was going to get in bed with him at his house? I was not going to do so, I was only fantasizing about it! He wasn't even taking me to dinner? I had not read him right. I had not figured he was this type of man. How could I have thought he was different from other *stupid* men. . . .

"Stevie, I know what you're thinking." Jake held up a hand. "Please, don't. I've set up dinner in my backyard. I promise it'll make you smile. I thought you would be more comfortable here at our first dinner than in a restaurant. . . ."

I couldn't move. Was he telling the truth? Was he sincere? He was right, probably. Going to a formal dinner, with Jake, in a formal restaurant, had darn near knocked me down with fear, but still. Our first date, *at his house?*

"Hang on." He got out of the car, ran around to the backyard of his house, then came back with a bunch of daffodils, irises, and baby's breath clutched in his hand. "Here, Stevie, these are for you. I wanted you to see them on the table when you came in. Please? Please come to dinner with me in my backyard."

I loved daffodils and irises and baby's breath. I saw earnestness in those green eyes, and I saw truth. "Okay. You're welcome. Yes. No."

He just grinned.

I have no idea why Crystal wanted to bring me to the Athertons to see Danny.

I told her that: "I don't know why you need me to go."

"I didn't ask you to ask questions. You're coming with me." She waved at the people in the Chinese food stand as we drove by. "I need to see for myself what kind of shape this kid is in. The parents say that he's all mentally messed up—well, let's go and see. Kids can't fake it for long, and I think these parents are exaggerating how bad it is and how much money they need for him. Millions of dollars for care? Give me a break. Can't Mom help out?"

"The mother has been helping out."

"Damn, Steve, whose side are you on?"

I wanted to say, "I'm on their side, you nitwit," but I didn't. I needed my job. "I'm giving you their side of it, Crystal, and they have good points."

She blew her bangs out of her eyes. "I have no idea why you're arguing with me." She stopped at a light and took long moments to admire herself in the rearview mirror. She drove fast, aggressively, and gave two drivers the one-fingered salute and mouthed, "Fuck you."

"I liked you better when you were fat."

I felt as if I'd been slapped. It was the same thing Herbert had said. And Crystal had never known me when I was *really* fat.

"You didn't cause conflict with me, or assert yourself. Now you lose some weight and you're not blubbering and lumbering around everywhere, true, but you used to be quiet. You'd do your work, turn everything in on time, and you were—invisible. You were there when I needed you but not in my face when I didn't."

"I still do my work, and I do it well, Crystal," I snapped. "I turn everything in on time and I was never invisible. *You* might not have seen me, but I wasn't—"

"Yes, you were. People don't see fat people, okay, Steve? They're there, but they're not there. People admire thin people. Pretty people. Rich people. Powerful people. No one registers a fat person unless you're sitting next to them on a plane and they've insisted you lift up the armrest so their fat can sit on your lap the entire trip. I've said no to that before. I don't feel obligated to have someone's fat on me. I paid for my whole seat and I should get a whole seat, but fat people . . ."

I wanted to kill her. At that moment, I really hated Crystal, and I try never to hate anyone. "Crystal, fat people have feelings like you. No, I take that back." I gritted my teeth, told myself to rein in my anger, but it unleashed, flowing and fiery. "You don't have any feelings, do you? You're a cold, self-centered, working machine. You don't value anyone unless they're young and pretty and thin and stylish. That's what you think is important. That person's intellect, their interests, what they do for other people, how well read they are, if they have cool hobbies, who loves that person, honesty and integrity—none of that means anything to you, does it? And you probably wonder why no one likes you at the firm."

She seemed confused. "What do you mean?"

I was baffled. "What do *you* mean?"

"When you said that no one likes me. What are you talking about?"

She didn't know? She didn't know how people constantly talked behind her back?

"Nothing, Crystal. I'm sorry. I shouldn't have said that. I'm angry about what you said, so I overreacted, said something mean, I'm sorry—"

"No, tell me."

"They all like you."

"You said they didn't." She pulled over onto a side street, ignored the blare of horns, flipped the other drivers off, again, and turned to me, eyes narrowed.

"Well . . . I'm . . . sure . . . no one l-l-likes me, either," I stuttered.

"This isn't about you, Steve, it's about me. Everybody likes you. Why did you say that about me?"

We went back and forth for a minute, and then I said, truly incredulous, "You don't know?"

"Know what?"

"Know that you're probably not the most popular person at Poitras and Associates."

"I know that. Cherie is. Or that Roller-blading dwarf, Zena, or maybe you, Steve. But why don't they like me?"

I hemmed and hawed and then I gave in, as I could tell Crystal was not going to move that car. "You can be a little . . . abrasive."

She thought about that. "And?"

"Perhaps a little . . . brusque."

"And?"

"Maybe you should say hello to people, or wish them a good day now and then. You know, smile . . . act as if you're happy to see someone . . . say thank you, give a compliment . . ." I felt so guilty, so terrible about what I'd said. What had gotten into me? Why had I let her have it?

She stared straight ahead for a while, then her head tilted up. "I'm not at Poitras and Associates to be Miss Congeniality. I'm there to win cases. I couldn't care less if the secretaries and support staff don't like me. I'm an attorney. I don't have to care about those people who are beneath me."

I had almost felt sorry for her.

Almost.

Danny Atherton was fed through a g-tube through his stomach, on a hospital bed, in the middle of the Athertons' dining room. Because Danny loved the University of Oregon Ducks, the bottom half of the dining room walls had been painted green and the top half yellow. Posters of Duck athletes were scattered across them.

Danny's parents were standing protectively on either side of him, their attorneys standing guard next to them, with a nurse next to Dirk, as Crystal and I entered. There were three other young kids, dark hair, green eyes, who stood in the hallway.

If there was any doubt that this child needed round-the-clock supervision and help, it was blown to smithereens in that second. Although Danny had the most angelic smile I believe I have seen anywhere, his gaze was fuzzy, he was tiny under the blankets, and there was medical equipment, tubes, poles, and medicines everywhere. Danny could not speak, eat, or get himself to the bathroom.

Crystal froze two feet in.

Dealing with reality is not something Crystal specializes in. The harder, darker, scarier, sadder parts of life weren't on her agenda. In her designer suit and four-inch heels and hard expression she was acutely out of place. And she knew it. This was above her, beyond her. She did not have the depth to deal with this.

"Seen enough?" Mr. Atherton snapped. "Do you understand now that we really do have health issues here or do you still think we're lying? Maybe we can show you a list of Danny's medications. We can show you his schedule for taking those medications, when the physical therapist comes, the nurses, the caregivers. We can show you how we change and dress him and how we change his diapers or sometimes use a catheter. One of us sleeps in here on that chair"—he pointed to a lounge chair—"every night. Every single night. Danny can never be left alone."

Crystal took a shaky breath. I stood frozen.

"Or maybe you two want to review his medical bills again," Mr. Atherton said. "We can show you the papers we need to fill out to file bankruptcy. Hey, you two are smart. How about if you help us fill them out?"

I didn't respond because here's the thing: Mr. Atherton's anger was justified. Not only at what had happened to their son, but at us. We were the law firm that was fighting them. Fighting this young boy who loved dragons, who went into surgery for a repairable heart problem and who ended up in this room, being fed by a tube with a bag for urine at his side.

"I'm sorry—" I started. Crystal was still frozen, staring. "I'm so terribly sorry."

"You're sorry?" Mr. Atherton said. "We're sorry, too. We're sorry that our kid can't play baseball and lacrosse anymore, can't play the tuba or have friends over. He can't even play checkers. He can't camp, he can't fish, he can't read his dragon books, can't play with his brothers, all because a bunch of high-paid doctors couldn't make sure he had oxygen during his operation. And now they're fighting us, trying to make us responsible for their mistake. You all want us to go away, don't you?" He crossed his chest. "Well, we're not going away."

"Mr. Atherton," Crystal said, voice weak, but still combative, that awful bitch, "you can't prove that the lack of oxygen was what caused this. We've discussed this before—"

"Ms. Chen?" Mr. Atherton said. "Get the hell out before I throw you out."

"But—" Crystal was rattled. How dare a plumber speak in this tone to her! She was Crystal!

"There's no buts," Mr. Atherton said. "You're here, you've seen our son, and I don't want you in our home. Go back to your firm and tell all the attorneys we're not liars, we're not trying to screw the hospital, not trying to pad our wallets, not trying to get rich over our kid's 'minor' health condition. Tell them the truth, but leave my home immediately."

I turned to go but looked back once at Danny, his head lolling about, his body weak.

He was smiling. He was smiling and angelic and sweet.

He couldn't eat on his own. He couldn't pee on his own.

And we were defending the hospital.

Crystal and I drove back in silence to Portland. She was nervous, agitated. I thought it was because she was as upset as I was about Danny Atherton.

Watching a young boy struggling to *be* a young boy, struggling to live, well, it rips your heart out, slings it around, and smashes it against the walls of your own protective shell until you want to curl up in a ball and cry your insides out. At least, that's how I felt. I snuffled and cried half the way back to the office. I thought I had a problem being so obese, missing out on life, feeling exhausted and sick from my diabetes and hypertension, but that was nothing. At least I was alive. I could see outside my window. I could go to work. I could speak and go to the bathroom.

I had spent so many years focused on me, and how miserable I was as a fat person, how isolated and lonely.

I was ashamed. Absolutely ashamed. Give me all of my weight back plus some and it would be only a miniscule bit of the heartache the Athertons were experiencing.

When we got out of the car in the parking lot across the street from the office, Crystal slammed the door, her high heels clicking as we crossed the street to our building, dodging oncoming cars.

"We can't get that kid into court or we'll be toast," she declared. "He'll have all the jurors crying. You never know what kind of uneducated, blue-collar saps you'll get on a jury. We have to lowball them and settle the case. Pronto. But first we have to bury their attorneys in papers and make the Athertons' life hell. Total hell. As soon as they're worn out, can't take it anymore, then and only then will that family be ready to settle. You see, people want to get on with their lives. They're angry and upset for a while and they're all fired up. They want justice, they want fairness, they want their stupid day in court. It's our job to dismantle them until they're left gasping on the floor begging for mercy."

I have tried not to be shocked by Crystal. It doesn't work.

"Crystal, I can't believe you want to make Mr. and Mrs. Athertons' lives more hellish than they already are. Offer them a fair settlement—"

"Steve, I know this is a little hard to understand without a law degree, without a college degree, I get it. Okay? But this is war. I'm not in this case to do some half-assed job. I'm in it to win it, no matter what it takes. We're not the ones having financial problems, they are. We can wait them out until they're eating their grass they're so poor. I can wait until the moon freezes over if I have to. They want this settled so they can spend time with their son, pay off some bills, and figure out the rest of their lives dealing with . . . dealing with . . . *him*." She spat out the word *him* as if Danny were a thing. "I can do it. *I will do it*."

"What you've offered isn't enough—"

She whipped around and glared at me, two inches from my nose. "It is enough; it's more than enough. I'm going to be a partner at Poitras and Associates, and this case is going to get it for me. Now get out of my way, Steve."

Her heels tapped on the floor to the banks of elevators.

"You have boxes and boxes of papers to get through. I suggest you get to work," she called over her shoulder.

"I'll take the next elevator up," I said.

"Suit yourself, but be at your desk in five minutes."

The elevator doors shut behind her, and I leaned against a wall, breathing hard, the image of Danny in his bed and his grieving parents stuck in my head.

I wiped tears off my cheeks.

The only good thing about seeing someone in a heart-wrenching position is that it makes your problems appear to be nothing, because, usually, they are. Somebody, billions of somebodys, always have it worse than you on this planet. Always.

They certainly did in the Atherton house.

I did not even attempt to stop the tears that flooded my hot eyes with my shaking hands.

The moral question of working on the Atherton case became paramount to me.

If I was working this case with attorneys who were trying to work out a fair settlement, given this terrible tragedy, and the hospital's fault in this, I would be okay with it. Being a legal assistant isn't always pleasant, but it's my job.

This was different.

This was Crystal Chen, on full-blast, vengeful, fighting, warrior mode. When she said she would smash the family, she would. She was making it personal, and she was attacking them with the full force of her rigidly ambitious, cold personality.

That I had a problem with.

I pondered all the boxes of paperwork, files, folders, exhibits, and so on, of the Atherton case by my desk.

Endless amounts of stuff.

And somewhere in there Crystal wanted an e-mail from Dr. Dornshire. Desperately. Why did she want it? What did it say?

Yoo-hoo, Dr. Dornshire? Where are you?

14

Ashville, Oregon

Grandma always took me with her to the city council meetings she presided over as mayor of Ashville.

"Women do a better job of leading than men, sugar, don't forget that. When you're older, it'll be common practice for women to be running or owning many companies. They'll be ambassadors, professors, heads of law schools, the president of the United States. Most men, excluding your grandpa, don't have half the working brain cells women do, and most of their brain cells have the words 'I am selfish' imprinted on them. They think of themselves first, second, and third. Don't forget I told you that." She held her hand up. "Praise the Lord for your grandpa."

I held my hand up the same way. "Praise the Lord."

"Praise Mary and Joseph, but especially praise Mary," Grandma said. "If you want something done right, ask a woman. Now take Mary. She gave birth, as a teenager, in a stable, after riding on a donkey."

"Praise the Lord for Mary." I raised my hand again. "And praise the Lord for giving Mary a good donkey."

"And praise the Lord, the next time Jesus comes, do not send wise men bearing impractical gifts."

"Praise the Lord, no bad gifts."

*   *   *

At the council meetings, everybody called Grandma different names, depending on their relationship with her. She was Mayor Glory, Mrs. Glory, or honey, depending on which one of her family members was present and wanted to make a point. Great-Aunt Chari called her Darlin' Girl. Second Cousin Twice Removed Ed Shantal called her Boot Kicker, in all seriousness, and her great-niece Tally, a born-again Christian, called her Aunt Glory Be to God. I'm told that before Helen sang naked on stage she would stand up and argue with her mother. "Momma, I don't understand why we can't . . . Momma, we need more money for . . . Momma, I don't agree with you. . . ."

Grandma also had a few council members up there with her. Two were women. One was a Latina woman named Connie Santiago, who was kind and sweet and could recite the federal, state, and local laws for you, verbatim, paragraph after paragraph, and often did.

And there was Evie Webster, who had a white mother and a black father, and owned tons of acres on the farm bordering ours. She bred race horses. Evie had straight black hair with gray streaks running through it. She was tough, smart, and had the word *compassion* running through her veins. Grandma had told me that.

There were two white men. One was Cason Phillips. He had seen action in World War I and World War II. Nothing fazed him and he was sharp as a whip.

There was also Devon Wilts, a shy young man who was a whiz of an accountant and could add, subtract, and multiply numbers in his head. "He's a genius," Grandma told me. "Don't forget it." He was Grandpa's top money man.

And my grandma? She ran a tight ship. Those council meetings had an agenda, and the agenda was followed. People had their time to speak, but there were rules. 1) Three minutes each. 2) Be polite and cordial. 3) No shooting of firearms. Ever. 4) Stay for the potluck dinner and dessert. Remember to label any food if there's nuts. Frankie's boy is allergic.

(Frankie's boy was in his twenties when I knew him, but the rule stood.)

To remind the townspeople of appropriate behavior, there was a bow and arrows on the wall behind Grandma. She was an expert, taught by her daddy, who was taught by his daddy, and up and up the line. Fact was, she won each year in the bow and arrow competition on the Fourth of July. Grandma won for best shot. She'd been mayor for years and someone hung the bow and arrows up as a joke saying, "Don't mess with Glory or she'll shoot ya."

It was only partly a joke.

One time three farmhands, their huge cowboy hats, and their flaming attitudes came to a meeting. They had clearly been tipping the bottle and they were shocked to see a woman mayor up there, and I don't know what hole or what time machine they'd crawled out of, but they didn't appreciate what they saw. They decided to test the authority of my grandma. They were rude, they talked out of turn, and they were clearly disrespectful of others, catcalling and sighing.

After they groaned and scoffed at eighty-five-year-old Maybelline Terrace, who wanted a giant, gated cat run built in the city park and who asked the council once a year to do just that, Grandma warned them a second time. "That's it. One more outburst of uncouth and demeaning behavior, and you will leave. You will pretend you are civilized people, gentlemen."

They scoffed. They leaned back. They were tough guys.

A woman, a single mother named Joey Whitefeather, stood up and said she hoped that Madame DePuis was going to teach ballet again this summer. Her son had loved the classes last summer.

Well, I'll be darned if those three tough guys didn't laugh out loud. No one else joined them. We all knew Skate Hutchings, anyhow. He was a star basketball and baseball player. He ballet danced, too. What the hell.

"Gentlemen," Grandma said, politely, as if she was serving tea. "I believe I will excuse you from our presence at this time."

The men were clearly baffled by that language.

"What? What'd that broad say?"

"I said, gentlemen, you may leave now. Thank you for joining us."

"I don't get this broad. All polite. Is she telling us to leave? She think she can do that?"

"Yeah, right. Who's gonna make us leave? We got a right to be here with Catwoman and with the dancing ballet boy." They snickered again. "Does the boy like boys?"

"I think I got me a Doberman that can help run your cats, lady," he said to Maybelline.

"Would you three please stand in the aisle for me?" Grandma asked, smiling.

"Why sure, pretty lady," one said. "I need more room anyhow. I'm damn squished here." He grinned, meanly, so meanly, at Florence Shing, who was a heavy woman. Florence ran the food pantry in town that families could go to when times got tough. She and her husband were multimillionaires. He had invented some farm machinery. He and Grandpa went fishing all the time. Grandma volunteered with Florence.

"We need a man to run this meeting," one of the cowboys announced as they went into the aisle. "She think she the damn-tootin' boss of me?"

"Stupid to have women up there." That cowboy smashed his hat back on his head. "This is men's business. They got no sense to run this."

"Women. They all gotta be in charge but they ain't got the brain mash to do it. It's insultin' to have a woman up there."

People later said that it was a good thing my grandpa wasn't there, because he would have "beaten the brain mash out of all of them."

So those three men were in the middle of the aisle, and Grandma called out, "Now, Uncle Danny and Bethie and Cousin Cal and Cousin Michael, you all clear out back there, will you?"

They laughed, and they moved. The only people who didn't know what was going on were those three semidrunken cowboys.

They stumbled into the aisle, hands on their hips. They were cocky, arrogant, obnoxious.

"Hello, gentlemen," Grandma said graciously. "My goodness, I can see you better now. I need you to apologize to the good people of Ashville for disrupting this meeting. We treat each other respectfully here and with kindness. We agree to disagree and we respect each other's opinion. This town has run well for 130 years by following these rules."

"I ain't agreed to those rules," one said, moving his tobacco wad from one cheek to the other.

"Me, neither. And I didn't vote for no woman. Why we got three women up there? One white, one blackish, one Mexicani. What the hell's this?"

"Politics is a man's job. You women need to get in the kitchen and stay there. And I ain't followin' the rules of a town with a color wheel runnin' it."

Oh, now, that did not go over well.

There was no rule against guns inside the council chambers, you just couldn't shoot them off. A number of people had their guns out whippety snip who were none too slow on the trigger. I knew this because a bunch of them were my relatives and they had hair-trigger tempers. Ran in certain lines of the family, that's what Grandpa said.

"Oh, now, now," Grandma said, smooth as silk, gentle lady. "You put those guns away. I'll take care of things. Come on, now, Grandpa Thomas. Put that away."

"You gonna handle this, Glory Be?" Grandpa Thomas croaked. He'd been in World War I and II, too. He was Cason's brother.

"I am." She eyed the three obnoxious cowboys. "Now, Grandma Lacy, you put that gun away, too."

"But they're shitheads," Grandma Lacy said. She's hard of hearing so the words binged around that room pretty good.

"Yeah, they're shitheads," Grandpa Thomas said. He couldn't hear too good, either.

"Shut up, old man . . . shut up, old woman," one cowboy said.

Grandma stood up. "I am done being polite. Excuse me to all

of you good townspeople for my language, but you three need to get the hell out now."

I could tell that her temper had been tripped. Grandma never swore.

"You can't tell me what to do, little lady," one cowboy said as he spit on the floor. The other two followed suit with the spitting.

The outrage in that room was not lost on me.

"All right then, gentlemen, don't say I didn't warn you."

And, with that, Grandma slipped that bow and those arrows off the wall, and before you could say, "Don't say I didn't warn you," again, she whooshed, whooshed, whooshed, and she shot off their cowboy hats. The arrows stuck in the wall behind them.

Then she pulled that bow back again and said, "Boys, you get on out of here right now or the next one's going right through those teeny, tiny dicks of yours. Excuse me again, good people of Ashville, for my coarse language." She whizzed on down the aisle, bow and arrow ready to rip. "None of you gentlemen appear very big in that department, so I'm going to have to get closer and aim careful, but I assure you that I will not miss, even when I'm hitting something the size of a toothpick."

Well, that seemed to be some sort of sign, because those townspeople, many of them our relatives, got their guns out *again* and darned if those cowboys weren't surrounded.

"Oh, shit!" one of them muttered.

"Shit yourself," Joey Whitefeather said. "You made fun of my boy, you ball-less wonders."

"Yeah, shit yourself," Grandma Lacy shouted. "I said you're shitheads, not just shits."

"Damn right. You're shitheads, not just shit. There's a difference," Grandpa Thomas said, and then he did what he was not supposed to do and he got suspended for a full town meeting and was not allowed in until dinner and dessert time.

Grandpa Thomas shot off his gun into the ceiling. Three times.

Those cowboys. They tried to force their way through a

crowd of pushing, pissed-off townspeople, but they couldn't. My relatives don't back down.

"One moment, please. I forgot something. I believe, kind sirs," Grandma said, bow and arrow still pointed, "that you all left your spit on our floor. Now you get that up, right this minute."

The cowboys were baffled. Pick up their spit?

"I . . . I . . . can't. I don't got a napkin."

"No problem," Grandma said. "We'll help you. Pally and Cousin Marie and Grandpa Kenneth?"

All three were huge. Cousin Marie won the hog-tying competition every year, and Grandpa Kenneth had been in the army, and Pally was built like a tractor, and they tackled the cowboys in a lick of a second and they helped all three of those cowboys to pick up their spit with both their cheeks. The face cheeks, not the butt cheeks.

Grandma examined the floor. "I think they've got it." She raised her bow again and pointed it at one cowboy's crotch. "Such a tiny target." She sighed. "Praise the Lord, I hope I don't miss."

Well, the cowboys turned around and flew out into the night.

The town requisitioned their hats and hung them up above the bow and arrows with nails. Above it, someone later made a lovely, hand-painted sign, complete with flowers, our white Schoolhouse House, and a garden. The saying across the middle was, "Don't mess with Glory."

The only problem was that Grandpa Thomas had to miss the town council meeting the next time. He protested his suspension twice. Grandma and the council did not give in. No guns could be shot inside council chambers. That was a rule. (There was no rule about arrows.)

He could, however, attend the potluck dinner and dessert after the meeting.

So saddened was Grandpa Thomas that he could not attend the next council meeting that he sat on the steps and played woeful songs on his harmonica the whole time, which we all heard.

Grandma said it added a "haunting, mystical moment" to the meeting, and she thanked him later for it.

He hugged her. Then apologized. "I'll try never to shoot my gun off again, Glory Be, and I apologize for it. My temper got a hold of me as the devil did in my youth, and I couldn't get a lasso around it."

"Don't you worry none," Grandma said. "Now, come on down. Ramon has made his marionberry pie and you know it's the best pie ever."

And that was that.

Grandpa Thomas didn't shoot off his gun for one full year.

Church seemed to calm Helen down, and we went every Sunday and sat with The Family.

Sometimes Helen sat quietly, but sometimes she didn't. She took to preaching a couple of sermons herself. "Everyone here: They're after you. They're everywhere. We're all being watched! Not by God, but by them. They are here. They are among you. Watch out!" she shouted. "Watch out!"

Thankfully, she would then settle back into her seat and go back to her incessant turning of Bible pages and not speak again. Several people commented that it was so kind that Helen was trying to warn us all of impending danger.

The minister knew he could go on without further interruption of his sermon. This did not extend to the singing part of the service.

During singing time Helen would wait until the choir was finished, as if they were the prelude to her act. With the exception of "Amazing Grace," which brought everyone to tears because Helen ended up crying through the "save a wretch like me" line, her songs were almost always show tunes, and she did a beautiful job, I will admit, even though it was humiliating each time. Grandma tried to stop her, but that made things worse, and Helen would have to start all over again. She usually patted Grandma on the nose first. "Pipe down, chicken," she'd whisper, then burst back into song.

She favored songs from *Cabaret, Hello, Dolly!* and *West Side*

Story with a couple of songs from *The Sound of Music* thrown in. Oh, and how could I forget *Jesus Christ Superstar?* That was a favorite of hers, especially right before communion.

She would stand, compose herself, smooth whatever she was wearing—overalls with a tutu, a slinky purple dress with a cape, or overalls under the slinky purple dress—and then burst into, "Jesus Christ Superstar . . . Do you think you're what they say you are . . ."

Thank the Lord that our minister was the brother of Grandma's best friend growing up and like a brother to her. He waited patiently. He was not irritated when people clapped after Helen's performances. She bowed politely, waved, nodded her head, often covered with her beaver hat and silver foil, and sat down. Grandma and Grandpa would exchange a glance, and Grandma would mutter, "Praise the Lord she did not swear." I'd hold one of their hands, and the service would go on.

When the baskets of communion bread came around there was a fifty-fifty chance that Helen was going to dump it on her head and then start examining each one, piece by piece. "I know there's a camera in here . . . you wait. You watch. It's a blimpomatic for spying on me."

The men passing the baskets from row to row would be ready with another basket of bread and everyone would move on, as normal. Helen would take little bites out of each piece of bread and examine the bite, hoping to find that elusive camera. When she couldn't find the camera, she'd toss the bread over her shoulder and grab another piece.

Grandpa always wrote big checks to the church.

Now it was said that people came to church simply to hear Helen sing. I would have laughed at that, but when we were at a cabin for a couple of weeks, and people in town knew we were on vacation for two Sundays, the church coffers went way, way down and Grandma got panicked calls from the minister for us to please return *immediately.*

I often heard people whispering requests to Helen before church.

"Sing that love song from *Fiddler on the Roof,*" old Mr.

Grotten told her one day, leaning heavily on his cane. "'Sunrise, Sunset' . . . It breaks me up each time I hear it."

"*The Sound of Music* makes my heart swell," Mrs. Chandler said, quite loudly because she is partly deaf. "Sing 'Edelweiss.' My mother's parents are from Austria, and it'll bring me back home. Or how about 'My Favorite Things'?"

"Why don't you sing 'I Feel Pretty' from *West Side Story?* I feel so fat today, I think it would cheer me up." Grandma steered her away from Clare Shoemaker pretty darn quick at that one, but that wasn't enough. After the choir finished that Sunday, Helen burst into, "I feel pretty . . . oh, so pretty . . . I feel pretty and witty and bright . . ."

I swear half that congregation was swaying to the music by the time she was done. Grandma glared at Clare after the service, and Clare held both hands up innocently. "Come on, now, Glory. It was a beautiful song, and you know it!"

"Are they after you, too?" Helen asked me one day in the car on the way home from church, where she'd sung a song from *Guys and Dolls.* "What is your true identity? Are you part of my tribe or theirs?" Helen had wrapped foil around herself to "ward off communications." She had also refused to brush her hair for three days, so it stuck up all over her head. She had dropped a toy crown over the top of it.

"I'm in your tribe, Momma," I reassured her.

"You don't look like me. You look like them." Then she swore. "Hell's bells are ringing. We don't look alike. I have blond hair, you have black hair. I have white white skin and your skin is darker. See?" She held our arms together. She was right, I was darker. "And our noses." She touched her little one and then mine, more of a beak. "Plus you have that." She poked the dimple in my left cheek, then poked her cheeks. "I don't have a dent in my cheek."

She stared out the window for a while, the sun high in the sky.

"Where are you hiding the listening devices?"

"I don't have any," I said.

"Yes, you do," she shouted.

"No, Momma, I don't."

"I know you do." She hit her fist against the car door. "I know it. You're lying." She hit her fist again and glared at me, and then she started fiddling with the door handle.

Grandma hit the brakes and tried to turn off to stop the car, but she was not quick enough for Helen.

"I am not staying with the spy," she declared, pointing at me. "Not when she's spying on me for the government!"

Then she unfastened her seat belt and leaped from the car.

I cried for days.

Helen was gone that time for four weeks. First to a hospital for her concussion and bruising and broken ribs, and then to an out-of-state mental ward because of the "sickness in her head."

It was the last two weeks of kindergarten. I remember because we had Clay Day the week before and I'd made a frog for Helen. Helen had turned that frog this way and that, then put the frog in her pocket and hopped off.

After she'd been there for weeks she jumped through a second-story window. I have no idea why that window did not have bars, but it didn't. She broke through the glass with her fists and a stapler and tumbled through the night sky right to the ground.

Helen came home drugged and mentally fizzy. That's the only way I can describe it. She came home *fizzy*, one foot sprained, a wrist in a cast. I heard Grandma telling Grandpa it was a miracle she was alive. "She had an angel with her, that's all I know. Praise the Lord."

Grandpa parked the pickup out front and, leaning heavily on him, Helen hobbled up the walk, her blond hair a mess around her shoulders, her blue eyes vacant. Grandma ran on out to give Helen a hug. Helen did not hug her back. Instead she leaned in and said, "I have to tell you about the cans of dead people."

"All right, sugar," Grandma soothed. "We'll talk about it inside. I'm so glad you're home. We missed you."

When Helen saw me, she opened up a huge flowered bag she had at her side, stuck her hand in, searched around, then brought out the clay frog I made her. The frog was missing an eye and a leg had broken off. "He's hurt," she told me. "He's hurt. He's very badly hurt."

I took the frog in my palm. "Hi, Momma."

She stared at me until her eyes got all fuzzy again, and Grandma and Grandpa led her inside. She was wearing a blue dress, plain and straight, and there was a brown stain on the back of it near her bottom. She must have sat in mud, I thought. She must have sat in reddish-colored mud.

It wasn't reddish-colored mud.

15

Portland, Oregon

The next morning I balanced my checkbook and paid the bills that were not withdrawn automatically from my account. I made a payment on my medical bills and dared to check the balance. Oh, lovely, this two-week cycle I had $162 left. I sent out ten more résumés, took a walk, did not see Jake—so disappointing as I'd put makeup on—and came back. I finished cutting the last of my raised beds, then started constructing the trellises for the climbing roses. I had gotten the wood when a neighbor had taken down his old patio covering.

I sawed and smoothed the wood, and later that week if it wasn't raining I would attach the wood pieces together, pour cement, and get the posts in the ground. My yard had patches of dead grass, weeds, and barrenness. It was my life in dirt, I noted. My garden was a metaphor. I blew hair out of my eyes. I am ridiculous.

But soon Ridiculous Me would plant the vegetables starts and seeds and I'd have roses climbing up my trellises on the way to Sunshine's garden.

Not bad.

I reminded myself to build the two crosses but not for who you think.

That night I lay in the bed that Jake thought was incredible and watched Polly on the news. Dressed in a green suit jacket and plain white silk undershirt and sedate pearl earrings, she managed to appear proper and professional, but she reeked sex appeal. The men loved her for that sexiness, and the women loved her because she took her job seriously, wasn't flirty or flighty, and reminded them of a well-loved sister. She couldn't help it that she was gorgeous, but she was on their side.

Polly was so Portland. She chatted about biking along the river and hiking in the gorge and fishing on the Deschutes River. She joked about having panic attacks and not wearing makeup around town and no one recognizing her. Now and then, during a rush of news, the darker circles under her eyes grew, and people knew she was a trooper.

Yes, Portland loved Polly.

But no one in Portland knew, except for me, Lance, and Aunt Janet, what was under the stylish jackets, the curly curls, and expertly sprayed on makeup: Polly was denying that she needed to fight for her life.

I was sick, sick, sick with worry. My hands shook.

Herbert ignored Polly's anorexia completely. His family didn't have problems. We were better. We were Barretts. We were pillars of Portland.

Pillars.

We were falling apart.

When Polly and I were fourteen, we were both disintegrating in our own ways. I was fat, withdrawn, depressed, prone to bouts of panic, semihysteria, and mood swings, and I studied all the time. She weighed less than 100 pounds. She was pale with a slightly bluish tint, with sunken cheeks, and often physically weak. I know she couldn't sleep at night. She was crawling in bed with me, and because she was so cold, her heart was constantly pounding, on a dead gallop. I could feel it. It hurt her to sit in a chair because she had no fat.

Kids called us the Fat Cousin and the Bones Cousin.

And still she ran and played basketball and piano.

I begged Aunt Janet to do something. She did. She took Polly to the doctors, repeatedly. The doctors told her to commit Polly.

She did. Herbert went and got her at the clinic and brought her home. Aunt Janet committed her again. Herbert brought her home, and actually hit Aunt Janet into submission.

"She needs to eat. Open mouth, insert food. Here, dummy," he said to a white-faced Polly at dinner one night. He picked up a spoon and started shoving food into Polly's mouth. Polly sobbed, then choked. Lance leaped over the table and tackled his father. I pulled Polly away from him and whacked her on the back until she could breathe. Herbert slammed his fist into Lance's face. Lance hit him back, twice, and Herbert was down. Aunt Janet leaned over Herbert and howled that he was "an abusive ass," and we hauled Polly up to her bedroom.

When Lance was at football practice the next night, Herbert tried shoveling food into Polly's mouth again. This time Aunt Janet, red with fury, leaped on his back and tackled him to the ground, calling him a "fucking bastard." He punched her in the jaw. I grabbed Polly and we ran from the house. Two doors down, Polly collapsed. The neighbors called the ambulance.

Polly was committed to a clinic for six weeks, which was extended to nine weeks because she wasn't doing well. At the same time Aunt Janet went back to rehab, too. She probably figured it was a safe time to go because the police were asking questions about her bruises and she told Herbert to leave Polly in the clinic or she'd tell the police everything.

The clinic didn't work for Polly. She came home and stopped eating again.

Herbert refused to send her back. "She's a spoiled, rebellious brat. When she's hungry enough, she'll eat. Why can't you be like Lance, Polly? Athletic, the star of all his teams, popular . . ."

The sick irony was that Polly was like Lance. Athletic, the star of her teams, popular, and a 4.0 grade point average.

Having Lance, the golden boy athlete of the school, as my older cousin, and having Polly, the beautiful cheerleader and prom queen, in my same grade meant that a lot of the teasing I normally would have gotten in high school for my weight was cut off. Lance pummeled two boys in the face and knocked out a total of four teeth when those boys teased me. He actually picked up one boy and dumped him in a Dumpster and flipped the lid down. He tied another kid to the flagpole outside school.

Polly verbally eviscerated the girls who made fun of me and then made sure they were ostracized so bad they came to me pleading with me to talk to Polly so they could be in the "in" crowd again.

"Listen, Stevie," Daly Howe told me one day, her blond ponytail swinging behind her, big eyes filled with tears. "You know the other day when I drew that picture of you in a bikini—I was kidding, but it wasn't funny. I know it wasn't, and it hurt your feelings and I'm sorry and I won't do it again, and would you tell Polly because she won't let anybody be friends with me."

But even though Lance and Polly had done what they could to shut down the teasing, I knew what I saw in the mirror.

A girl who was fat and getting fatter.

Now and then, when the sun was up and the shadows were right, I'd see my momma in my cheekbones, my eyebrows, my profile, and that made me eat more. She could not be in me. She was not me, I was not her. I would erase her from my life, certainly from my face, by eating. Those recognitions scared me, completely irrationally, to pieces, especially since I worried constantly that schizophrenia was lurking in my genes, too, waiting to spring to life, and that I would soon be hollering at Command Center.

And when the sun was slanted on Polly? She could hardly make a shadow she was so thin. She passed out twice at school. It was only when several teachers and the principal said that if Herbert didn't commit her to a hospital they would report him for child abuse that he did so again. "What will everyone think?" he roared. "I've got a kid who refuses to eat and one who eats everything in sight and is getting so fat we can hardly keep her in clothes. Mental problems. Runs on your side of the family, Janet, not mine."

Polly was a girl who was being killed by anorexia, I was eating my way into oblivion, and Herbert was worried about his reputation.

"I have one fat cow and one skeleton," Herbert said to us.

"This psychosis is from your side of the family, Janet, and you're your crazy mother, Stevie. I can see your mother in you."

"And I can see why my momma thought you had a stick for a dick," I said, my pain for Polly finally making me speak up. "And that you're a short weasel fart. You *are* a short weasel fart. She was right. My grandpa called you Hatchet Face and said God knew he'd blown it with you. He was right, too. Grandma wanted to cut you up and put you in the pig trough."

Herbert shook me till my teeth rattled and I was grounded and not allowed dinner for two weeks.

No matter—Aunt Janet, Polly, and Lance snuck it to me.

Here's the thing: Polly and I are on the same spectrum. Both of us suffered from appallingly low self-esteem, tragedy in our pasts, devastating losses that we couldn't speak of or we'd "shame" the family, an abusive relationship with Herbert, and Aunt Janet's alcoholism.

We were a mixed-up clan—not in a funny, we'll-laugh-at-these-stories-when-we're-older kind of way, but in a diseased, rotting, maggot-infested way.

Polly stopped eating for control over her life.

I shoveled food into my mouth for comfort and so I could forget my past.

The public response to us was always different. Anorexia, oh, how sad. How terrible. But, hey! She's a size 2, or zero. Isn't she svelte? Slim as a whip! There's the pity element, but she is, *thank God,* not fat.

Morbidly obese? The public response is completely different: Gross. Disgusting. Get some self-control, why don't you? Lazy lady, dumb, a burden on society, you're responsible for our soaring health costs, and so on.

But what's behind both problems, now that's about the same. No one gets that part.

It's a spectrum, folks, and what's behind the spectrum isn't pretty.

I received another note on my door from Jake when I got home from work. He enjoyed our last date. Could he take me out on a river boat cruise in Portland? Would I want to come?

Figuring yourself out will come easier on the river,
I guarantee it. Plus, the dinners there are good. My
brothers and I went last month.
Sincerely,
Jake

Rein your heart in, I told myself. I so did not want to make
another mistake as I had with Eddie. I so did not want to get
hurt again, to have to deal with grief or loss or the pain that
would come like a roaring train when Jake was no longer interested in me.

But I couldn't help myself!

I e-mailed him. Yes, I would love to come. Thank you. I was
so glad he couldn't see me jumping up and down for joy, doing
a wiggle dance, then pretending to play an air guitar.

Our backyard date had been a night I will never forget. Want
romance? Here it is: Jake had hung his own trellis with white
lights. He had a caterer come in with dinner and dessert. The
tablecloth was white, my flowers went into a vase off to the
side, there were candles all over the backyard, and he even had
music on. Piano solos, blues, rock.

We had shrimp and lobster pasta, salads, hot breads, tiny
chocolate pecan pies for dessert, coffee, wine. So scrumptious.

The conversation was better. "Tell me about your family," I
asked.

He was one of four boys. They all lived in Oregon, his parents were still married, and they travelled together. "You mean,
your family is normal?"

He laughed. "Your family isn't?"

I laughed. I tried not to be bitter. I noticed that he noticed,
but I changed the subject. He turned the conversation back
around to me. He somehow knew I was a legal assistant. I told
him where I worked. After I got done being petrified I told him
some amusing stories from work and, surprisingly, he found me
very amusing. I asked what he did, and guess what?

He's an engineer. He builds and repairs bridges.

A bridge builder. Now, isn't that perfect?

He played songs on the piano, and I sang along with my scratchy voice. He didn't sing so well, either, but it was funny, and fun, and by the early morning hours we were into some of the grit of real life.

"I was married when I was twenty-five, Stevie. We were officially divorced when I was twenty-seven. I thought I would be married once, that I would stay married for the rest of my life. I never, ever thought I would be divorced. My parents have been married forever, and I assumed, and wanted, the same happy life and marriage."

"What happened?"

"My ex-wife decided I did not need to know a number of things about her before we married. She was a kleptomaniac, she had massive credit card debt, she'd been married twice before and neglected to mention it, and she had a criminal record for check fraud. I'd had no clue. None. I was an idiot."

My stomach clenched with sorrow for him. "I'm sorry."

He nodded. "It's fine. It was a long time ago. I don't see her, I don't talk to her, but I thought you should know."

We talked about her for a while, and how one lie after another had been discovered. "What about you? Married before?"

"Yes, I was." I gave him the bare outline of the information that he needed.

"There's more you're not telling me, isn't there?" he asked.

I stared up at the stars. Truckloads. "Perhaps I've left a few details out. I can't talk about them quite yet, Jake, I'm sorry. I'm not trying to be mysterious, or cagey, I just—"

"It's okay." He picked my hand up and kissed it. "You can tell me when you're ready."

We talked and laughed until three o'clock in the morning, and he walked me home. He didn't try to kiss me, but by then I was envisioning jumping into bed with him and rolling around until the roosters cock-a-doodle-do-ed.

That night I pored over the new clothes I had bought with Phyllis. I tried all of them on again with my new haircut. I thought of Jake. I wasn't comfortable yet with my new body, but I couldn't continue to be such a massive frump when around any corner at all—even in Portland, because he was working there for the time being—I could run into him.

So. My clothes. I would wear them, starting tomorrow. I got two trash bags and whirled through my closet tossing out all the plain, ill-fitting stuff.

In my bed that night, staring at the Starlight Starbright ceiling, I asked myself if I could ever trust enough to fall in love. I hadn't been in love with Eddie. I don't even think I loved him when I married him.

So was I capable of letting go enough to fall in love with a man? My answer: I don't know. Trust has always been an issue for me, a debilitating, gnawing issue, and you need trust for love.

But Jake? The man with daffodils, irises, and baby's breath in hand?

Maybe, oh, maybe.

I saw my uncle's ads for his state senate campaign on TV.

He was shown on the steps of the state capitol, buttoned up in a suit, his white shock of hair perfectly brushed down. He was the Establishment, a group of wealthy, influential white men who do all they can to keep the status quo, to keep women and minorities down, down, down, down below them.

But Herbert knew what was best! He stood for morals and values. He slapped a hand into his palm. He had the Bible to back him up. "This is about keeping marriage honorable, a union between one man and one woman. Not two men, not two women, not a woman and her dog. This is not about discrimination," he said, sanctimony dripping from his lips. "This is about upholding our moral values. This is about not sanctifying what is wrong, morally wrong. "This is about keeping marriage the blessed event that it is. My wife and I have been married for forty years. We have two children and one adopted child my wife and I took in out of the goodness of our hearts. We're a family, a traditional American family. Let's keep it that way."

I thought about "our family," our "traditional American family." I thought about the anniversary party.

Vomitous, all.

If Jake found out that Herbert was my uncle, would he run for the hills?

I planted blueberry bushes for Lance and three camellias for Polly. The blooms were pinkish reddish heaven. I cut back a bedraggled trumpet vine that I had faith would grow again, and I planted marigolds and a pink clematis near the picket fence. I planted sunflower seeds in a sunny spot and hoped for the best.

I also had sod delivered. So I cheated and didn't plant grass seed. I found the sod by chance. A neighbor's son's friend was planting it on the property of a shoe company, and they had extra and needed to get rid of it. They hauled it over, all stacked up, and dumped it off. I was so excited I nearly did a jig.

Now, it was a terrible amount of work over many long days. I had to rent a rototiller, get all the weeds out, flatten up the property, blah blah blah, but when I laid it down, exactly as instructed, voilà.

Instant pretty.

The best part? Jake saw me with the rototiller and said, "You are a woman after my heart, aren't you?" He helped me with the rototilling and I got to watch his muscles flex, and ladies, if I could have swooned away, I would have. He helped for hours while wearing a black tank top, which made me feel faint. And afterward we sat out on my deck and ate chicken sandwiches, and he was still sort of sweaty, and messy, and I'm surprised I didn't pass out, my sexual emotions getting the best of me.

When he left that night he said, "There's nothing sexier than a woman with a rototiller," and I said, "Your rototilling could make me roar." He laughed, winked at me, confirmed our date, and went home while I blushed so hot I thought I had internally combusted.

I stared at the Starlight Starbright ceiling for a long time that night, visions of muscles and a sweaty man tickling my mind.

When I walked into work with one of my new outfits on, Cherie stopped in her tracks, a bunch of stressed-out, slobbering newbies around her, and said, awed, "Would you look at Stevie? Wow! *Wow!*"

And the stressed-out newbies took a minute away from their stress and grinned at me, and so did other people, who came out to see what the commotion was about and told me I looked great, and then Zena sauntered up and said, "Hey, Sex Goddess! Seeexxxxx Gooodddddesss!"

I giggled and felt myself blush, and people clapped and cheered, which made me feel as if they liked me, so I blushed more.

I loved my job but I needed a second one, so I sent out more résumés and applications that night.

The economy is terrible here in Oregon. Twelve percent unemployment. But still. There had to be something out there.

I looked at my budget again. Anemic. Frightening.

I have mentioned that, haven't I?

Okay. I took a deep breath.

Maybe I could be a chicken.

I typed out another letter.

Cluck cluck.

I stripped and sanded a rocking chair with a broad headrest.

I asked it questions: If you had to compare your life to a garden, what would you see in it? Dead trees and bushes, stuck in the middle of winter? Weedy? Swamped with too much water? Drought filled? Blooming with a pink dogwood tree, tulips, daffodils, and gladiolas? What do you need to cut out of your garden to make it better? What do you need to add?

What is your name, chair?

My name is Hope.

Flowering purple vines, huge pink blossoms with red centers, yellow daisies, bees, butterflies, a tiny turtle, a blue birdhouse and birds.

Hope. I painted it as such.

On Monday I dressed up in my new clothes and was buried in paperwork on the Atherton case.

On Tuesday and Wednesday I dressed up in my new clothes and was buried in paperwork on the Atherton case.

On Thursday I dressed up in my new clothes and was buried in paperwork on the Atherton case.

And on Friday evening, dressed up in my new clothes and working late for a case for Cherie, I took a few minutes to sort through the boxes and I found it.

Hello, Dr. Dornshire. Good to see your letter.

It was a miracle.

It was case-shattering. It was harsh and blunt, and it was damning against the hospital because they were clearly at fault.

It was damning against Crystal, because a copy had been sent to her.

She had never disclosed the letter, which she is required, *by law*, to do.

What else could I find?

I pulled my keyboard toward me and got on the Internet.

How funny that the hospital had been "unable" to locate Dr. Dornshire.

He was right there. I was staring at a photo of his face, surrounded by a whole bunch of African children outside a medical clinic. He was smiling in his green scrubs. They were smiling.

I was not smiling.

I spent a lot of time staring at my Starlight Starbright ceiling that night. Interestingly enough, my hands were not shaking.

On a Tuesday night, Portland's most loved TV anchorwoman passed out, on camera, live, her head hitting, then bouncing off of, the desk in front of her, her auburn curls spilling about.

The cameramen and producers were so shocked they initially didn't do anything. It was Grant Joshi who immediately helped her, ordered an ambulance, and cradled her in his arms.

Some viewers later thought the tears falling from Grant's eyes indicated he was madly, passionately in love with Polly. See? Those rumors about them being lovers were true! He was heartbroken! He loved her! They were incorrect. Grant and Polly were simply, truly wonderful friends.

And his wonderful friend had almost starved herself to death. I flew to the hospital.

Polly took time off immediately from the station, and me and Lance drove her from the hospital to the clinic four days later. I drove The Mobster. Lance couldn't drive, because he couldn't stop crying and actually had to lie down on the backseat because he was hyperventilating. "Honey, pass that bag back," he called to Polly. Polly did so, pale and weak. He breathed in and out of it, passed it back. She breathed in and out, then Lance took it back. She patted her heart. "We're going to get help, heart. We'll be okay."

Her boss, Leroy Mussen, was an asshole and started threatening her. If Polly didn't come back to work by the following Sunday there would be an "or else" she would have to deal with.

But even Polly knew that she was done.

Simply put, she would die if she didn't get help.

Me and Polly held hands as I drove. We didn't say much.

We had been through this before. What else was there to say?

Jake and I had talked by phone many times, and he was waiting outside my house when I drove up after returning from the clinic, as we'd discussed. He took me right into his arms as I cried for Polly. When I was done crying on his shoulder and his shirt was a wet rag, he brought me inside and made me chili and cornbread. We ate together, he lit a candle, he cleaned up, and I cried some more. Honestly, I wasn't even sure Polly was going to live. She was so thin, so frail, that I worried she'd have a heart attack.

That man got me into bed by myself. "Sweetie, you have to sleep now. I'll lock up and I'll call you tomorrow."

At midnight he left and I curled up into my pillows and thought of Polly and felt sick, and then I thought of Jake and I felt warm and cuddly . . . then I felt guilty for feeling warm and cuddly and fought with my insomnia, and then I dreamed about Sunshine not eating until she fell into her own shadow and died.

16

Portland, Oregon

The response to Polly's collapse was immediate and loud. The station was besieged with calls about her health, and gifts and cards arrived by the box load. At the end of two weeks, Leroy Mussen was raving and told her that if she didn't come in, *that night,* to do the news, and all future nights, he would fire her.

I begged her not to leave the clinic, and so did Aunt Janet and Lance. Herbert wasn't there because Polly had told him not to come. I'd heard the phone conversation. "Dad, you're a leper. I can't stand you. Thinking about you makes me want to blow in a bag. If I envision your face, I want to hide. If I think of how you smell like a pipe I want to puke. If I think of that mausoleum-slash-prison that you live in I want to swallow Drano. Don't come."

But Polly was resolute about going back to work. "I'm going."

"Honey, please!" Lance said. "I've got enough money for all of us. Quit the job. I'll give you $1 million! Two million!" He wrung his hands. He was serious. He regularly offered to give us money. We always, always declined. "I can barely knit anymore I'm so worried about you—I can barely knit! See my hands, they're exhausted! Blistered!"

Polly got dressed up and put on her makeup, even as a barrage of doctors, nurses, and counselors urged her not to.

"Don't worry," she told all of us worried people. "I believe in vengeance, and I'm going to go out and get it."

We had no idea what she was talking about, and she wouldn't give us any more clues. I drove her to the station and stayed with her.

Polly was treated as the well-loved celebrity she is at the station, mobbed by people hugging her, telling her they hoped she was better. Grant didn't bother to hide his rampaging feelings. He hugged her, cried, asked how she was—could he do anything for her?

She thanked him and Kel for the flowers, two bouquets. The candy. Two boxes. The books, crosswords, and other things they thought might relax her, which filled two boxes.

Leroy Mussen came around, with his small, thin, beaked nose and balding head, and said, "Get ready, Polly."

She did the news with a smile, but at the end of the newscast she had a surprise for all the viewers. (This would be the vengeance part.)

"And now for a bit of personal information, folks." She smiled, but her eyes were sad. "You may have heard a few rumors about my abrupt departure and my head-banging incident recently. You may have heard that I've had a nervous breakdown or I'm on drugs. Neither is true. What is true is that I suffer from anorexia nervosa. I've been fighting this terrible disease since I was thirteen years old. I remember looking at myself in the mirror at the age of ten and believing I was fat. My father told me that I was and I believed him. (More vengeance.) My body issues have been long lasting and, frankly, now and then, they seem to take over my life and I can't control them. This is one of those times. I have been in a clinic since leaving the station, getting treatment and counseling."

She paused for a moment, smiled through sad eyes, and said, "Unfortunately, though, our station manager, Leroy Mussen, has told me that if I don't leave the clinic and come back to work full-time tomorrow I will lose my job."

I heard a collective gasp in the control room.

Ahhh. I sat back, crossed my arms, and laughed. Here came the vengeance on hyper-speed.

Leroy hissed, "Goddammit. Shit."

"Although I love my job and I love working with Grant, and all my coworkers here at the station besides Leroy, I love staying alive more, and as much as I will miss all of you, I am going to have to quit work here. I hope that after my six-week stay at the clinic I will be better, and with the support of my family and friends and a good counselor, I hope to conquer this disease once and for all."

Leroy Mussen screamed, "Take her out! Close off! Go to commercial!"

Oh, but people there must have hated Leroy Mussen. Perhaps this was their vengeance? It was obvious they loved Polly. No one moved. They didn't go off the air, they didn't go to commercial. The cameras stayed steady.

"And," Polly said, with a cheeky smile, "it would be nice to have a job. In six weeks, if you know of anyone who is hiring, please let me know!" She smiled again. "For KRNZ News, this is Polly Barrett. Good night and thank you, Portland. Thank you for the kindness you have shown me these last two weeks." She turned to Grant, waiting for him to say good night to the viewers.

Grant did not say good night. Instead he got all choked up and wobbled out, "Polly, you are the bravest, kindest, most beautiful woman I have ever known. And"—he turned back to the camera—"if Leroy Mussen, our station manager, fires Polly because she's going to a clinic to get better, then I'll quit."

Leroy Mussen was almost purple. "I said to get the fuck off camera!"

Gee. No one must have heard that order, either.

The weatherman was not to be outdone. He stepped into the frame and said, "Me, too. I support you, Polly. We should *all* support you, including Leroy Mussen."

The sports announcer swiveled in her chair. "Polly, I'm with you, too. Good luck. I know you can do this." She reached out a hand and squeezed Polly's hand. Polly got all teary and had to wipe her eyes, her chin shaking.

I put my hand over my mouth so I didn't cry. I'm such a wuss.

Leroy Mussen was having a purple fit. "I said go to commercial, dammit! You stupid people, move, move, move!"

No one moved. There was definitely vengeance in the air that night.

Then Grant smiled at the camera, as did Polly through her tears, and the weatherman and sportscaster all smiled too and said, "Good night, Portland!"

Leroy Mussen was flaming red-hot and out of control. Raving. "I will sue you, Polly, do you hear me? I will sue you for breach of contract. Get a lawyer, because you're outta here! Did you hear me? You're the fuck out of here."

He did not get any further. Grant grabbed him and shoved him up against a wall. "You. Will. Shut. Up. Now."

Leroy started to struggle and curse, but he is a short, thin man and his face was turning red-purple. He did not appreciate Grant, manly and strong, showing all his employees who was physically dominant. He swore something vile.

"When you stop swearing, I'll let you down," Grant said, voice reasonable, "but you must promise not to verbally abuse Polly."

Leroy swore again. Grant lifted him up higher, his little feet dangling. Leroy had no choice—everyone was staring, giggling, smirking as he was hung up on the wall like a prisoner in medieval times. Leroy closed his pinched mouth.

Grant waited ten seconds, then lowered Leroy's feet.

"Both of you," Leroy blustered. "Both of you will lose your jobs, Grant and Polly. And you, too!" he screamed at the weatherman, news staff, and sportscaster. "Did you see that? Did you see that?"

Some people sure had the giggles.

"I didn't see nothin'," Bertie, the camerawoman, who was one of Polly's best friends, said. "All I saw was a short man screaming hysterically at Portland's most popular anchors."

"Nope. Me neither," Jules, an associate producer, said. He had five kids and a stay-at-home wife. It was very brave of him to take a stand and risk being fired. "I didn't see anything except you destroying staff morale."

"I didn't see a thing," Jenny, a reporter, said. "Nothing except you throwing another fit and using the F word and harassing Polly because she has anorexia. Why would you harass a woman who has anorexia?"

Leroy glared, his beady eyes swiveling from one person to the next. He realized he was cornered. Perhaps at that second he understood how deeply well hated he was at the station. Not a person stood for him, especially not Grant, was steaming mad three feet away and said, "You're a moldy piece of crap."

"You're all gonna be outta here," Leroy warned, his bottom wiggling in indignation. "All of you. All of you!" He came up on his toes, finger pointing, swaying back and forth.

"I don't want to work for a station that puts the health of their people behind ratings," Grant said. "I don't want to work for a man who is so obnoxious and uncaring that he'd have someone who clearly has an eating disorder working here instead of being in a clinic."

"Me, neither," I heard, all around.

Leroy glared, his eyes beady, then threw his fists in the air and said, "You'll regret this. All of you. Start scanning the want ads for jobs as trash collectors." He stomped out, butt wagging.

But that was untrue.

There was only one person who lost his job that night, and that was Leroy Mussen.

The second Polly and Grant went off the air, the phones lit up as if a spaceship had landed on the Willamette and the e-mails came pouring in, the complaints loud and clear. The newscast hit YouTube, the national air waves picked it up, and the howl of protest at a newswoman getting fired because she had committed herself to a clinic to conquer her anorexia was deafening and furious. Advertisers threatened to pull their money quicker than you could say, "Leroy is moldy crap."

The owners were so backed into a corner that they fired Leroy immediately, and by the next night the lead story was . . . themselves. Shi Makowski, the owner, apologized for the "misunderstanding." Polly Barrett was not going to be fired! Not at all! They loved Polly! In fact, Polly was to take all the time she needed and they would still pay her full salary and pay for her stay at the clinic! The station couldn't wait for Polly to come back, when she wanted to, when she was well and healthy and happy. Her job was still there for her. The door was always open. She still had her job, people, do you hear that? They wished her the best. Please. Please! Keep watching our station. By the way, Mr. Mussen has decided he wants to spend more time with his family so he will not be working for the station anymore. Not one more day. Go, Polly! Up with Polly, down with Leroy!

So Polly kept her job.

And she kept her place at the clinic.

She would come out only to attend Herbert and Aunt Janet's nightmare party and then Lance's Hard Rock Party. She'd get a weekend pass. Then back in she'd go.

Afterward, she said she wouldn't have missed the anniversary party for the world.

Me, neither, I told her as I drove her back to the clinic afterward.

Oh, that party.

It was a doozer.

If we had only known what was going to go down. . . .

Jake and I were talking by phone, he was joining me for walks, we were e-mailing from work, we were . . . *dating!* Me, dating Jake!

I told Zena about our dinner date on a boat on the Willamette when we were eating lunch at Pioneer Courthouse Square and watched her eyebrows rise straight up into her bangs. "Good for you, you lusty loon," she said. "Don't forget that you can get sparkly colored condoms nowadays."

"A, I don't need condoms now and B, please, Zena, let me envision a red-striped condom."

"Birth control is archaic. The pill makes me nauseated. Diaphragms are a smelly mess. I don't want anyone giving me a shot in my arm, an IUD freaks me out, I won't put a ring in my vagina, and condoms are strong tube Baggies. Who wants to wear a Baggie even if there's stars on it?"

"Let's take this one up with the president of the United States. Get it on his agenda." I handed her some cherries. She gave me a yogurt.

"Did you know they've also come out with something a man can put over his penis and it vibrates? It's a vibrating penis. Now, who sits home and thinks up this type of thing? And wouldn't a guy feel that his unit was going to be vibrated right off with that on?"

"Do you think insurance would cover it if it did fall off?"

"Oh, heck no, the insurance company would say that it was a cosmetic procedure, unnecessary. . . ."

I felt this rush in my body whenever I thought of Jake—although not in a red sparkle condom—which was all the time. I was on fire, even though I was so worried about Polly, sick of my uncle, and despairing about the Atherton case.

Jake was separate from the rest of my life. He was a gift, a break. He was just for me. He was behind another door, that door was yellow and bright, and everything else was behind other doors. He was joy for me.

He was joy.

"Want me to run a check on him?" Zena bit into an apple. "You know how I did on your amour who had a thing for fast planes and Central America?"

I shook my head.

"Don't be stupid, Stevie. Most men are utter, undeniable creeps."

I shook my head.

"Don't get hurt here, Stevie. It's plain dumb. Don't let your vagina think for you. A vagina will always get you in trouble when you let it near your brain synapses. Let me check him out."

It was the "don't get hurt" part that got to me. I nodded.

I had a job interview Thursday evening at six o'clock to be a chicken.

The manager was a round, chipper, funny sort of nerd who clearly got his identity from working at Aunt Bettadine's Chicken Dinners.

"We're a family," Marty Pingle said during our interview, pushing wire-rimmed glasses up his long, beaklike nose. "Family!"

"A happy family!" I enthused.

We chatted for a bit about my job at Poitras and Associates and how I wanted to pay off my medical debt.

He nodded soberly. "I understand, I do. We chickens have to stick together." He brightened. "Do you like chicken?"

I assured him I loved chicken. Chicken sandwiches, fried chicken, baked chicken, chicken in my pasta, chicken strips, chicken salad . . .

"How about a cluck-cluck chicken test run?" he asked me. This involved me getting dressed up in the chicken outfit to see if I was chicken enough.

He grinned and handed me a giant chicken head.

The chicken head went over my head. The chicken head had millions of brown and gold feathers; big, yellow, maniacal eyes; and a gold beak. I put it over my head. I could barely see out of the eyeholes.

Mr. Pingle helped me get into the rest of my full-bodied, multifeathered chicken outfit, then turned me around and made sure that the back of my chicken head was in line with my chicken body. Over my tennis shoes I wore red chicken feet. I flapped my arms and tilted my head back and forth.

"You're a natural!" Mr. Pingle shouted. *"A natural."*

I stomped my chicken feet.

"I knew you would be one of our best chickens!" he announced, stomping back. "I knew it! Cluck cluck!"

I clucked, clucked, clucked at him.

He clucked back, did a stiff chicken dance.

I danced back at him with my red chicken feet.

He handed me a sign that said, "Chicken meals only $8.99!" and turned me toward the door. I was to dance about for thirty minutes at the corner, "to get a feel for being a chicken before the grand event!"

I stood at the corner, waved my wings, and held up the sign.

I passed the cluck-cluck chicken test and I had my second job.

Friday nights for four hours and four hours each on Saturday and Sunday. I would make $10.00 an hour.

I sighed.

Cluck cluck.

Zena dropped an entire box of condoms on my desk. They were the fun type, colorful, sparkly. "I checked out your friend Jake Stockton. Go ahead. He's cleaner than a whistle. Now let him whistle your whistle."

I leaned back in my chair, threw my arms and legs up in the air, and wiggled. I leaned too far back, though, and fell all the way over, somersault style.

I suppose this is dating in this century. You don't just take men's word . . . you take what you find on the computer about them as "word."

Zena grabbed a condom and started blowing it up with her mouth.

I ripped it out of her hand.

I was ready to rock and roll in my garden. I'd used two-by-twelve-foot lumber and angle brackets to create the beds. I had used a soil–compost organic mix. I knew that I would have to plant my seeds and seedlings a week or two apart from each other so I wouldn't be buried in lettuce all at once and have none weeks later. I knew I had to figure out which were weeds to pull and which were vegetables and how much water the whole thing needed.

I squished a gardening hat on my head. It wasn't yellow. That I could not do.

I dug into my raised beds and prepared to plant seedlings for tomatoes, squash, zucchini, radishes, carrots, peas, beans, etc., so I, Stevie Barrett, could have a vegetable garden with no corn. No corn at all.

17

Ashville, Oregon

When Helen returned from the mental ward with the reddish-brown stain on the back of her dress, she refused to shower or enter the bathroom alone. She insisted that Grandma or Grandpa or me stand inside the door frame, door open, to "guard her from the voices." We initially turned our backs to give her privacy, but that made her cry out in the most pathetic voice, "They're coming. They're coming. Help me, help me." She would leap off the toilet, midstream, if there was the slightest indication we were leaving.

"Look at me," she'd beg, scared, sometimes shaking, way too skinny.

I went eye to eye with her the whole time she was doing her business. I don't think she noticed my tears at all.

"Don't leave. I can't be alone." Then she would lower her voice and hiss, "Barry might be coming, Barry might be coming, Barry might be coming. He's always after Tonya."

I nodded. I didn't know what else to do. I still played with stuffed animals.

"And me," she breathed, nervous. "But especially Tonya."

"Who's Tonya?"

"Tonya. You know. With the long brown hair and the big lips? She cries all the time."

"Oh. She's sad."

"Yes, she's sad because of Barry. He's mean. I hit him when he grabbed her. That's how I got that." She pointed at her wrist cast. "Then we both had to go in the dark room with the pads. They turned off the lights."

I studied the wood floor, not understanding, scared, confused.

"Look at me! Look at me!" she shouted, fear crushing her. "I don't want Barry back." She hobbled up, her sprained foot hurting her, and wiped.

Helen insisting that someone watch her while she did her business on the toilet was especially hard for my grandpa. He was an old-fashioned gentleman, and a woman's business was a woman's business. A lady was a lady and should be treated as a lady at all times.

But Grandpa did it. He stood in the bathroom door, his wide shoulders almost the width of the doorway, his cowboy boots spread apart, and he watched his daughter urinate and wipe her bottom, often saying, "Yuck. I've been poisoned with brown."

I don't think Helen noticed his tears, either.

"What did they do to her?"

I was supposed to be in bed, but I had come downstairs for milk. Grandma's anguished cry made me sit down in a tight ball on the stairs to listen.

"She's worse than she was before," Grandpa said, his voice gruff. Through the doorway I saw that they were holding hands across the table. They always held hands. Good or bad, my grandparents always held hands. "This new medication isn't working any better than the old stuff. In fact, I think it's increased her paranoia, her suspicions, her fear . . ." Grandpa brought their clasped hands to his forehead and Grandma leaned toward him.

"You've talked to Chad?"

Chad was Grandpa's best friend and our lawyer.

"Yes, I talked to him. He says the head of staff there is watching Barry and they'll have an answer for us soon."

"And what about this Tonya she keeps crying about, telling

us we have to save Tonya? I can't bear the thought of this Tonya being hurt. Honestly, Albert, I know we don't believe most of what Helen says, but this has a ring of truth to it. She's honestly scared to death for her friend Tonya."

"Chad says he's trying to get a report on her, too."

"I can't believe this. We met Helen's doctors. We met the nurses. They seemed competent; they seemed as if they knew what they were doing. They reassured us she would be safe, that they would try new medications. . . . She's crumbling, her mind has crumbled."

I saw Grandpa's huge shoulders sag. "I'm afraid you might be right, Glory. I'm afraid you might be right."

Grandma wrapped her arms around his shoulders, and then I heard a sound I never wanted to hear again: Grandpa, strong and mighty Grandpa, who ran a company and a farm, sobbing.

He sobbed and sobbed, shaking, rocking, keening, and Grandma joined him, her tears running with his, the two most miserable people I have ever seen in my life clinging to each other.

I crept upstairs, crawled deep into my covers, and cried till my eyes swelled.

The light of the moon shone on my broken frog.

"They put the dead people in cans."

Helen rocked on her rocker as me, Grandma, and Grandpa turned to her in shock.

The sun was going down and it made the sky behind our cornstalks turn into brilliant golds and yellows and oranges. We had Helen's favorite opera record on, too, and she was singing along.

She had let me and Grandma get her in the shower to wash her hair earlier that day, although I had to get in there with her with my bathing suit on because "Barry might come, Barry might come. I think he's spying on me here."

"You need to eat more cookies," I'd told her, water streaming down our faces. She was too skinny and I could see her ribs.

"I'm not going to eat brown cookies," she told me.

"How about pink?"

She nodded. "Okay to pink cookies."

We made pink sugar cookies.

She ate one of the ones I'd decorated. "I did that one," I told her.

Surprisingly, she smiled at me. "Very delicious."

Grandma sniffled when she heard that.

The day would have ended so well, one of our best, had not Helen decided to tell us, "They put the dead people in cans."

Grandpa put his beer down. Grandma put her drawing of the cornfields aside.

"What do you mean, Helen?" Grandma asked.

Helen continued rocking in her chair. "At the Bad Place"—that's what she called the mental ward—"there was a man named Andrew. They put him in a can."

I put my pink heart cookie down on my plate. I wasn't so hungry anymore.

No one said anything for a while.

"I saw him. I saw Andrew in a can."

"Do you mean that Andrew went to a room by himself? Do you call the room a can?" Grandma asked, knitting her hands together.

"No. That's not it. Andrew died."

My throat felt like it had a fist-sized gumball stuck in it.

"When did he die?" Grandma asked.

"He died at the Bad Place on a Wednesday. Barry killed him. He sat on him. Squished him. Andrew couldn't breathe."

Grandma and Grandpa exchanged a horrified glance. I hugged my knees in close as the sun kept sinking toward the corn and the dark blue started blocking out the yellows.

"Andrew said, 'Help me Tonya,' but they grabbed Tonya. The men in the white coats. They always grabbed Tonya. Me, too, sometimes. They grabbed these." She held her boobs. "And this." She stood and grabbed her butt, then sat back down. "He said, 'Help me, Helen,' and I tried but the men threw me on the wall."

Grandma cried. Grandpa made a roaring sound, but Helen didn't notice.

"Tonya tried to save Andrew. She tried. His face turned red, then purple, then good-bye." Helen snapped her fingers and her chin wobbled. "His tongue came out like this." She dropped her tongue in the corner of her mouth. "And his eyes were like this." She rolled her eyes back in her head. "I miss Andrew. Barry is mean."

"Was Andrew a friend of yours?" Grandpa asked.

"Yes, he was my friend." Helen's eyes flooded with tears. "He watched when I was in the bathroom so Barry wouldn't find me again. He watched out, and that made Barry mean mad."

I saw Grandma lean over, her hands on her head. Something was wrong with Grandpa, because even in that dim light I could tell he was white as a ghost.

"I sung Andrew songs. He gave me crossword puzzles. I didn't do them. All the noise in my head made it too buzzy, but I have them still." She reached into the flowered bag by her side and pulled out crossword puzzles. Each of them had a picture on it. I could tell that she'd done the artwork because of the minute detail to each one, every line and dot perfect. Over one crossword, she'd drawn a stark bed, but the bed was twisted into a pretzel. Another one had a window, crooked, swerving, done in blacks and grays.

"They put Andrew in a can after they squished him," she said.

"How do you know this, sugar?" Grandpa asked.

Helen hummed part of the opera song that came floating out to the porch. "I know because Barry took me and Tonya down to the room. Down down down the stairs." Helen bit her lip as her voice cracked. "He made us!" she shouted. "He made us! I didn't want to. I said no and Tonya said no, Momma, but he made us!"

Grandma reached out a shaking hand and put it on Helen's arm. The cornstalks swayed in the distance as the sun continued to sink.

"Me and Tonya held hands, we held hands, but Barry said we needed to know what would happen!" Helen wrapped her arms around her head and rocked.

"What do you mean, what would happen?" Grandma asked.

I felt sick. I knew that Grandma and Grandpa had forgotten I was even there.

"He said if we were bad, if we were bad! *If we were bad!*" Helen started keening back and forth, her voice a low, raw rumble. A bat flew across our field.

"What, honey? What did he say?" Grandma asked. I saw her hands shaking. I saw Grandpa taking deep breaths, as if he didn't want to hear what she was going to say but knew he had to.

"He said if we were bad, if we told, *if we told what happened,* that he was going to put us in a can, too! Me and Tonya! In a can." She stomped her feet in place, her face twisted. "He did it to our Andrew. They put Andrew in a can. I saw it, I saw it in that dark room."

Another bat followed, then a third.

"What room? Where was the room?" Now it was Grandpa's turn.

"In one of the houses. Outside. Down the long, dark hall. All the dead people that got squished. They burn them up and put them in a can and put them on the shelf and I saw Andrew's can. He was there."

Helen started crying, quietly, her shoulders shaking. "I saw Andrew's can. It said his name. There was a date. A number. When he died. Yep. They squished him and put dead Andrew in a can. He saved me from Barry. The voices told me to kill Barry, but I couldn't." She cried harder now. "I wanted to."

Grandpa and Grandma were up and hugging their daughter, rocking her back and forth. "Sweetheart, sweetheart."

"Poor Andrew, poor Andrew with the crossword puzzles. I don't want to go in a can. Do you think Tonya's in a can now? You know, Tonya? My friend?"

We were out there till the sun dropped away, the darkness descended, and the bats flew in swarms.

*   *   *

The next afternoon Helen started drawing on a canvas with a charcoal pencil. She drew a row of silver cans. The tin cans were labeled, "Charlotte. Andrew. Patty. Harry." Sticking out of the cans she drew fingers or toes, human hair, and a hand. A left hand, I noticed. Each rim was painted red.

"That's blood," she told me. "Blood of my friends and the friends I didn't meet there."

The background was black and brown. In the upper right-hand corner there was a window with bars over it.

"You can't escape. The bars will eat you."

In the left-hand corner there was a door leading into a black room. Sitting on a bench in the dark room was a woman in a blue dress, her blond head buried in her hands.

"They put you in there first," Helen told me. "That's where you wait before they squish you and put you in a can on a shelf."

Then she painted her left hand with red paint and pushed her hand over Harry's can. "He's dead. He's gone. I'll be gone soon, too."

I was so scared I didn't know what to do. I still played with clay and jump ropes.

"But I'll save you, girl kid," she told me. She put her red-painted hand right over her face and held it there. When she pulled it away I could see the handprint.

Red. A bloodred handprint over Helen's face.

"I'll save you."

Whenever Helen got her period she informed my grandpa, not my grandma, that the enemy was "bleeding her, torturing her, stabbing her stomach. Can you help me?"

The enemy did not arrive after Helen returned home from the mental ward.

So besides carrying a number of drugs, the tortured vision of Andrew in a can, and injuries from her leap from a window with no bars that would eat you, she was also carrying my sister, Sunshine.

Sunshine's father, we learned later, in all likelihood, was Barry.

Barry the rapist.

Andrew's murderer.

Grandma was one tiny step from hysterical.

18

Portland, Oregon

"You don't seem as harried today, Stevie," Eileen said. "Last time I saw you . . ." She let her voice wander off. She couldn't bear to say anything further.

"I don't remember being harried. I was working in my garden." She had come over, unannounced, as she had many times since our last "incident" with the chocolate cake, but I hadn't heard her this time, so I didn't have time to hide in a closet and wait till she left. She had arrived at my house this morning at nine o'clock and insisted I go with her to this teahouse with white tablecloths and tiered, sugary, rich desserts.

I hadn't wanted to go. I told her that. She argued, and she pouted. I said no, thank you, again. Then she'd said, "We're going or I'm staying here all day."

The thought of her lounging around my house all day was depressing, but I was steamingly frustrated with myself because I had allowed her to bully me into coming. I had wanted to work in my garden and attach crossbeams to my rose trellises, one for me, one for Grandma, one for Grandpa, before going to my chicken dancing job.

And yet here I was, in some teahouse out in the suburbs. Why didn't I say no to her?

"Oh, yes, the garden. You hardly ate vegetables before the cheater operation. You said they were the devil's brew, I think.

And now you're Miss Organic Carrot. Digging in dirt, slamming things together with your hammer."

She turned and waved, both hands, at the young, blond waitress. "Yoo-hoo." Under her breath she said, "The service here is terrible."

"What's terrible about it?" I asked.

Eileen sighed. "If you had spent more time in the high-end restaurants you would know what respectful service entails. This gal . . ." She rolled her eyes.

"She brought us the tea and teapot on a tray, she's brought you extra lemon for your water, more strawberry lemonade when you drank the first glass, she exchanged some of the pink cakes for carrot when you asked, when you said something was "rotten" about the blackberry tea she brought you lemon tea, she mopped up when you knocked over your cup . . . she's still smiling. What's wrong with the service?"

"It's her attitude. You know, the fat attitude."

"I didn't see it."

"Well, you wouldn't. After your cheater operation . . ." She eyed my outfit. "Hello, Mrs. Tomisson," she murmured.

Before I could respond, the waitress came over. She smiled at Eileen, but I could see the strain. "Young lady, I need you to take away these berry muffins. They're awful. Dry. Stale. We'll have more of the chocolate fudge pieces."

"I don't think I can do that," the waitress said. "We don't have enough and we're still expecting a number of other guests—"

Eileen glared at her, hands clasped over her mound of stomach. "Do it now, young woman, or I will speak to your manager."

"Okay." The waitress tipped her chin up. She kept smiling, to her credit.

"Now."

The waitress turned. Eileen thought she was getting the chocolate fudge pieces. The manager came instead.

"Can I help you?" The manager, a thin, blond woman with bell-shaped hair and a soft face, stood before us.

"I'm fine," I told her, smiling. "Everything is delicious." No way was I going to get caught up in this.

"It's not fine," Eileen snapped. She listed her complaints. The manager nodded. Eileen ended her complaints with a diatribe against the waitress. "Lazy, poorly trained, snobby—"

The manager lifted one finger. "Stop."

"I beg your pardon?" Eileen said, her chins quivering in indignation. She was Eileen Yorkson. No one interrupted her.

"The waitress did all she could to make you happy. We haven't had such a demanding guest in here, and we're unsure how to handle this situation."

"I'm happy with it," I said. "It was delicious."

"I'm not happy with it," Eileen snarled at the woman. "Your waitress should be fired. She obviously has trouble with serving others. She has an attitude problem and talks back to customers."

"The waitress is my daughter," the woman said, so coldly anyone else would have frozen in their seat.

"Then she should be taught manners." Eileen's words came out weak. Even she was taken aback by this change of events.

"She has been taught manners and she has been taught to serve. In fact, she recently returned from a month in Mexico where she built a church. Last summer she was in Guatemala doing the same thing. During the school year she divides her time between sports and volunteering at a food bank and teaching Sunday school. Giving back and serving is what her whole life is about."

Eileen was staring off into space, her face flushed, chins quivering.

"Her manners were impeccable," I said to her, "and I apologize for my . . ."—I paused ever so slightly—"friend. I am so sorry she treated your daughter rudely. I tried to intervene."

I had.

But had I tried hard enough? It's one thing to take it yourself, but what had I done to keep Eileen from the poor waitress? Wasn't continuing to go out to restaurants with Eileen allowing the mean behavior to continue? "I'm truly sorry. I should have done more to control her."

"Do not ever apologize for me," Eileen snapped.

"Get out," the woman said to Eileen.

"What?" Eileen gasped, throwing down her napkin, crumbs flying.

"Get out. My daughter has perfect manners, but I don't. You're obnoxious. You're demanding and rude. Get out." Her voice cracked, her body rigid with anger. "Out. Go. *Go.*"

Eileen's face registered her shock. "No one talks to me like that! Do you know who I am?"

"I don't give a holy shit who you are," the owner hissed at her. "None. Get out of my teahouse and don't come back. I will not have anyone attacking my daughter."

"I'll bet you were a working mother, never at home, and that's why she turned out as she did," Eileen muttered as she struggled to heave her body up. "She thinks she's better than everyone, and so do you."

"I don't think I'm better than anyone," the woman said.

"Your daughter's a brat—"

Well, that did it. The woman picked up not one but two cupcakes and smashed them both, at the same time, into Eileen's face.

"Get out!" she ordered. "Get out!"

I walked around the table, and heaved a fighting, infuriated Eileen up on her feet as she hurled expletives, her face bursting with rage, icing dripping off her chins and diamond necklace. I manhandled her out of the crowded teahouse as she hollered that she would sue the woman from here to hell, she would "close her down," and she would regret the day she ever opened her doors. Did the woman know who she was, dammit? "*Do you, you skinny bitch?*"

It was ugly. It was beyond ugly. Eileen was huffing and puffing and could hardly catch her breath by the time I shoved her in the car, helped lift her feet in, and slammed the door.

I scuttled back in and saw the mother hugging her crying

daughter. I grabbed Eileen's purse, opened up her wallet, and handed $40 to the owner for the food. To the girl I handed the rest of Eileen's money: $500.

"You deserve this and more. I am so sorry for my horrible, terrible, truly rude friend." I reached out and hugged the girl, then turned to her mother. "If she sues you, and she won't, but if she does, call me. I promise you I will testify on your behalf." I scribbled down my name and number.

The owner nodded.

"I'm sorry. I am truly, utterly sorry."

I wanted to kill Eileen.

Eileen's father called me later and asked what happened.

I told him everything.

By the time I was done, he was crying.

"I don't know what to do, Stevie. She's so unhappy. She's angry all the time. She's making all my employees miserable, I've had three of my best people leave in the last three months. Twelve are threatening to quit, most of them women. The morale is horrible. And yet, if I let her go, I think it'll kill her. But my company . . ."

We talked for more than an hour and then I had to garden my way back to mental health. I changed clothes, grabbed a bucket, and started weeding. I threw a few handfuls of weeds into the bucket.

Why am I such a wimp with Eileen? Am I afraid of her anger? Do I feel in some inexplicable way that I deserve her comments? Do I feel guilty about the weight loss when she hasn't experienced the same? Is she a link to my past and I can't let go of the link, as I've had to let go of other people, however unwillingly? Do I stay friends with her for purely altruistic reasons, which is that I am her only friend, and I think she would implode if I walked away? Is that a good-enough reason?

I have lost so much weight and it has been a wondrous miracle, but I'm still trying to find myself, trying to find the new Stevie.

She has been lost for so, *so long,* and I need to find her.

Did this new Stevie want to be friends with Eileen?

I pulled out a mongo-sized weed and tossed it in the bucket.

On Friday night I clucked and danced on a corner dressed as a chicken with scary yellow eyes. I was almost hit by a motorcyclist who called me a "chicken shit." I sweated profusely. An old man with a cane tried to pinch my chicken butt. Mr. Pingle said I did an outstanding job, outstanding! Sales were higher than on any other Friday. "Cluck cluck!"

On Saturday morning and Sunday morning I walked starting at six o'clock. My whole body was tense from my chicken-arm-waving exercises, my chicken dances, and my exuberance with the sign. My whole mind was numb.

Numb.

I was a dancing chicken. I was so utterly humiliated. What if Jake found out? He was out of town for the next ten days, in San Francisco for work, but eventually I would have to tell him.

I figured I could pay off around $4,500 of my medical debt, barring any unforeseen problems, like The Mobster dying, by the end of the year. But was it worth the humiliation?

Probably. It probably was. I hate debt. It makes my nerves jingle and jangle.

Before I went back to being a chicken that night, I gardened. I pulled up weeds that outrageously decided they had permission to be in my vegetable beds in the first place and I laid stone down for my pathway. I had gotten the stone for nothing off a job site I saw on the way home from work. (No, I did not steal it.) The pathway led under the three trellises and then to a corner of my yard. I wanted that corner to have a circular patio where I could make a mosaic design out of cracked china plates I had. Sunshine and I used to play tea party with Grandma's china plates.

I had a late lunch under the canopy of my old, white, flowering cherry tree. I loved that tree, as I loved my two pink cherry trees and my tulip tree. After lunch I planted a few geraniums that my neighbor had given me, then hung up two birdhouses I had bought for $3 at a garage sale on my walk on Thursday.

As I was driving to my chicken job early that evening I briefly wondered if there was anything I could do to make more money.

I could sell the eggs from my ovaries, but I think my eggs are probably too old.

Maybe a kidney? My brain?

I hated that my thoughts kept circling around money, I did.

But money is one of those triggers, I think, for all of us. Except for the insanely greedy, the ones who would sell their own sister if it could bring in an extra hundred, I think most people simply want to survive, not owe anyone money, and go on a nice vacation now and then.

My feelings about money could be summed up by a quote I saw on a napkin years ago: "Money Isn't Everything, But It Calms My Nerves."

That's how I feel.

And my nerves were shot.

Despite our fun, witty phone calls and e-mails, ten days was an awful long time without Jake. An awful long time. I ached for him.

Zena and I saw Crystal dart up to the Chinese food stand again in Pioneer Courthouse Square. The man stepped out of the stand and gave her a hug, then lunch, and she teeter-tottered on her heels back to work.

"It's surprising she's nice enough to anyone to earn a hug," I said. "She's all needles and ticks to me."

"She's the type that shoots poison darts and flings snakes," Zena said.

I handed her some orange slices.

"Okay, here's the question of the day. Plastic surgery."

"You know I had my boobs done."

"Yes, but you had to. You were the size of a rhino, and now you're the size of a flamingo and your boobs were dropped to your waist. I mean, if you ever wanted to have sex, you had to get those girls yanked back up to their proper position in life."

"True." I wasn't offended.

"Women do all sorts of stuff to make themselves younger. They use needles to inject stuff, they go under sharp knives while unconscious, have strange machines suck them out, but for who? *Men.* Men, shallow and testosterone-dripping men with testicles in their craniums. Men often want their wives to do it to turn them on, but don't you see the hypocrisy here?"

I thought about hypocrisy and men, an easy topic. "Yep. I do. What do men do to make themselves younger and sexier, and why don't women insist on it?"

"Bingo, dearie. I have a friend in her early forties who has had all kinds of stuff injected into her face. She got her butt lifted, she's had liposuction, a boob job, all for her husband, who constantly criticizes her. He's in his fifties. He's almost bald except for a rim of gray. He has a gut and a face like a squished bulldog, and there he is criticizing his wife."

"And she takes it."

"I think she takes it because after seven years she's going to divorce the guy and take the house in Tuscany. She loves Italy. Says the wine is better there. I was there when he came home from work and told her she should get her poofy lips done again because they were, in his words, 'flat and tight.'"

"What did you say?"

"I told him that as soon as he dyed his gray hair brown so he didn't look so, so old and Grandpa-ish, and grew more of it so that when he was going down on my friend she wouldn't have to be disgusted by the sight of his bald head rooting about, and as soon as he got rid of that gross gut that would squish my friend in bed and firmed up his flubby bottom, then he could suggest Botox for his wife's lips."

I choked on a slice of pepperoni, then I laughed. "What did he say?"

"Let's put it this way: I wasn't invited to dinner, but my friend called me later that night and we laughed so hard we sounded like hyenas."

Polly was no longer scratching on death's door from not eating, but she was not feeling well. She'd had a bad run of it the first weeks at the clinic, as usual. She did not want to eat, she did not want to go to counseling, she did not want to talk in group with "I Feel" statements, she did not want to talk to her psychotherapist or go to lectures on nutrition or drink supplements or weigh in, and she did not want to do Tray Watch, where a nurse sat with her until she ate every bite even if it took three hours.

She did not want to do family therapy, and she forbid Herbert from coming anywhere near the place. She called him herself and told him. I was there for the call. "Dad, don't come anywhere near this place. I do not need you to come and tell me what a disappointment I am, how craziness doesn't come from your side of the family, it's from Mom's. I don't need a lecture or criticisms, and I don't want to hear any more about your anti-gay senate campaign and how I might have hurt your reelection chances and damaged the Barrett family name, you narcissistic moron." Then she grabbed a bag for her face.

She told me and Lance as we sat with her in a courtyard garden, the trees rustling above, birds tweeting, "I'm still in my rebellion and denial stage."

"How's it going?" I asked her. Lance started knitting faster. He had brought a blow-up with him named Lucy Desiree so Polly could again see "the curves that real women should have."

"How's it going?" Polly asked, pushing her curls back. "Oh, splendidly. I'm enjoying all these doctors and nurses and counselors perpetually bugging me to address my issues. Looking at their food makes me feel sick, I can't indulge my food rituals, and I feel as if it's getting stuck in my throat. I shake, I'm cold, I seem to be growing fur on parts of my body, and I'm weak but want to run. It's been so pleasant, thanks for asking." She took a bag out of her sweater and breathed into it.

Polly's weight, at five foot seven, same height as me, was about 100 pounds. She was skeletal, deathly, sickly.

It wasn't pretty. It hurt me to see what she'd done to herself.

I held her hand. Lance knitted faster. Lucy Desiree grinned maniacally.

"Remember when I was younger and I had to eat all my food

in tiny bites? Or six peas only, no more? I pushed my food around my plate, then had to divide it up in equal parts. I used to think about food all the time. Certain foods I would not eat. I would count calories obsessively, usually when I was on one of my long runs. And then I'd come home and have to deal with Dad." Her eyes focused on the tangled branches of a tree. "He wanted me to be perfect. When I started getting breasts I remember he seemed so angry at me. He told me he didn't want a 'slut' for a daughter and yelled at Mom to get me a tight bra and 'hide those things.'"

"He told me I was a half-assed athlete and could do better," Lance said.

"He told me I was a disgrace to the Barrett family," I said.

Lance stopped knitting and pulled Lucy Desiree into his lap. She grinned maniacally at us. "Hey, ladies! Can we talk about my Lance's Lucky Ladies Hard Rock Party to launch my business? If I think about Dad for too long I'll get cramps. Let's go as triplet punks! We'll all dress exactly the same—what do you say? I'll get us black wigs and leather and boots and we'll put on our makeup together. I'll even dress up one of my dolls so she's our twin. We'd actually be quadruplets then, wouldn't we?" He pondered this.

"Or we could each hold a doll and then we'd be sextuplets," Polly said. "Sextuplet hard rockers. That'd be a first."

Lance drew in his breath. "That's an awesome idea, Polly. Awesome." He shook his head. She was so brilliant! "And my ladies are going to be all around at the party. I've got three hundred people who have already said they're coming. The band— oh, man, the band! They're playing eighties music only. AC/DC, Def Leppard, Blondie, Queen, Kool and the Gang, and some love songs from Air Supply. We gotta have them. Slow dances, you know, romantic. I won't be dancing romantically, though." He bent his head, sighing.

"Maybe you will, Lance," I said, hope in my voice.

"Oh, no. Couldn't do that. Don't know what to say, how to dance, no—but we're gonna have those little white lights, and I called the caterer. Only steak, and salad for the vegetarian people. Can't understand people who don't eat meat. I like to sink my teeth into a cow sometimes. Lambs are yummy, too, right on the tongue. And I got five giant guitar cakes coming."

"What about the invitations?" Polly asked. "When are your invitations with the electric guitar and the skull going out?"

"Soon. I talked to Trixie. She says they're all going out right away." He started laughing. "We thought of this funny thing. When people open the invitations for the Hard Rock Party, they're going to get a lapful of these tiny naked ladies in pink and purple glitter to advertise my dolls, plus the pop-up doll in the middle. Isn't that, well, genius?"

"Genius," I said. It was hilarious.

"And then we also got this tiny recorder in each card, and it's going to play that song 'Big Balls' by AC/DC. You know the lyrics, 'I've got big balls, she's got big balls. We all have big balls.' People are gonna dig it."

"I love it." Polly laughed.

"I do, too. I can't wait to come," I said. "We'll need to celebrate after the anniversary party."

"No, we'll need valium sandwiches," Polly said.

"So you gave Trixie the photographs of Janet and Herbert, and she knows to put their wedding picture on the front, that it's to be a formal white color with gold engraving around the edges and on the inside there's to be the photo of them now with the party date and time and all that?" I asked.

"Yes, the photo where Mom is choking back tears, or it looks that way," Polly said. "She's wearing that pink blouse buttoned to her neck and clearly can't stand Dad's hand on her waist and Dad looks like the arrogant shit that he is."

"That's the one. Trixie'll do it. She's smart." Lance rubbed his head. "I think she's pretty smart. . . . She got a little confused about a couple of things . . . flipped around some information, addresses . . . but I think we've got it now—yeah, I think we do. Yep."

"Are you sure?" I eyed him as two birds noisily flew back to the tree branches above us.

"Yeah, you bet, sure, all wrapped up." He appeared worried,

then it vanished and he sat forward and grasped our hands. "We're gonna get through the anniversary party torture on Friday night, and on Saturday night, we're gonna rock out, the three of us!"

"Rock out," Polly said. She leaned over and kissed Lucy Desiree on the mouth. Lance was clearly touched. Lucy Desiree smiled maniacally.

I had sanded and primed the chair and painted it blue and now it sat there, waiting for me.

I remembered Herbert's rant against Aunt Janet and her college classes. How he was going to cut her "allowance" and "forbid" her to go to school in the future if her "domestic responsibilities" were not met.

I thought of her going to school on that beautiful campus in Portland. I thought of her in class, participating in a discussion, and chasing her dream that she had finally dared to chase. I thought of learning and growing and how your mind opens up in school, whether you're studying literature or history or politics, and how your classmates and their diverse backgrounds and opinions make you think, and think hard, about the world, and life, and yourself, and where you are and want to be.

I painted until one o'clock in the morning. I couldn't stop.

I called it my Learning Tree Chair. The legs became the roots, the seat the trunk, the back of the chair—which was a full wood back—an old oak tree with books hung from the branches. The titles of the books were *Shakespeare, World War II, Spanish, Central America, The Revolutionary War, Feminism, The Sixties, Jerusalem, The Depression, Current Events.* I had sawed off another piece of wood in the shape of an apple, attached it to the top, and painted the word *FREEDOM* in black.

Because that's what Aunt Janet was getting, freedom.

Freedom from the life she had led to this point.

She had dared, she had insisted on change, she had—on her own—decided to be more.

More than she had been, more than her fears, more than the forces that held her back.

She was more.

I crossed my legs and stared at that chair, the light of the moon tunneling on in.

Who knew that the woman I had always seen as meek, weak, and scared would motivate me to be more, too?

But it was the truth. Aunt Janet had motivated me to be more of me.

More of Stevie.

19

Ashville, Oregon

For some reason, a bunch of priggish white executives came to town and decided that Ashville needed chain stores.

They had to go to the mayor, Grandma, and town council with their idea. The men wore their fancy-pants suits, hair slicked back, shiny shoes. They smiled but, as I told Grandpa, leaning across Helen on the bench that evening, "I think they're human snakes with teeth."

"I think so, too, honey. Now you listen to me. If your gut level about a man is that he's a snake, believe it. Don't you try to convince yourself he's not. Listen to your gut. It's not gonna lie to you."

"Snakes rakes," Helen said, fiddling with the wildflowers she'd stuck in her dress. "Rake the snakes. Bake the snakes. Put the snakes in tiny cakes and burn them up to tiny stumps."

So the snakes began their presentation with their shiny pictures and their cheesy smiles and their ingratiating airs, with most of the town watching.

"You need more shopping—"

"Hell, no, we don't," Shade Diamond said, standing. "My wife shops enough. We got all we need right here. We got Chris and his family running the hardware store. Mabel and Sister and Dot run the clothing stores. We got two families running grocery stores, which have been in business since my great-granddad got here. What do we need more shopping for?"

"We have better shopping, a wider selection. You only need to go to one place—"

"Excuse me," Katy Wy said. "You say that you got better shopping than my store?"

"We know what we're doing. We've made studies of towns and people, we know the numbers, we know how these things work, and you'll be glad that we're here." Mr. Snake smiled. His co-snakes smiled. "You haven't experienced this type of shopping, so you don't know what you're missing. You don't know how great this is going to be!" He fisted his hand and raised it in the air.

There was silence and then, as if the entire town was thinking together, they all raised one fist in the air and hollered.

It about scared the pants off Mr. Snake and crew, but then he reddened and started to reargue his points. He was frustrated with us country bumpkins.

"You need the money here, the taxes, the income."

Grandma nodded at Devon Wilts. He recited, in detail, how Ashville was quite on top of things financially. He knew all the info down to the cents, and he regaled us with those numbers and the amount in our savings.

"Don't you get it?" the Snake said, gritting his teeth, his hair thick with goo. "Your town is gonna go belly up without us. You have an antiquated system of doing business."

Grandma nodded at Evie Webster.

"Nothing antiquated about it," Evie said. "We bring in the modern and new when needed, and we keep the traditions and the values that are important. Sprawling, ugly stores are not something we value, young man." She then detailed Ashville's comprehensive business plan.

"We don't have to follow these laws. We're trying to be nice," the Snake snarled.

Grandma nodded at Connie Santiago.

"Oh, yes, you do have to follow the laws," Connie Santiago

said, then launched into said laws and repeated the ones that applied, verbatim, by number, with all the tricky language.

"Hey! People, we don't want to get nasty here. We don't want a fight," Snake said.

"Then don't pick one," Cason Phillips cracked out. "If you do, you'll lose. Simple. Now get your heads out of your asses and go home. We've got the town picnic to talk about."

Helen was examining a piece of silky purple material she'd been hauling around with her for about a week but when Mr. Snake raised his voice at Grandma and said, "Mayor, this is not the end of this issue," his flushy face flushed, Helen's head snapped right up. "I don't know what kind of town you're running, I don't know who you think you are to stand in our way—"

"What?" Helen hissed again. "What?"

I knew she was talking to the voices.

"Oh, shut up," she hissed. "You can't tell me what to do. I'm taking care of this. *That's my momma.*" She got up and quick as a wink was in the aisle. She marched halfway up and then shouted, "You! Hey, you!"

The snakes turned around and stared. Helen must have made quite a picture. She was wearing a pair of blue fairy wings and a black coat, with her polar bear hat on her head. As usual, she had on her boots and chicken wire to stop the voices from being so noisy. "You! You asshole! *Asshole.*"

"Excuse me!" Snake said. "Do not call me an asshole."

"I have to!" Helen said. "Command Center told me to do it. You pipe on down. That's my momma." She pointed at Grandma. "And you are a Kaboomerat. That's it. A Kaboomerat. A rat."

Mr. Snake turned to Grandma and raised an eyebrow. "A problem child?" he said, smirking.

Oh, how that pissed people off, especially members of The Family.

"She's not a problem!"

"You're the problem!"

"Don't you dare speak to Helen or Glory with that sneer in your tone—"

I stood up before I even knew what I was doing and said, "Shut up, snake faces!"

My grandpa was up and standing behind Helen in a flash, but Helen was not to be swayed. As you know, she had an innate talent for rhyming, and so she made up a song, singing it to the tune of "I Could Have Danced All Night" from *My Fair Lady*. I don't remember all the words, of course, but I do remember a few lines.

"You're a snake, you freak, you're a snake." Her voice deepened, then climbed, the notes reaching each corner of that building as she threw her arms out. "Slimy and sneaky, poked with a rake." The rest of the song was about the size of his balls (small), the size of his dick (a thumb tack), and the size of his nose (gargantuan). She made mention of a flopping bottom, ears like a donkey, sloping shoulders. Her chorus was, "You're a sly one, wet and slick. We don't trust you, tiny nipples." Her notes soared and dipped and swirled around, and if you didn't listen to the words, you would think you were at a Broadway show listening to a Broadway star, which you were.

At the end she hit a high C and ripped open her coat, showing off a fluffy pink negligee over her rainbow pajamas. She carried that long note until the rafters shook.

It was a stunning performance—funny and theatrical, with words perfectly rhymed, and right on target.

There was a standing ovation, and the applause was deafening. She tossed that silky purple material into the audience and bowed.

The Snake and his cohort snakes hardly knew what to do.

When it was over, Grandma said, "Gentlemen, the answer is no." She brought her gavel down again. "Get out."

They started to argue. Stupid people.

Then Grandpa Thomas got in trouble again, darn it. He shot off that darn gun. Three bullets, one for each fancy-pants slicker, straight at the ceiling.

The snakes slithered right on out, lickety-split.

Later the snakes complained to the sheriff.

But, funny enough, when the sheriff went to talk to the people at the meeting, no one saw Grandpa Thomas shooting his gun off. Not one. Not even the sheriff's wife, who was there that night.

"Case closed, boys," the sheriff said. "Now you head on out of town. Your business is finished here."

But poor Grandpa Thomas.

He was suspended for two town council meetings, and he so enjoyed them.

The harmonica songs he played, right outside the doors, were more woeful than ever.

Grandma made him a chocolate banana pie. His favorite.

Helen had been complaining about feeling dizzy in the morning, and then she started throwing up on her bedspread.

"I'm being poisoned!" she hissed at me. "Poisoned! I think it's the CIA!"

"It's not the CIA," I told her, patting her shoulder with one hand, holding my nose with the other. I thought I was going to be sick, too.

Every morning Grandma washed that pink flowered bedspread. By the end of the week, she gave up, threw it out, and bought two more. Helen refused to get up and run to the toilet to vomit unless someone was in the room with her because she did not want to be in the bathroom alone in case Barry came.

"I'm being poisoned by the CIA!" Helen told us, sitting on the toilet later, not letting me or Grandma move an inch as she did her business. "But don't put me in a can when I die." She pointed at both of us, then her lips trembled, and her voice shook. "Do you think Tonya's in a can yet?"

There were many conversations between Grandma and Grandpa that I needed to hear around that time, because Helen had got a baby in her stomach when she was at the mental ward even though she had no husband. I spent a lot of time hiding near the stairs late at night.

"We have a mentally ill daughter who was raped in a mental ward and now she's pregnant. . . ."

"I don't know what to do about the baby, I'm so worried. . . ."

"The baby may already be damaged from the drugs she was on. . . ."

"Can we raise another child? Can we even handle a baby here with Helen?"

"Remember when she was pregnant with Stevie? She thought she had Punk in her stomach."

"The baby may be mentally ill, too. . . ."

"Stevie's not, honey."

"Stevie's not now. But Helen seemed pretty normal up until her last couple of years of high school. . . . She did get awfully depressed now and then, she complained about a buzzing in her ears, she didn't want the TV on, she had some grandiose plans, but she did okay."

I put my hands to my face. What were they talking about? Would I end up like Helen? Did I have the fighting-with-voices-disease, too? Would I end up wearing tin foil and getting the bugs? Would I end up in a corner crying? I felt my whole body go cold with panic and dread.

I saw Grandpa shaking his head, then tears coursed down his cheeks. "But she's almost three months along. My poor girl." He slammed his fist three times into his open palm, his face twisted in grief and anger, and my grandma linked her arms around his neck.

Later, as an adult, I grew to understand him better. He loved his girls. Loved his wife, loved his grandchildren. And he had not been able to protect Helen. In fact, he probably felt as if he'd handed his daughter over on a platter to a rapist. He was not to blame, but he never would have stopped blaming himself.

Never.

That guilt sat on my grandpa's back like a serpent, I'm sure of it.

I didn't speak for days.

Grandma and Grandpa grew more worried, constantly asking me what was wrong.

Finally, in the living room of the Schoolhouse House, which

was where the students used to study (I swear I still smelled that chalk), with the sun shining through the stained glass, I told them.

"I'm afraid I'm going to become Helen."

They didn't understand what I meant at first, but then their faces cleared and raw pain creased every line.

"Am I going to have a Command Center when I'm older? A Punk? Am I going to hear voices and wear weird clothes and throw things?" I was distraught, almost beside myself.

Grandma and Grandpa comforted me, told me that I wouldn't. "Honey, you don't have the same thing. . . ."

"But I might get it!" I insisted. "I heard you talking! It might come out when I'm in high school! Helen was in her twenties!"

"Sweetie, you don't have it. . . . You won't be like your mother . . . I'm sure of it. . . . We thought something was off when Helen was a little girl, didn't we, Glory? She was different at your age, way too imaginative, talked to imaginary friends. . . . She'd be happy one day, sad the next. . . ."

They tried to reassure me.

But I was smart. I could spell schizophrenia, and I could read their loving, frightened eyes. I saw the desperate hope that what I was suggesting wasn't true, but I knew that there was at least a possibility that I could end up having the same problems as Helen.

That overriding fear, the fear of becoming Helen, chased me down my entire childhood and into my twenties. I read about it, I learned about it, and it shook me to my core. The fear of a collapsing mind, the fear of a Command Center and a Punk, were a huge part of my eating problem.

And the primal, all-encompassing fear of living in a mental ward as Helen had and facing nightmares of my inner mind and nightmares on two feet stalked me like a phantom stalks his victim for decades.

Helen was the one who brought the baby to Grandpa's attention weeks later as she was sitting on the toilet. Her fear of being alone in the bathroom continued. Sometimes she refused to go to the bathroom unless Grandpa was home. She'd started peeing outside rather than be in the bathroom without him. Even in her delusions, she knew that Grandpa would protect her at all costs.

"The enemy didn't come to bleed me," she told him. "Did you see that? There's no blood. And there's a mystery here." She pointed to her stomach and stood up, straddling the toilet. "I think they put something in me. It's right there. It's moving."

She bent down to see herself and poked her stomach with her pointer finger.

"What. Is. That?"

She glared at Grandpa.

"What the hell is *that?*"

Grandma and Grandpa took Helen to see Dr. Lindy Woods, an OB-GYN in the city. Lindy was a cousin on Grandpa's side and used to hang out with Helen in high school.

Helen wore her hair in six braids, lay down in the backseat of the car, and made up poems. Most of her words rhymed with the F word. She was mad at Punk, one of the loudest voices in her head, because he was "so bossy, so rude. Always bugging me, he's crude. Punk the funk, soon I'll give you a deep dunk."

I was dropped off at the house of my best friend, Lornie Rose, but later, when we were back home, I heard Grandma talking on the phone to my great-aunt Cinnamon, who was an attorney, when she thought I was out in the vegetable garden pulling carrots and onions and squash.

"We took Helen to the clinic to see Lindy. She was fine for a while, she sat straight up in Lindy's office, hands clasped tight in her lap, but when Lindy and another doctor and a nurse entered in white coats, she started screaming, backed right into a corner and covered her head with her hands. She was terrified, absolutely terrified. Then she started yelling, 'I'm not going back there! You won't put me in a can! I don't like that dark room, I don't like the hall. He's bad, he's bad! Help me, Dad! Help me, Dad!'

"She grabbed Albert and would not let him go, her arms and one leg wrapped around him. So I pushed Lindy and the others out and explained how Helen was scared of people in white coats because of her experience at the mental wards. So Lindy, I swear I thought she was going to cry, she changed into a University of Oregon sweatshirt and jeans and then she sat down and talked to Helen, as they did in high school, and eventually Helen got out of Albert's lap and she let Lindy put her hands on her stomach. I think that somewhere in her mind, Helen recognized Lindy. She said, 'I remember you because of lemonade and horses.' They used to ride our horses and then drink lemonade."
I heard Grandma's voice crackle, then she sniffled.

"Anyhow, Helen got on the table but told Lindy she wasn't going to allow them to put any 'tracers' in her, and Lindy said, 'We never put tracers in anyone. We're the good people.' And Helen said that the enemy had put something in there, and she knew because they weren't 'bleeding her anymore.'

"Lindy told her that there was a baby in her stomach and . . ." Grandma choked on her tears. "And Helen sat up straight and said, 'There is no baby in my stomach. I don't have a husband.' And Lindy said, 'Yes, there is, honey. There's a baby in there. Do you remember how it got there?' And, Helen did, she must have, because her eyes got wide, and I knew she wasn't with us anymore—she was somewhere else—and her whole face crumpled up and she pulled her knees up and started crying, keening back and forth, then she pulled at her hair, and fiddled with her toes, and kept crying, these mewing, sobbing sounds, and yelled for Albert to help her, help her."
Grandma slumped onto the floor, still holding the phone.

"It about destroyed Albert. Anyhow, when we finally got Helen calm, Lindy asked her if she wanted the baby, and said if Helen didn't want the baby that Lindy could take it out. Helen completely lost it. She started shrieking, high pitched—it was like listening to an animal. She wrapped her arms around her stomach and tried to kick Lindy. 'You won't take it. I won't let you take it. You get away from me. You aren't going to hurt it, it's mine!' Helen knew. Somewhere in the back of her mind she understood she was pregnant, she had a baby, and she wanted to protect it, above all."

I thought of that baby in Helen's stomach. Would we look alike? Was it a girl? Was it a boy? How did it get in there?

"So we're keeping the baby. Lindy talked to her about eating well and resting, once Helen wasn't hysterical, but then she started rhyming words again, and asked Lindy if she wanted to hear her poem. Lindy said yes, and Helen said, 'Babies, babies, babies. How do they jump in your stomach? You must be a bad girl. Or get them from throw up.'"

Grandma rubbed her forehead. "Lindy started to cry—she and Helen were such wonderful friends—but Helen didn't notice. She said another poem. It was about a black room. 'Black room, slimy room, hurt room. Stick in your butt, stick in your front. Always ouch, always mad, I tried to kill that hairy crab,' and then she started singing that song, 'When You Wish Upon a Star' from *Pinocchio,* and Lindy cried again. Before we left, Helen actually let Lindy hug her, and said, 'I like lemonade and horses.'"

Grandma listened on the phone for a minute. "How do I feel about another baby? I don't know how we're going to do this. But what else can I do? She refused the abortion. The baby is coming, so we'll deal with it." She paused. "I love all of our grandchildren, and having Stevie live with us has been a gift from the second she came into our lives. We'll hope this baby has the personality and cheerfulness of our Stevie. I love that child to distraction, and so does Albert. Without Stevie we would never have been able to handle all this grief with Helen, never. Stevie has saved our lives. She's an angel, right from God to us."

I went to sleep that night, after Grandma and Grandpa kissed me good night, then kissed each other, and the last thing I heard were Grandma's words in my head. "I love that child to distraction, and so does Albert. . . . She's an angel, right from God to us."

I believe, I truly do, that the love of my grandparents is what saved my life.

Even after they were gone.

Grandma and Grandpa watched Helen very carefully.

And who knew why—maybe it was hormones or maybe Helen was hanging on to a shred of sanity, or maybe God stepped in and answered Grandma's incessant prayers to Him, Jesus, Mary, Joseph, the Apostle Paul, and the Prophets—but Helen did eat, she did rest. There were incidences, but the voices in Helen's head seemed to grow dimmer. They didn't tell her to stand in the middle of the street and flap her arms or climb a tree and jump from a branch or pick at her fingernails till they bled. They didn't tell her quite so loud that the CIA was after her.

Until the seventh month. That's when things fell apart. That's when she tried to get Sunshine out of her body. All by herself.

I loved first grade, although I did get some teasing about Helen at first. Some kids called her a "crazy lady," and one girl asked why she shouted at lampposts and why she wore a cape, but I could deal with that. Plus, a bunch of cousins and kids of Grandpa's employees were in my class, and they told the kids teasing me to "shut up or lose a tooth" or "Tease Stevie and I'm going to smash your nose inside out," and that took care of things, even when Helen danced into my classroom wearing antennas on her head and a set of black spider legs from my last year's Halloween costume. Grandma rushed in and escorted her out pretty quick.

First grade was all day, not like kindergarten, which meant I was out of the house for hours. My teacher, Mrs. Zeebach, had been a student of Grandma's and she had me reading novels and doing advanced math worksheets, but the best thing was that I won the school's art competition in the fall and in the spring with my work. When my name was announced, the kids in my class stood up and cheered because that meant I had beat the sixth graders, too. I won $5 and chocolates. I shared all the chocolates with my classmates.

Grandma and Helen usually met me at the end of the drive-way where the school bus stopped.

One afternoon Helen was waiting for me with two pencils behind her ears. She was carrying a lunch box. "Stevie Stevie. A beehive girl. You won't give a monster a swirl. Buzz buzz buzz, beehive girl, you don't make me want to hurl."

She poked me in my stomach, then she poked her own stomach. "I got a beehive in here. It's moving. I can feel them. I think they're going to sting me so I'm going to have to smother them." Then she softly hit her stomach, got all teary-eyed, and said, "Barry's bad, Barry's scary, Tonya's in a can, not one that you can carry."

On a sunny Friday, though, Grandma's friend Mrs. Wong came and got me before school was out. It was Song and Music Day, where we spent an hour in front of the piano that Mrs. Zee-bach played. It had been my turn to sit next to her on the piano bench, which was the first good thing. Another good thing that happened: We had found Herschel, our hamster, who had myste-riously escaped during the night two days ago. Phuc Do found him behind the bookshelves and caught him, only dropping him once on his head when he wriggled out of his hands.

Right after we got back from Mr. Wright's PE class, I heard the sirens.

I later learned that Helen had gotten ahold of a knife and tried to take the baby out of her own stomach. "The bees are all cooked," she'd told Grandma. "All cooked. I tried to take them out so they wouldn't get burned."

That night I studied the stain of blood on the carpet of Helen's room.

I don't know why I did it—maybe it was simply years of liv-ing with someone sick and how it makes you see almost every-thing differently from anyone else, how it makes you feel crazy, too, and your world shakes and sputters, and reality is topsy-turvy and confused—but I got my paints out.

I drew petals in purple, blue, and green around the circular red stain.

I made a flower out of the blood, complete with a long stem. That night I kept thinking about flower blood.

And I kept thinking about how my own mother used a knife on herself to get her baby out of her stomach.

I wondered if it was ever possible to run out of tears.

I sure hadn't.

When the sun came up, I was still up, too, and when Grandma and Grandpa saw the blood flower, I thought I was going to get in trouble, but I didn't. The three of us stood there, and then Grandpa pulled me into his strong arms for a long hug and Grandma kissed my forehead.

Helen came home about three weeks later from a special hospital in Seattle. She was, miraculously, still pregnant. But her fear of chairs had grown exponentially.

"I am not going to sit in a chair again," she told Grandma when she waddled in the door, a plain green dress over her skinny but pregnant frame, her blond hair in a ponytail. "No. I didn't like that. The chair wouldn't let go of me. It hurt me."

"Sugar, we have different chairs here," Grandma said, wiping her hands on her flowered apron. "These chairs are comfortable and friendly."

Helen eyed her suspiciously. "I think you're from the other side."

"No, sugar, I'm on your side. I'm always on your side. And these chairs are nice chairs. They won't hurt you."

"Have you gone to the CIA?" she asked Grandpa.

Grandpa shook his head and put his cowboy hat on the coatrack. "No, baby, I haven't. I'm with you. I'm on your side, and you can sit in this chair. Your mother made your favorite dinner again, oatmeal with cinnamon, no white sugar."

"I don't eat white sugar because of the noise, and I'm not going to sit in that chair because of the foobadurang."

"Sweetie, how about this chair?" Grandma pointed to a big, comfy red chair in the living room. "There's no foobadurang."

Helen stared at that chair. She went over and peered underneath it, then she sniffed it. "There's no ropes here."

"No, no ropes. There are no ropes here," Grandma said. Helen didn't notice Grandma's voice wavering. She didn't notice Grandpa's exhausted, shattered expression.

I did. I held Grandpa's hand.

The way I understood it later is that Helen had had to be held down sometimes in a chair. They didn't want to tie her to a bed because she clearly already had nightmares about beds. But she also kept trying to hurt the baby with her fists. Helen had told the doctors the bees were "ready to come out and knocking on their door."

"I am not going to sit in a chair with ropes or octopus tentacles again. Are there octopus tentacles on this red chair?"

"No, sweetie. Not at all," Grandpa said.

"Where are the tentacles?"

"They're not here. We don't have tentacles on the farm. We only have chickens and goats and pigs and horses. That's it. Remember?"

Helen nodded. "All right. I remember. We don't have octopus here. I can sit in this red heart chair if you check it each day for tentacles and ropes."

"I'll do it now, sweetie," Grandpa said.

I watched him examine that chair. He even turned it upside down. "I'm checking ... still checking ... almost done checking, Helen. Okay, sweetie. It's safe."

Helen nodded. "Are you sure?"

Grandpa checked the chair one more time, every inch of it, his hands running over the whole thing. Do you see how family members in the house can get caught up in someone else's mental illness? How you start talking the language of a schizophrenic? Try doing that at seven years old. I am living proof: It knocks something sane right out of you.

"Yes. We're safe."

"Okay. I have to get the devil's water out of me now. Come and watch," she told my grandpa. "I don't want Barry to come in."

So Grandpa watched his daughter pee, never taking his eyes from hers, so Barry wouldn't come and get her, and then we had dinner. He moved the red chair to the kitchen table. That seat wasn't as high as the others, so Helen's face was only a little bit above the table, but she sat down at each breakfast and dinner with us, after Grandpa checked the chair.

The other chairs in our house did not fare well. Periodically, and without warning, she would throw the kitchen chairs, the chair by Grandpa's desk, a small stool that Grandma used for gardening, the Adirondack chairs on the deck, and the two antique chairs by the small table near the front door. The throwing was unpredictable.

"This one has to die," she would say, lifting it up. Helen was not a big person at all, but in her demented rages she seemed to become stronger.

"This one is trying to hold me down."

"This one won't shut up. Shut up, chair! I'm not going to let you hit me with your wood. Quit screaming at me."

She broke a couple chairs, scratched a bunch up, and chipped wood off others.

She was distracted only by her pastel crayons or paints.

"Draw a picture of that chair, Helen," Grandma told her one time as she spun my wooden kid's chair above her head. "Then I'll be able to see what you see."

"No! I'm not going to draw today because of the kicking of the bees."

"I'd love a picture by you."

"No!"

"You can get back at the chair by drawing it," Grandma cajoled. "You can show it who's boss, that Helen's in charge."

"I'm only going to draw a bad picture," Helen replied, slamming the chair down. "A bad chair. A chair with arms and handcuffs and chains and some snakes and not you, Command Center."

"Well, that will be very creative. Not boring at all. I always love your pictures."

"Everybody does, because then they can see the mess." Helen kicked the chair, then pushed her black top hat back on her head. She had wrapped foil around her neck and tied it in a big bow. "They can see the mess in my brain."

"You draw the mess well. You're an artist."

"I'm telling the truth about chairs, so the truth isn't invisible anymore." She stuck her lower lip out, then scratched her arms. "Shut up, Punk! I'm not drawing for you!"

"It's good we have you to tell the truth, honey."

Helen grunted, but she took the pastels and the big canvas Grandma had been holding.

"You sit here, girl kid." She pointed to a chair. I sat down. She nodded at me, then adjusted the tin foil tie.

Out of the swirls and curls and tiny, twisting, spiraling crayon marks came a chair. It was my wooden chair, although it had morphed into a chair in three different colors of red, a chain wrapped around the back, handcuffs lying on the seat, and two detached arms on the floor. I thought of the blood flower upstairs in that room when I saw those arms and had to run outside and sit in the corn by myself for a while.

Helen morphed, twisted, elongated, shortened, stretched, and zigzagged each chair she drew. The background was one of two things: She drew weather, thunder and lightning, rolling clouds, or a sunny day that somehow, in some sneaky way, foretold something ominous. Or her backgrounds were full of squiggles. Long, short, fat, thin, all mixed together forming a moving, fluid, disturbing background.

The background of those pictures was a hint of what was going on in Helen's mind. The hint was enough to scare us all to pieces.

Helen was relatively calm for a few weeks. We even talked about the baby.

"There's something in there," she whispered to me while we walked around the farm one morning, feeding the horses, petting the cats, and watching the corn sway. She pointed at her stomach.

"I know," I whispered. "It's a baby."

She nodded at me, quite serious. "Someone tried to take it

out before it was baked. It's not baked yet. When it is, it's coming out."

I didn't know what to say.

"It's a baby. It's crying right now."

"Why is it crying?"

"It's crying because it's lonely and scared and its head is filled with mean people fighting and telling it what to do. Bad things."

"That's sad." I wanted to cry for the baby.

"Yes, it is. It's a baby and a few bees." She sighed, then squished her yellow floppy hat down on her head. She was wearing two bathing suits over a ski outfit. It was warm out.

I did what Grandma did then. I changed the subject. "I'm glad you're home, Momma. I like your hair."

She raised her eyebrows, confused. "You do?"

"Yes, it's pretty." It was pretty. Helen was pretty. If she wasn't wearing a confused, angry, demented, drugged-out, or fizzy expression, and if you could ignore whatever weird outfit she was wearing, you would say that Helen was gorgeous. She had high cheekbones and full lips and a small nose.

"Hmmm . . ." She stopped and stared at me. "You're a girl kid that's mine, aren't you?"

"Yes, I am. I'm your daughter." My voice caught. I knew she had a sickness in her head, I got it. Grandma and Grandpa always answered all my questions about that, but it still hurt. I was only seven, and I played hopscotch and four-square.

"You like my hair?"

I nodded again. "It reminds me of gold."

"Your hair is black and you have a dent in your cheek." She touched it, then stroked my hair. "Pretty."

That night Helen cut off her hair and gave it to me in a Baggie. "I have a present for you," she said. Then she kicked a chair and said, "Command Center says you're an octopus in disguise!"

I burst into tears.

20

Portland, Oregon

Saturday morning I was a totally hungover chicken from my previous night's work. Saturday evening Mr. Pingle greeted me with tremendous excitement, his high-pitched exuberance cutting right through the fog of my chicken hangover like a sumo wrestler grabbing onto my cranium. I held my head tightly.

"Cluckers!" he declared. "You're already in chicken mode, I can tell! Already thinking as a chicken!" He clucked at me, louder and louder, and I pressed my hands to my head tighter and tighter. "You, I think," he told me proudly, quietly, so as not to offend any other employee there, "are the best chicken we've had. There's something so authentic about you! So authentic!"

He pushed his glasses up on his nose and grinned at me.

"Thank you, Mr. Pingle. I appreciate that." I stomped my chicken feet.

"Here ya go, Stevie." He held out the chicken outfit. I closed my eyes. "I love it, your concentration! I'll be quiet so you can situate yourself, grow into your role, think as a chicken thinks."

He helped me into the chicken outfit, the big red feet, the feathered body, the chicken head, and, to his credit, he didn't speak.

When I was all chickened out I grabbed the sign he held out to me—CHICKEN DINNERS ONLY $8.99!—and headed out to the street. I danced, I jived, I waved, people honked. I jumped off the sidewalk to avoid being hit by a swerving pickup, ran away from a group of drunk teenagers who tried to take off my head, and tripped over a stroller. The mother hit me with her purse.

At the end of my shift, I went home and flopped into bed, visions of chicken feet and mommies with feathers hitting me with purses dancing through my head.

The Atherton case dragged on, as did the depositions of anyone having anything remotely to do with Danny's operation, the protocol for these operations, safety guidelines, oversight, the doctor in charge of the unit, president of the hospital, and so on.

We learned later that Mrs. Atherton was being sent to a clinic for a week for exhaustion. She had been hospitalized two nights before when she'd collapsed. I pictured her life, caring for Danny round the clock, not sleeping, desperate in those dark night hours, praying for a miracle, the miracle unresponsive. I thought of the medicines she had to administer, the IV that needed changing, and the constant threat that her dear son, the one who loved dragon stories and baseball and music, would die in their dining room, in his hospital bed, and on the other end of the spectrum, her horrified fear that this would be his life forever. Her grief and her anger and the stress that this entire lawsuit must be taking on both of them had me glued to my chair, staring into space and hurting for her.

I thought of the father, working his plumber job. He had recently been hired to work at a hardware store, so he was doing that, too.

I thought of the three other young boys and how their lives had been affected by this tragedy, and again I wondered how a country that could spend hundreds of billions of dollars on wars and war machinery to kill others can't figure out a way for a young boy to get all the medical care he needs, *and deserves,* without the entire family collapsing financially.

And I thought of that paper. The Dornshire letter.

I knew what to do.

I so knew what to do.

*   *   *

After work I changed into blue jean shorts and a purple T-shirt. Zena had invited me to watch her roller derby competition, and I was going to eat a salad before scooting off to watch women try to kill each other.

For a minute I paused in front of the mirrors on my closet doors.

I still could not believe I could fit into shorts.

The body staring back at me, slender, with legs that had curves instead of globules of fat and dimples and wrinkles, still shocked me. Part of me would always believe that the mirror was an illusion. To go from being 320 pounds to 150 pounds was nothing short of a mind-blowing miracle.

Or a few cuts here and there and a stomach band during my first surgery, and another surgery, more risky, that whacked off many pounds of sagging skin that used to be puffed out with fat.

My weight after the operation slipped off like water on a water slide. I could drink only liquids at first, then pureed food, soft and moist foods, and not much of it or I would get dumping syndrome and vomit. I lost 40 pounds in three months. I lost more than 100 pounds the first year, and my face emerged from my fat.

I did not expect my operation to solve everything in my life, but my diabetes poofed into thin air, my blood pressure is normal, I won't need knee or hip replacement surgery, I can breathe when I walk, I don't feel another heart attack is imminent, and I do not ache or puff when moving. All incredible. Each day I'm grateful. Breathing is sweet.

But there have been more than physical differences in my life. The difference in how people treat me is stunning . . . and hurtful and aggravating and frustrating. And nice, too, if I can disregard the fact that when I was heavy they probably would not have paid any attention to me at all.

When I weighed 320 pounds I was constantly waiting for attacks from strangers, Herbert, acquaintances, coworkers, you name it. People say the rudest things to heavy people. "Have you tried this diet? My cousin did this. . . . You're going to die if you don't do something. . . . You have such a pretty face; if you lost weight it would show. . . . God, you're fat. . . . She's gross. . . . Why is she eating a hamburger. . . . She's taking up way too much space on this planet. . . . I cannot believe that fat butt. . . . tub o' lard. . . . Oh, my God, I've never seen thighs that big. . . . She can barely walk. . . . Her arms are the size of my waist. . . . Eww!"

It's devastating. You try to build your armor up, but all those comments bypass the armor, each and every one, like sharpened spears.

Now, at five foot seven and a hundred and fifty pounds, I suddenly count, as if I didn't before when I was heavy. Strangers chat with me downtown, my neighbors call me in for lemonade, and the checkers at the grocery store or waiters in restaurants regard me with friendly smiles instead of disgust.

Eileen tells me all the time that I cheated in order to lose weight, but here's how I see it: We have surgery and go under very sharp knives for all sorts of things: appendectomies, heart operations, brain operations. Many times the surgeries, health issues, and injuries that Americans have are caused by being overweight, smoking, drinking, doing drugs, or being involved in accidents caused by our own stupidity. They're preventable problems we bring onto ourselves. We undergo procedures to live or to improve our health. I did it for both.

What was I supposed to do? Stay that size my whole life and, possibly, die decades earlier than I would normally have? Continue to live in pain, unable to breathe right because some people out there would think I had cheated to lose weight? Try another diet that didn't work, would never work? Was it my fault I was addicted to food? Yes, I thought instantly. Yes, it was my fault.

And no.

You try going through what I went through and you might find yourself addicted to something, too. There was no way I could look inward until I looked outward and fixed what soon would have killed me: my weight.

I had done that.

Somebody doesn't approve? Somebody thinks I took the easy way out by getting bariatric surgery?

Their problem.

Not mine.

It was Eileen's problem, not mine.

I had scars, the scars would never disappear, but I figured that was life. I had scars on the inside, scars on the outside.

Doesn't everyone? And, in some way, don't the scars make us stronger? Even if the scars caused us near-mortal heartache? Don't they?

I had to admit, I was still standing. Still upright.

And I was wearing a pair of blue jean shorts.

Wasn't that something?

That night I cheered until my throat was raw.

Roller derby is not for wimps. The building was jammed with rabid fans. We watched Zena tackle another skater she was ticked off at. *Tackled her to the ground.* Then those two rolled—*rolled*—on the floor while their teammates cheered them on. Zena was penalized and threw a fit. We booed, then we laughed. We waved at Zena. She smiled and waved back, cheerful, happy.

Zena's team didn't mess around. The stay-at-home mothers obviously had a lot of aggression because they skated as if they were at war against the ravenous lions in a bloodthirsty Roman arena. The brain surgeon was no slouch. At the end of the night she might well be operating on someone's head that she herself bashed in.

It was so much fun.

I don't even remember who won.

"You gotta try this, Stevie!" Zena yelled at me after she crashed into the side, face-first. She smiled her huge smile. It took up half her face. "You'd love it. You can kick some ass!"

Oh, I couldn't.

I couldn't!

* * *

Jake was coming home the next day. His bridge-building work had taken more time than expected. We'd been calling and e-mailing and texting. All these modern ways to communicate. "I want to take you up to Trillium Lake, Stevie. Have you been there?" I had not. "You'll love it."

But if Jake had said, "I want to take you out to a vacant lot and dig a hole to Germany and fill it back up," I would have said yes to that, too, and loved it.

I could hardly dare to believe that I might, *might,* have met someone special.

But would he think I was special once he knew about my past? Would he think I was special if he ever saw a photograph of me at 320 pounds? How would he feel about the anchor scar on my body? How would he feel about someone bad in bed?

My doubts slid onto me like a landslide down a ski slope until the snow was choking me.

"Can you take a day off work when I get back?" he asked.

Could I? I never took a day off. I rarely took vacation days. Work was me; it made me feel safe. "Yes, I can," I heard myself singing. "Yep."

When he returned, we drove up to Trillium Lake at Mt. Hood. It sparkles, it's blue, and it's surrounded by trees with Mt. Hood rising in the background—a white, pointed gift for Oregon. There's a trail around the lake, and we started off on that. Honestly, it's so pretty you feel as if you're part of a post-card.

"What are you hiding from me, Stevie?" he asked partway through, taking my hand. Oh, stop, my fluttering heart!

I automatically gripped his fingers tight.

"I know there's something. I can tell."

We stood together, right next to the blue water, fishermen in the center of the lake, the sun casting white diamonds on the water. "Can I tell you another time?"

He turned me toward him, tilted my chin up with his hand. "You sure can, honey, you sure can. Tell me when you trust me."

He is so darn sharp.

And he is such an outstanding kisser. There is nothing better than a kiss at Trillium Lake, with Mt. Hood glowing in the distance, especially when you're being held firm and warm against a giant of a man, his lips soft and sexy, and you're melting.

I corralled a group of men with a cement truck who were working down the street. I told them where I wanted cement, they poured it in a circle, and I paid them in cash. While they were pouring I pounded china plates to medium-sized pieces.

I placed the pieces inside the circle—biggest pieces in the center—and worked outward. The cement guys stayed for a while. "Are you an artist?" one asked. "I wish," I told him.

When I was done, I was crying, my hands were shaking, but I felt . . . better.

I was acknowledging what had happened, but in a pretty way, a peaceful way.

I touched each piece of china.

They reminded me of the tea parties that me and Sunshine had with our stuffed animals. I let myself think of those happy memories, tried to block out the rest, and sat there, the wind breezing on by, my wind chimes tinkling, a distant lawn mower humming.

I sat there.

That night I dreamed of her.

We were sitting in a cave having a tea party with our stuffed animals, who had come to life. The monkey with the pink polka-dotted dress was, indeed, prissy, lifting her pinkie finger when she drank her tea. The giraffe was a tomboy, elbows on the table, a baseball hat on her head. The polar bear was very scientific and talked about the Arctic ice. We all wore crowns on our heads and ate gingerbread men and women.

And then Helen came, dressed in black, no expression on her face, and she took Sunshine and stuffed her in the teapot while she sang "Amazing Grace."

I tried to pour Sunshine out, but she was stuck. I tried to lift the lid, but it was nailed on. Helen said, "Command Center did it, I didn't."

I could hear Sunshine begging me to save her, then gurgling. She was drowning in the tea. She couldn't breathe. I smashed the teapot on the table and the giraffe, polar bear, and monkey cried because inside the teapot there was nothing, nothing at all, not even Sunshine, and the giraffe said it was my fault for not saving Sunshine, and I knew she was right.

I woke up crying, my hands shaking as if they were being electrocuted, my heart pounding.

Do you ever get over the trauma of your childhood? Is it possible? Does it stalk you forever or are you eventually able to sleep normally?

I stared up at the Starlight Starbright ceiling and tried to breathe. I needed more than a wish fulfilled. I needed a miracle.

The next day in Pioneer Courthouse Square I asked Zena if she wanted to go to Lance's Hard Rock Party.

"Sure," she said. "I'll come as one of the KISS men. One of them grew up here. I'll be the female Oregon contingent of KISS. Cool and rad, I'll be there." She linked an arm around my shoulder. "But you have to promise me, Stevie, that you'll join the Break Your Neck Booties roller derby team."

"Uh. No." I handed her some pumpkin bread.

"Uh," she mocked me. "Yes. Say yes, Stevie. Say yes."

"No."

"Yes." She handed me some grapes. "When are you going to dare?"

"Dare?"

"Yes. When are you going to dare? Dare to live? Dare to dare?"

"Soon," I promised. "Soon."

He was so furious, he was speechless.

How can you hear speechlessness over a telephone?

I heard it when his voice blistered out, "Stevie, for God's sake!"

And then I heard it in the heavy breathing and the stinging, rigid silence.

"Herbert?"

He swore.

"What is it? Is something wrong?" I clunked my coffee cup down. I had been up late working on a chair. I had painted it pink, then painted roller skates on it with flames shooting from the heels. I was going to paint fishnet stockings on the legs and give it to Zena. The chair's name was Booty. "Is it Aunt Janet?"

He made some strangled sounds, like a monkey was pinching his esophagus, then seethed, "You know what it is, young lady! *Dammit!*"

"I . . . I don't . . ." I searched my mind. What could it be? What happened? The party was planned, the white tents and chairs were ordered, the flowers were coming, I'd been on the phone with the caterer so many times dealing with Herbert's changing, picky requests, the caterer herself had even muttered, "This party is going to drive me back to drinking," and Lance told me the invitations were out.

"This was a simple task, *simple*. A retarded child could have handled this!"

I put a hand to my head and held the phone away from my ear for long, long seconds as he ranted. Did I hate the man? I didn't want to hate anyone. Hate hurts the hater, not the one you hate, but he pushed it, he so pushed it.

"I called you because of these monstrous, *demonic* invitations. How could you screw this up so badly, Stevie? This is totally inappropriate! A disgrace to the Barrett family name."

I thought of how many hours I had had to spend talking with Herbert about which recent picture he was most handsome in for the invitation. "We had a photo of you and Aunt Janet on your wedding day, on the front, as you requested, and a photo of you two now on the inside of the invitation. You wanted white, we made it white. You wanted gold detail so it would reflect 'your place in society,' your words, not mine. So what's wrong with it?"

"Young lady, I will not tolerate your insolence. We received an invitation today, and we are thoroughly disgusted. We're beyond embarrassed. We are livid. Did you hear me?" he shouted.

"Janet and I are livid. I should never have put you in charge of this, ever. It was a poor choice on my part, Stevie, but I have learned my lesson."

He hadn't put me in charge of this. I had taken it over for Polly because she couldn't do it because it made her want to breathe in a bag, and Lance took over because I was doing everything else.

"You did this to hurt me, to hurt my reelection campaign. Indeed you did this to hurt all law-abiding heterosexual married couples in Oregon. It was a calculated attack on me. You're campaigning with the Democrats, aren't you?"

There was something amiss here. I was not getting this. "Hang on."

"Hang on? Hang on?" he shrieked. "Don't you dare walk away from this phone. I'll not have it!" I dropped the phone on my butcher block island, grabbed my keys, and hurried out to my mailbox. I hadn't picked up my mail in days. There was the usual array of advertisements, bills, including the dreaded medical bill statement. . . . And then, there it was. Lance and I had actually mailed ourselves invitations. It was quirky and odd, but we'd laughed as we'd done it.

"We should both return the RSVP card and mark 'Nope, can't make it,' " Lance said.

"Sorry," I chuckled, "I'll be cackling in a bar in Mexico with a margarita in my hand that night."

We'd laughed about it in a rather sick and sorry way at the time.

I raced back to my house, dropped the mail on a dresser I'd found at an estate sale ($8) and painted green with white stripes, and ripped open the invitation.

And there it was. Herbert and Aunt Janet's invitation to the renewal of their vows celebration.

"Oh. My. God," I breathed. "Oh. My. God."

And then I laughed. I laughed so hard I had to cross my legs. I picked up the phone and told Herbert, "I'll call you back," my voice squeaking as he continued his harangue. I shuffled out to my deck, planted my butt in an Adirondack chair and, as Herbert called back, laughed my head off.

I laughed and laughed.

I lay between my growing vegetables, on my new grass, under the sun, and called Lance. He hadn't gone through his mail, either, he'd been so consumed with his blow-up girls. I waited on the phone, still cackling.

"Ah, Stevie, gal, gimme a second. I haven't slept in about two days. . . . We've been working our tails off . . . had to hire three people. They're all radical. Are you sure you don't want to work with me? I know how you feel. You're not taking advantage of the relationship, okay . . . all right, here's the invite to the torture chamber."

I heard him rip open the envelope. I heard some hard rock music, the song "Big Balls," and he drawled, "Well, now, shit."

And then I heard it: laughter.

Loud, gasping, sucking-air laughter.

Oh, I couldn't help it. Somehow it was even funnier the second time around, especially with Lance's belly laugh booming in my ear.

"Lance, I'm wetting my pants, gotta gotta gotta go!"

That made him laugh all the harder.

I didn't even make it to the bathroom.

I took the invitation to Polly the next day during visiting hours. She was still ticked, still rebellious, still wanted out, out, out, she could handle this herself, herself, herself.

Polly opened the invitation, then dropped it on her lap, shocked, that "Big Balls" song rumbling from the invite, tiny naked ladies sprinkling out.

Then she laughed and we laughed together, forehead to forehead, collapsing back on the bed.

This time, it was Polly who didn't make it to the bathroom in time.

Weak bladders must run in the family.

* * *

I propped the invitations to Herbert's anniversary party and Lance's Lucky Ladies Hard Rock Party on my kitchen counter for laughs.

Trixie had somehow gotten the information for the invitations crossed. Switched. Vice versa. Mixed up.

The wording was correct, so all of Herbert's cronies and political allies and country club snobby friends knew to come on Friday night, to the house, at six for an anniversary celebration involving Uncle Herbert and Aunt Janet.

But they received the invitation with the white skull on the front and the silver electric guitar. When they opened the card, tiny pink and purple, glittery naked ladies slid out and a blow-up doll popped up. Then the recorder burst into AC/DC's hit song "Big Balls."

Lance's Hard Rock Party friends and acquaintances received the invitation with a photo of his parents on their wedding day on the front and their current photo on the inside. The date, time, and location was also correct, and the wording did indicate they were to wear hard rock outfits or they wouldn't be let in and to be ready to "freakin' dance all night! An awesome party with Lance's Lucky Ladies!"

Lance's friends, he told me, seemed to think the invitation was very cool. A wild party, with a picture of a "wickedly uptight couple" on the front. "What's wrong with that woman? Is she a robot? Is the dude a sado masochist? Yeah, Lance, we're coming. I'm gonna be Def Leppard. . . . I'm comin' as Hagar. . . . I'm going to be Madonna with the pointy bra!"

Herbert was beyond steaming.

Aunt Janet laughed. "It's a sign, Stevie."

"A sign of what?"

"When my anniversary invitations get screwed up, naked purple ladies fall in my lap, I'm listening to 'Big Balls' and thinking that these invitations are so much better than what Herbert's planned—well, that's a sign."

Perhaps it was.

"I love my Jane Austen class. Did I tell you I got a new haircut? I'm wearing it down from now on. I threw out my blouses, too. Virginia and I agreed that I'm a throwback to a fifties mother with a bosom. We went to the raceway the other night. She got her Corvette up to a hundred miles an hour."

As for Herbert's "friends"? I'm sure they were all scuttling to the bathroom quick as a wink before they wet their pants, too.

"I called Dad, Stevie. Took the blame. Told him I had arranged for the invitations, not you," Lance told me the next day.

I couldn't even answer him. We both cracked up so hard, we couldn't speak.

Should I invite Jake to the parties? To one? To both? What would he think of me when he met Uncle Herbert? Would he hear anything about my prior weight? Should I tell him first? Was it relevant? What about my past? We still hadn't discussed that, either. I knew that Aunt Janet, Lance, and Polly wouldn't talk to him about it, and he wouldn't ask them, out of respect for our relationship. . . .

Jake took me on a river boat ride at night. I took him to a play in Portland. He took me out to dinner afterward, then to a fancy coffee café where they pour the coffee from three feet above your cup. I made up a picnic and we ate together early Saturday afternoon in the hills above Portland. I dodged his questions about what I was doing on Friday, Saturday, and Sunday nights. I could tell it puzzled him; then I could tell he was wondering if I was dating someone else, and I knew he wasn't pleased about that. I changed the subject.

Cluck-cluck. Lord, how I did not want Jake to know I was a chicken.

I had bought a flat of pink and purple petunias, marigolds for a border, and yellow daisies on my way home from work last week to shake off the gloom and stark fear I felt about Polly. I pulled out two stacks of clay pots I'd bought at garage sales for cheap ($1 each). I mixed in dirt and fertilizer and planted pot after pot. Call it flower power without the drugs.

I put some of the pots on the front porch, others on the back deck, one on a wire table I'd found ($2), two at the base of a trellis, and more on a bench I'd put together with scrap wood.

So much prettier.

I do love spring.

Spring gave me hope.

Hope that my guilt, guilt for not saving Sunshine, guilt for hating Helen, guilt for the other thing, which was probably caused by my weight . . . maybe spring would take some of my guilt away.

Maybe it would be sucked up into one of the tulips that was blooming along the edge of my property, or wrapped up in the yellow petals of the daffodils or the sheen of my tomatoes or the curve of my zucchini. Maybe it would fly up into my pink cherry trees and get lost for good among the branches.

I hoped. I hoped it would.

Hope did not take care of my flashbacks or my nightmares. I had a duet that night, so to speak. Before I went to bed I remembered how tiny Sunshine was when she was born and how I felt when she finally smiled at me. Her smile was crooked, I remembered that, but her eyes were bright and shiny. I was the one who taught Sunshine how to hug when she was a baby, placing her arms around my shoulders.

I read a book about a woman obsessed with gardening until I couldn't keep my eyes open, turned off the light, then stared at the Starlight Starbright ceiling. When my hands started to shake because my memories came sliding in, I got up and stared at the stars in the night sky, then stared at the darkened corner of my yard where there was a bunch of weeds. I still didn't know what to do there.

When I finally went to sleep I dreamed of Helen and Sunshine.

Helen was eating Sunshine, knife and fork in hand.

"I even tried painting therapy," Polly said, waving her hand in dismissal. "And visual therapy. I have a counselor and a psychotherapist and a group leader. I'm supposed to talk in 'I Feel' statements. I've done all this before. Did I tell you that yesterday I did yoga? Boring. Then I had two sessions with two different counselors to help me modify my behavior. I felt like a rat in an experiment." She snorted. "Geez. I need to gain a few pounds and I'll feel fine. I got out of whack again."

Still. In. Denial. "You're still in denial," I said. "Still. In. Denial."

"Not much."

"Yes, you are."

"I know I can handle this myself, and I'll do better if I'm not here. I hate it here—"

Lance got up and strode to the window of her room, arms crossed in front of his huge chest.

"Lance?" Polly said, stopping in the middle of another rant. "Is something wrong?"

Lance didn't answer.

"Lance? What is it?"

Still silence.

Then, finally, he turned around. "I've been talking to your counselor, Annie Sinclair, and I'm angry."

"You're angry?" Polly asked.

"Yes. She helped me figure it out. I'm angry. *I am angry.*"

"Why are you angry?" I asked. "I mean, I can think of a number of reasons, but which one in particular?" Lance did, indeed, seem angry today. He had been quiet on the ride out to the clinic and hadn't said anything since the three of us were in Polly's room together.

"I'm angry—" He stopped, breathed through his nose, tractor-sized shoulders back. "I'm angry because you two always scare me. I'm angry because, Stevie, you ate so much you almost died, and Polly, you don't eat so you almost died. I'm angry because I'm tired of worrying about you two."

Polly and I glanced at each other, pretty darn shocked. Lance never got angry at us.

He stuck his chin out. "Since I was a teenager, Polly, I've watched you get skinnier and skinnier and I watched Stevie get heavier and heavier. Do you girls know what you put me through? Do you girls have any idea how it feels to watch this semisuicidal stuff going on and I can't do anything about it? It kills me." He thumped his chest. "Right there. You're killing me. Stevie, you're not killing me so much now, but Polly, you are."

"Lance, I'm sorry," Polly said. She patted her heart. "I don't mean to, Lance, you know that. I got this when I was so young. I wanted to be perfect, Dad was always making comments about my body, I was depressed. . . ."

"I know, I get it, and I'm sorry. I'm sorry Dad was such a shit. But you're an adult, Polly. You gotta get a grip. You gotta take responsibility for this—if not for you, sister, for me. Do you know how long I've felt guilty about you two and your eating diseases?"

"Why have you felt guilty?" Polly asked, clearly distressed.

"You felt guilty?" I asked, incredulous.

"I felt guilty because I couldn't help you, Stevie. You were eating because of this tragedy with Grandma and Grandpa and your mom and Sunshine, and I couldn't fix you. I couldn't help you get better. I was totally helpless. No matter what I did in trying to protect you two from Dad, making him get mad at me instead of you two, bringing you food to your room, buying you ice cream, nothing worked. Polly, you got skinnier. You were a bone. A skinny bone! I grew up scared that you were going *to die*. I would feel so mad at you for not eating, but I couldn't show it because I thought it would make things worse for you," he moaned. "You were a bone who wouldn't eat. Even your hair was falling out then! And you were pale and weak . . ."

"I'm sorry, Lance." Polly shook her head, her chin wobbling.

"You're sorry? I'm sorry, too." He ran a hand through his hair. "I'm sorry because for years you've had to battle this thing, but honey, I gotta ask you—you say you're trying here to get better, but are you?"

Polly stuttered, then said, "What do you mean?"

"I mean, I don't think you're really trying. I think you're clinging to your anorexia. I think you're scared to do the hard work you know you have to do, and I can't take this anymore. Do you know how much stress you've caused me? Both of you?

Have you ever thought about what you've done to me? Polly, did you ever think of what you were doing to Stevie, and Stevie to us?"

I had thought of it, and I was ashamed. They had watched me get so big they probably wondered when I'd pop. And I had popped. "Yes."

"Yes?" Lance asked. "What about you, Polly? I know, I know you're sick. I know you have a disease. I know I'm probably supposed to treat you softly and gently, but I can't anymore." He sniffled. "Are you ever going to reach outside that disease long enough to fix yourself so the rest of us don't have to stand around and watch you try to plant yourself in the ground because you've starved yourself to death? Are you? Aren't we important enough to you, Polly, so that you'll truly and sincerely help yourself get better instead of simply playing the game here until you can get out?"

"Lance—" I said, my voice creaky.

"After the last time you were in the clinic, did you keep going to your outpatient meetings? Did you keep seeing your counselor? No, you didn't, and then you slipped again, and I had to watch you, on TV, when your head thunked that desk, and I thought you were dead. I screamed, Polly, then I almost wet my pants. I drove to the hospital so fast I got a ticket." He squared his shoulders, then rolled his lips in tight so he didn't cry.

"I love you, Polly, and I love you, Stevie, but my heart"—he thumped himself again—"I can't take this anymore. You two are my best friends. You two are the only reason I'm not lonely all the time. I know you're out there. I know I can call you. But what happens if one of you dies, especially from something you could have prevented but you didn't love me enough to save yourself? I want to cry when I think about that, and I'm angry. Very angry."

"Lance," Polly whimpered, patting her heart rhythmically.

"Sometimes I'm up all night worrying. It makes me vomit. After Stevie's heart attack I had to go on antidepressants, and that's not the first time. I do it with you, too, Polly, and I hate taking drugs, you know that." He sniffled, ran a fist over his eyes. "I knit blankets all the time and give them away. See my fingers." He held them up. "They're tired. They're tired of knitting. I'll wait for you in the parking lot, Stevie. I'm angry at you girls."

The electric silence in that room probably could have been blown up with a match.

I climbed on Polly's bed and we sat there, numbed, holding hands.

"He's right," she said, her voice exhausted, defeated. "I know he's right." She patted her heart. "Calm down, heart, pump the blood, relax."

"I'm not one to talk, Polly. I was within an inch of eating myself to death. Absolutely to death." I coughed, trying to get the lump out of my throat. "And Lance watched every minute of it."

"And he's watched me morph into a skeleton with a head for more than twenty years." She brought our entwined hands up to her face, then we both lay down on that twin bed, together, and didn't move.

The next morning I walked in the rain. I felt terrible about Lance. If guilt could physically knock people to their knees, I'd have been walking on my knees that whole walk.

I put myself in Lance's position, something I should have done a hundred times before, and I hated myself. I did. I saw everything from his eyes.

When I got home, I went to bed for about twenty minutes, pulled the covers up, and stared at the Starlight Starbright ceiling. Within ten minutes I wanted to conk myself on the head. Wasn't I done with this yet? Done with literally and figuratively pulling blankets over my head?

I showered, pulled my sweats on, had two pieces of toast, and headed to my garage, where I kept my obsessions. I would build and paint Lance a chair. No, it did not make up for the years I had hurt him, but it was something. An acknowledgment of my realization of what I'd done. An apology.

First, I cut off the legs of a chair with an abnormally large seat I'd bought at a garage sale ($2). Next, I attached new legs, about four feet tall. I cut out four guitars from wood. Two were about two feet long, two were one foot long. I painted the chair black and the next day painted a skull on the seat. I painted the guitars with red, purple, and green swirls, then attached the guitars to the front and back of the chair and painted the long chair legs with red squares.

Across the middle slats I wrote, "Rock your own life. Always."

I drove it over to Lance's and put it on his front porch, with a note attached. The note was simple. "I'm sorry. I love you. Stevie."

My phone rang later that night.

I heard muffled words, a sniffle.

"Lance? Lance?"

More muffled words, another sniffle, and then, "I can't talk right now, Stevie. Oh! You've made me cry! Cry! I love my chair! If my house burns down tonight, I'll take it out first! Oh! I can't talk right now, I can't talk!"

Muffle, sniffle.

Jake called. He wanted to take me to a piano concert downtown on Sunday night. I almost laughed. Huge, athletic, rough and tough Jake, loving piano. I had to turn him down. He asked about Monday. I said yes. "Busy Sunday night then?" he asked.

"Yes, I am."

I could feel his question, his frustration. He was not pleased. I just couldn't tell that man I was a chicken yet. There was a lot I couldn't tell him yet.

Cluck and cluck.

21

〜

Ashville, Oregon

Helen escaped.
Despite my grandma and grandpa's best efforts, she slipped out the door. She'd been pointing more and more at her growing stomach, saying, "The bees and the babies are trying to kill me." And she'd whisper, "Command Center doesn't like it. I'm going to pop. I want it out. So does he."

Grandma grew pale trying to calm her, and the creases in Grandpa's face grew deeper. Both of them had aged during Helen's pregnancy. You could almost see them changing overnight. They were scared to death and had every logical, rational reason to be so.

One rainy day, after I won the first-grade spelling bee, I got off the school bus, walked up our driveway, and saw Grandma sprinting for the Schoolhouse House from the fields, her cowboy boots flying. I had no idea my grandma could run that fast.

"Search inside. Don't miss a corner, Stevie," she told me, panting, frantic. "I can't find your mother."

Soon Grandpa came roaring up the drive in his pickup truck with six of his employees from work. We searched all over our property, then Grandpa told me to call Uncle Peter, the chief of police, and the minister at church and to tell Aunt Terri to call The Family. Within an hour we were mobbed with people going out on search parties to find Helen.

No one paid any attention to me as I huddled in a corner.

I didn't know what to do. I was scared. Scared for Helen, scared for the baby in her tummy, scared with all the people around, scared because Grandma and Grandpa, although standing tall, were clearly covering their panic.

And then I thought of the cave.

Sometimes, on lucid days, me and Helen walked across the property, Grandpa or Grandma behind us, and explored. One day Helen took me to a cave, hidden in the hillside. In front of the cave there was a giant rock, so it could not be easily seen. Helen had gone there as a girl many times, apparently. She called it her secret cave.

The first time she showed me the cave, she showed me a metal box where she had saved photos of her, Grandma, Grandpa, Aunt Janet, and her many friends. She also had dried corsages from dances, dried wildflowers from our farm, a few love letters from various boys, two necklaces that had been gifts from girlfriends, shells from a trip to the beach, rocks from a campsite on Mt. Hood, and a whole bunch of pretty cards. There was also a pennant from her college and playbills from shows she had been in on Broadway in New York. There were playbills about operas, too, a man's face on the front. She held those in her hands and touched his face with her finger. "He's nice," she told me. "He sings. We sing together."

I took off running for the cave. To this day, I realize how stupid it was for me not to tell them where I was going. Perhaps I had some grandiose notion that I would find Helen and bring her home myself. Remember: I was seven.

I ran as fast as I could, arms pumping, past the vegetable garden, past the sunflowers, past the barn with the horses, past the corn, past the cattle, and up into the hills.

It was very difficult to see the slit of the cave from anywhere on the property, so the only people who would ever know it was there had to be told by someone else. Helen and Aunt Janet knew about it because Grandma had told them. Grandma knew about it because her mother told her. And her mother's mother found it, rumor has it, when she was running from an angry boyfriend who had a scythe in his hand.

Once through the slit, however, which was about six feet long and two feet high, you could stand up in the cave. It was about twelve square feet wide and probably eight feet tall, although my memory probably isn't very accurate. It wasn't as dark as you would expect, because the top of the cave opened to the sky through a small tunnel. Native American artwork adorned the walls, which Grandma told us never to touch, so we didn't. There were horses, Native Americans with spears, Native American families, buffalo, teepees, moons, and stars. We'd even found arrowheads on the floor. I had one in my jewelry box and Helen put a couple in her box, too.

But I wasn't thinking of Native Americans or arrowheads at all as I scampered up the hill and crawled behind the big rock. I didn't need to ask if Helen was there, because I knew she was. I heard her wailing, loud and guttural, intermixed with sobs and yells to Command Center to stop hurting her with the "stinging, biting bees."

I slithered through that slit, shaking at what I'd find, and stood up. I had a hard time seeing at first, because I went from the light of the day to the semidarkness of the cave, but then my eyes adjusted.

I saw Helen's box, which was open, all the letters and pretty things strewn about, and I saw Helen, holding the playbill with the opera man's face.

She was sitting up, hands on her stomach, sweating, panting, sobbing. She was wearing a green plaid maternity dress Grandma had bought her, one tennis shoe and one flip-flop, and tin foil wrapped around her chest.

"Get it out!" she hollered. "Get it out! It's killing me!"

I scrambled over to Helen in the semidarkness of that cave, her knees up, teeth clenched in pain, panting. I instinctively hugged her. "It's okay, Momma, I'll help you. I'll go get Grandma and Grandpa."

I pulled away, ready to run, but she grabbed my wrist and yanked me back, our faces two inches from each other. "Don't leave me don't leave me don't leave me." Then she let out a piercing scream, that scream lancing through me like swords swishing through my insides. I can still hear it, deep within me, echoing through my nightmares.

"Don't leave! Do you hear me, girl kid?" Her eyes were crazed, her breath coming in gasps, her knees trembling by that big belly of hers. "There's an alien in there. A bee alien! Command Center doesn't like it. It hurts! It's hurting. I can feel it coming out! It's coming out."

Well, I was pretty smart—I even knew my multiplication tables and could spell *schizophrenia*—but I wasn't sure how the baby got in her stomach without a husband, and I sure didn't know how it came out. Did it come out through the stomach? Was there a zipper? I had heard they came out "down there," but what did that mean? There were so many questions in my life already, living with Helen, and the baby issue had not been a priority to address.

Helen's wracking scream brought me back to reality on the double, the noise echoing off the dark, wet walls of that cave as she yanked me back to her face, only inches away.

"I can't breathe," she said, her face a scrunched mask of misery. "I can't breathe. Ohhh! Stop it, Punk! Stop it!"

"It's okay, Momma, it's okay." I pushed her hair back from her sweating face and she groaned as she collapsed to the floor. "It's okay."

"Take it out," she demanded, pale, sweaty, deathly, her beautiful blond hair caked with dirt and sweat. "Take it out and kill it."

In my quaking fright, I knew two things: I didn't have the slightest idea how to get the baby out, and I wasn't going to kill it.

I found out a lot that night.

Seconds later Helen sat straight up again, dropped her head back and sobbed, grunted and moaned, breathed in and out like a freight train, and screamed again, mouth open all the way, eyes lost.

I stroked her hair with shaking hands, my mouth dry as sand. "Momma, let me go and get Grandpa—"

"No!" She sucked in air through her mouth, her lips bloody where she had bit down. "Don't go. Don't leave me with this thing. It's killing me!"

She collapsed back on her elbows, her knees still up, her whole body heaving.

I decided then and there, almost comatose with fright, that I was not ever going to have a baby. I wasn't going to go to the store or go to a baby doctor or go to a stork and get one of those things put in my stomach, no way.

She let out a primal, raw groan, then started crying, tears streaming down her face. "Save me, save me, girl kid!" This whole scene repeated several times, the freight train breathing, the groaning, until she yelled at me, "It's coming! It's coming!" Helen pulled up her dress to her waist and pointed at her naked privates. "Get it out. The aliens put it there. Pull it out. Out!"

I was used to seeing Helen's privates because of her fear of bathrooms and showers, but her stomach was shocking. It was huge and seemed to be moving, her knees wide apart, shaking as if someone had put a wiggling worm in them. I put my hands on her stomach. Where was the zipper? Where was the opening? How was that baby going to get out? Would it be naked?

"Pull it out, girl kid, pull it out!" she hollered at me, her face white, eyes pooling with tears.

"I don't know what to do, Momma," I whimpered. "Where is it? Where's the baby?"

She couldn't answer for a second, her white face tight as she contorted in pain, then another tortured shout erupted, seemingly from the center of her ragged soul.

"It's right there!" She swung an arm around, leaned toward her knees, and pointed at her privates, way "down there."

"Get over there! Pull it! Get rid of it!"

I scampered around between Helen's legs. She grabbed my shoulders and shook me until my teeth ached. "Help me! Help me!"

And then I saw something coming from between Helen's legs. I felt sick. I felt ashamed. I shouldn't be looking this close at Helen's privates, and there was something wrong with them!

They were huge and something moved down there, something I didn't recognize. It was gross. It was all red and wet and gooky. What was going on down there? What was that?

"Pull it out. Pull it out pull it out pull it out," Helen told me, her voice weakening, her face pale, so pale white, sobbing.

I started to cry, the tears slipping down my face. Pull what out? Pull that thing?

But Helen was insistent. She rose up again, a wild animal in pain, grabbed my hands and shook them. "Pull it out, pull it out!"

That cut through the dense fog of my own terror. I peeked again and saw something coming out of Helen's body. I put my little fingers on both sides of that hard thing and I pulled gently. Helen moaned between clenched teeth, and I stopped and cried and ripped my hands back.

But Helen was insistent, crying, begging. "Take it out, kid! Help me! It's going to rip me apart! They're going to kill me!"

I swayed, so nauseous, and scared, all the way to my petrified bones. Helen kept making guttural, animalistic sounds, and I put my hands down there again, and I could see that it was a head. A tiny head. I pulled and I didn't stop pulling even though Helen was shrieking, her eyes wild as she dipped into hysteria, her hair sticking up all over, her mouth gaping open as her body shook and strained and arched. I pulled, so gentle, and a tiny baby came out, first her head, then her eyes and mouth, then shoulders and a tummy and two legs and teeny toes and all.

Helen heaved one more time, then collapsed back onto the dirt of the cave, panting, moaning, exhausted. She whispered, "It's all over now. You can kill it."

I held the baby on my lap, ignoring the rope that connected her to Helen. It resembled a brown snake and I thought it was gross, but I didn't pay too much attention. The baby was red and wet and bloody and goopy, her fists flailing, and I could tell it was a girl, and I fell in love with her.

Right at that second.

I fell in love with my sister.

I heard voices and yelling outside the cave but I didn't say anything because my baby had taken a deep breath, and sighed, and now she was sleeping. She made cat sounds, and I could see her chest going up and down, up and down. I held her up in my arms as I did with one of Grandma's friend's babies. Her name was Chloe and she was tiny, too.

Grandma had told me to be gentle but hold Chloe close enough so I didn't drop her. So that's what I did with my baby, too. I was gentle but I held her close enough. I was glad I was wearing a sweatshirt, because I think that kept her warm. I brought her up close to my face as I heard Grandpa and Grandma and other people scrambling into the cave through the slit and kissed my baby right on the nose. She made that meowing sound again.

She was the cutest baby that has ever been born on this planet, that I was sure of.

I smiled up at Grandma and Grandpa and the other people. "I have a baby!" I whispered to them. I didn't bother to wipe the tears off my face. I couldn't. Grandma had taught me how to hold a baby, and I knew I needed both hands. "I have a baby!"

Later, as an adult, I remembered the stunned, stricken looks on all of their exhausted faces.

At the time, though, all I could remember was what my grandma and grandpa said to me. "Stevie," Grandpa said, then he stopped, because he got all these tears stuck in his eyes. He tried again and wiped his eyes as he cradled Helen, who was moaning softly against his chest, still holding the photo of the opera man. "Stevie, you are the bravest person I know."

And Grandma said, as she put an arm around me and my baby, "You are a gift from God, Stevie, an angel." Her words all wobbled and pitched and dipped. "We love you so much, sugar."

I thought of what I loved the best. Grandma and Grandpa. The farm. The horses. The white Schoolhouse House. Pretty much everyone in town. Daffodils and tulips and playing outside on the hills and in the fields on sunny days. And my momma, Helen, even though she made me confused and scared.

"My baby's name is Sunshine because I love the sunshine." I kissed her little head again and her nose. "I love my baby."

Sunshine had to go to the hospital for a couple of weeks to get bigger and better. Helen had to go to the hospital, too, but not to the one my baby was in.

Every day I asked Grandma and Grandpa when Sunshine was coming home.

I did not ask about Helen.

I didn't want to know when she was coming back.

When Helen wasn't home, I realized how tiring it was when she was home. I went to school, I came home for cookies, helped in the garden, rode the tractor with Grandpa, ran in the fields, played in the corn. I could invite friends over who loved to come because we had animals, and Grandma always had a craft or sewing project for us to do.

My grandparents had The Family over for barbeques. Helen was frightened of crowds of people. She called them "an army out to get her blood," so this wasn't possible when she was home.

I did not have to worry about her pouring shampoo into a teaspoon and taking little sips of it. I did not have to wonder what embarrassing thing would happen when we took Helen into town. Would she stop at the TV shop and say, "They're talking about me, can't you hear that? Why can't they stop talking about me?" I didn't have to worry about her putting her hands up like claws and hissing at my girlfriend, Toby Mae. And I did not have to figure out how I would react when she kicked a lamppost and said, "Get out of here, Command Center. You're not supposed to be here. This is my planet."

I didn't have to examine her coat for large black spiders before she put it on or check her chair. I didn't have to witness her breakdowns, or how she cried and grunted in corners sometimes and nothing I did comforted her, which made me feel useless and sad.

On the most basic level of emotion I did not have to deal with the fact that my momma did not love me, didn't appear to like me that much, and gave me little warmth. Now and then she would hold my hand, which gave me a warm glow initially, but then she would turn my palm up and study it, often saying, "You have knife marks on your hand" or "Are you spying on me?"

A child's bond to her mother cannot be understated, and my bond with Helen was a ragged, baffling, disheartening, chaotic mess. I felt crazy, often, around my own mother. I grew up questioning what was normal, asking what reality was and wasn't, and not trusting the outcome of different situations. She scared me and I couldn't predict her behavior, so I was often off-kilter and worried.

Anxiety followed me around as if I were wearing an itchy blanket I couldn't shake off. I dealt with anger, too, which I felt I had to smother. Anger at how much in my life Helen spoiled, how she needed so much attention, how she wouldn't take her medications so she could act nicer, how she argued with voices.

I told myself that I loved Helen, but sometimes I thought I hated her. That made me feel guilty, and I was sure I was going to hell.

Had I not had my grandparents in that house, constantly, *constantly* telling me that Helen had a disease in her head, that it wasn't my fault, that I didn't cause it, that they loved me dearly, and had they not shown me that love each and every day in a hundred ways, I do not think I would have been sane by the end of my childhood. As it was, I constantly danced around my own breakdowns, especially after the bridge incident.

But my grandparents' love saved me.

That is the truth.

In a couple of weeks, after we visited Sunshine in the hospital every day, my baby came home. It was the best day of my life. Sunshine wore a pretty pink outfit with bunnies that I picked out and pink booties. On the deck that evening watching the sun go down, Grandpa put Sunshine in my lap and I held her close and gave her a kiss on the forehead. One of my tears dropped on her small nose. "I'm so happy I have my baby," I said. Another one of my tears dropped on her nose. "Hey! She smiled at me! She smiled at me!"

Grandpa cleared his throat and wiped at his eyes. I thought he'd gotten something in his eyes. "Makes sense that Sunshine would smile at Stevie first, wouldn't you say, Glory?"

My grandma must have had something in her eyes, too, because she was also wiping away a tear. "I would say so."

I kissed my baby again and tried not to let another tear fall on her face.

So we kept the name Sunshine. We all called her that, not Sunny, but Sunshine, the name I gave my baby when she was born in a hidden cave with Native American drawings on a hill behind a rock on Grandma and Grandpa's farm.

She was Sunshine to everyone.

Except Helen.

Helen didn't call my baby Sunshine.

Helen called her Trash Heap.

Trash Heap.

Her first words to Sunshine? "Command Center sent you to kill me, didn't he?"

We naively believed that she would not hurt her. Grandma and Grandpa could not get their minds around their daughter hurting their granddaughter.

That was a mistake.

If I went back to Ashville I'd have to deal with this type of memory. I couldn't do it.

Could I?

22

Portland, Oregon

"What is that?" She giggled, then covered her mouth. My eyes followed Eileen's gaze to my latest house decoration. I'd found two white pillars at a rummage sale, placed them on either side of my fireplace, and wrapped them with white lights.

"They're pillars. I think they came from an old building. You can see the carvings on the top and bottom. It's fun. I have a piece of Portland history right in my house—"

She smothered her laughter. "You have very . . . *creative* tastes, Stevie. Who would ever have thought to thunk down two pillars in a living room when they have nothing to hold up?" She smiled at me with patent condescension. "Here, eat one of these doughnuts. They're from that great bakery you love off Hall Boulevard."

"No, thank you." Sugar had not tasted the same to me since my operation. In fact, sometimes it made me get dumping syndrome. I braced myself for her response.

"You're obsessive about your weight, Stevie. It's disgusting. One doughnut won't make you fat." She ate another doughnut. She had come over uninvited. She was doing that more and more. It was nine o'clock in the morning on a Saturday. She was wearing an overly large green shirt and matching green pants. She had beautiful jewelry—all jade—on her ears, neck, and wrists, along with her usual collection of diamonds and another $1,000 purse.

She was panting as she'd come in from her car, and she settled in my rocking chair. It groaned.

"No, they're not going to hold anything up, they're there for . . ." My words dropped off.

"For?" She arched an eyebrow at me.

"It's decoration, Eileen." I hated the way my voice sounded so insecure.

"Decoration? Honey, a $2,000 glass vase made by Michel Solange is decoration. So is a handmade sofa by Nick Tatakanos imported from Greece. My marble surround in my bathroom from Italy is decoration. So is the wood floor from Central America in my den with its carved inlays. Now that's decoration. Quality. Class. Decoration is not something you find off a demolished building."

"It depends on who thinks it's decoration—"

"No, it doesn't, Stevie." She slapped her thighs as she laughed. "Honey, I'm not being mean, but the way you decorate your house—"

I peeked at the white outdoor lattice I'd propped against a wall and hung with hats, the long white shelf I'd built on three of the walls, one foot from the ceiling, so I could display my colored glass collection, my eclectic collection of clocks, and my antique books. In a corner was my comfy purple chair with a leopard print blanket. "What's wrong with it?" My voice: weak.

"I know you're on a budget." She reached over and patted my hand. "But less is more, and you need . . . less. For example, those birdcages. Gotta go, girl. They gotta go."

I loved the three old birdcages I'd hung in a group in a corner. One was iron, one was blue, one was made of wicker.

"Haven't you noticed the way I decorate, Stevie?"

I had. I had noticed the cold formality, the pristine cleanliness (Two maids. Both "lazy girls, you wouldn't believe how lazy"), the dark artwork next to modern monstrosities in loud colors.

Eileen's bedroom, covered in mauve and white flowers, was almost the size of my house. Her living room was pure white.

Nothing went together. All expensive, then thrown in.

"Yes, I've seen it." I smiled cheerfully. I could not be mean.

"About a million times you've been there, but sometimes, it takes a while to rub off, don't you think? Finding your own style can be difficult, and you're in the middle of it right now. Plus you've been so busy with other . . . things."

"Yes, I have. I work a lot, Eileen, and—" Why was I trying to defend myself or my home?

"You think you have the lock on working?"

And we went from there. I wasn't a good friend, where was I at night, she called and I never called back. . . . She ended up slamming my door and stumbling down my steps. I ripped open the door.

"Are you all right?"

"Shut up, Stevie." She struggled to her feet, hands down, butt in the air, huffing and puffing. She got to her feet, wobbled, and said, "Shut up, you stuck-up, skinny snob."

Mr. Pingle was so pleased with me. Ever since I started prancing and preening on the street, their sales had increased twenty percent. I cannot take full credit for this, nor can I be proud of my rhythmic efforts, but he was ecstatic.

"You're my good-luck charm, Stevie! My good-luck charm!" He clapped his hands together. "I don't think we've ever had a better chicken!"

I thanked him. As I left the joint, two young employees with piercings flapped their wings and cawed at me. I rolled my eyes.

I studied my vegetable garden that night in the dark. It continued to grow, colors flashing beneath the leaves, my sunflowers coming up, and I felt this rush of pride. I had shown Jake my garden recently, and he'd loved it.

"Who made the trellises?"

"I did."

"Who made the pathway?"

"I did."

"Did you make this mosaic design?"

I nodded, grinned.

He shook his head, amazed. "I think you're pretty special, Stevie Barrett."

"I think you're pretty special, too, Jake Stockton."

Right on my mosaic design we kissed, slow at first, then with such passion it made my toes tingle. The wind ruffled on by, the cherry blossoms floated down, and the birds flew to my bird-houses.

With the moon winking at me, I decided to get one other thing done I'd been meaning to do.

I grabbed four sticks in my backyard. With simple raffia I tied them together to form two crosses. I dug two holes and stuck them in the ground by the back fence, under the tulip tree.

Then I sat there with them, my arms around my legs, the darkness wrapping me up tight. They looked lonely, and lost, and alone. Those crosses are not for who you think.

His last words to me were, "Good-bye, fat cunt."

I don't know why Eddie was so furious. He got the house. He did have to write me a check for half the equity, so I received about $20,000, but he got to keep his old boat, his fancy car, and his motorcycle. I left with my clothes, my car, all my saws and paints, and my retirement account from my job, about $50,000. He took the $25,000 in credit card debt, which he'd run up, not me. I had no credit card debt.

He did end up with a huge bill from his divorce attorney. If he'd done the slightest bit of research he would know that Tito Zaro was the Supreme and Glorious Leader of all Greedy Attorneys and overcharged men going through a divorce by making them madder and madder and inventing dire problems and angst and testosterone-driven macho emotion where there should be none. Tito charged him $42,000 for the divorce. Cherie charged me nothing.

"You and Zena are the best legal assistants in this galaxy," Cherie told me. "No way am I going to charge you a penny for this, Stevie, but you have to promise me you'll stay and work for me till you're a hundred."

My problem with Eddie Norbert came about because I had refused to follow the advice of my grandparents.

My grandpa told me to marry a man with integrity, who would give me a happy marriage like he had with my grandma. "The glorious love of my life, she is my life."

I did not do so.

He told me to marry someone honest and smart, who knew how to treat a lady.

I did not do so.

Grandma told me to marry a man who would dance under the stars with me but still get up to milk the cows the next day, praise the Lord.

I did not do that, either.

She told me to use my brain. "Fall in love with your head first, honey. Know beyond a shadow of a doubt that he will love you forever, be loyal and true, and then let your heart sing with his, let your destiny be bound from now till heaven, like it is with your grandpa and me."

Nope. Not that.

Because I blocked out the sweet voices of my grandparents, because it hurt too much to do otherwise, I followed my own, depressed, desperate, semicomatose, troubled self into a relationship I never should have been in. I had never been on a date, didn't think anyone would ever want to date me, and didn't really care that much, either. So when Eddie asked me out, it was a shock.

Eddie worked for my uncle. He was an average man, sort of paunchy, with narrow eyes. He thought I'd come with money. He told me that later. "You mean your uncle isn't going to help us buy a house at all?" He was aghast, furious. He threw a clock across the hotel room. We were on our honeymoon.

"No, we both work. We can do it, Eddie. I'm not taking a penny of his money. Ever. Not that he would offer it. You know how I feel about him. I told you how he treated me as a child, how he treats me and Lance and Polly—"

"Get over it, Stevie, I don't give a rat's ass about that. You suck up to him. I work for him, I want to be vice president in his company, and your attitude is not going to stand in my way, got that?"

I nodded meekly.

I tried to be a good wife to him. I was pathetic.

I made his breakfast, his dinner, kept the house, worked full time, washed his car, took his shirts to the dry cleaners. He took my check and put it into his account. He handled the money. He gave me an allowance. Forty dollars a month. He refused to allow me to see where the money was going. I allowed him to refuse me that information.

"Get me a beer. . . . Get your ass home. . . . Rub my feet. . . . Where's your check? Why haven't you asked for a raise? . . . You embarrass me, Stevie. . . . God, you're getting fatter every day. . . . Why the fuck can't you keep beer in the fridge? Is it so damn hard? . . . I don't know what went on in your past and I don't want to know, but get over it. I'm sick of you acting like a whipped puppy. . . . Here, doggy, here. . . . You looked at my cell phone calls? How dare you, you bitch. That's none of your fucking business. I don't have to tell you who Morgan is. I don't have to tell you who Elisa is, either. . . . You can't satisfy a man, Stevie. You'll never be able to. Deal with it. . . . Shut up. . . . Close your fat trap. . . . Talk to your uncle. I want that promotion. . . . Ask him for money. Tell him you want to buy me a boat. No? What the hell do you mean, no? I'm not giving you any money for clothes. I don't care if it's been two years. You're fat, woman, and nothing you wear is gonna slim down that ass."

I was heavy on our wedding day and gained 100 pounds during my marriage. I ate everything. I could consume large pizzas by myself, half-gallon ice-cream tubs, an entire batch of chocolate chip cookies, bags of chips. I hated myself afterward, but during my eating, everything went away, the memories, the sadness. I was lost in a blurry, distant land of binging bliss.

We had agreed not to have children. I love kids, but mental illness was speckled all over Grandma's family line and no way was I going to risk having a child who had to endure what my mother did. It wasn't fair to the child. My first pregnancy was within the first year of my marriage. One night I told Eddie to get the condoms, but he refused because it wasn't "as slippery" for him, especially since he had to deal with "all your rolls of fat." I tried to push him off; he refused and slapped me. Twice. Then he finished his business with a groan and rolled over with a fart.

Eddie was so ticked at the pregnancy. "This is your fault. We can't afford it. You're hardly making any money, and you sure as hell aren't going to stay home with it. . . . Find a day care. . . . Don't expect me to help with it. This was your idea, not mine. I'm not ready to be a dad. You're too fat already." He was so mad, he wouldn't sleep with me for two months. "You've pushed me out of bed, Stevie, so now you're responsible for the consequences."

Except for his response, though, I was thrilled . . . and scared to death for the mental health of my child. Memories of my experience with Helen in the cave deluged me, and that brought on another wave of emotion that I battled back down with piles of food, but the joy was still so . . . present. Continual. At the end of three months, he moved back into our bedroom and forced himself on me. "You better lose weight after you have this brat or we're done."

That was his foreplay. I was dry because I wasn't remotely turned on, and he told me, "You can't even get yourself oiled up, can you? God, you're bad in bed. You can't even move. You squish around. You're gonna smother me. I can't even find your hole!"

I cried into my pillow. The next day I lost the baby.

Eddie said, "Good. We weren't ready. Don't screw up on the birth control again, Stevie. That was stupid of you. How come you haven't got that raise yet?"

I mourned for the baby until I thought my heart would burst.

Another year into our marriage, I got pregnant again. The pill had made me sick, so I had gotten a diaphragm. He had refused to get off of me so I could put my diaphragm in one night.

I had told him I didn't want to have sex with him because he was drunk so he had to exert control. He told me I was getting to be a shrilly, fat, fishwife nag head. (His father had been a fisherman.) I told him to get off. He told me he was my husband and that was his right and he hated working for Herbert and had I bought more beer?

That was his foreplay.

He blamed me when I told him I was pregnant. I lost that sweet baby in the fourth month. I bled profusely, left work, called him.

He never showed up at the hospital.

In fact, he came home drunk, and I mourned that baby until I thought my heart would burst a second time.

And I still stayed with Eddie.

If that, folks, doesn't give you an idea of how screwed up I was, how profoundly depressed, I don't know what will.

In the middle of the night, for weeks on end, I blamed myself for both miscarriages. The doctors had been blunt: I needed to lose masses of weight. I wasn't healthy enough to be pregnant. I was high-risk. I could put the baby at risk and my own life. Don't try to get pregnant again, Stevie, until you've lost weight.

Devastating.

My fault.

My guilt. More guilt.

I went on a low-dose birth control pill that made me nauseated only one week out of the month, and stayed for another miserable year, sinking deeper and deeper into a sludge-filled emotional pit. I quit thinking, quit reacting, quit making chairs out in a shed in our backyard that Eddie had reluctantly let me have for my "fucked-up brain." I quit being a person the second I walked into our home each night after work. I could help handle the complex litigation at our firm. I had attorneys tell me all the time that I "saved their lives," I had attorneys (seriously) fight over who got to work with me, and Cherie told me repeatedly that Zena and I easily do the work of four people.

But at home, with Eddie, I was a profoundly scared,

continually-on-alert, mentally battered shell of a woman. In the back of my mind I knew I had to leave, but I couldn't.

What made me finally take that step?

My near death.

Besides Lance hitting Eddie in the face twice, "knocking the snot out of him," as Lance put it, and Polly screaming at him on multiple occasions that he was a "short, hog-faced, abusive, cigarette-sucking, slobbering drunk, and I hate you and will always hate you. What the hell is wrong with you, Stevie, why are you still with him?" the defining moment was my heart attack.

I said to Eddie, "I think I'm having a heart attack."

He grabbed a beer and said, "It's all your fat squishing in on you."

I said, "I can't breathe."

He said, "Shut up. The game's on."

I said, "I've got shooting pains."

He said, "That's your arteries cracking from fat."

I called 911. Then Lance and Polly.

I was wheeled away to the ambulance on a special stretcher for obese people who weighed 325 pounds or more. I thought I had a rhino lounging on my chest. I could hardly suck any air in, and there were shooting pains down both arms, like knives had been stabbed into my veins. Both Lance and Polly came running toward me after screeching to a halt outside my house in Lance's Porsche. Both were crying, giant Lance crying harder than Polly.

And there was Eddie, sitting on our front porch smoking a cigarette as they loaded me up into the ambulance. Polly got in with me, hysterical, saying over and over, "I love you, Stevie, I love you, oh, I love you," and Lance would follow in his car. My last vision before the ambulance doors slammed shut?

Lance hit Eddie, twice. Boom boom. I think it knocked the snot out of his nose.

Eddie never came to visit me at the hospital.

Polly, Lance, and Aunt Janet hardly left my side. Several

friends, neighbors, and coworkers came by. Even Herbert came and, I was surprised to see, had to leave the room when his eyes filled up with tears. Before he left the room he did manage to utter, "This is what happens when you get so fat, Stevie. It's not a surprise."

Cherie Poitras visited. I remember she was wearing ankle boots, a brown leather skirt, pink lace shirt, and matching brown leather vest.

She brought me all the divorce papers to sign.

Herbert was there when I signed the papers. Cherie said to him, "Hello. I'm Cherie Poitras. It says a lot about you that a man who has abused your niece for years is still working for you. How strange that is. How peculiar. How unprotective and unmanly."

Herbert blustered, turned all red. He hardly knew what to do with this woman towering over him in leather and ankle boots.

"I know many people who know Eddie." She put her manicured fingers to her chin, as if thinking. (This wasn't true, she told me later.) "Everyone knows that deceitful, hunk of hairy prick works for you only because he's married to Stevie. With this divorce, which will be very, very public (It wasn't; Cherie was blowing smoke), are you concerned that people will think less of you if he still works for you? But maybe your reputation doesn't concern you. (She knew it concerned the egomaniac immensely.) Maybe you're not worried about what the people at your club and at private dinner parties are saying about you and the terrible way Eddie treats Stevie. Good for you not to care what anyone thinks!" She poked him in the chest, and he stumbled back.

Herbert blustered again, turned redder. Fired Eddie that day. Eddie eventually ended up in Louisiana after the house sold.

I went home and cleared out all my stuff with Lance, Polly, and a bunch of Lance's ex–pro football friends. Eddie came home when we finished. He was semidrunk.

That's when Eddie said, "Good-bye, fat cunt."

Lance helped the snot fly out of his nose again.

Twice.

Then one of the pro football players, now a curator at a museum, tripped him flat.

I had clarity for the first time in years.

And this is what the clarity told me: You will never be with a man again who doesn't treat you as Grandpa treated Grandma, complete with the dancing under the stars. That man probably doesn't exist, but being alone is far better than this.

And then I cried, thinking about Grandpa and Grandma, how this marriage would have been such a disappointment to them, how I was a disappointment, how I had failed them. I cried about that, then cried for them, and somewhere in that mess I swear I could feel their arms around me.

Six months later, I had my stomach-shrinking operation. I had this choice: lose weight or die.

After some debate I chose the former.

As I was rolled down the hospital corridor on a stretcher by a nurse, my IV line pushed by a second nurse, I remember a woman self-righteously announce, "Whoa. I can't believe that! It's a *woman!* How does anyone get *that* fat?"

"Ohhhhh. Myyyyy. Goooood!" the woman next to her gasped, not bothering to lower her voice. As if because I was fat, I was deaf. This is a common misconception in America. Fat people can *hear.* We hear what you say, and we know what you think of us. "She's huge! That stomach! It's a human mini-mountain. I'm surprised she's not dead."

"That's gross, that is *so* gross! Eww!"

"They should have stapled her up a long time ago."

I tried to shut out their voices, their giggles, their snorts of laughter. One of my nurses, an African American with the most gorgeous, greenish eyes I've ever seen, said to them, "Thank you for keeping your rude, judgmental comments to yourself."

My other nurse snapped, "Be quiet this instant." We stopped to glare at them, and then I said, "Guess what? I can hear. Fat people have ears. They work." I flipped my middle fingers up, which is so unlike me, and said, "Let's see if you have eyes. Can you see this? That's right, my fingers are saying, Fuck you. Do you see that? Fuck you."

My nurses laughed and we turned the corner.

I felt bad instantly for using that language. I could almost hear my grandma saying, "Never cuss unless it's at Herbert, praise the Lord. The Lord knows what Herbert's like and He'll give you a pass."

But here's the thing that obese people live with: I am enormously fat; therefore, I do not exist. I do not have value in a society that judges thinness and money above all else. It's the last acceptable prejudice. You could never say about an African American, a gay person, a Hispanic or a Jew what people say about fat people. Never. You'd be considered a raving racist.

But to address the woman's question in the hallway of the hospital: How do you get as fat as I was?

It's not too hard.

Eating copious amounts of food will do the job splendidly, and avoiding the gym as one might avoid a cobra having a menopausal hot flash might be another.

But that's not the right question. The right question is this: *Why* did I, why does anyone, get this fat?

Why is the question.

And for that, I am convinced, you have to go way back, for most people who are morbidly obese, into the depths of their childhood, no matter how dark and murky and disturbing, and you will find that answer.

How do I know? Because I've been in group counseling for ages with obese people. With rare exception, they all had trauma in their childhoods: Abandonment. Poverty. Neglect. Abuse. Parents on drugs or alcohol. Sibling sicknesses or deaths. One woman's mother beat her until she passed out on a regular basis. Another was attacked each morning by her brothers. One man ate because he lost his father in a war and his mother dealt with it by dropping him off at a series of relatives' houses. He was on his own at the age of thirteen.

Yes, pause a second and take a peek into their pasts, if they'll let you, and you will find the answer to the fat question.

You will also find, almost without exception, the answer extremely, horrifyingly, ugly.

A few days later I ventured to my garage, pulled out a rocking chair, and asked it: Have you ever lost yourself in a relationship? Has the most lonely part of your life occurred while being married to someone? Have you ever been married and sucked it up but in your truest heart you knew you would never marry that person again if God gave you a second chance?

Is there someone you wished you had married instead? If you had to do it over, would you marry at all? What is the purpose of marriage? Who does it benefit?

What's your name? Answer: Question Mark. I laughed.

I decided to carve a giant question mark for the back of the rocking chair. I would paint a bride and groom on the seat. The bride would wear a short, fluffy red dress, the groom a tux. In a balloon above her head the bride would be thinking of a beach in Mexico and the groom would be thinking about a beer. The armrests would be painted with pink and white flowers.

What would it be like to be Jake's wife?

I would not need a question mark for that, I would need an exclamation point! See, like this!!

Lance and I went to visit Polly at the clinic.

Polly told us she would have to drink three scotches on the rocks, not many rocks, before coming to the anniversary party. "Maybe a daiquiri, too. I could come in stumbling drunk. Then Dad would tell everyone he had a 'mentally ill, alcoholic daughter who refuses to lift her fork to her mouth and put food in it. It's an attention-getting mechanism. She gets it from her mother's side of the family. They're insane. All men carry a burden, this is mine, but I will shoulder it, as is my duty.'"

And Lance said, "I would rather have a vampire bite off a testicle than go to this party." He snapped his fingers. "Do you think that there's a market out there for vampire blow-up dolls? I'll bet there is!"

And I said, "I hate the Atherton case," and then told them about Danny, the boy who loved dragon stories. Lance blubbered. Polly said she would have her henchmen kill Crystal as soon as she got out of the clinic.

Polly had finally agreed to work with Annie Sinclair. She was humbler this visit, more emotional. Broken, but in a good way. She was finally, finally trying to save herself.

Annie was half Hispanic and half African American. She had a long black ponytail and huge, dark eyes. I talked with Annie in her office for about an hour, answering all the questions she had about Polly. In particular she focused on Herbert.

Then she asked me about me.

I clammed up.

In a gentle way, she asked again.

I sidestepped.

A third and fourth time, a gentle prod for information.

I declined.

I think it was on the fifth time around that I caved.

I think I had been wanting to cave, probably for my whole life. I had had some counseling before the bariatric surgery, but not much. I had said I hadn't known my dad and my momma drowned. I left out a couple hundred other details.

I filled in a few of those details for Annie.

I was a mess when I left.

She agreed to see me through her private practice.

I agreed that was a good idea.

Jake called and asked me out to dinner for Friday. I had to decline, but said, "How about Saturday around eleven for brunch?"

He said that was fine, but I could tell he wasn't happy. On Saturday he took me out on the Willamette on a boat his brother owned, and the weather cooperated—blue skies, sunny day.

We talked about his bridge-building work. He loved it; he travelled all over and would be going to Venice in late fall. We talked about my work. We talked about politics and social issues and even about art, and we agreed to go see a new display at the museum. I don't think that Jake and I ever stopped talking around each other, ever.

"Tell me about your family," he said.

I told him about Herbert, referred to him as a cannibal who did not exactly eat people, simply chomped around the edges, and Aunt Janet. I did not mention the alcoholism. He knew about Polly, but I told him how I could not have had a better cousin in my life, the same with Lance. He knew who Lance was. "He's your cousin? I met him a few times at meetings in Portland. He's a great guy." I told him about the blow-up dolls and said he was not allowed to have one. He said he did not desire one.

"What about your parents?"

I did not want to lie. But I didn't want to talk about it, either. "My mother's dead, and I didn't know my father."

He stared at me pretty intently, then linked an arm around my shoulders. "Anytime, sweetheart, anytime."

I had to be back in the late afternoon. He didn't question why, but I could tell that this man was not going to be put off much longer. It wasn't in his nature.

We did, however, have the very best kisses on the boat, hot and delectable, made better by wine and cheese and turkey sandwiches he'd brought.

I was beginning to think I could fall in love with this man, I could.

Crystal was in full-blast, Victory-Is-Near mode.

I felt that victory was not near.

Since the case started eons ago, she had smothered the Athertons' attorneys in paperwork, engaged in aggressive discovery, required depositions of eight million people, filed a barrage of motions in court, continued to argue that the medical outcome could have been expected because it was detailed in the paperwork the Athertons signed, etc., etc.

"Smother them into submission until they can't breathe and

are totally broke and despondent. That's how I work," Crystal said.

We had another meeting with the Athertons, which for some reason Crystal wanted me to come to. Sonja Woods and Dirk Evans were working out of Sonja's garage so they had no office.

Crystal had told them she wanted to meet them on their "turf," and as Sonja and Dirk had no turf, we were now sitting in an office they had borrowed. You see, this was Crystal's way of sticking it to them. "Let's see where you all work. You've seen the glamorous place where I work in downtown Portland. You're obviously nothing. I'm something, so roll over and die."

The office was in a worn-down office building. There was a table that wobbled and eight wooden chairs. I would be delighted to have those chairs for my obsession.

Crystal rolled her eyes when she saw their "office." "Nice, glamorous."

Sonja and Dirk did not comment. Both of them were exhausted, grayish, and sported huge circles under their eyes. Sonja was bone thin and Dirk was gaining weight. The Athertons were sagging.

"I and my firm are losing patience with you people," Crystal said.

I wanted to groan.

"We understand," Sonja said, tipping her chin up. "But we refuse to compromise on the original amount."

This went on and on, grandstanding and rudeness by Crystal, class and quiet determination by Sonja and Dirk. On and on till I wanted to bang my head on the table.

"That's enough, Crystal," I whispered.

She kicked me, hard, under the table, pontificated and threatened on and on, and finally said to the Athertons, "Do you people think, for a minute, that you can win a case against us?" She glared at the Athertons. "Give up. You're up against the big guys and we always win. *I* do not lose. I'm sorry about your boy, Dan, but accept things as they are and move on."

She swung her designer shoe, plucked at her $800 suit, and pushed her black hair back.

"Don't attack my clients," Dirk said.

Crystal snickered. Long, lean, glamorous. "Your clients need to be educated about this issue. We have a *housewife* (Slimy vermin. Lazy loser. Bottom-dwelling infected crab) and a plumber here, and they don't get the legal ramifications. If we go to trial, you can, Mr. and Mrs. Atherton, *you will*, walk away with nothing. Got it? All this for nothing. You, Dirk and Sonja, need to explain this without the legalese so these two"— she jerked her head toward the Athertons—"can understand."

I leaned forward and grabbed Crystal's arm. "Crystal, close your mouth." She yanked her arm away, glared at me, kicked.

At that, Mrs. Atherton, wearing jeans and a yellow T-shirt, her face pale with worry and defeat, started to cry. Quiet, hopeless, hot tears.

"Oh, dear," I said. "Oh, dear." I reached across the wobbly table and grabbed her hand. I could hold on for only a second, because the table was lifted up, up, up, then smashed back down by Mr. Atherton, the noise thunderous, papers and folders flying everywhere.

"You are a bitch," Mr. Atherton seethed, his muscles flexing under his blue T-shirt. "In my life, I have never met anyone more obnoxious, condescending, and cruel than you. You are absolutely heartless. I never thought I'd meet a person who truly had no heart, but now I have. You are a cold, manipulative person, and if you can go home and stare at yourself in the mirror and be happy with what you see, then more power to you. But, me, I see someone that makes my wife—" He paused, tried to hold in the tears that suddenly sprung to his eyes—"You are someone that makes my wife—a woman who is so much smarter than you, funnier, kinder, *better than you*—you make her cry. You have made her cry a hundred times, Crystal. Every time she leaves this office, *and you,* she cries."

He brushed a hand across his face.

Dirk jumped up next to him, ready to hold him back physically, but not verbally.

Crystal's mouth hung open in shock, as if she were trying to catch wasps or mosquitoes in it.

"And you know what?" Mr. Atherton continued, his voice splitting down the middle with pain. "This didn't need to be this way. It didn't. We have a son, Crystal, a son we love dearly, Danny, who fights for every single breath he takes. Every single one. We are on our knees, every day, praying for a miracle and none comes. None. We pray for strength to get through the day. We pray for work for me. We pray we have enough energy for our other kids. We pray in thanks for all the people in our lives who help us, who bring us meals, who entertain the other boys, who even come and clean our house and mow our lawn, and the guys who washed my truck the other day."

I could hear Crystal's breath, ragged. She tapped her heels.

I glared at her, arms crossed.

Mr. Atherton picked up the table and smashed it down again, then stuck his square chin out. "And you know what, Crystal? My wife makes me pray for you. *For you.*"

Wow, I thought. I couldn't do that. No way. Praise the Lord.

"I wouldn't do it at first, I couldn't. *I can't stand you.* You have stood in the way of me being able to help my son for a wrong that was done to him in a hospital that promised to fix him, not hurt him. But my wife—" Again he swiped at his eyes, then put a hand on her shoulder. "My wife insisted that I pray for you. We pray, Crystal, that you find happiness. We pray that you learn how to feel, to be kind and compassionate and giving. We pray that our hearts will forgive you and that God will forgive you. My wife only had to pray the prayer of forgiveness twice. I still have to pray it every day. But I do. I am trying to forgive you."

I was so struck by that, I started to cry, and I grabbed Mrs. Atherton's hand again. She was startled, but she did not pull away.

"My beautiful, strong, courageous wife has more class, more character *in her ear* than you will ever dream of having. And here you are, making her cry." He picked up the table again and slammed it down once more. Our hands lost touch again as the table cracked, all the way down the middle.

Crystal made gaspy noises in her throat.

Mr. Atherton stood straight, shoulders back. "Crystal, you rotten person, I'm not arguing with you anymore. Our church gave us a check to help us through. We can pay our mortgage with no worries for a full year. Our cars are paid for. If I have to declare bankruptcy because of this medical debt, I will. No skin off my nose. I'm not moving or buying anything new at all. But I will not"—he bent over and pounded both sides of the cracked table, which then collapsed—"I will not give on the amount that we are requesting. Not one cent. It's fair. It's just. It's accurate. Danny will need care the rest of his life and that is the minimum amount of what it will cost. If you can't agree to it, that's fine. You want to fight this out some more, we'll do it. I will fight you until I die, and even if my wife makes me pray for you every one of those damn days, I'll do it."

He breathed hard for a second, piercing Crystal with those bright green eyes. She made more gaspy noises, mouth still trying to find that pesky mosquito!

Then Mr. Atherton, a husband, father, plumber, friend, gallantly pulled out his wife's chair, helped her up, hugged her close because she was still crying, and kissed her on the forehead. "I'm sorry I swore, honey," I heard him whisper. He glared at Crystal, and I knew he wanted to fry her on an open spit. Then they left.

I wanted to cheer.

What a stud.

Now that's the kind of man my grandpa would have wanted me to marry.

Crystal jabbered about the case incessantly in the car on the way back to the office, but I could tell she was rattled. Her hands shook and she couldn't catch her breath.

She was also, I think, thrown by Mr. Atherton. Strong. Courageous. Loving.

And there she was. Cruel. Heartless. Mean.

And somebody out there was praying for her.

Sheesh. The devil would have to be standing over me with a

pitchfork to my neck, flames shooting from his mouth, before I would pray for Crystal.

Praise the Lord, as my grandma would have said. God screwed up on Crystal, too.

The anniversary party planning was exhausting. I was getting calls from many people who had many problems.

For example, the tent people. One of their tents had collapsed at a wedding. The big one. The bride had a "hissy fit," so they would be bringing three smaller ones. Their people would be coming to Herbert's early in the morning the day of the party. It was scheduled to rain. Was I aware of this? Had I planned for it?

The ice sculpture people called. The owner was from Russia, and I could not understand his accent very well, although he seemed very apologetic. Their ice sculptress, naughty girl, had run off with her boyfriend to, of all places, Alabama, so they would not be able to provide two swans with their necks entwined. Their other ice sculptor refused to do swans—the necks drove him crazy. Crazy! Would a grizzly bear do? He could carve ferocious grizzlies! Sharp teeth! The owner growled.

No, a grizzly wouldn't do.

How about a tiger, long tail? Another growl. A sphinx? Zeus? Naked Zeus?

No.

What about gnomes? Two gnomes?

Double no.

I imagined two male gnomes side by side at an anti-gay marriage political rally/anniversary party. I imagined a naked Zeus, well endowed, sexy. Whew, boy.

We settled on two doves with a heart between them. At least, I think it was two doves. I couldn't understand him well. We did, definitely, though, have the heart. I understood that part. "Okay, miz. Is good. Is all good. We do." Click.

The florist called. The red and black flowers would be ready to go.

I did not order red and black flowers.

Yes, you did.

No, I didn't.

Yes . . . let me double-check. Oh! You're right. You didn't order red and black carnations. That's for the hard rock party the next night. Same last name, so there was some confusion. . . . Here's your order. Pink and yellow flowers for the anniversary party? Gee whiz. They weren't prepared for that. They'd have to order more. Okay! They'd do it! Had I ordered red and black roses surrounding a giant, white plastic skull? No? That was for the other party, too, then? What about the guitar wreaths? Also for the hard rock party that Saturday?

They'd fix it!

The one thing that was taken care of was the music. I called and asked the quartet if they were ready for the anniversary party. My cell phone connection wasn't very good, but I heard what I wanted to hear. They were organized. They would be on time. They would play classical music.

So, all was ready.

Except for Aunt Janet.

Aunt Janet was not ready.

I found that out at the last minute.

Annie Sinclair called and asked me and Lance to come together for an appointment with her and Polly. We both agreed immediately and met on Sunday at one o'clock.

You know how some families bury their secrets?

How the secrets implode and morph and turn into underground volcanoes and infected sores?

That's how our secret was, complete with shame, guilt, and a truckload of insidious grief that had magnified exponentially because it was "a secret."

Annie started us off. "As you know, Polly is making some progress here. A lot of progress." She smiled. Annie was a gentle soul.

"Good job, Polly!" Lance exclaimed. "Good job. I love you!"

"So although Polly has addressed some of the issues in your

family, including her issues with Herbert and Janet, you all have not addressed the tragedy in your past, have you?"

I felt myself sinking.

Lance covered his face. "I should have brought my knitting and a girl."

Polly said, wringing her hands, "I know, I know! I don't know if we can talk about it. I thought we should leave it where it is, but I think, I think—" She gasped, held her throat. "I think this secret is making me sick, it's keeping me sick! I need a bag."

"This is gonna hurt," Lance said. "Oh, poor, poor Stevie! I love you, Stevie!"

"We were never allowed to talk about what happened to your mom, Stevie, or Sunshine, or our grandparents," Polly said, holding a bag Annie handed to her. She patted her heart with her other hand. "Be still, heart, quiet down. All is well." Then said to us, "Dad told us never to talk about it, to keep it secret, to forget it happened, *or else.* I know you and I have talked about it a little bit, Stevie, and you with Lance, but we've basically shoved this scary, horrible thing away and tried to make it not there anymore."

"But it is here," Annie said. "It's always been here. You've never dealt with it, never tried to work it through, because you couldn't. You were forbidden to under threat of the gravest punishment, and yet it's continued to cause you the gravest pain."

"It never should have been shoved away," Lance said, pushing his shoulders back. "And I'm going to be a man about it now. A man. We've all circled it. We've smashed it down like a spiked football and it keeps coming up. It's freakin' followed us our whole lives. We've had a murder, a suicide, an attempted murder, and our grandparents died, and it's out there. Hurting us, here." He pounded his chest.

"Stevie," Polly said. "Honey, I don't want to hurt you, I don't, but . . ." She took a shaky breath in. "Can we quit circling it? Please?"

Two tsunami-sized emotions were sweeping through me. Grief, as usual. Grief over the secret. Secrets will kill you. If not physically, they will kill your insides. They will kill the life you want to live.

The second emotion I felt? Relief. Relief that someone wanted to say Sunshine's name, and talk about Grandma and Grandpa, and hear, even, my momma's name, and how Lance and Polly felt, and a million other things.

"Polly, let's talk about it." I pulled my lips in tight, feeling those tears edging on in. "Lance." He got up to hug me, not bothering to hide those ol' emotions rolling through him. "You're right. We can't circle this anymore."

"I love you, girls!" he declared. "I love you!"

We started then. We talked, hesitantly, about Sunshine, how cute she was, what we used to all do together on the farm with the animals and running down the hills together and playing in the hayloft. We talked about Helen. We laughed, not in a mean way, but in remembrance of her singing in church, her beaver hat, her necklaces. We cried for her. We tried to imagine that piercing, intense anguish she must have felt all the time, the fear, the aloneness, how she said many times that she was "just a Helen, a no-love person, I should be dead." We talked about our anger and our loss over her death and Sunshine's, and we talked about our grandparents—everything they tried to do to help, how they must have felt so hopeless and scared and devastated.

Grief killed them. We knew that.

We were there for hours and hours.

We would be there, in the future, for hours and hours.

But at least the secret was no longer a secret.

That was something.

I asked a chair a lot of questions that night:

Do you have any family secrets? What are they? How have they affected your life? What will happen if you talk about them? Is it better to talk about them or keep them buried? What are the consequences of both? Is it eating you?

I started painting the chair red. On the seat I painted a sunrise. I painted the legs with orange and yellow stripes. Later I would cut off the back and cut out a yellow ball for the sun for the backrest. I thought I'd carve out angel wings, too, and attach them.

Because don't we all need an angel hanging around when we want to start over?

The chair's name was Maybelle Swan.

I wished my insomnia would go away. It's exhausting. I thought of Jake. When he had tucked me in I hadn't had any nightmares at all. He was calling me every night to chat before we both went to sleep. It was a melody in my ear to hear him tell me good night.

But I still couldn't sleep very well.

I had a nightmare that night. I saw my mother. She was wielding a cornstalk as one would a sword. "You shouldn't have told!" she whispered. "You shouldn't have told!"

I cringed in the cave. She followed me in and put the cornstalk through my heart, and I died.

23

Ashville, Oregon

The love of sisters can transcend the mountainous difficulties of life.

Herbert, Aunt Janet, Lance, and Polly visited us about a week after Helen got home from another mental ward. Aunt Janet wanted to see her sister and the baby, as did Lance and Polly.

Helen let Aunt Janet hug her. She actually put her arms around Aunt Janet and said to her, "You smell like corn. I like corn."

Aunt Janet cried, and Helen wiped the tears from her face and licked them off her fingers. "All gone now," she said. Then she tapped Aunt Janet on the nose and Aunt Janet hugged her again. "I love you so much, Helen."

Helen nodded at Lance and Polly, the floppy yellow hat on her head bopping about. She was wearing a peasant's dress from her time on Broadway and a flowing pink cape. "You are a boy and you are a girl," she told them. "We have a Trash Heap here. Watch out." She pointed at Sunshine, asleep in a crib. "She bites."

Helen let Aunt Janet wash and condition her hair and even cut a few inches off where the knots had grown. She let Aunt Janet cut her scraggly fingernails and toenails. When we had dinner the next night, Helen looked so pretty. I've never forgotten it. Her hair shone, her makeup was perfect, her nails polished. She was wearing her pink tutu, but underneath it she had on an elegant green silk dress.

I noticed that Herbert stared at my momma for a long, long time at dinner.

In the middle of it, though, Herbert said, "Glory, more lasagna here." He did not bother to glance up from his plate.

"It's in the kitchen, Herbert," Grandpa said.

Herbert glared at him. "Women should be pleased to serve the men in the household, Albert."

"The women in this household are not required to serve the men. In fact, it is men, Herbert, *men* who should serve and protect women. It is the husband's responsibility to make sure that his wife is happy, that she has a full life and the freedom to become whoever she wants to become."

Herbert made a sound through his nose that said, essentially, "That's asinine, you old man." Then he said, "The man is the head of the house. All are to follow his lead, his rules, his direction, without question or dissent."

"Yes, and if you want everyone to hate you, and you want to lose your relationship with your wife and with your children, be sure to continue insisting that your family follows your arcane, abusive rules. You're going to end up alone, Herbert."

He snorted again. "*My* wife knows her place."

"I wish my daughter would find a new place," Grandma said, trembling she was so mad. "Preferably one quite a long ways away from the place she's in now."

Helen decided to show off her poetry skills then. "Herbert Herbert. A herb. A Bert. A Bert Herb. A tiny stick, for a dick. A little man, a skinny thing thing, he'll wind up playing with his bang bang." She swirled her spaghetti noodles. No sauce. She was not eating red or pink food today so Grandma gave her plain noodles. "He has a mean voice. He has a mean heart. He'll stick his thingie in your part."

Aunt Janet gasped. Lance and Polly giggled.

Herbert swallowed hard and flushed bright red. "Control yourself, Helen—"

Helen threw her fork and it landed in the middle of Herbert's plate, then skittered off into his lap, bringing lasagna with it. "He wants to be a big man but he's not. He's a little man with lots of snot. Hooked fat nose, loose jiggling bottom. Fingers like worms, a dick like cotton."

"You crazy bitch—" Herbert started.

Oh, now, that was it for Grandpa. He grabbed Herbert under his shoulders, yanked him out of his seat, and dragged him to the front door, his feet barely touching the ground as he cursed and squirmed. We heard fighting outside, then Grandpa came in, by himself, and sat down. He bent his head, crossed his hands, and prayed. We crossed our hands and bent our heads, too. Grandpa's prayer was, "Lord, help me to control myself around the Devil's henchman. Amen."

Grandma flicked back her white curls and said, "Lord, please do Your work as You see fit with an evil person who is short and who was sitting at my table a second ago. Perhaps he needs to meet You face-to-face soon. Just a suggestion. In Your son's name I pray."

Ten minutes later we heard Herbert honking the horn of his car. In a flash, Aunt Janet was up, flustered, hurriedly gathering up her things, tripping on her feet.

Lance cried, "We're in trouble now!"

Polly whimpered, "Help me! Now we're going to get it. Help!"

They all popped up, pushing back their chairs, in the middle of dinner. Lance's chair tumbled over. Polly ran into the couch. I was aghast. No one left Grandma's table in the middle of dinner!

Grandpa stood up. "You all stay right here. I'll take care of this."

Grandpa shut the front door of our Schoolhouse House and all of us scrambled to the window and peeked outside through the lace curtains. I thought Grandpa was going to talk sense into Herbert, who was sitting in the car, horn on full blast. He didn't. Grandpa had something in his hand, a tool of some sort, and he used it to pry open the hood of the Cadillac, then reached under it.

Within a second the honking stopped. Grandpa slammed the

hood back down and marched back up the steps, the porch light illuminating his angry expression. He threw the tool onto the porch.

When he came inside he sat down, calm and quiet, and said, "Please, Janet, Lance, and Polly, enjoy your lasagna. You will not be leaving at this time."

Aunt Janet sunk down into her chair. Helen reached across the table, grabbed Aunt Janet's hand, and said, "Get rid of that snake. If he was my snake, I'd cut his head off."

Grandma patted Aunt Janet's shoulder. "This situation can be remedied. I have already prayed about it, and God told me to tell you to divorce him. He said you will be much happier without him. I heard it loud and clear."

Lance's and Polly's mouths dropped to huge O's.

Aunt Janet hung her head, chin to buttoned-down blouse. Herbert made her dress so frumpy.

"Glory, this is delicious," Grandpa said, smoothing over the awkward moment. "You are the best cook this side of the Mississippi." He took another bite. "No, I'm wrong. You are the best cook on both sides of the Mississippi."

Grandpa had another bite of lasagna. "Rats. I'm wrong a second time. You, Glory sweetie, are the best cook on both sides of the Mississippi, the entire North American continent, and in all of Europe, including Turkey. A country called Turkey," Grandpa mused. "How come we don't have a country called French Fries? We have a country called Chile. We need a country called Chocolate Milkshake."

Polly giggled.

Grandma laughed, a curl falling into her face.

Lance grinned.

Even Aunt Janet smiled.

About twenty minutes later we heard Herbert pounding up the steps.

He bellowed for Aunt Janet and the kids to come outside right that damn minute and get in the damn car.

"Janet, Lance, and Polly, you are to stay right here," Grandpa said as he opened the front door and stepped out. We all, even Helen, scrambled to the windows to see the action and got there in time to see Herbert punch Grandpa in the face.

Grandpa's face didn't even move, that's how solid my grandpa was. But then Grandpa's fist came up and Herbert went flying off the porch, landing on his buttocks.

That's when Helen took charge. "I'm going to take care of that snake. He makes me booger mad." She gave Aunt Janet a kiss on the lips and a hug, then stuffed three napkins into her bra and darted out through the kitchen door to the garage. About one minute later we saw Helen skipping from the garage, her pink tutu bopping about over her green silky dress.

She was carrying an ax.

We all scrambled out to the front porch.

When Herbert saw that ax, he got behind his Cadillac and shrieked, "Albert, get your crazy daughter away from me."

Well, now, Grandpa apparently had no inclination to do so. As we watched the scenario unfold, he said, "Glory, I would get out there and try to control our daughter, but I am so full of your delicious lasagna, I cannot move. Might give me indigestion." He patted his stomach.

Helen released a long, pitched Tarzan cry.

And Grandma said, "I understand, sweetheart." She wrapped an arm around his waist. "The cheese was very heavy tonight. Oh, my goodness, I can barely move myself."

Helen pointed the ax toward the sky with one hand and stuck her middle finger up at Herbert with the other. She yelled, "An ax and a booger and a bottom-faced man, I'll cut you up and dump you in a can."

"Here, I'll call Helen back into the house." Grandma cleared her throat once, twice, then whispered, "Helen, please come back inside, dear."

Helen started swinging that ax around her head in a circular motion.

"You think of everything, Glory," Grandpa said. "I'll help you out." He sighed, then whispered, "All right, fun's over. Come on in, Helen."

Helen shrieked, "I'm going to cut off your stick, snake!"

Aunt Janet and Polly and Lance were gaping, but after a second they started laughing, trying to muffle the sound with their hands over their mouths as Helen chased Herbert. I laughed, but I didn't bother to cover my mouth. I cheered, "Go, Helen! Get the snake! Hiss hiss!"

Helen stopped running for a mere second, turned toward all of us out on the porch, and bowed, quite elegantly, tutu bopping. She continued chasing Herbert around his Cadillac, and when she couldn't catch up, she smashed the ax into the hood of the car.

Herbert shouted in protest, and she sang, hitting a high C, "Snake, snake, slimy snake, I'll cut off your head and make a cake!"

She swung the ax onto the trunk.

Herbert screamed and swore.

Grandpa stroked his stomach. "Still too full to move."

"Cakes are good, cakes are bad, I'll use your balls and not my dad's," Helen trilled out. She broke the front windshield. "Sugar, salt, and flour, I'll have you chopped up within an hour."

Herbert swore.

Grandma whispered, "I think we're done, Helen. How about some pie?"

"You can say luck." Helen's soprano dipped into the soft darkness of the night. "You can say muck. You can say duck, but you can't say fuck." She brought the ax down on a door. "You fucker. You're bad to my Janet."

This went on for quite a while.

I was so entertained. "Good work with the rhymes, Momma!"

Aunt Janet giggled.

"Do you think she'll kill him?" Lance asked.

"Maybe," Polly said. Neither seemed concerned.

"It's cherry pie, Helen," Grandma whispered.

Eventually Herbert escaped into his car, screaming obscenities, and took off.

He went straight to the police.

Grandpa called Uncle Peter, the chief.

The chief arrested Herbert for assault against Grandpa.

That night, me, Polly, and Lance listened against the closed door of the den while Grandpa and Grandma told Aunt Janet to divorce Herbert. I heard the same arguments. Something about a man named Victor. . . . Herbert would declare her "unfit". . . . Her alcohol problems . . . He would take the kids. . . . She had to protect them from him. . . .

In the middle of it Helen walked in and declared, "Get rid of that snake! He poops the devil."

For the next two weeks, Aunt Janet, Lance, and Polly were at our house. We all spent time with Sunshine. Polly, especially, loved Sunshine, loved holding her. We called her "our baby."

At first they were nervous, all of them, jittery and unsmiling, as if they couldn't get Herbert's terrible aura off.

But then they let go of it, and we played in the stream, in the barn, on the property. We went to church, we made cookies, and we hung out with The Family.

When Herbert came back to get Aunt Janet, me and Polly and Lance had become blood brother and sisters.

I never forgot it.

Neither did they.

And, against my grandpa's and grandma's advice, Aunt Janet went back to Herbert, taking Lance and Polly with her, both crying.

We were careful with Sunshine around Helen. The baby's crying sometimes made Helen run from the house. "Too noisy. A siren." Her size made her nervous. "Too small," she said. "She'll break." Her smell at times was not favorable, either. "Something is bad in that thing. A rotten egg or a skunk." And the kicker: "They sent Trash Heap to watch me. I think she took my coat."

She watched the baby from afar. Sometimes she'd wiggle her fingers in the air at Sunshine, her face intense, worried, confused. And sometimes Helen would wave at her. That was truly sad, Helen standing ten feet away and waving at her own child. When I saw her blowing Sunshine kisses as she lay in Grandma's arms one time, but not coming near to hold her or hug her, I had to run outside to the garden and bury my head in my knees and cry by the carrots.

Even then, I got it. A mother, so whacked out by disease that she couldn't have a relationship with her own child, was waving at her. "Hello, Trash Heap," she called softly. "Hello, Trash Heap." And then, "I don't like you. You need to go home. Punk said bye. Get out. Good-bye."

One fine day, when Grandma, me, Helen, and baby Sunshine were in the grocery store, Helen decided there were microphones in the bread loaves.

"Honey, there's no microphones," Grandma said. She put a calming hand on Helen's arm. Helen was wearing her black rubber farm boots with the chicken wire and a trench coat over a lacy red negligee. On the way into the store she'd opened up her coat as if she was flashing people and sauntered on in, hips swaying.

"Yes, there are microphones," Helen whispered. She had refused to button the trench coat. "They're spying on me. They're here to watch me. It's a cushintong."

"No, honey, they're not spying. There's no cushintong. It's bread. Now, come on over with me and Stevie and let's get a doughnut. You love doughnuts. Do you want a chocolate doughnut or a white sprinkled?"

But Helen was not to be dissuaded. Grandma had done up her blond hair into a bun and she ripped that bun down, her blond waves falling to her shoulders. She lunged for the shelves and started climbing them. Grandma reached for her and grabbed her around the waist. I grabbed at her boots. "Helen, come on, honey, let's go have a delicious doughnut."

"Momma, get down, please, please," I begged her. I was so embarrassed. I saw one of my friends, a girl named Heather who lived on the next farm, staring at Helen, her eyes wide. "Momma, there's no microphones."

Helen kicked at me and Grandma until Grandma had to let go, and she scrambled to the top shelf in the bread aisle. Once there, she started throwing the bread off, then lay on her stomach, reached down to the second shelf, and started throwing the bread off there, too, despite our begging her not to. When all the bread was on the ground, she lay on the top shelf and covered her eyes with her arms. "I need my helmet! Get me my helmet! They're trying to read my mind with the microphones."

"Helen, I have your helmet at home. We'll go home and get it lickety-split," Grandma said, her face and voice calm. The helmet Helen wore was Grandpa's when he was a football star at Ashville High School.

"You can come down, Momma. Here. You can wear my ribbon over your head until we get home. It's okay, Momma, it's okay. Please come down." I glanced down the aisle. Heather was gone. Heather's mother was friends with Grandma. Maybe she'd pulled Heather away to spare Grandma.

"I don't want a ribbon. You'll use it against my neck. Did you get my doughnut? Is that girl kid getting a doughnut?" Helen asked, pointing at me. "If she gets one, I get one."

"You'll get a doughnut—"

"First I'll get my helmet on, then we'll get a doughnut."

"Helen, that's right. Now, come on down."

"No. Helmet first." She punctuated her desire with a piercing, high C.

By this time several employees, including the manager, Stan Blackhawk, were there. Stan's brother was one of the executives at Grandpa's company. He was Native American and wore his hair in a long ponytail, as Stan did.

"Hello, Glory," he said to Grandma, nodding to Helen on the top shelf, her arms covering her face. "Hello, Helen. Hello, Stevie." He smiled at Sunshine in the stroller.

"Hello, Stan," Grandma said, turning to shake his hand. "Oh, and hello, boys!" She smiled warmly. The two young men standing next to Stan were former students of Grandma's.

They both grinned and hugged her. They all greeted me with cheerful hellos, and wasn't I getting taller. I sure resembled my Grandma's family line. Isn't that dimple cute?

Well, you would have thought we were at the town picnic then. Grandma chatted, at length, with Stan and the young men. I heard about their mothers. One was having problems with her bladder; the other one was having problems with toenail fungus and had had a fight with her sister, Scootie. They still weren't speaking.

Then she talked to Stan. Stan's wife, Camille, was well. They had six kids and another was on the way. This one was clearly a "whoops" child, but he was happy about it. "The wife is not happy about being pregnant while having hot flashes, though."

So they all chatted, and other people stopped on by and saw Helen lying on the top shelf, now singing, "We're off to see the wizard." They waved at her, ignored all the loaves of bread on the floor, and joined the conversation. Jackie Klind (a doctor in town) had discovered the greatest cure for warts, and she had fixed up two of the neighbors' kids recently. Could Grandma come and help settle a dispute between the Phillipses and Montezes? They were having trouble with cattle crossing each other's property and Jeremiah was threatening to shoot. How about that Fourth of July parade coming up, wouldn't that be fun? Wasn't it sad that Pho and Julie had broken up? Julie was heartbroken, hadn't left her home for six days. Six days!

About an hour later Grandma decided it was time for us to move along. Helen had sung a number of songs, and you could believe you were listening to the radio, her voice was so haunting and lovely. But then Helen started making up her own love song and inserting swear words. It was something like, "Tulips and daffodils and bridges over blue streams, sunny days and raindrops and cartwheeling in the park, my heart is breaking. . . . my heart is so sad. . . . my heart is fuuucckkkkeed uppppp, it is so fuuuuccckkkked upppp . . ."

Grandma did not appreciate swear words. "Sugar, come on down, now. I'm hungry. Let's get those doughnuts."

"Not unless I can get a helmet," Helen said, stopping her

song abruptly. "I'm not coming down. It's dangerous. I need to smother Command Center. Punk, too. He's back. Red eyes."

Well, we all thought on that, and then Derek, one of the young men, decided he would run home and get his football helmet, and he did and he brought it back and he climbed up to the top shelf and helped Helen get it on. She had to move her foil hat around a little bit, but then we were all set.

She sat up, fiddled with the helmet, declared, "I've got some control now," and came on down. Everyone said hello, Helen said hello back and, "I've got some songs in me." She sang another show tune. We clapped at the end. Mr. Tsong cried. His late wife loved that song.

"Now, Stan, you be sure to charge me for this mess."

To which Stan said, "I wouldn't think of it, Glory. Not a chance. We'll clean this ol' place up in a jiffy." And all our friends grabbed some bread and it was cleaned up in a jiffy. Then Grandma took Helen's arm, took her leave of everyone with an I can't believe how big you boys are and thanks, Stan, say hello to Camille for me, and it was lovely to chat with you, Barb and Chris and Sandy and hug hug hug, and off we went after they told me how pretty I was and growing so tall. Wasn't that dimple cute?

We got the doughnuts, which Helen licked, and our groceries.

The checker was a friend of Helen's from first grade.

"Hello, Helen," she said. "How are you?"

"Shut up," she said. "You can't convince me to give up my brain."

Danka nodded. "Okay, Helen. I won't even try." She didn't say another word.

Helen did not want to take off the helmet for a week. She even insisted on showering with it on. Grandma and Grandpa did not fight this because the helmet did, indeed, seem to be helping. Maybe it muted the voices. Maybe it simply made Helen feel safer or more protected. Maybe she needed the weight on her head. Who knew?

What soon became clear, though, is how much she did not like Sunshine.

* * *

When Sunshine was about a year old, Grandma found Helen leaning over her crib one morning in the bedroom we shared, growling at her. A couple of months later, Helen put a sheet over Sunshine's whole body when she was sleeping and told us, "Trash Heap is gone now."

I have never in my life seen Grandma and Grandpa move so fast as they sprinted into our room.

Another time she poked Sunshine in the stomach when she was resting in Grandpa's arms. "She's a gadget. She's a sooterdorfmanz."

"What's that, sugar?" Grandpa asked her, so gentle.

"It means she's after you." Helen touched the hearts she'd drawn on her cheeks that morning with a blue marker. "I think she's stealing my money! I think she is. She's a money stealer."

"I don't think so, sugar," Grandpa said. "Sunshine loves you. See how she's smiling?" And, indeed, Sunshine was smiling at Helen.

For a second, Helen froze, then she touched the baby's nose with the tip of her finger. "It's squishy."

"Sure is. She's a little one," Grandpa said.

She touched Sunshine's fingers. "Small fingers." She stroked her cheek. "Soft." She pushed the wisps of blond hair back. "A bird is soft. A chick is soft. Punk is soft with his red eyes."

In one lightning-quick move, she yanked the baby out of Grandpa's arms, whipped around, and ran for the door, moaning deep in her throat.

I screamed, terrified. My worst nightmare was that Helen would take my baby away from me. Sunshine screamed, too. "Give me Sunshine! Give me Sunshine!" I yelled.

My grandpa, built like a mountain, but strong and quick, had both Helen and the baby in a firm hug within seconds. "Get your grandma," he told me, and I ran off, hysterical, and found Grandma in the barn with the horses. "She's trying to steal Sunshine! Help me, Grandma!"

We ran for the house and I ate Grandma's dust as she sprinted to the door, her cowboy boots flying.

Helen was baring her teeth, growling, clicking her teeth together as if she wanted to bite Grandma and Grandpa. They were pleading with her, soothing, cajoling, but Helen wasn't having any of it, holding Sunshine way too tight while my baby screeched.

Grandpa had an arm between Helen's chest and the baby, but I knew that you couldn't yank a baby away from someone else without hurting it. Helen made a *yip yip* sound, like a coyote, then bared her teeth again, straining away from Grandma and Grandpa.

Well, I'd had enough. She was not going to take my baby. I grabbed a wooden spoon from Grandma's kitchen and the stool and I put the stool behind Helen and brought the spoon right down on her head as hard as I could.

She let go of my Sunshine and Grandma caught her.

"Don't you hurt my baby!" I shrieked at her, near hysteria. "You stupid Momma! You stupid Momma! Don't you hurt my baby!" I hit her again on the head, all of my rage and fear coming out through that spoon.

A surprising thing happened then. Helen closed her mouth. She didn't growl or grunt, and her body sagged, almost to the floor. Grandpa caught her as her tears smeared the blue hearts. Then she said, her voice cracking, "I'm bad."

"Yes, you are!" I raged. "You're bad!"

"No, sweetie," Grandpa said, breathing hard, "you're not bad. You're a good girl."

"It's the truth! The truth!" she cried out, her hands to her heart. "I'm bad! I'm a bad girl."

"You're a bad momma!" I told her, still shaking, still scared, Sunshine's choking cries hitting me hard.

Grandpa pulled her up straight. "Come on, honey, let's go lie down."

"No, no, no," Helen said, bringing her blond curls to her eyes. "I'm bad. I'm a no-love person. I have no love in me." Helen's head jerked a couple of times. She said something, but her speech slurred and I didn't get it. I heard this: "Thubada-wagon. You're a terrible thubadawagon."

She turned, lashed at the air with her hands, as if she was scratching someone invisible standing in front of her. "I can't stand you," she said to the air. "You shut up! I know I should die! Die, die!" She got down on her hands and knees and whispered to me, her eyes imploring, "You hear them, too, don't you?"

I swallowed hard and shook my head, some of my fury draining away. "No, Momma. I don't hear the voices."

"What do you mean you don't hear the voices?" Helen asked, her voice now strident. "You have to hear them. I hear them all day long. They're bugging me, being mean, telling me what to do, and I can't stand it! You don't hear them?" Her voice pitched and she shouted at me, hands cupped around her mouth, as if she was trying to make herself heard over a cacophony of noise. "You don't hear them? They're yelling!"

I shook my head. "I'm sorry, Momma."

"How can you not hear them?" Tears sprung to her eyes. "They're everywhere. All the time. No one can think, no one can talk!" She turned to my grandma. "Can't you hear the voices?"

"No, sweetie, I can't," Grandma soothed. "Now hang on, let me hug you. We'll make the voices be quiet."

"Can't you hear the voices?" she yelled at Grandpa, cupping her hands around her mouth again.

"No, sugar, all I can hear is my love for you."

Helen froze, her face crumpling, her body sagging. "No one can hear the voices? No one but me! Only me. Why me?" she asked Grandpa, her voice breaking. "Why me and the voices? Why? Am I alone?"

"No, sweetie, you're not alone," Grandpa said. "Not at all. We love you."

"I'm all alone," Helen said, not giving any indication she had heard my grandpa. "I am all by myself. And them!" She fisted a hand. "I'm all by myself with them! And I don't even like them! I don't want to be with them!"

"You have us, sugar. Me and Grandpa and Stevie, we're here. We're always here."

"But the voices, they keep us apart." She stomped her feet

again, wobbled her head, because she wanted to get the voices out through her ears. "I know they do. They're here now. Being mean. They want me by myself so they can kill me."

"No one wants to kill you, darling, no one. We love you. We need you," Grandma said, blinking tears out of her eyes.

"They want me to give in and do bad things to that Trash Heap and that girl kid." Helen sobbed and pointed at me. "They're an army and I'm just a Helen."

"We know you won't do bad things. You're a good person, a strong person, my darling."

Grandma was pale, and Grandpa was gray. They both sagged. Maybe the army was beating them, too.

"I'm just a Helen. I'm a no-love person. I have no love in me. Who can love me? They won't go away. Never will they go away."

At that moment, on Helen's devastated face that day, I got my first, true understanding of how sad, how *unutterably* sad, her life was.

In the next moment I realized that she knew it, too.

"I'm just a Helen," she said again, broken, shattered. *"Just a Helen."*

It was one of the most devastating moments of my life.

Most people, maybe even everyone, would think that my grandparents' decision to keep Sunshine in the same house with Helen, who was suffering from schizophrenia, was a colossal mistake all the way around, even if now and then they could get her medicine down Helen. (Medicine that had its own set of lousy side effects, by the way, and which was often changed, for a variety of reasons.)

The schizophrenic person should be sent to live with someone else, somewhere else, they would say. Other people, my grandparents, or people who were living the nightmare, people who knew of the complexities of this terrible disease, people who were in the position to know there was no black or white here, only a very murky, painful gray, might choose to make another decision.

My grandparents, into their seventies, learned the hard way about the horrific, appalling conditions in the hospitals, asylums, and treatment centers for the mentally ill at that time. Put Helen back in one of those? Put Helen—their beloved, cherished daughter, who had been raped, impregnated, beaten up, locked up, attacked, neglected, overdrugged, poorly drugged, tied down, handcuffed, isolated, and shattered—back in "treatment," knowing she would resume living in a constant state of well-founded fear, pain, and hysteria?

"What should we do?" I heard them asking, again and again, their hands clasped together. "What should we do?"

Save a baby granddaughter at the expense of their daughter, when their daughter might well die in such a place? Endanger the granddaughter by leaving the daughter at home? And what about Stevie, they kept discussing. What's the impact on our "darling Stevie"? The impact now, the long-term impact. Do we have Helen leave so the granddaughters' mental health is saved? Can we counteract the negatives that Helen heaps on them by wrapping them up with love and kindness? Are we making a terrible, terrible mistake that will have awful repercussions we can't even see?

These, folks, are not the conversations anyone ever wants to have.

Eventually they told themselves they could keep the baby safe because they could not get their minds around committing Helen to hell again, and they decided to double their efforts to keep Helen from Sunshine, her Trash Heap.

I don't blame them for their decision. Even now, even after the bridge incident. They could not have possibly conceived of what was going to happen.

But they blamed themselves every single day afterward.

I loved Sunshine and spent all my time after school and on weekends with her. I pushed her stroller, I rocked her to sleep, I read her stories. As she grew older I taught her how to play with stuffed animals and how to kick a soccer ball. Grandpa or Grandma would take us to family parties in town, and all my cousins hugged her. We worked with Grandma in the garden and we played in the stream.

"I love you, Sunshine," I'd tell her.

"Love you, Evie." She couldn't say Stevie, so that's what I got. "Love you, Evie."

I taught her what the animals were and their names.

"Bob the Horse," I'd say.

"Aw da Hor," she'd say.

"Sheba the sheep," I'd say, pointing.

"Eba da eep," she'd say.

"Horny is Grandpa's dog," I'd say.

"Porny pa's da," she'd say.

I taught her songs, too, and I was teaching her the alphabet and numbers.

We continued with art time together.

Grandma was a talented artist. She could draw anything—the Schoolhouse House, the barn, the town, our wildflowers that sprung up every summer—but she always put a fairy-tale spin on it. She hid a gnome behind a flower, a leprechaun on a leaf, a magician casting a spell on a frog. Watching Grandma work was like watching a storybook come to life.

This is what Grandma told me about art: "Make it your own, Stevie. . . . Let the art tell people who you are, what your mood is, what you think of life, the world. . . . Your art can be serious or funny, or both. It can tell the truth or poke fun. It can be sad, or it can offer joy. Make sure your art is true to you, Stevie, *it must be true to you.*"

One afternoon, on a four-by-four-foot canvas, Helen painted a cliff. It was black, gray, jagged, dangerous—even the grass blades were sharp and dangerous. Around it were thick, looming, curving trees, resembling the bars of a jail cell, a dark shadow looming between the tree trunks.

At the very bottom of the rock was an arm. No body, only an arm and a hand. A left hand, I noted.

She named the painting "Night Night."

Then she glared across the table at Sunshine, who was two years old, and whispered, "Night night."

*   *   *

A few months after that, Helen's behavior escalated. At dinner one night, the rain drumming against our windows, she decided she didn't want her left hand.

She was eating toast and raspberry jelly because it was red, Kool-Aid because that was red, and an apple, also red, when she suddenly slammed her left hand on the table and said, "Who put that there?" She held up her hand and studied it, teeth bared.

We explained that was her hand, but that didn't work. "I don't like it. It's a spy tool, isn't it?" She shook her hand. "I want that off." She slammed her hand back down, three times, then picked it up, keeping it limp. From then on, she carried her left hand limply, halfway up, swaying back and forth.

In an abrupt change of subject, which I was so used to, she glared at me and said, "I don't have a daughter. I don't want a daughter. I want a shoypertobarn," she told us.

"Helen, that's enough," Grandpa snapped.

"Helen, do not say things like that, sweetie," Grandma said, angry. "I forbid it."

"Fuck you, sweetie," Helen said, gently, sweetly, reaching out to grab my grandma's hand with her right one. "Sweetie, fuck you."

I swallowed hard and then coughed. I tried to clear my throat, but I couldn't do it. I started crying at the table, the tears streaming out of my eyes. Helen had said mean things so often, but this one stuck. I cried because I was so worn down from the constancy of Helen's delusions, illusions, shouting at voices, strange reactions, hitting, and her hatred of my sister, my best friend. And I cried because I could feel something black and sinister lurking over all of our shoulders. *I could feel it.*

Grandma grabbed my hand, then said, her eyes furious, "Helen, leave this table right this minute."

And Grandpa said, his voice raised, "Out, Helen, now. Right now! You will not hurt Stevie!"

But Helen didn't move, even though Grandpa yanked out her

red chair from the table and grabbed her under the shoulders to haul her out.

"There's water coming out of your eyes," Helen told me, astonished, peering straight at me.

"I know that." I hastily wiped the tears away.

"Why is there water coming out of your eyes?" Helen asked.

"Because I'm sad. Don't you get that? Don't you get sad?" My voice raised, a rush of emotions flowing right out, a waterfall of pain.

She looked confused, then suspicious. "Why are you sad?"

What to say? I'm sad because you're my momma and I don't have a normal mother and maybe it would have been better if I had no mother, as I have no father? I'm sad because I'm so tired? I'm sad because you hate my sister?

"I'm sad because you make me cry a lot."

Helen didn't say anything, but her eyebrows rose and her mouth opened a little bit. She reached a hand out to me. "I'm sorry I make you cry, girl kid. I'm sorry."

I was too shocked to say anything.

And I could see her then, in a flash, the mother I wanted to love. I could see a little bit of sanity in the backs of her eyes.

"I don't want to make you cry." She let go of my hand and slapped her cheek, one, then the other, quite hard, then held the heels of her hands to her eyes and arched her neck. "I'm just a Helen," she whispered. "I don't know. I don't understand. All the voices. It's so noisy in my head. They're telling me what to do. I'm scared. I'm scared all the time, and I'm wet and I'm gooey and I don't want to be in a can. Do you think my friend Tonya is in a can? And I don't like your chairs and this thing"— she waved her limp left hand—"and it's a bad thing in me. I'm bad. Bad Helen. I am a bad girl, and I made that girl kid cry." She conked her head on the table. "He's going to kill me. He will. I will be dead."

I felt my breath catch and that familiar feeling of sickness overwhelmed me. Through the tangle of my harsh emotions, I often felt overwhelming pity for Helen. How would it be to be her? To listen to that cacophony in her head twenty-four/seven? She was living in hell. Absolute, white-hot, nightmarish hell.

Why can't the voices that schizophrenics hear be kind and gentle? Why couldn't they praise my momma, encourage her, tell her to hug her daughter and bake cookies? Where did those vicious, violent voices come from? Why?

She whipped up her head and wiped the tears off my cheeks, so gentle, so sweet. "You're a good cuddly animal." She cupped her hands around my face, and for a sweet second I let myself believe that Helen was the same as all my girlfriends' mothers, kind and nice, the type who made cookies and wore blue dresses with heels, who smiled and helped out at school.

"I like you," she told me, her eyes slipping back into nowhere again. "But not her." She glared at Sunshine, who was clutching a stuffed tiger. "I don't like that one. She's a chair. She has tentacles. Trash Heap has worms. I think she eats them. Kerboomalot."

Shortly thereafter, Helen kidnapped Trash Heap and hid her on the cliff near the trees that looked like the bars of a jail cell.

24

Ashville, Oregon

Helen continued to hold out her left hand in a weird way and told us it didn't belong to her. "Get this off. It isn't mine."

I said, "Okay, Helen, I'll take it off for you finally, but I have to find a hand screwdriver."

Do you see how I had to buy into her insanity at times, how I had to talk to her, manage her?

"A hand screwdriver?" she asked. She tilted her head. She was wearing a kids' red cowboy hat.

"Yeah. Grandpa has one, but it's a special one to get rid of hands and he's not home, so I can't get it." I pushed back my hair, and the charm bracelet that Sunshine gave me clinked.

"You'll get the hand screwdriver later?"

"Sure, I will."

We sat down and did our artwork. I drew a picture of a miniature fairy village. Sunshine painted with her fingers. Helen drew a picture of a black bridge with a turbulent, dark sky and a moon with a reddish-orangish haze. Under the bridge, in the cresting waves, she drew two left arms and two red dots. I knew the red dots were eyes.

On Monday Helen felt bugs running up and down her body and scratched herself so bad she bled.

On Tuesday she tried to climb up on the roof of our barn to jump. Grandpa scrambled up behind her and caught her in the nick of time. I saw the whole thing. He could have died trying to rescue his daughter.

On Wednesday morning she said, "I will kill myself before I let Command Center get me." She was eating blueberries in a row, one by one. The row stretched across the table. Every time she ate a blueberry, she ate a bite of peanut butter. She stopped abruptly and put her hands in her lap. "I'll take you away from Command Center."

"Thanks, Momma," I said. I wished Helen had slept in. I could get off to school without talking to her, and then I wouldn't have her voice and all the other voices she was fighting with in my head. It helped me get 100 percent on my spelling and math tests if she wasn't around when I was eating my cereal.

"He's coming for us. So I'll save you."

"Good."

She put the salt and pepper shakers up to her ears and listened to them. "Nothing there." Then she dumped a load of sugar into her bowl and listened to that. "Only one voice." She picked up her spoon and clinked it on the glass. "I can hear the voices, but they're quiet today."

"That's good," I told her.

Her head snapped up. "I'll take you with me, girl kid, away from Command Center, but not Trash Heap. I won't take her." She took an eyeliner and small mirror out of her pocket and drew an eye on her forehead in brown. "Now I can keep a better eye on that small thing."

I shuddered. Sick and scared.

On Thursday she smashed the TV because she was being watched.

On Friday she tried to beat up a cow.

On Saturday afternoon, in town, she whacked seventy-five-year-old Mr. Shiminsky with a spatula because he had "coughed," and that was a signal that it was he who had tried to take her kidneys last night in her bedroom.

That afternoon I ate three cupcakes and tried to calm the nervousness that stalked the better part of my childhood on the farm.

I knew something bad was going to happen.

Two weeks later, on a sunny, serene Saturday morning, Helen tried to cut off her hand with a piece of glass.

I was curled up in bed next to Sunshine, who had crawled into bed with me, as usual. She smelled of lemon-scented shampoo and soap. The light was flowing through my window, highlighting the dust fairies dancing around. The Schoolhouse House was quiet, the birds chirping. I remember those birds. Later I would always associate the early morning chirping of birds with fountains of blood.

I woke up to the sound of shattering glass. Helen had broken her window with a hammer. I got up carefully, not waking up Sunshine, and ran for my door. I heard Grandma and Grandpa pounding down the hall at the same time that Helen started hollering, "Get out of me, Punk! Get out of me! I know you're spying on me!"

It is not normal for children to see their mothers covered with blood. These images stay with you, burned and red and jagged, pricking at your innocence like a butcher knife against skin.

But there was Helen, a spurt of blood greeting my eyes. She was on the bed wearing a queen's outfit that she'd worn onstage on Broadway. She even had a crown on over her dirty hair.

She held up her wrist as blood spilled out. "Hey, kid. It's coming off. It's not mine. The short spy, Trash Heap, put it there, I think."

Then she passed out onto her bed, the blood seeping into the mattress.

I dropped to the floor as Grandma and Grandpa flew in. The last thing I remember is Grandpa picking Helen up and running out the door, blood flying everywhere.

Weeks later, when Helen drew an eye on her forehead and on her chin, because the government was spying on her and she wanted to "spy back," I took Sunshine upstairs to our bedroom to play with the dollhouse Grandpa had made us. She sat in my lap. At first she wouldn't play with any of the little dolls. I did it all. I walked the plastic girls around, put them at a table, had them take a nap. She watched me, her shoulders down, her body hunched in on itself, her unhappiness palpable.

"I love my charm bracelet, Sunshine, that you gave me, and I love you."

She didn't say anything.

"You're pretty. Your hair is gold and sunshiney and yellow." I pushed one of her curls back. I had put her hair in a little ponytail with a pink ribbon that day. "You're the prettiest three-year-old in the world."

She leaned her back against my stomach, and I gave her a hug.

"What's wrong, Sunshine?"

She turned around and rested her cheek against my chest. I put the mother from the dollhouse back at the kitchen table.

"What's wrong, Sunshine?"

She hugged me close, her tears flowing into my shirt.

"Why are you crying?"

She didn't answer.

"Sunshine, what's wrong?"

She said a few words, but I couldn't understand what she was saying.

"What? What did you say?"

She lifted her head, her big blue eyes drowning with tears. "Momma hate me. Punk hate me, too. She told me. And Command Center hate me, too. Why everyone hate me?"

I was stunned. It felt like my heart had been hit with a nail gun. "Sunshine, Momma has a sickness in her head. She doesn't know what she's saying. She doesn't understand. She says bad things, but she's not bad. She does love you, but she's messed up. . . ."

Sunshine wasn't buying it. "She hate me. She say I going night night soon. Good-bye. Command Center take me, that what Momma say. Night night."

I hugged her close and rocked her back and forth.

She picked up the momma doll and threw her across the room.

Grandma overheard that conversation. I knew because I heard the stairs creak, and then I peeked out my window and saw Grandma running to her garden. When she got to the middle of it, she leaned her head way back, hands over her face, and cried, eventually sinking to her knees near the lettuce.

Grandma and Grandpa were up against a wall and the wall was bending, curving, squeezing them. Our family was going to be suffocated by that wall if it didn't smash the life out of us first.

After many discussions that I eavesdropped on, and many tears, they took their last option: electroshock therapy.

Helen was going to be tied down to a hospital bed and electrical currents were going to be shot through her brain.

Not generally something one wants to do on a Thursday afternoon.

When we got Helen back from being electroshocked, she did not appear to recognize any of us for days.

I don't think she even knew where she was. She'd been gone for three weeks. Grandpa flew her to Seattle to a very expensive place for the mentally ill whose families have lots of money.

Grandpa gently helped her out of the car. Grandma went right up to hug her. Helen pulled back, hands up. "Don't touch me," she whispered. "Not now. No touching."

Grandma backed off and brought her right into the house, fussing over her.

I said, "Hello, Momma."

She tilted her head, quizzically. "Yes. Hello, girl kid."

Then she studied Sunshine, who said, "Hi, Momma," in a quiet, little voice, her lower lip trembling.

"What is that?" Momma asked, pointing at Sunshine. "What is that? Is she wearing a worm? I think she's trying to kill me."

* * *

The electroshock therapy and yet another round of new drugs did nothing for Helen except flatten her out for a bit. Grandma had to mix the drugs in with her food because she refused to take "tiny spy pills," so who knew if she was getting the right amount of drugs with her strange or nonexistent eating habits.

For the first few weeks it was like watching a zombie who had a penchant for ball gowns and chicken wire.

Helen didn't protest as much. She didn't shout to her voices, although sometimes I saw her lips moving, a whisper coming out now and then, her made-up words slurring with the real ones, as if she'd forgotten those, too.

She did remember one word, which she whispered to Sunshine often: Night night.

Night night.

About three months after she had her brain electrocuted, Helen started seeing Command Center taunting her.

The first time it happened, we were eating dinner. It was Chinese food, I remember that. I had opened up a fortune cookie, and it said, "Accept your blessings."

That night she let Grandma shower her. Grandma had gotten into the shower with her bathing suit and Helen smelled nice afterward. She'd even sniffed her hair. "I smell lemon," she told me several times. She put on a blue flowered dress, a red velvet cape, her boots with the chicken wire, and a tin foil necklace.

Helen looked up from her fortune cookie and released a bloodcurdling screech.

It about gave Grandma a heart attack. Her wine spilled all over her lap, and Grandpa jumped straight up, ready to protect his ladies.

Sunshine moaned in fear, scrambled off her chair, and hid behind me. I couldn't move I was so scared.

Helen climbed on the table, her face twisted with rage, and yelled, "Shut up, Command Center."

I hugged Sunshine close to me, her skinny body trembling.

"Get back in the hole. You're not taking me with you, gosh dammit!"

She picked up a dish and threw it at the corner. "Get out of here. No one wants you around."

She picked up another dish and threw it.

I told Sunshine to run upstairs to our room, and she did.

Grandpa and Grandma tried to reason with their daughter, but she wasn't listening to their pleas, their entreaties to calm down, relax.

She rearranged her foil necklace, then raged, her fists clenched, "Oh, no, not you, too, Punk, not you! Get out of here."

"Momma, it's okay. Nothing's there. No one's there—"

"Oh, you don't know that, you don't know that at all. He's invisible to stupid people, but I see him."

I felt my stomach clench with hurt. *Stupid.* I was stupid.

"Punk, I can see you," she hissed, ignoring Grandpa's hand as he gently tried to get her off the table. "You're hiding behind that couch right there. I see you spying on me. I can see your red eyes! I can see your green nails. Get rid of him, Command Center, or we're done. Put your cloak over him! I'm telling you right now!" She arched back, her hands out like claws. "Damn shit. You're a damn shit."

Grandma tried to calm Helen, but it wasn't working. Grandpa said, "Sweetie, come on down. I'll take care of them." Nothing.

Then Grandma held herself up to her full height, stood in front of Helen, and said, "Command Center, leave. Punk, out of the house, right now!"

"Yeah, get outta here!" Helen yelled, her thumb in the air pointing toward the door, as she swayed back and forth on the table. "They're still here, I can see them. Command Center is behind the lamp, and Punk is under the couch. I can see his red eyes!"

Grandma ran around the lamp, punching her fists, peered under the couch, and said, "Punk, get out of here!"

"I am not a slut!" Helen argued. "No, I'm not! Quit shouting at me! Make the others shut up! I said, I'm not a slut! You can't torture me with your knives!"

Grandpa said, in a threatening, mean voice I'd never heard before, "Punk, I'm going to get my gun. Now get the hell out before I shoot you." Grandpa went to a wall, grabbed one of his grandfather's unloaded guns, and aimed it at the couch.

Then Grandma said, "If you don't leave, Command Center and Punk, I will cast my spell! Do you hear me? I will cast my spell."

"Yeah, she's gonna cast her spell," Helen yelled, punching the air with her closed fists. "You'll be turned to dust!"

I watched, confused, bewildered, scared. Before my eyes, Grandma and Grandpa seemed to be morphing into Helen.

Grandpa ran forward and pretended he was shooting Punk and Command Center. Grandma waved her hands around while she was casting her spell, and Helen declared, "It's three against two. It's three against two!"

Now, why did that work? Was Helen exhausted because she'd been up all night? Maybe. Was it the medication, perhaps, recalibrating something in her mind? Were her demons suddenly, for a reason we'll never get, mentally scared off? Was it Grandma praying not for total healing but simply for peace this one night that did it? Who knew?

But it worked. It absolutely worked.

Helen abruptly froze, then bent to stare at the lamp, climbed off the table, and peered under the couch. She blinked a couple of times and fiddled with her necklace "They're gone," she whispered, in awe. "They're gone. They're away." Grandma and Grandpa each put an arm around her and laid her on the couch. "Finally, they're gone."

Grandma pulled two blankets up to her chin, and Grandpa stroked her hair. Helen closed her eyes and Grandma got her a fruit drink, mashed up her medicine, and had her drink it. "I'm not a slut, and I'll bet the damn fried shits will come back to kill us on the cliff," she said sleepily. They would, we knew they would—they always did—but Helen went right to sleep.

Grandma collapsed on the floor, and Grandpa stumbled to his chair.

I went outside and swung on the porch swing and tried not to let my mind crack open.

About fifteen minutes later Grandma came out to visit me. I was still shaking and asked her if she'd actually seen Command Center and Punk. I knew she would say no, but that's what living with someone with schizophrenia can do. Every day the whole situation tests your sanity. Every day you question what's real and what isn't, and you teeter on the edge of keeping your mind together.

I snuggled into my grandma's warmth as she reassured me she hadn't heard or seen anyone else, because they weren't real. A few minutes later, Grandpa came out and sat with us, his arm around my shoulder. He dropped a kiss on Grandma's lips.

"Hardship, honey, builds character. Having struggles in your life, dealing with your mother, will make you a stronger, more courageous adult. Learning how to find joy in the little things, the stream that runs through our property, the mountains, art, animals, the weather, this will set you up for a life of gratefulness, and that will give you happiness. People who don't have to deal with heartache, or don't allow themselves to reach out to other people who are enduring heartbreak, end up being shallow, superficial, boring people, sweetie. They never truly live. They never get what life's about. They never become full, compassionate, caring people able to live with wisdom and grace."

We rocked on the porch, amidst the darkness and the sprinkling of stars, the white shining moon, the howl of a coyote, the whinnying of the horses in the barn, and the meow of a cat.

"Praise the Lord," Grandma said. "I try to thank Him all the time for what we have and ask Him for strength to deal with what we don't have." She sighed. "But I've never thanked Him for Punk and Command Center. Damned if I ever will. Punk's got those weird red eyes and he's slithery, and Command Center is obnoxious. Such terrible manners! A horrible house guest!" She winked at me.

Grandpa chuckled. "I feel sorry for Punk's wife. He's creepy. I wouldn't want to sleep with anyone with red eyes."

I giggled.

Grandma said, "Yes, and Command Center is so noisy. I'll bet he's single. Who would ever marry *him?*"

I giggled again, and then I said to them, "Punk's a punk!" And for one shiny moment I thought I was clever. My grandparents laughed at my joke.

"You're right, Stevie. Punk *is* a punk!"

Schizophrenia is never pretty. It's a disaster, plain and simple.

But it is easier when you have a grandma and grandpa to sit with, on a deck outside the Schoolhouse House, near a garden full of flowers and vegetables, their hands in yours.

25

Portland, Oregon

I had put the Dornshire letter into an unmarked manila envelope and dropped it off at the post office.

Legally, and playing by the rules, we were required to disclose everything to the other party during the discovery part of the lawsuit with the Atherton family's attorneys.

But I knew, without a shadow of a doubt, that if Crystal found that letter, she would destroy it. She would not disclose it. She would do a skinny-ass victory dance in her high heels, close the door to her office, and shred it faster than you could say, "You lose, Danny boy, tough luck."

And that would be it. My goodness, that would be *it*.

Would the Athertons lose their case without the Dornshire letter?

Maybe.

Maybe not.

It was a tough case. They did sign off on the medical paperwork, acknowledging the danger of the operation, and Crystal would make sure that the jury felt the evidence was "squishy" on whether Danny's problems were because of a natural, although unhappy, outcome of the operation or the placement of the breathing tubes. She would have medical witnesses paid to say it was the former.

With the letter, would the Athertons now win?

Yes.

They would win. Slam dunk.

I opened my garage, pulled out a plastic sheet, dropped an old chair on it, and started my questions.

"Are you happy? What does that word mean? Should we strive for it? Should we be content with contentment? If you're not happy, how do you become happy? Is happiness a choice? How so? Is it necessary to live a good life?"

The chair's name was Stacey. I don't know why. I painted it yellow and later would paint a fat raccoon on the seat eating a chocolate bar and grinning, and I would attach willow branches in an arc above it.

I don't know why.

In the morning, on my deck, I found rain boots with red roses on them and a ribbon. The card said they were from Jake. I smiled. Inwardly, I did a jig.

At night I dreamed I was in a cozy house in a huge tree in the sky with a well-tended vegetable garden, golden sunflowers, pink roses, petunias, and marigolds. From the house you could see the sun rising up and down, pastel colors waving across the sky. There were other houses in the tree, and me and Sunshine would fly to visit our friends and neighbors, glittery wings on our backs. Butterflies would sail past and wave their wings at us, bluebirds sang trilling songs, and hummingbirds darted to and fro. We had tiny pink pastries and tea in blue and white china cups.

It was all lovely until a black cloud came and settled on the tree and shook it. The houses fell out of the tree, and the black cloud reached down and ripped our wings off our backs. We tumbled to the ground and smacked it and died, and I knew I should have saved Sunshine. It was my fault.

The black cloud was Helen.

I didn't sleep the rest of that night.

I slept fitfully the next night.

In the mornings I got up and walked in my rain boots with red roses.

And walked.

I tried to chase the nightmares down.

I kept clucking. I wrote checks for my medical debt. It was going down. In my chicken suit one night I thought of the chickens on our farm in Ashville. I could not go back there.

Could I?

Could I do it?

Why would I do it?

Did I want to do it?

I called Aunt Janet to see how she was doing with her classes.

"I love them! But I love the people more. Everyone's so different, not the old fuddy-duddies Herbert and I hung around. One of my and Virginia's best friends is a woman from Iran. She wears a burka. We have another friend from Mexico, and two gentlemen are from Somalia. They're teaching me how to think and how to have an opinion and how to understand debates. I didn't get that before, dear."

"That's because Herbert squashed that in you."

"Too true, sweetie." There was a silence and I waited. "But I let him. I let him squash me. I'm having a hard time forgiving Herbert for being such a mean, selfish person, but I know I'm going to have a harder time forgiving myself for being so weak."

"I know how you feel. I have the forgiving-of-self problem, too." I changed the subject. "How's everything else going? How do you feel about the anniversary party?"

"The anniversary party? I feel sick about it, sweetie. Sick. It makes me feel like vomiting."

On Tuesday night, Jake and I went to watch Zena at another roller derby competition.

She'd only needed to borrow a scarf from me that morning when she'd hissed at me from behind the pillars in front of our building. You see, she is so slender, she was able to wind the scarf around and about her black T-shirt with a giant lipsticked mouth on it so it didn't show. She'd flipped her black skirt inside out so the skulls were hidden.

"Nice, Tinkerbell," I'd told her.

She'd kissed my cheek. "You have to go clubbing with me one of these days, Stevie. You can dance until your brains fall out."

"Thank you, but I need my brains in my head."

"Overrated," she'd said, popping in breath mints and swiping on lipstick.

The roller derby women were, again, dressed in fishnets, short black skirts, and red satin shirts. Some of the women wore striped socks. A couple were in black tutus. Tonight, they were out for blood. They screeched around the track, tackled, flew, crashed, hit, got penalized for intentional tripping and intentional falling, and swore at each other.

"Go, Zena!" I hollered, then corrected myself. "Go Badass Z Woman!" Jake cheered for the team, too. Badass Z Woman was penalized twice and then expelled for "unnecessary roughness." There was only a minute to go, and when her team won, Zena skated to the middle of the track where the women had actually made a pyramid pile, their joy at winning overflowing.

I wish I had the courage to do what Zena did, I wish I did.

I wrapped my arms around myself. I was breathless. That bout had been breathtaking. One of the stay-at-home moms had broken her arm, and she was pissed. "How the hell am I going to change diapers now? *Shit!*"

Afterward, Jake drove me to a hill above Portland.

"Let's dance," he said, holding his hand out for mine.

"Here? Outside?"

"Here and outside." He pulled me in close, one arm behind my back, our hands clasped.

And there we danced, under the stars, under a white moon, lights twinkling in the distance. I thought of how often my grandparents danced together on our deck at the Schoolhouse

House, toe to toe in their cowboy boots. They knew how to love each other, they did.

Jake's kiss met mine, and I closed my eyes so I could feel every delicious curve, his heat, his taste, his passion.

Man, that man could kiss.

And, okay, his hands wandered well, too.

I wanted to use the sparkly, glow-in-the-dark condoms, but I couldn't.

Something held me back. I can only compare it to being corralled by invisible reins and yanked on. My body wanted to fling myself onto Jake, but my mind was scared to death, almost hyperventilating at the thought of getting that serious with anyone, with opening myself up physically and mentally to so much . . . unknown, to possible hurt and emotional destruction. Being with Jake meant that eventually I would have to tell him all about myself. All the secrets, my past, my weight issues, my shame, my guilt, the babies, everything.

It was too much. I hoped I would be ready for the sparkly condoms later.

I did notice something, though. My hands weren't shaking as much anymore.

I thought of Jake's smile.

The next time Crystal met with the Atherton family, I told her I wanted to be there because I was learning so much from her about how to nail a case.

"Winning, that's the only thing you need to do as an attorney, Steve. That's it. *Win.* Crush the opposition. Mangle them up and spit them out. Doesn't matter who they are." She put her high heels up on her desk. I was sitting in front of her desk so I was staring at the bottoms of them, Mt. Hood in the distance. "You can come, but I'll need you to stay late to get your other work done."

I agreed. I could barely contain myself, I wanted to go to that next meeting so bad.

"I heard about Polly. I didn't know she was your cousin. Didn't put it together until yesterday. Also didn't know that you're Lance Barrett's cousin, either. I had no idea you were from such a prominent, wealthy, old Portland family." She narrowed her eyes at me, as if I'd deliberately hidden something from her. "Isn't Lance a multimillionaire because of his companies? Didn't he play pro football?" She tapped her toes together and said, "Is he single?"

"Yes, he is single."

She stared up at the ceiling, and I could hear her brain grinding away. A Rich. Single. Man. And she'd been treating his cousin pretty darn bad. "Well, you and I get along well, don't we, Steve? Why don't you set me up with Lance some night?" She smiled thinly.

"No." The word dropped out of my mouth as if it had been sitting on my tongue.

"What?" She removed the bottoms of her shoes from my vision and leaned forward, like a viper ready to puncture flesh. "Why not?"

"Because I don't think you'd be good for Lance. I love him, I know him, and you and he would not be good together."

"We would be fabulous together. Two driven people—both highly successful, well-respected, intelligent people who are connected socially and politically. We both play the game, and we play it well. Together we'd be on top of this city, probably this state. We get money. We get business. *We get it.*"

"That, Crystal, right there, is why Lance would not want to go out with you. You're not what Lance needs."

"And what does Lance need, Steve?" she snapped.

"He needs someone who is caring and kind and funny and understanding. He needs someone who's tough, but compassionate and interesting and engaged with living, not making money. He needs someone who loves him for all he is, and all he isn't, and who will love him no matter if he lost everything tomorrow or decided he wanted to go and live in a tiny town in eastern Oregon with cattle circling his home."

"Well! That's a nice vision, Steve, but I don't think that's what he needs."

"How would you know? You don't even know him. All you know is that he's a millionaire businessman and you love the sound of that."

She sputtered, she huffed, she puffed, and I walked out.

Darn but I hoped she wouldn't exclude me from the Atherton meeting.

Zena and I had lunch at Pioneer Courthouse Square three days later.

"Why would a woman get a Brazilian wax?" Zena handed me a handful of blueberries.

"What's that?" I bit into my tuna sandwich.

"It's when a woman goes to a waxer lady and they take off all her hair around her privates, except they might leave a little strip of hair."

I stopped chewing. "How do they do that?"

"They put hot wax on your privates and—"

"They put hot wax on your privates?" As my grandma would say, "Good Lord." I handed her a tangerine.

"Yep."

"You mean like melted candle wax?"

"Think so, Stevie."

"And then what do they do?"

"They pat it with a cloth, then strip the cloth up, and all your hair comes out."

I dropped my tuna sandwich back in my bag. "You have got to be kidding."

"Nope. Heard about it the other night. One of my roller derby friends does it. It's the stay-at-home mother. She says she dyes the remaining strip of hair pink."

My mouth dropped. I hardly knew what to say.

"She does it because then she can remind herself, every time she's sitting on the toilet, that she's still a wild gal, still young and hot and sexy."

"Does it work?"

"Probably not. She's got four kids and she runs the Parent–Teacher Association at school. She says a lot of the women there are sharks. One of the women actually threw an entire PTA notebook at someone else because that woman didn't vote to sell wrapping paper for the school fund-raiser."

"Aren't there other ways to feel young and hot and sexy that don't involve hot wax on your vagina?"

Zena took a sip of her strawberry banana fruit drink. "Not for her, sugar. Not for her."

We pondered that.

With visions of a pink private dancing through my head, I hurried back to the office for the Atherton meeting.

It started out much as before. Mr. and Mrs. Atherton appeared as exhausted as ever. They were both a palish-gray color, the lines etched even deeper into their faces. I again thought of their son, in their green and yellow dining room, hooked up to all those machines. There cannot be anything more wrenching on this planet than watching your child in that state. *Nothing.*

And yet.

In their eyes was a light, a light of . . . could I say, *victory?* Of hope? Of enjoyment? I clicked my heels together under the table. Why, by golly, they had gotten the Dornshire letter. I'll bet they loved it. I'll bet they treasured it. Was it framed yet? I bent my head to hide my smile.

This was gonna be fun.

The negotiations started again.

"The Athertons, on our recommendation," Sonja said, her head held high, the circles under her eyes not so bluish, "have decided that we will not mediate this case any further. Our initial demand of ten million still stands. It is a reasonable request due to the severe and expensive nature of Danny's medical problems caused by the hospital."

Ha! I'll bet Sonja danced a jig when she got the Dornshire letter.

Crystal laughed. Then she made this sighing sound that said, loud and clear, "Stupid people. You're so stupid, it's laughable." She laughed again. "We're going to trial then." She flicked her black hair back. "There is no way in hell we're going to pay you that much. None. Nada. Forget it. There are reasonable people in this city who will sit on the jury and they'll see through this for the shakedown that it is."

I heard Mr. Atherton grumble. His wife put a restraining hand on his arm.

Dirk, their other attorney, who did not appear so grossly exhausted anymore, said, "Do not use the word *shakedown,* Crystal. That's not necessary and it's inflammatory."

She rolled her eyes, straightened the perfect lapel on her ultraspendy suit. "The hospital is well known and well respected, and this *is* a shakedown. A con job. A frivolous lawsuit filed in the hopes of hitting the lottery. We'll see you in court."

Crystal stood up and started gathering her folders and papers.

"If I could beg for one more minute of your time," Dirk said, leaning back in his chair. He smiled. He was confident. He had adored the Dornshire letter!

"No. I am done with giving you my time," Crystal said.

"All right, but I thought you might want to review one last document."

"Unnecessary."

"I think it's necessary," Sonja said, as she tried to rein in her smile. It was difficult. She held out a sheet of paper. I was familiar with that sheet of paper, and it was delightful to gaze upon it once again.

Crystal scoffed. She held out her manicured hand. It was clear that she wanted Sonja to bring her the paper. Sonja refused to do so. She gave it a little push across the table.

For a second Crystal paused, her face twisting into a disgusted mask. She couldn't bear the thought of this ridiculous meeting with these ridiculous people going on for one more ridiculous second. She stared straight up at the ceiling, so put out, then deigned to walk two steps and grab the document.

And that's where everything got funny.

Funny in a horrible, tragic way, because this was a horrible, tragic situation.

But still. Ha! Ha ha!

Crystal eyed the paper.

We all heard her intake of breath.

She muttered, "Shit!"

Her hand shook. She went pale, about as pale as Mr. and Mrs. Atherton.

Her body trembled.

She swallowed and coughed, swallowed and coughed again, as if something was stuck in her throat. Perhaps it was a rifle or a fence post.

She tried to sit in a chair, missed, and fell to the floor.

She scrambled back up, quick as she could.

"Shit!" she yelled. "Shit!"

Ha! What a lovely day.

Two weeks later, Crystal was forced to settle the case the Atherton family had brought against Harborshore Hospital for ten million dollars. Crystal tried to get a gag order, but it was denied.

The evidence was overwhelming. The hospital had screwed up. Tragically, irrevocably, horribly screwed up, as detailed in the Dornshire letter. Dr. Dornshire had come in at the end of the operation to oversee how two of his medical residents were doing. It was he who had discovered poor Danny disintegrating, medically speaking, on the table because the breathing tube had been poorly placed. It was he who had saved Danny's life. It was he who knew of the anesthesiologist's drug problem and had reported it to the hospital the previous month. He was shocked to find the man still there.

Dr. Dornshire detailed, in blunt, harsh language, what happened in that hospital room to the president of the hospital and had sent copies to five other doctors/administrators.

His wording? "Inexcusable neglect . . . The impact on this child's life was not only tragic but preventable. . . . Basic safety steps were not followed. . . . Procedures were ignored. . . . Anesthesiologist is an addict. . . . Reading a motor cross magazine . . . No one paying attention to the patient . . . Liability is enormous. . . . Pay up to avoid a costly, public PR nightmare."

Within two weeks he left town for Africa to help open up a

clinic for suffering/starving children and had assumed that the matter was taken care of.

The case, with all the gory, depressing, captivating details, hit the newspaper. There was a photo of Mr. and Mrs. Atherton and Danny, before and after his heart operation. There was the Dornshire letter, printed out, probably courtesy of Sonja. There was a photo of the anesthesiologist, who had been caught stealing some ultrapowerful drug from the hospital, and five of the doctors/administrators who had officially received the Dornshire letter but then smothered it.

Many people at the hospital lost their jobs. Poor them.

As for the Athertons, they got their money. Sonja and Dirk's attorney fees were paid by the hospital, and I heard they immediately paid off their homes and rented office space complete with a table that didn't wobble and chairs that swiveled.

How did the Dornshire letter get in the files in our office in the first place without first being destroyed by Crystal?

I have no idea.

Praise the Lord, Grandma would have said. He knows how to step in when the devil has stepped out and he can perform miracles any day of the month.

It appeared that the Athertons had had their day.

After all that hardship, however, the Athertons' grief was not over.

Danny Atherton, baseball player, fisherman, Frisbee thrower, lover of dragon books and music, outstanding big brother, and loving son, passed away a week after the papers were signed.

I was so upset I had to leave work.

I worked in my garden, cried, and held the shovel with shaking hands.

A bowl full of my own beans, peas, tomatoes, squash, and lettuce did nothing to lift my mood.

When I came back to work Cherie asked me about the case. Crystal was fired.

"Damn, but I love to smear the competition into the ground

until they're eating dirt, but we as a firm will do this with class and dignity, and we sure as hell are not ever going to let anyone attempt to annihilate, through deception and lies and unethical work, an innocent family." Cherie shook her head. "Crystal'll be disbarred, and we'll be sued by the Athertons for malpractice, rightfully so, because it's clear Crystal knew about the Dornshire letter but did not disclose it. Oh, well. Our insurance will cover it, and I will tell them to pay up without delay."

"Can I ask you something?" I said.

"Sure."

"Why did you hire Crystal? She's not our usual attorney here."

Cherie nodded. "I made a mistake. Her parents run the Chinese food kiosk in Pioneer Square. I've known the whole family for years. I told Crystal when she was a young girl that if she did well in school, and went to law school, that I would hire her. I wanted her to see outside of her own life. I kept my promise. I regret that I made it."

"Ah, I see." That explained Crystal hugging the owners of the kiosk.

I turned to go.

"Stevie."

I turned around.

"About the Dornshire letter." Cherie leaned back in her chair and swung an ankle, clad in a shiny purple and red heel.

I froze.

"It's interesting how that letter ended up in the Athertons' hands, via the mail. So very unusual. Almost unheard of." She tapped her polished nails on her desk. There was a purple strip across the tops.

I couldn't speak because my throat was constricting.

"Someone must have mailed it to them. Someone at the hospital, maybe. A sympathetic administrator, perhaps?" She stared up at the ceiling, raising her eyebrows, as if contemplating this mystery. "A secretary there? A doctor? Doesn't seem likely. Hmmm."

More constriction.

She turned those bright eyes on me. "The law is the law, Stevie."

I nodded. My throat strangled me.

"We have to follow it as everyone else does, even if I find it agonizing to do so upon occasion." She rolled her shoulders. She was wearing a red leather jacket.

No air. None. I was going to suffocate myself.

"But sometimes, Stevie, one must bend, perhaps *massage,* the law in order to do the right thing, the ethical thing."

I coughed, tried to breathe, put a hand to my throat.

Her gaze caught mine for very long, poignant seconds while I fought to inhale air. Any air.

She smoothed her skirt, cleared her throat. "Now, don't forget to put on your calendar that we're all going to the beer gardens next week. We have a separate tent. I've arranged for a rib and potato dinner."

My knees almost gave out as relief swooshed through me as wind would swoosh through a tunnel. I turned to go, my body stiff. How long could I stand without breathing?

"Stevie."

Oh, no. Here it was. She knew. I knew she knew. She knew I knew she knew. She was one of the smartest people I've ever met. I weakly faced her.

"Nice job," she said quietly. "Very nice."

I closed my eyes, breathed.

"But let's keep this between us girls," she whispered. "It's a girl secret."

I nodded. "Thank you."

She grinned. "No problem. I love girl secrets!"

"Come to one practice," Zena told me one day in Pioneer Courthouse Square. A man walked by muttering. It reminded me of Helen and it hurt my heart.

"No. I can't roller-skate." I handed her tiny tomatoes I grew in my garden.

"Didn't you skate as a kid?" She handed me graham crackers.

"Of course I skated as a kid."

"This is the same thing, only now you get to push and shove, roll on the floor, trip, attack, push, elbow, swear, dive, and fight for victory." She did the peace sign with both hands, her vogue haircut spinning around her grooving head.

"I'm not violent."

"You'll learn how to be."

"I don't want to hurt anyone."

"You'll enjoy hurting people, trust me." She grooved her head up and down.

"I'm not fast."

She thought about that one. "You could be, if you wanted to be, Stevie."

Could I?

"Give it a shot." She pretended she was shooting a gun.

"Stevie, roller derby is about women becoming more of who they are. Braver, stronger. It's a sisterhood of kick-ass women who can get on the rink, put everything crappy behind them, and concentrate on knocking someone else's teeth out." She said this in all seriousness.

I pictured teeth flying. "Okay, Zena. I'll do it."

And I did. I started practicing with the Break Your Neck Booties roller derby team one Saturday on the weekend, one weekday night, with one game.

Me. Stevie Barrett.

Wimp.

After forty years, Aunt Janet finally found her roar the day of the party.

Not her voice, her roar.

In the truest sense of roaring.

One could make the argument that this was not the best *time* to find one's roar, but surely, better late than never, and I did enjoy the fireworks.

Herbert was mighty shocked about that roar, mighty shocked.

I enjoyed it, personally.

Now, that sounds vindictive and vengeful on my part. And petty and small.

But sometimes one has to delve into one's vindictiveness and vengefulness and petty smallness, if only to be honest with yourself that no, your name is not Pollyanna and you are not perfect, especially when it comes to insufferable cockroaches named Herbert.

I could not work the weekend of the anniversary and hard rock parties and informed Mr. Pingle that I would need time off.

That man is a geek to his core, so I related to him big-time, and he is so kind. "You're not ill, are you, Stevie?" He wrung his hands. "You're not hurt? You'll come back, won't you?" He pulled me aside. "You're my only employee I can talk to, do you feel the same?"

I assured him I did.

"It seems, it terms of chicken, that we can relate. Do you feel that, too?"

I assured him I did.

"I know there's a promotion for you coming soon in our family here."

I thanked him but explained that I had to attend family parties.

His unhappy face cleared instantly and he clapped his hands. "I *sooo* understand, I do. Have a lovely time, then, Stevie, and we'll see you next Friday. Friday! I feel so much better now." He wiped his brow. "Can't lose my best chicken friend!"

We clucked at each other and waved our chicken wings. I put on my chicken head and did the chicken dance on the corner. An old man told me grumpily to "get a real job—join the Marines," a group of teenagers threw a beer can at me, and a kid came over and gave me a quarter so I could buy myself some candy.

When I came in that evening from my chicken gig, he was triumphant, almost tearful in his joy. "I have talked to corporate, Stevie, and I have secured you a raise!" He put both hands in the air. "We have victory! I know you're a new employee, but your dedication to Aunt Bettadine's Chicken is extraordinary. You're going to make $12 an hour now."

"Cluck cluck!" I told him, winging my elbows up and down. I knew that would make him happy. What a geek. I so relate to him.

He clicked his heels as he clucked.

Eileen and Jake were bound to meet, but I was putting it off as long as possible.

I came home from my chicken job, stuck one of those nerdy miner's flashlights on my head, weeded my garden, and adjusted some of my pathway stones until late. About two in the morning I went to sleep, the incessant ringing of my doorbell waking me up a few hours later.

Eileen brought me flowers in a pot because "you're an organic garden hippie woman now, Stevie. Dirt under your fingernails, leaves in your hair, but whatever. Here."

She had many complaints that morning, her "prominent" job, the screwball stockbrokers, the screwy women at work, the screwy stepmother, and finally she was leaving and Jake, dear Jake, was coming up my path. He had asked the night before if he could bring me brunch. It was such a nice offer, on top of so many other nice things he'd done, that I burst into tears because I am a wreck. He kissed the tears and handed me a carrot from my garden.

I had not told Eileen about Jake for the obvious reasons you can think of yourself.

"Well, chicken, have a good time at your chicken job tonight," she said, winging her elbows up and down as she walked down my path to my white picket fence.

I followed her down the path as Jake smiled at Eileen, held out his hand, and introduced himself as a friend of mine.

All I could think of was, "Damn."

Eileen, still clutching his hand, turned to me. "I didn't know you had a friend named Jake," she said accusingly.

"Yes, I do." I made further introductions, and I could see

Eileen's face going red. "Now I understand why you're so busy, Stevie, that you can hardly see me anymore at all. Why you've dropped me. It's a man, isn't it? So typical." She glared at Jake.

"I'm sorry, Jake—"

"Nothing to be sorry about," Eileen snapped. "Well. I think I have the full picture now." Something in her eyes changed, she got this sneaky expression, and she wiggled her elbows at me and made the sound of a rooster. "Don't work too hard tonight at your job. I'll drive by and wave hello when you're waving your feathers!"

I felt sick.

"Excuse me?" Jake said. He didn't understand what was going on, but he understood Eileen's tone.

"Oh!" Eileen put her hands over her mouth, diamond bracelets sparkling in the sun. "You didn't know? Our Stevie here is a chicken! A chicken!"

I felt sick and nauseated.

Eileen waved her chicken wings again. "She wears a chicken outfit every Friday, Saturday, and Sunday afternoon and dances around on a street corner advertising chicken dinners." She gobbled. "Only $8.99!"

Jake glanced at me.

I felt sick and nauseated and vomitous.

"You should see the chicken head she wears. It's Jake, isn't it?" She circled her eyes with her hands. "The eyes are these huge yellow blobs, the beak is pointy, and she even has chicken feet over her shoes! I drive by every time she works and honk at her."

I felt sick and nauseated and vomitous, and my head was now way, way down.

Out of the corner of my eye I saw Jake cross his arms over that muscled chest of his that I wanted to see naked. I was sure I would not see it now. Nor would I see that smile aimed at me again. I mean, who wanted to date a woman who danced as a chicken?

"Hmmm," Jake said. "And what is your name again?"

"I'm Eileen. I'm Stevie's best friend. We've been friends forever! Right, Stevie? And, I must say, you make the best dancing chicken ever! Ever! Gobble, gobble! Why, between your chickening and this guy, no wonder I hardly see you. I thought it was because you were being snotty because of your weight loss, but noooo—"

"Excuse me, Eileen," Jake cut in.

"Excuse me!" she trilled, flapping her wings again. "See, she has to work a second job as a dancing chicken because she bought into this asinine notion that you have to be thin in this country to be worth something, so she spent tons of money on operations to get thin! Two operations! Two! And she had her boobs done, too. Those girls were spendy! But I bet you know that already. All bought but not yet paid for!"

"Stop it, Eileen!" That was enough. I'd had enough. "Who are you to come to my home and speak to me like this—"

"Who am I? I'm your best friend!" she shouted, all false humor gone.

"No," Jake said, his voice low, tough. "You are not. You're not a friend to her at all, are you?"

Eileen's mouth twisted. "Yes, I am."

"You come to Stevie's home, announce that she's working as a chicken to someone who clearly didn't know, you make fun of her, and her job, and then you tell me about operations that she's had, which are absolutely none of my business, and it's appalling that you would share someone's medical history with anyone else because it's private, and all the while you're gobbling and flapping your chicken wings. A friend. It's Eileen, right? A friend wouldn't do that."

Eileen blustered and blustered. "A friend would have been honest with you—"

"Stevie didn't tell me what she was doing for her second job because she didn't think I needed to know at this time. I understand why. When she wanted to tell me, if she wanted to tell me, she would have. As for her operations, same thing. It's not even my business to know."

"Well, I . . ."

"Well, you what?" Jake's face was so hard, and I could see

the longer he thought this out, the madder he was getting. "I've never had a friend who would try to embarrass me in front of someone else. I've never had a friend who talked about my medical history to others. I've never had a friend who made fun of me as you're laughing at Stevie, so maybe you should go now and think about what being a friend means."

Eileen's eyes narrowed. "You're going to let him talk to me like this?"

I nodded. "Yes, I am. I should have done it myself, but I'm not as quick on my feet as Jake is. That was mean, Eileen, so mean."

"I don't give a shit!" she said, but I could tell she did. I could tell in the way her whole face wobbled, how she jerked her body. "I'm leaving you and your fake boobs alone now, Stevie." She cock-a-doodled, flapped her elbows, turned on her heel, and left. Right by the garden gate she caught an edge and tumbled down.

Jake and I ran toward her and helped her up. She needed our help, but she struggled anyhow. "Let go of me!" She was crying, the tears running down her face along with her mascara.

She banged her car door shut and roared off.

"How about brunch?" Jake asked me. I nodded, and he pulled me and my trembling body in close for a hug.

"Three hundred and twenty-five pounds." Why lie to Jake? "I had a few problems and I buried them with eating."

Jake pulled me onto his lap. "I cannot even imagine you at that weight."

"You moved in about seven months ago, though. I wasn't weightwise where I am now. . . ."

"I thought you were gorgeous then, and I still think you're gorgeous."

"But does it bother you that I was that heavy? That I couldn't control myself? That I ate that much?"

"Honey—"

That did give me a trill, that word, *honey.* . . .

"I'm taking you where you are now. Not two years ago, not

five years ago, not ten years. We can't go back and change who we were. I think we have to take each other where we've met, right here."

"But how do you feel about dating a chicken?" I was still mortified.

"Stevie, you took on a second job to pay off two operations, is that right?"

I nodded.

"And you had the operations because you'd had a heart attack when you were thirty-two and if you didn't you probably would have died, is that right?"

I nodded.

"You don't want debt, you want to get rid of it. That's honest. You're working hard at both jobs."

I nodded again.

"I understand why you didn't tell me about the chicken job and the operations, Stevie. But, maybe some day in the future, you'll trust me enough to tell me everything."

"I think . . . I think I might." He made my boobs twitter, he did.

"I wish you didn't have to work a second job, and I have to say that it worries me that you're working that much, but the truth is"—he kissed me on the lips, long and slow, and then murmured—"I love chickens. Especially chickens with big yellow eyes."

26

Portland, Oregon

The morning of Herbert and Aunt Janet's anniversary party dawned bright and clear. No clouds.

It would rain.

I knew it. Literally and figuratively.

I drove The Mobster to Herbert and Aunt Janet's house in jeans and a sweatshirt, my dress and high heels in a bag along with a makeup case and jewelry.

I had dared beyond daring and invited Jake to both parties. He'd said yes, and smiled, and kissed me on my grass and we'd rolled on it, pressed in close together, so I'd had to go and get a dress. I knew exactly the one I wanted.

I'd held my breath as I entered the retail store and went to the same rack. That slinky, silky red dress with a draped V-neckline, spaghetti straps, and a ruffle at the bottom was still there. Better yet, it was on sale. With my coupon, well, now, we were in business.

Phyllis had been there. "That one is perfect. Try it on."

I'd stood staring at myself in the dressing room mirror, turning this way, and that, and this way again. Phyllis had heard me crying and walked into the dressing room and hugged me. "You are one gorgeous woman."

Gorgeous? No. I wasn't. But I was . . . better . . . maybe even pretty.

I'd taken a close-up peek at my face. There she was. I could see her in my cheekbones, my nose, the arch of my eyebrows.

There Helen was.

In me.

I was Helen.

I shuddered.

If I went back to Ashville, could I get the image of Helen off of my own face? Was there the slightest chance it would bring me peace?

"Go get 'em, darling," Phyllis had said. She slapped me on the butt.

When Herbert saw me coming up the walk to his cold and formal, dreadful mansion/mausoleum, he did not say hello or good afternoon. There was no, "Stevie, thank you for all the time you have put into planning and executing this party for me and Janet. Thank you for leaving work early." He tilted up that jaw of his and said, "Please tell me, Stevie, that you will not be wearing *that* to my anniversary party."

I took a deep breath, feeling my anger rise. I was bone-deep exhausted from planning this party, working full time, being a chicken, and going back and forth to visit Polly at the clinic. Sunshine kept coming to me in visions and nightmares, followed by Helen, who wreaked destruction. I kept seeing the bridge, and my mother was in me.

"No, Herbert." I pushed my hair behind my ears. "I won't wear this. I have a dress."

"Good. Now, the tent people have sent the Mexicans and they've been here for half an hour. I'm surprised you weren't here to meet them. I had to deal with them myself."

"I'm here now." *I am so sick of pandering to this man.*

"Yes," he drawled, "I can see that. You have called the caterers again, I presume, to make sure they're coming on time?"

"They'll be here on time, and I called them again yesterday to make sure that all your new requests were met, including white and wheat rolls but no sourdough, salad with no nuts, only tomatoes and chopped onions, the onion pieces should be a quarter of an inch at most, pasta salad tomatoes should be cut in two long strips—"

"Stevie," he clipped as he stared over my head and scanned his estate, not meeting my eyes. I was nothing, that's what that said, *nothing*. "I know what I ordered. I depended on you to get it done right. Let's hope you did."

"Let's hope," I said. *He's insufferable.*

"I didn't know there were three tents, did you?" He rocked back on his heels, hands clasped behind his back. "I think that's awkward, don't you? Poor planning. One would have been best. That was my expectation."

"I understand that one would have been best, but their large tent collapsed and they're expecting rain, so we set up two more—"

He studied the sky. "There's not going to be any rain, Stevie, I can tell. I understand that the flowers will be here shortly?" He arched an eyebrow at me. "They're not here now."

"They're coming, Herbert, in the colors you ordered." Not the colors that Aunt Janet had wanted. I had ordered the flowers that Aunt Janet had wanted, and he had called the florist himself to check, shouted at the florist, then shouted at me. "I'm sure Janet will be disappointed, but at least you have the flowers you want." *Is there a more obnoxious man on this planet?*

"Correct. I'm paying for this celebration and I know what works best. Janet's choice, of wildflowers mixed with daisies and sunflowers, was ludicrous. We're not a hippie couple."

"No, you're not." *Aunt Janet is a gentle soul who has been smashed to smithereens by you, and you're a runty boar.*

He continued to peruse the grounds around my head, as if I didn't exist. "See to it that the virginal white roses I ordered are on the arbor. They're symbolic. I want them in the photographs when I make my announcement against gay marriage. That's very important, Stevie. I'm a man of means in this community, and I want it clear that Janet and I celebrated in style, not with some barbeque where we flipped hamburgers."

I had to get out of there. "Where's Aunt Janet?"

"Hmmm?" His attention was already elsewhere, probably trying to find something else that I did wrong.

"Where's the bride?"

His mouth tightened. "I believe she is finally preparing herself."

"What do you mean?"

"Janet gets nervous at these gatherings of people—so many important people in one place it's intimidating for her, she's a quiet, anxious sort of wife—and I told her to go and lie down and take her medicine so she does not embarrass us. I also sent Ellen Tofferson up to help her."

Bad idea. "She hates Ellen Tofferson."

"Ellen knows how to handle my wife with discretion."

"Ellen is condescending and rude to Aunt Janet. She's grim and bad tempered and uptight—" I felt the anger bubbling in me, hot and acidic.

"She is a pillar of this community."

"Everyone hates her. She's obnoxious. They only put up with her because she writes checks from her late husband's estate."

"Ellen is proper, understands how important maintaining our society is—"

"She brags about her money, drops names, and has made it her life's work to launch vendettas against other women—"

"Your opinion is unnecessary and unwanted. I will handle Janet. Now, I'm sure you have things to do." He turned on his heel and left.

I glanced up as a curtain moved in Aunt Janet's window.

Aunt Janet glared down at her husband, and I saw it then: Raging fury. Bitter resentment. Disgust.

Not good.

I should have taken it as a warning sign of the upcoming roar, but someone else needed me, so I turned to help.

Minutes later I saw Ellen Tofferson stomping down the stairs, her bosom shaking with indignation. She announced to Herbert that Janet was "throwing her usual fits."

Herbert rolled his eyes, sighed heavily. "All men have a burden. This is mine."

Ellen put her hand on his upper arm, her wrinkled, blobby face heavy, serious, sympathetic. She is built in a pear shape with a bobbing bottom and gray hair. "I'm with you, Herbert. I am *with you.*" Her bosom shook indignantly again of its own accord.

I was not *with him,* I wanted to hit him.

Someone came up and asked me a question about the placement of tables and chairs. Another person, from the caterers, had a different question. My phone rang. It was the florist. My phone rang again. It was the ice sculpture people. They were on their way. "We had inspiration! Big inspiration, Stevie! We come down now. You love it!"

The party was starting, officially, at six P.M.

This would have been a fine time for the party if Aunt Janet was not roaring.

"Heavens to shit!" she said, throwing her powder box across the room.

Aunt Janet never swears.

"Heavens to shit!" she said, louder this time. She threw her compact blush. I ducked. "It's been forty shitty years!"

Polly lay back on the bed and fiddled with her necklace. She was stunning. Her curls were pulled back in waves. She was wearing a burgundy-colored dress, no sleeves, golden piping, gold shoes. On anyone else it would have been silly, but she looked like an ultrachic gypsy. "Uh. Yeah. It has been. You chose to stay for forty shitty years. You stuck yourself there and didn't move and we got stuck there, too, for our entire childhood. We were all whipped dogs, and now we're celebrating. Hoo-ha!"

Aunt Janet gripped the edge of her vanity, her robe hanging open, and exhaled. "Heavens to shit, I hate what I am about to do. I told him I didn't want to do this, I told him many times. And here we are. *Here we are.* He didn't listen. No, worse, he did listen, but he didn't take into account what I was saying. He didn't care. And I don't care enough about myself to stand up to him and say, 'Heavens to shit, I don't want to remarry you.'"

Her chest heaved. "I don't even want to *stay* married to him. Not for one more heavens-to-shit minute!"

She hurled three lipsticks. One hit Herbert's pillow. Another hit a huge photo of his parents that he insisted on keeping in their bedroom, *right across from their bed*. Now that is a sexual turn-on. The third lipstick flew right out the window and landed in the wedding cake that an employee from the bakery was carrying out to the tents. No one noticed until the guitar player bit down on it later that night.

He was a bit drunk so he flipped it open and tried it on.

The raspberry glacé color went very well with his eye color.

The cake was delicious.

While Aunt Janet continued to disintegrate, which included ripping down the portrait of Herbert's parents and dumping shampoo over their faces, I rushed back downstairs to check on the party details. The last thing I heard from Polly was, "Mom, it's about choices. Here's your choice: Do you want to recommit yourself to a venomous tyrant? No decision here *is* a decision, you know what I mean? I think your decisionless decisions gotta stop. That's a thought for you to throw around."

"Holy damn," Aunt Janet said, as if she'd been hit by a bolt of enlightenment. She yanked her hair out of the bun Herbert had insisted the hairstylist make. "Holy damn, I don't want to be here, and holy damn, I can't be decisionless for one more blasted minute."

The tables were set on the sprawling grass under the tents with the white twinkle lights and the floral arrangements, boring but pink and tidy, as Herbert had ordered.

Out of the corner of my eye I saw Lance, gorgeous in a gray suit, strolling along the back perimeter of the property. I snickered, couldn't help it. I saw a few boxes under his arms, tucked in tight. I watched as he settled himself at a back table, then opened the boxes and popped something out into the three chairs. Next, he fiddled with something under the table that he'd brought in a bag. I had to struggle to keep my laughter to myself as before my eyes three different "girls" appeared in the seats.

Right there, right then, Lance was blowing up his dolls.

Ah, wasn't that sweet! He had brought Lolita! My, her breasts had grown!

And there was Norway. I called her that because she was six feet tall with blond hair and a toothy smile.

And Sabrina Dina. Wasn't she spectacular this evening?

I wondered which guests would willingly sit next to the "ladies." I envisioned the head of one of the ultraconservative political parties here. She was a rabid, half-cocked nut. Or the president of the anti-gay group, a snivelly, tiny, whiny man with a wife who resembled a zombie corpse.

I was distracted by a balding man, short and smiling, leading three younger men.

"Hello," I said. Aha, the ice sculpture people.

"Yes, yes! You Stevie?" the Russian man said, arms thrown out wide. "We done. It beautiful. A song. A siren. You love, yes, I know you love."

I directed them to one of the long buffet tables and thanked them profusely for their time. I was actually looking forward to seeing the two doves with the heart between them.

I was distracted again by the caterer, who had another question about one of Herbert's endless changes. She had brandy on her breath—she had warned that this party might drive her to drink, and I could not blame her. When I turned around, the ice sculptors had unveiled their creation.

My breath caught smack in the middle of my esophagus. Right there.

I so wanted to laugh, but I couldn't. I held my mouth tight as a lid on a can of carrots so as not to offend the four men staring at me, eagerly awaiting my effusive praise.

Clearly, there had been a misunderstanding between me and the Russian gentleman. These communication problems!

"It magical! Some mystery there, too, you no think?" he asked. "It in the eyes. Mystery! Romantic!"

"Uh, yes, mysterious! Definitely mysterious." I clamped my teeth together on my giggle.

"It a sea fairy tale!"

"You're right," I said, muffling a chuckle. "A sea fairy tale."

"A sea legend!" he gushed. "An enchantress of the fishermen for hundreds of years!"

"Definitely an enchantress." I lassoed my laughter.

Hoo boy. The ice sculpture was an enchantress. In the middle of the buffet table lay a five-foot-long ice mermaid with a secretive, sexy smile on her secretive, sexy face. She had flowing hair, a curving fish tail, and she was topless, as you would expect from a mermaid.

The Russian and his employees stuck their chests out. Proud. Confident. Manly. Waiting for profuse praise.

She had voluminous boobs, that was a fact. The nipples were quite large, too. But, perhaps seawater changes the composition of those things. Herbert would . . . well, there were no words to describe what he would do when he saw those boobs and nipples. And the tail.

"It's a work of art," I told them, suddenly enormously pleased. "A work of art."

The Russian beamed with pleasure, standing up on his toes. "I so glad you like. Took long time. The breasts"—he cupped his chest in all seriousness. "They take long time. Must be smooth. Soft, yes?"

Yes, I nodded. Oh, yes. I gripped my giggles. "They must be soft."

"Soft and big." He cupped himself. "Mermaids big. Shells right there sometimes, so big."

"Absolutely."

"But not tonight. No shells. This art. Mermaid art."

"Mermaid art!"

I snuck a peek over at Herbert, who was upbraiding one of the Hispanic employees of the catering company. "Herbert will pay double for your efforts."

The Russian man beamed again, then said, "Masterpiece, no?

She masterpiece. Those breasts! Perfect! Take long time." He wiped his eyes.

I patted his shoulder.

"I miss her already," he weeped.

Minutes later I was on the phone, frantically trying to get ahold of the quartet that had still not arrived. I finally reached them. They were not coming. On the way here, the driver had hit the accelerator instead of the brake and they'd driven through the front of an adults-only club. "We completely smashed a display of sex toys," one of them said. Minor injuries, but all were in the hospital. "I had no idea those things even existed! Have you heard about this new toy for men called a Pink Princess? Guess I've been inside too much playing my violin. So sorry we can't be there."

Lance heard the conversation, saw my stricken face, and said, "I'll take care of this," and ambled off, phone to ear. I grabbed our neighbor, Mrs. Bunce, none too gently, and asked her to play piano for the vow part of the ceremony. The piano was right inside the door, in the living room, feet from the now-virginal-rose-drooped arbor on the deck where Herbert and Aunt Janet would renew their vows.

"Sure I will, darling, but this is not a happy day for me. Your aunt is simply retrapping herself, married to a rabid alligator. Virginia and I don't get it. She should be tramping around the world with us on one of our trips." She sighed, waved her hand. She was wearing beige pants and a beige shirt, her hair in a long beige braid, and hippie sandals. She was a multimillionaire. "I'll do it, but I'd rather play the death march, that black and morbid song. I was hoping your aunt would make a break from that stiff-assed anteater. . . ."

Herbert came up behind me seconds later, then signaled with his pointed finger for me to follow him. We ducked into the den. "Where the hell is the symphony quartet?"

"They were in a car accident."

"Damn." He shook his head. He did not even ask if they were hurt/mangled/dead/decapitated. He didn't care. "Stevie, I was counting on you to do this, this one small thing for your

aunt and me, to make a few calls to arrange my anniversary celebration, and apparently it's too much for you, isn't it?" He
glowered at me. "After all that I have done for you, taking you
in, raising you, dealing with your weight issues, your emotional
issues, putting you through college—"

I was furious. Suddenly, stunningly furious. Maybe it was my
weight loss that had given me confidence. Maybe it was dealing
with Crystal and the Athertons and Polly and watching Aunt
Janet finally grow a spine. Maybe it was because of Jake and
this golden glow he'd brought to my insides, but I let that leechy
cockroach have it.

"Let's get something straight, Herbert, right now. First off,
yes, you took me in. It's my understanding that you didn't want
to, but Aunt Janet said she would divorce you if you didn't."

He paled. It was the truth. Polly had told me she'd overheard
a conversation.

"So don't pretend you're this magnanimous, generous man.
You made sure I never felt part of your family. You made me feel
fat, dumb, and unwanted, a burden. I knew, from the second I
stepped into your house, that you didn't want me there. How do
you think an eleven-year-old feels, knowing that?" My lungs
constricted. "I was *a little girl,* Herbert. Helen had tried to kill
me. She killed Sunshine." My voice broke. "She killed herself.
My grandparents died shortly after that, one after the other. I
lost everything. Do you get that? Are you capable of getting
that? You even took away my name after shaking me every
night for months."

Something flashed in his eyes. Maybe it was emotion, but it
was too quick for me to catch, and he slammed his sausage lips
together. "I provided for you—"

"You provided for me?" Can a body turn red-hot with anger?
"Hardly. You received social security payments for me each
month. You had the proceeds from Grandpa's business. There
was the Schoolhouse House and all the land that you sold. The
farm equipment. The cars and trucks . . ."

"I told you, the business went bankrupt. I had to sell *everything.*" He shook his head sadly, but he was suddenly as pale as

a mean ghost. "Your grandpa was not a businessman. Way too generous with his employees. He was in the . . ." Herbert coughed. "I know you don't understand business, but your grandpa was operating in the red, and that's why the company went . . . uh . . . under two years after he died."

"You know what, Herbert?" I could barely speak, but I was finally going to voice what I had always suspected. I had checked up on my grandpa's business online. It was sold two years after Herbert got his hands on it, and it was still there. "I don't believe you. It was a thriving business. I think you ran it into the ground, that's what I think happened."

He turned a sickly white-green color.

"I think you're the one who's not a businessman. You're the one who ruined it all. When your own father died ten years ago he specified who was to run each section of your family's company, and you were not named. Yes, I know that, we all do. You're a figurehead. That's it."

He stumbled back, stunned.

"You probably went into my grandpa's company, and when the employees hated you and your smug, superior attitude, you probably cut their pay, fired the older people, brought in your own people, and sank the place. That's what happened, right?"

His head jerked, right and left. "I won't discuss this with you. You don't have a head for business. You wouldn't understand the mess that I found there. I have acted as your father for years—"

"No, you haven't. I know what a father is, what he does, because I had Grandpa. You're not a father to me. You're not even an uncle I want to claim as my own. The only reason I have contact with you at all is because of Aunt Janet, Lance, and Polly."

"You ungrateful—"

"Ungrateful? I am ungrateful?" I fought back tears. "I wish that you had refused to take me in. I wish you'd let me stay in Ashville with The Family. Me, Lance, Aunt Janet, and Polly would have been better off without you, even if we lived in a tiny house and had no toilet. I might never have had the extreme eating addiction I did, and Polly wouldn't have anorexia. Am I grateful for you? No, I'm not. You have hurt me thousands of times, and I'm done. I am done with you. You are a toxic person, and I will not have contact with you again after tonight."

"You're done with me after tonight," he scoffed, but he looked scared. His eyelid twitched and his hand shook when he pushed his white hair back.

"Yes. I am. I regret all these years that I've put up with your cruelty, your overbearing, critical personality. I regret that I didn't have the self-confidence to walk away from you. But what I regret the most is not being part of a healthy family, and now I'm fixing that." I could hardly believe what I was saying. Was I ready for this? Could I do it?

"What are you talking about now? More nonsense."

I took a deep breath. "I'm going back to Ashville."

He sucked in his breath, his head snapping back as if I'd slugged him.

"My family has tried to contact me as an adult, through letters and phone calls, but I avoided them because I was huge and fat and I didn't think I could stand the pain of talking to them again, remembering. I thought I was a disgrace to Grandma and Grandpa. You've told me that for years. 'You're a disgrace, Stevie.'" I mocked his voice. "I closed them out as I closed out all my grief, but I am done closing anyone or anything out, no matter how much it hurts. I'm going home, Herbert. Home to Ashville."

He staggered back and put a hand on his desk for balance. "You can't."

"Why can't I?" Why was he so . . . *scared?*

"Because . . ." He cleared his throat. "It's not necessary, Stevie. We're your family. Put your past behind you. Put those people behind you. They were all odd, strange. Your grandparents' people are backwoods, uneducated, uncouth people."

"No, they aren't. I knew them. That's what you forget. I knew them and I loved them. I loved The Family. I belonged in Ashville."

He sank into his leather chair, knees collapsing.

What was going on? Why was he so averse to my returning?

Then it dawned on me: He was afraid I would find out the truth, wasn't he? There were secrets in Ashville he didn't want me to know.

"No good will come of it."

"Yes, it will. Even if it's painful, good will come of it. I'm disgusted with myself for not going sooner, but I let your lies become my truth."

"Don't go, Stevie. I'm warning you. Stay away from that town. They don't want to see you."

That hit me in the gut, but I no longer believed it, no longer believed what he'd told me as a kid. "You're lying. I know that. I think you've lied to me since I set foot inside your front door, but I was too grief stricken and young and lost, and then as an adult I was too screwed up and miserable to see it, to deal with it. But I am strong enough now. You're a liar, and I am going to Ashville."

I turned and left the den. I briefly thought about being classy and shutting the door quietly, but I didn't. I slammed it so hard I heard something fall off his shelves and break.

I would not associate again with Herbert. Not ever.

Family is the most difficult relationship of all, I think. There are some family members we love dearly. We believe we can't live without their kindness, wisdom, humor, insight, their very presence. With others, they're irritating and disagreeable but we can suck it up, limit contact, and smile now and then. And then there are family members that we cannot stand. They're verbally abusive, unkind, or throw barbs and darts while smiling. They subtly or blatantly put us down, criticize, destroy, and destruct.

Society says we should keep in contact with them. Set up boundaries, try to control how we respond to them, be friendly and civil. They are, after all, family.

This is what I now believe: That is bullshit.

Complete bullshit.

No one should be around anyone who is abusive, mean, or dickheaded. Life is too short. I could have easily died when I had my heart attack, and thinking of all the time I'd spent with

Herbert, hurting or angry from what he'd said or done . . . well, I was done with that.

As I left the den, crossed the deck, and glared at the "virginal white roses" climbing up the makeshift arch for the ceremony that Herbert had ordered, I was hit in the shoulder. I stared at the eye shadow container that clattered to the ground, then up at the window. I heard Aunt Janet shriek, "Heavens to shit," and ran on up to her bedroom.

There would be trouble tonight, I knew it.

And it certainly would not be limited to the big-nippled mermaid and blow-up dolls.

But my, Sabrina Dina was spectacular!

Herbert stormed into their bedroom about fifteen minutes later. He was grossly, sickly white. He glared, pointed at me, and shook his head. I swear I saw rampant fear in his expression, his hands shaking. "Dammit! What's going on? How long does it take you to get ready, woman?"

Aunt Janet sat up in bed in her robe and said, "There had better be no newspaper reporters and no photographers down there, Herbert. I have told you how I feel."

"Why aren't you in your damn dress," he thundered. "You're supposed to be ready!"

"Did you hear me, Herbert?"

"Hear what? All I need to hear is that you're going to be ready in five minutes. You got that, Janet? We're starting in five minutes with or with—"

She raised her eyebrows. "With or without me?" Her whole body shook. "Herbert, you will listen to me. I have already told you, and I told the quartet over the phone last week, that I do not want them playing 'Here Comes the Bride.' I'm too old for that."

"Get ahold of yourself!" He threw a trembling hand in his wife's direction. "Polly, why are you lying on the bed? Stop this laziness this instant."

"I'm lying here because I'm hoping Mom will change her mind and avoid the public spectacle of a marital hanging," she drawled. "Then we can all take a nap or get drunk. I vote for drunk."

"We are renewing our vows, young lady, and our commitment to each other."

"No, you're making a political statement. You're a whack job, you know that, right, Dad?"

Herbert was so mad I thought he might hit Polly, so I scrambled to stand in front of her. "Get out, Herbert," I said.

"Yes, do," Polly drawled. "You can take yourself, your own self-made whack job, and go whack."

"I have told you, Herbert, I'll have no political statements," Aunt Janet said. "Do not make any of your anti-gay speeches. This is not a campaign rally."

"Woman, I don't know what's gotten into you, but you will stop speaking to your husband in that manner and accept my authority. Do you understand?"

"No, I don't." Aunt Janet threw her foundation bottle at him. "Tell me, Herbie, what would you do if I walked out? Right now. Would you care?"

"He would pop a gasket in his head and die," Polly said. "Not because you left him but because of the humiliation and waste of political capital it would cause. He's a pillar! He's running for reelection!"

He scoffed. "You won't leave me. You know the consequences of that action. I've told you before, I have been clear, so I won't even entertain the notion."

"Entertain it, Dad," Polly drawled. "Please."

"I'm sick of you telling me what to do," Aunt Janet said. "Sick of you ordering me around. Sick of your disapproval and disappointment. Sick of you running my life, and I'm sick of myself for letting you run it. I am sick of myself!"

Now Herbert's jaw dropped open.

"And I don't want to do this. I don't even know why I'm here and not in . . ." She put a hand to her mouth.

"You will not embarrass this family with all of our friends here—"

"They're your friends, Herbie, not mine. You took all my friends away from me."

"I took the friends away from you who were inappropriate for you and would lead you astray, into a life unbecoming of my wife, inappropriate for a woman in the public eye—"

"Yes, she could have hung around with Ellen the Emasculator," Polly drawled. "Now that would be enough to make me want to swim in a pool full of vodka rocks."

"She's so splendid," I added. "Her bosom shakes with indignation."

"Bosoms can do that," Polly noted.

"I miss Virginia. She won't be back for six weeks!" Aunt Janet said this almost to herself, then the fire was back in her eyes. "Six weeks! She's leaving for an African safari tomorrow! She invited me and you said I couldn't go!"

"That's right. I won't have you gallivanting around the world with Virginia. Plus, there's no reason to go to Africa. Heathens, unsafe, unhealthy, diseased, superstitions, poverty stricken."

"Why do I let you tell me what to do?" she asked, almost to herself. "Why have I let you bully me my whole life? When do I get to become myself and do what I want? Do I have to wait for you to die to do it?"

Herbert hardly knew what to do. To say he was stunned down to his shiny black shoes and tuxedo would be an understatement, but he was a wily man, and he realized ruling by force and threat weren't working here. Polly started singing a song about a husband who was shot by his unhappy wife, Janet was having a meltdown, and I had somehow scared the crap out of him with my announcement about Ashville.

"You can do as you wish, within reason, and within what I feel is right for you as my wife."

Aunt Janet threw a perfume bottle at Herbert, who ducked in the nick of time, then said, "You even pick out my clothes! You hired a personal shopper for me, and when I wanted two new skirts in a different style, you had her pretend they didn't have my size! Don't pretend you're shocked, Herbert, I knew! I knew! I hate my clothes. I hate them. I hate that stupid dress, too!"

The "renewal of vows" dress hanging on the hanger was stiff, proper, a heavy flounce of off-white yuck.

"You're going to resemble an aged Little Bo Peep," Polly said. "And there's your wolf." She pointed at Herbert. "He's gobbled you up already."

"I will not allow you to have one of your mental meltdowns at my party!" Herbert seethed.

"Your party, Herbert? I thought it was *ours.*"

I put my slinky red dress on about fifteen minutes later, and it was a clothing miracle. I felt liberated. Free. Sexy! Except for the fact that my aunt was renewing her vows to a weasel fart, I was a new Stevie.

When I came out of the bathroom adjoining Aunt Janet's bedroom, Polly said, "You are flat-out gorgeous."

Lance wobbled out, "I think I'm going to cry."

Aunt Janet sighed. "You are beautiful, Stevie. You remind me of your mother. It's your lovely face, Stevie. . . ." She touched my dimple.

I thought I'd choke on that comment. For decades I had fought against that image in the mirror. I didn't want to be her and had spent years running from the resemblance, denying her, burying her under food. As I had lost weight my momma's face had emerged from my own, and she had killed my Sunshine. I had struggled and struggled. How could that be beautiful?

"Never forget that your mother loved you, sweetie," Aunt Janet said. "She was so sick, but she did love you."

"No, she didn't," I croaked out, but part of me, way deep inside, said real quiet, "Yes, she did, she loved you as much as she could."

"Yes, sugar, she loved you," Aunt Janet said, tears pouring out. "It was in her eyes when she looked at you, when she held you when you were a baby, when she sang to you, when she painted with you." Aunt Janet kissed, then hugged me. "That's from your mother. She was too sick to do it herself, but I know, dear, I know that she would have kissed you with all she had if her disease had not taken her away from us."

I put my hand on my cheek, covering the kiss.

Then me, Polly, Lance, and Aunt Janet turned and stared into the mirrors on the closet doors together.

I saw my momma's face in mine, but Polly leaned in and kissed me, and I smiled and saw my dimple, and Aunt Janet linked an arm around my shoulder, and in the blue eyes I shared with my momma I saw my own expression, the pain I figured I'd always carry with me, but also a new strength and determination there, and maybe, finally, a dose of courage.

And then Lance said, blubbering a bit, "Stevie, you're way prettier than any of my blow-ups," and I laughed, and in the laugh lines around my eyes, and in my black curls, the strength of my chin, I saw myself.

Finally, in the mirror, after so long, I saw me. Not Stevie and Helen, but Stevie.

Aunt Janet kissed me again.

I headed back outside to direct people, answer questions, say hello to early guests, make sure all was right, and then I saw him.

He was standing near the tables under the white tents, staring quizzically down at Lance's dolls. For a second I admired that he-man the size of a redwood, with shoulders like a tractor, blondish hair, a tough face and a tough jaw, with eyes that turned me to mush. I admired the man who danced with me outside, and made me pasta, and held me on his lap, and said he wanted to start with me from right here, right now.

He turned, then, because you can always tell when someone is staring at you, and he smiled. I smiled back, in my red dress, with the ruffle at the bottom.

"Thank you again for coming!" Herbert boomed to the guests, all properly seated in rows, in white chairs, on either side of a strip of white satiny material, on the perfectly manicured grass, awaiting the bride, currently having a fantastic meltdown. Herbert stretched out his arms, loving the attention, the man of the house, leader of the pack. "This is a celebration of what marriage should be."

I heard three camera snaps and saw two quick camera flashes. The photographers and reporters were all from local newspapers.

Aunt Janet was going to be unhappy.

"This is a celebration of what a solid, old-fashioned American family is, and should always be." He turned to me and Polly, holding our bridesmaids' flowers on his right, and Lance, on his left, the best man. "A long, happy marriage, between a man and a woman. One man. One woman. Children." He smiled piously when certain members of the audience cheered, then grew somber. "I have no idea what's happening in this state. This liberal, free-love, anything-goes state. I have no idea what's going on in this country, where there are no moral standards, no values, no boundaries of what is right and wrong, and a general disregard of the biblical structures that built this country!" His voice rose and fell.

I watched Jake's face as it hardened. I had warned him about Herbert and his upcoming political statement against gay marriage. It hadn't gone over well with Jake. His brother was gay. That was the brother who owned the boat we borrowed on the Willamette.

Beside me, Polly said, without bothering to lower her voice, "Dad sure knows how to roll out the romance, doesn't he? Set the mood. Praise his wife, talk about their decades-long love affair, their life together. . . ."

Herbert glared at her, pious smile frozen tight.

We smiled back angelically.

Aunt Janet was going to be extremely unhappy.

"But we're better than that!" Herbert boomed. "We know what America is about!"

Lance was starting to boil. He was sweet and kind, but once that temper switched to high, watch out. Please.

"We're not here to celebrate only my and Janet's long-lasting, happy, fulfilling marriage, we're here to celebrate what marriage is, what it should be, what all men and women should commit to. A loyal union. Faithful to one another. Blessed. Fruitful!" he pontificated, then held out his hands to us.

Perhaps we were supposed to wave our fruitiness to the clapping crowd, but none of us felt the urge.

"Yes, fruitful," Polly drawled. "As in, we're all fruitcakes."

"Nuts. We're all nuts," I said, glancing at Lance, whose face was tight and reddening. Would he hit his father in front of all these people?

We got the glare from Herbert.

We smiled back, angelically.

"And now, let's begin this ceremony and let's hope and pray that others will join us in our battle against gay marriage! An abomination! A curse! Against the Bible! Anti-American."

There was weak, scattered applause, the photographers took a few pictures, the reporters scribbled their notes.

Oh, Aunt Janet would be steamingly unhappy.

I peeked at Jake. He was staring pretty hard at Herbert, that jaw rock hard.

Herbert nodded at Mrs. Bunce, the multimillionaire piano player, who glowered at Herbert, then started playing. I had told her to play the song Aunt Janet requested, not "Here Comes the Bride," which Aunt Janet thought was a ridiculous song to be played for a woman of her years.

Unfortunately, that was the song that was played. Later Mrs. Bunce told me, with an enormous amount of huffing and puffing, that Herbert had told her to play "Here Comes the Bride," and told her how "romantic" it would be for his wife, that Janet wanted to reenact her wedding day. Mrs. Bunce was so mad that Herbert lied to her that she let the air out of all of his tires the next day with her steak knife.

I froze, absolutely froze, when I heard those notes, and said, "The bride's gonna be pissed."

Beside me, Polly wailed, "Oh, you are a polluted moron."

And Lance said, "You bastard. She said no to that song."

He did not say it quietly. Herbert's head swiveled toward Lance before he forced that lizardish smile to his mouth again.

It was all a control-freak game to him. He'd wanted that song, and he was going to get it. He'd wanted the reporters, and they were there. He'd wanted to renew his vows for political gain, and he would do it. To hell with Janet. I was disgusted. Absolutely disgusted.

The "Here Comes the Bride" song played out.

No Aunt Janet.

I heard Herbert clear his throat under his arc of virginal white roses.

He nodded at Mrs. Bunce a second time.

She glowered, then played the full "Here Comes the Bride" song again.

"The bride's not doing what she was told," I said. "Betcha she's in trouble now."

"You screwed up, whack job," Polly said.

"She didn't want that song, Dad," Lance said again, louder. "You knew it. She told you. She had another song picked out."

This time, as the song finished, I noticed a line of sweat across Herbert's brow, the top of his cheekbones flushed.

Would Aunt Janet actually stand him up? Would she dare? Had she finally had enough? Had she heard "Here Comes the Bride" and that was that?

For a third time, "Here Comes the Bride" was pounded out again while Mrs. Bunce continued to perfect her glower.

"Bad choice, Herbert," I drawled.

"Typical Dad behavior," Polly said. "Tyrannical, titillating, tortuous, taboo."

"You don't even love her, do you, Dad?" Lance said. "You love you. It's all about you."

No Aunt Janet.

Jake leaned back in his chair, crossed his arms. I dare say his expression said, "You deserve this, asshole."

Herbert was livid. Flushed, tight-lipped, about to blow. He knew the game was up. He had lost this tiny battle. Amidst the whispers and the turning heads, he stalked over to Mrs. Bunce and whispered something to her. She nodded, glowered at Herbert, and began another song. This one was cheerful and upbeat, from a Broadway show, the song that Aunt Janet had requested, one I remember my mother singing.

We waited halfway through that song.

Finally, Aunt Janet appeared at the end of the rows of white chairs.

She was roaringly unhappy.

Her off-white dress with its high collar, poofy sleeves, and thick flounce was hideous. She charged up the aisle, her face stormy, one hand holding her bouquet straight down. If I had thought she was mad in her makeup-throwing mood, that was nothing. Ten feet from Herbert, she threw her bouquet at his face. He was so shocked, he didn't even put a hand up to protect himself.

"You asshole! I told you not to play 'Here Comes the Bride'! We agreed on it!"

"Now, Janet, calm down. I thought it would bring you beautiful memories of our wedding day. . . ." He did the pious lizard smile, but the smile wobbled.

"No, you didn't. Our wedding day was a joke. I hated it. I told you I hated it. Your mother planned everything. I had no voice. I hated your mother, and I have hated being married to you."

Herbert's mouth opened and shut, opened and shut, a sea snake trying to catch a worm.

"You wanted this stupid ceremony. I didn't. I told you that, and yet you still planned it. You wanted an event for the press, a launch against gay marriage, a PR hit for you and your stupid campaign. Hell, Herbert, even your own vow renewal ceremony has to be part of your political plan!"

"I'm sorry, friends," Herbert intoned, trying to be magnanimous, the pitiful victim. "My wife has had too much to drink—"

I saw two more camera flashes. Flash, flash. Aunt Janet whirled around, furious, then turned back to Herbert.

"Nice try, Herbert. I haven't had a thing to drink, not a thing." She threw something else—it was blue, and it shattered against the steps. It was the blue drinking glass Herbert always made Aunt Janet drink from to remind her of her "weakness."

Herbert jumped in shock, then sighed and said, "All marriages have challenges. This has been mine."

"You idiot, Herbert!" she shrieked. "You and your anti-gay marriage initiative. As if our crappy marriage should be an example to others. Where the wife struggles against her own suffocation, is not even allowed to have an opinion, or to be a person in her own right. Where she's supposed to be pretty and docile and smile nicely and all the while she has become no one, no one that she herself can respect or recognize. I don't even know myself, because I allowed you to take me away from me."

Finally, Herbert was stunned speechless under his virginal white roses.

"I like the new you," I said.

"Way to go, Mom," Polly cheered. "We have a decision!"

"Kickin' ass," Lance said. "Spike that football!"

"You think that two men defile traditional marriage?" Aunt Janet said, shaking with fury. "Or two women? What a joke. What defiles marriage is when one person doesn't respect or love the other. It happens when one person forces another to live in a mausoleum, and pick up his shoes each night, and is expected to roll over for sex every Thursday night at ten o'clock and Saturday night at nine-thirty, on the dot, precisely. And she's supposed to roll with joy for sex that takes approximately four minutes with no foreplay." She took off a high heel and threw it at him.

"I'm leaving for Africa with Virginia. I'm calling an attorney before I go. And don't you dare tell me, again, as you have a hundred times before, that I can't divorce you, that you'll take everything and leave me penniless. You used to tell me if I left you that you would take the kids from me because I'm an alcoholic, and because I fell in love with Victor. Well, they're grown and beautiful people, despite what a lousy mother I was for not leaving you, and I know they won't leave me, even though I deserve it for what I put them through with you! I'm going to travel, and write, and dance the mamba, and listen to jazz music, and read what I want to read, and I will never, ever wear the smothering clothes you buy me again."

With that statement, she whipped off this lace veil thing Herbert insisted she wear because it had been his mother's, whom she hated, and threw it at him. Then she took off the other heel and threw that at him, too, before charging off. "Fuck, fuck you, Herbert!"

No one moved for long, tense seconds, then Polly grabbed a microphone, smiled like an ultrachic gypsy, and said, "Isn't this pleasant? Welcome to the Barrett family. We've tried so stinkin' hard to appear perfect, but we're rotting from the inside out. So many secrets, so many problems, so much energy expended trying to pretend. Hello, everyone. I'm Polly. I'm anorexic." She smile angelically, waved.

About ten people, clearly those who had been in twelve-step programs, automatically answered, "Hi, Polly," then slunk down in their seats.

Lance, so handsome in his suit, recovered quickly and said, "Hello, everyone, I think you know me. I'm Lance, and I want to take a moment to introduce Lance's Lucky Ladies, blow-up dolls that all can enjoy. If you all would care to turn around, there are several in the back there, under the first white tent. I have brochures on the tables, and I'm happy to answer any questions . . . and, oh, I knit. I love knitting. And I cry easily. Whew! That felt good to get that out in the open. Right there." He pounded his chest. "Honesty feels right."

And then it was me. What to say? I used to be obese because I ate my grief? I've had some ruckus in my childhood? This whole family has been living a lie about how and why I came to live with them and here's the truth? I think my uncle is hiding something from me in Ashville?

Nah. I thought I'd skip that part.

"Ladies and gentlemen," I announced, smiling angelically, proud of my red dress with the ruffle, delighted that Jake was there, even though he had a close-up shot of the Barrett family insanity, "dinner will now be served. We'll be having salmon with a light covering of pesto, marinated chicken with teriyaki sauce, salad with no nuts, and pasta salad with tomatoes cut in long strips, as per Herbert's instructions, followed by wedding cake. It's all delicious and there's plenty, so please stay, have a wonderful time—"

I stopped midsentence as a drumroll echoed across the lawn, followed by another drumroll. Electric guitars screeched, then a keyboard, something else that was clangy and loud, and then they all smashed together at one time. Next there was a throat-tingling scream, you know the scream that rockers scream before they launch into some head-banging hard rock tune?

That was the one.

Our musical entertainment had arrived. Only it wasn't the quartet from the symphony who had crashed into an Adults Only store and knocked over the sex toys.

No, there were no tuxedos and well-groomed men and women, with proper and polite smiles plastered on their faces. There were no violins, violas, or cellos. There were no music stands, no musical notes floating through the air adding peace and tranquility to this hellacious day.

None of that.

Lance had taken care of the problem, as he said he would.

These "musicians," who were dressed in leather and torn clothes, with long, stringy hair, dark glasses, an assortment of tattoos, various piercings, and makeup, were from the band that was playing tomorrow night for Lance's Lucky Ladies hard rock party. Black liner and black lipstick were de rigueur.

Another head-banging scream pierced the evening, followed by a roll of the drums and the thrum of the guitars. "Hey! You guys wanna party?" Rock star cackling. "You guys wanna rock? You guys wanna jam it out and shake your titties?" More rock star cackling. "Let's see you guys showin' some skin! Get down, everybody, *get down!*"

Drums. Bass. Screeching. Those guys rocked out.

Oh, how they rocked.

Herbert gaped at them, then at his stunned audience, and at us, eyes wide open. He was more stunned than if I'd hit him with a Taser. The man was gobsmacked.

Humiliated under his virginal white roses.

"Happy anniversary," I told him.

"Congratulations," Polly said.

We smiled angelically.

"I think you need one of my dolls, Dad," Lance said. "You can try out Thunder Thighs and Patrice. I think they'll fit your needs."

"Shake your titties!"

It was Mrs. Bunce who had the last word, though. She played what she wanted, which was the death march. Nice and gloomy. Three times.

The party did make the paper the next day, but not in the way that Herbert had planned. The decorations, the food, the cake, even the hard rock band made the news. All of that, however, was dwarfed by Herbert's rant against gay marriage before the ceremony and Aunt Janet's screeching diatribe against Herbert and his anti-gay initiative, complete with the heel-and-bouquet-tossing incidents, the blue glass flying through the air, the African safari, the mamba, scheduled sex, and jazz music.

Herbert's support plummeted. Soon after that, his political party asked him to step down. He did.

Me, Jake, Lance, and Polly had an amazing time, along with the three hundred other proper, uptight guests who decided to let it all hang out. It's amazing how people will talk to you when you are honest about your own problems. By the end of the night, we learned of a shoplifting habit, a drunken mother, a father who was jailed for being a serial killer, a husband who had a cheating wife on his hands, and another one who was addicted to painkillers.

For the first time, I actually enjoyed a few of Herbert's stuffy friends. Herbert hid out in his home, but the rest of us danced, laughed, ate, and drank champagne. The guests loved the mermaid with the enlarged nipples, Lance got a lot of orders, and it did rain, as if buckets were being poured down from above, but the tents held.

At the end of the night, when all the guests were gone, me, Jake, Lance, and Polly each danced with Lance's Ladies, in the rain, while drinking champagne, until we were soaked through.

*   *   *

Lance told me later, "Stevie, I talked to Jake."

"And?" I bit down soft on my lower lip. He liked him, didn't he?

"My left ankle twitched. Three times." Lance sighed, so relieved. "I trust my left ankle. You're good to go, Stevie."

Polly told me later, "Stevie, I talked to Jake."

"And?" I wrung my hands together. Polly liked him, didn't she?

"I think he's like Grandpa."

I nodded. Definite similarities.

"But he's Jake, too, and I like him a lot." She grinned at me. "I'd wrap that man up pretty quick if I were you."

27

Portland, Oregon

It was time. I would plant the corn. I would do it. I could do it. I had gone to the nursery the previous week. I told them I wanted to plant corn. I bought the kernels and there they sat, waiting for me.

That morning I ran the dirt in the upraised bed through my fingers and didn't bother wiping the tears that fell into that dirt as I dropped the kernels in.

As I smoothed the dirt over each kernel, I saw my grandparents' cornfields, the green leaves, the yellow and white kernels, the stalks swaying in the wind, the pathways they'd plow through it for corn mazes at Halloween for me and my cousins and friends before we carved pumpkins.

I was back in my grandma's kitchen, bringing the corn to the table on the white platter. I was sitting with Sunshine and Helen, painting on the deck, the corn tall and straight in the fields. I was running through the corn, chasing a cat, and driving along the edge of our property, knowing we were home when I saw those green stalks. I was smiling at Grandpa as the butter on the corn slipped down our chins, The Family talking and laughing around us.

My tears watered the kernels and my hands shook with lost memories, but it wasn't too bad, and remembering all the happy memories, well, it reminded me that I had let the hard memories suffocate all the joyful memories that had come before it. I vowed not to let the suffocation go on anymore. I had had enough suffocation in my life.

I gardened until I had to get ready for Lance's Lucky Ladies Hard Rock Party. By the time I was done, I felt so much better, cleaner, my thoughts less jumpy and chaotic. At the end I was thinking of the earth and, my, isn't that a slinky worm and, oh, there's a red-feathered bird at my bird feeder, and I think I'll pull some zucchini for zucchini bread and pick blueberries for breakfast.

I stared out at the raised bed where I'd dropped the corn kernels in. They would grow, green and strong, with floppy leaves, and those leaves would turn to yellow and white corn cobs.

I would eat them with a light coating of butter and salt. And maybe I would think of Helen and remember her in the garden, the floppy yellow hat on her head, without the rage and sadness that had followed me my whole life.

Maybe I could.

Maybe I would.

"We rock," Lance said in wonderment.

"We do," Polly agreed, as we all admired each other in the mirror.

When I had agreed to dress up as a hard rocker for Lance's party, I was actually scared to death. It's a scant bit out of my comfort zone, but I had to say that with the costumes Lance rented for us, and the makeup artist he had hired to completely paint our faces in black and white and red, the three of us could go out there and bust a move and bang some music.

"There's something awesome," Lance breathed, "about being unrecognizable. Awesome."

"There certainly is," I breathed. "I love it." Stevie was gone. Hard rocker was here. I mimicked playing an electric guitar, then I jumped in the air and thumped my head up and down. Ouch. But still. I tried.

Polly hit imaginary drums, Lance picked up a banana and started singing into it, and then each of us picked up a nearby blow-up girl, outfitted much like us, the sextuplets, and danced with her.

I got Canada Katie. My, wasn't she so squishy soft.

The huge ballroom on the McMannis Brothers' property had been transformed. A long white and black banner read, WELCOME TO LANCE'S LUCKY LADIES HARD ROCK PARTY! At the entrance there was a guitar wreath made of flowers sitting between two blow-up ladies outfitted in black leather. One had a whip in her hand.

There was a blow-up girl at each of the tables in the main room, which were covered with black tablecloths. In the center of each table was a three-foot-tall, white skull with a candle in it, surrounded by red and black flowers. Guitars hung from the ceiling. Outside, steaks were on the grills and the tables practically bent with potatoes, salads, and breads, Lance's favorite foods.

Hundreds of people filed in, all decked out in rock's finest. The band was as sizzling hot as they had been the night before at Herbert and Aunt Janet's party.

It was, without question, the funnest party I have ever, ever been to.

I danced all night with Jake (the sexiest rocker I've ever seen), Lance, and Polly.

Me, Stevie, who had been afraid to dance, danced all night.

In the middle of the evening I noticed that Lance was hanging out exclusively with one person who was dressed up like the KISS band member with the silver star makeup and a black wig.

It was Zena. I could tell by her size and her strut.

Lance and Zena. They weren't speaking, but they were standing next to each other, sort of gazing into each other's eyes, and one time I saw them dancing, close, Zena chatting, Lance nodding. Even through the makeup I could tell that Lance had a stricken expression on his face.

Now, why hadn't I thought of them together before?

Lance called me at three in the morning.

The phone woke me and Jake up. No, I had not used a

sparkly condom. I hadn't needed one, because I had been honest with Jake.

"I'm not ready."

"I know, honey." He smoothed my hair back.

"I'm sorry, but I can't make love to you. I don't know when I'll be able to."

"It's okay. I don't need a commitment from you on that." He kissed me. "Stevie, you're not going to be able to make love to me until you're able to trust me. And I'll know you're able to trust me when you tell me about yourself, and your past, everything that's happened, all of it, not bits and pieces. I want to know. I want to know you."

"It's a lot."

"I had a feeling it was."

I about drowned in those eyes. "Stevie, it's gonna almost kill me to sleep next to you tonight and not make love to you, and I don't think I'm going to be able to do this again, so enjoy it while it lasts," he joked.

"I will," I said, "I will." I snuggled up to him, and went to sleep, and had no nightmares.

When Lance called, I fumbled for the phone. "Did you see me? I danced with a lady! I didn't know what to say. She did most of the talking, which is good. I couldn't even open my mouth. We ate together, but I was nervous, so nervous, I couldn't even eat my steak. She invited me to her roller derby competition. You have a friend that does roller derby, don't you?"

"Yep. I do."

Lance groaned. "It's Zena, isn't it? This is a tragedy. A tragedy! She's too much for me. I met her downtown that one time with you. She wears the beautiful clothes and her hair is so pretty—it's liquid black gold—and her smile is friendly and she's funny and smart. . . . This is a tragedy."

I knew he was getting teary.

"Lance, you can do this."

"No! I can't. I don't know what to say around her. I'm intimidated. I'm scared."

"Lance, you own companies, you're a successful businessman. I've seen you give so many speeches, you're in command of the whole room, you know all the numbers off the top of your head, you know where your business has been, where it's going, you get all the technical stuff. . . ."

"That's business! This is . . . this is"—hard exhale—". . . *this is a woman!*"

After a half hour of reassuring Lance he was a stud, I hung up the phone and snuggled next to Jake. "I like your cousins," he said sleepily. "I do not, however, care for your uncle, and that's not going to change, Stevie. The man's a disease."

"I don't like him, either. Give me a kiss."

Zena said to me, "I met someone at your cousin's party."

I feigned innocence, took a container of fruit out of my bag, and stared straight ahead at a bunch of men in kilts playing bagpipes in Pioneer Courthouse Square. They had nice legs. A man in a skirt is kinda sexy. Do all women want to flip that skirt right up or is it just me? "Who did you meet?"

"It was a dude dressed up in this way-out rock outfit. I mean, it was one of the best ones there. His face was all painted in black and white and red, same as your face, now that I'm thinking about it. Anyhow, I said hi, and he said hi, but that was about all he said." Her brows came together. She was puzzled, baffled. "Anyhow, I asked him to dance, and he said yes. The guy's huge—building-sized—but he could dance okay, sort of rigid and robotic. After we danced I asked if he wanted to get something to eat, and he nodded, so we sat down and ate these incredible steaks—my favorite food—and he still didn't say much at all, but he kept smiling at me." Her brows came together. She was puzzled, baffled. "Actually, he didn't eat."

"So he was a quiet sort?" I handed her some carrots from my garden.

"Yeah, so quiet." She crossed her arms, figuring that one out. "So, anyhow, I told him about roller derby, and he seemed to enjoy hearing about that. I invited him to come to the next match and I gave him my cell number, and he nodded. He seemed nervous. What's there to be nervous about? I dunno.

Maybe he won't come. I don't even know his name or what he looks like. He doesn't know what I look like, either, because I was a KISS band member, but he knew a lot of people there because people kept coming up and talking to him, hitting him on the back. . . . So a lot of people think he's cool. That's good, it's a good sign. Probably not an ax murderer."

I tried to figure out what to do here. Should I tell her? If she knew he was my cousin, would that interfere with how she felt about him? Would she think that was weird to be dating my cousin?

"I don't think he said much of anything at all to me. Maybe he didn't speak English?" Her brows came together. She was puzzled, baffled. She pulled at her fishnets, her purple boots crossed at the ankle, then shrugged. "Well, whatever." She handed me a cookie.

I smiled.

The bagpipes blared.

I did want to flip those skirts. One flip. One peek. A small peek.

Cherie had a divorce case that was "on fire," so to speak.

She was representing the wife, Claudia.

Claudia wanted a divorce.

Terrence, the husband, did not want a divorce, although by all accounts he was a difficult son of a gun. He had agreed to move out only because Claudia told him she *might* think about a separation, not a divorce, if he did.

The Colliers had a sprawling home in the country, horses, and a popular pumpkin patch called "Collier Family Pumpkin Farm." The place came complete with a train that took kids out to the pumpkin patch, hay rides, a barn filled with goodies, jellies and flowers and gourds, and a petting zoo for the kids.

"I respect this client because she's so creative," Cherie told me. "You've got to love the ingenuity I've seen here."

Cherie had me come to the meeting between them and the husband's attorney to "enjoy the fireworks. This'll crack up your day."

"I don't want a divorce," Terrence said. He had a gut and a balding head, and his attorney resembled a dazed crocodile. "I know you're upset about the porn, Claudia, but we can reach a compromise on it."

"No compromise," Claudia said. She was elegant and refined. I could not imagine how those two got together. "I will not have women in my home with their legs spread, tickling boobs the size of Rhode Island. I told you last year when I found out about your porn to get rid of it."

"And I did!" He spread his arms out wide, like a drunken eagle, his eyes earnest.

"Dumping it in a storage locker is not getting rid of it."

Porn Husband went pale.

"Yep. I found it."

"I was . . . I was . . ." He struggled. "I was going to sell it."

"Sell it?" She arched her eyebrows. "Great. And what were you going to do with the money?"

He swallowed hard, his eyes jittering back and forth. "I was going to take you to Hawaii."

He was a poor liar.

Claudia shook her head sadly. "Well, no Hawaii for us."

"Why not?"

"I used the pickup truck to unload all your porn for you." She made the sound of a revving pickup truck.

Porn Husband made a strangled sound.

"Then I used the tractor to gather it all in one place." She snapped her fingers three times. "I lit a match. Burn, baby, burn."

He gasped. "You didn't!"

"I did!" She grinned at him. "Whoosh whoosh! All up in flames. And then!"

"You burned my porn collection?" He was appalled. Mystified. Devastated.

"Yep. And then I accidentally drove your motorcycles into the pond." She made the sound of a motorcycle, low and deep. A close likeness of the engine.

He slapped a hand to his forehead. "You drove my motor-cycles into the pond?"

"Yep. And I learned that our pumpkin shooter can do a lot of damage. Bang, bang, bang." She imitated shooting the pumpkin shooter.

"How does our pumpkin shooter do damage?" He started to sweat.

"Especially to your Ferrari." She made the purring sound of a Ferrari. "When pumpkins are shot at it at high speeds, it dents. Me and my girlfriends had a Shoot the Ferrari Party. It was so much fun. We had daiquiris while we did it. Coraleen got so drunk! Bang, bang, bang."

"How could you do this to me?" Porn Husband was dis-traught, poor dear.

"Here's the thing, Terrence." Claudia leaned forward. "You're trying to roadblock this divorce. I want out. I'm dating a gor-geous guy ten years younger than me, and I don't want you in the way. I need vigor and a man with staying power in my bed from now on, you get what I'm saying? I need a man with hair who's not carrying a dead deer in his gut. I want a man who can hike and boat and doesn't want to sit in front of his computer jacking off. It's not attractive. You seem old to me. Rigid. Unex-citing. Dry. I want to feel young again, and he makes me feel young and sexy and vibrant, like I'm the coolest woman he's ever met. I'm keeping the Porsche, by the way. I need a sports car to drive fast."

Porn Husband was shrinking in his seat. "You're leaving me for a younger man?" He was aghast! He had never in his wildest dreams believed his wife would leave him! She simply needed time to get used to his porn collection!

"Yes, I'm leaving you for a younger man. He is delicious. So tasty. My girlfriends are at *my* home right now. Cherie?"

Cherie turned on a TV. There were the girlfriends, waving, laughing. They were behind the pumpkin-shooting gun. I couldn't tell if Coraleen was drunk again. Out in the middle of the pumpkin patch? Three sports cars.

"Now you listen here, you porn-hungry, saliva-dripping, fart-dropping, acid-belching old man," classy Claudia said, as polite as you please. "You will give me a divorce or I will tell them to start shooting those pumpkins till each one of your sports cars might have been dropped from Pluto, got it?"

Funny how sports cars motivate men.

We wrapped up that divorce with no further ado.

I love my walks. Have you ever noticed the geometric shapes in nature? The triangles that tree branches form? The oval-shaped yellow petals of a flower? The circle of a bird's nest? Have you ever noticed that birds flying in a flock sometimes form the outline of a fish? Have you noticed raindrops plopping off leaves and the twirl of leaves as they fall and the scent of honeysuckle and jasmine?

Have you noticed?

"I have something to explain to you, Stevie," Herbert intoned, his voice black and gooey on my answering machine days after the renewal of vows disaster. "It might be difficult for you to understand the extreme circumstances surrounding your leave-taking of Ashville as a child. I'm going to have to ask you to trust me and do as I say: Do not take yourself to Ashville and awaken all those memories of your deranged, demented mother and your grandparents and your sister. That's a part of your past you don't need to bother with again. It's done. In fact, I forbid you to go, young woman. I forbid it. Call me back immediately." He cleared his throat. "Have you heard from your aunt Janet?"

I did not call him. And yes, I'd heard from Aunt Janet when she was in Paris en route to Africa. "It's divine here. I had no idea this whole world was outside, outside the door of my airplane. . . ."

While I sanded a chair late the next night, after Jake had left me with a passionate kiss to rattle my brain, I thought about Herbert. He hates himself, I knew that. Herbert is the most unhappy, angry, bitter person I have ever met. No one in our family wants him around. He knows this. He's smart enough to get it but mean enough, controlling enough, for whatever reason, to not stop the behavior that makes everyone hate him.

And now his wife had left him, his kids wouldn't have anything to do with him, and he was sunk politically and publicly disgraced.

I tried to feel sorry for him.

Couldn't quite get there.

I saw Sunshine that night in my dream. She was sitting on the front step of the Schoolhouse House. She smiled and waved at me, the charm bracelet she'd given me on top of her head like a crown. Behind her was the vegetable garden. Beyond that, the corn. In the middle of the corn was a painting Helen had made. It was one of the Schoolhouse House, the only thing she ever painted that didn't reflect the insane cubicles and hallways of the ongoing hell in her mind. The picture was bright and pretty, wildflowers spotting the landscape. The picture grew and grew until it took over what I was seeing.

Helen came flying out of the hills, only she was a hawk with her own head, and kidnapped Sunshine. She dropped Sunshine on a cliff and whispered, "Night night." She flapped her wings, harder and harder, until the edge of the cliff started to crack. Helen the Hawk stared at me and said, "I don't like this Trash Heap," jumped on the edge, and the cliff broke off. I tried to reach Sunshine, but my feet wouldn't move out of a teacup. In my dream I knew it was my fault that Sunshine died.

When I woke up, sweating and panting, I knew what to plant in the corner of my garden where the weeds are.

28

Ashville, Oregon

The kidnapping of Sunshine happened on a Friday. That day I made Sunshine a heart collage. I used tissue paper, sequins, broken sticks, a pink button I ripped off my sweater, tiny bits of construction paper, and a red pencil I used to draw a miniature picture of our barn. I was ten years old.

My teacher held my heart up and announced, "Now, this is an artist. Stevie, *you* are an artist." My classmates, many of them relatives, clapped for me. I thought I'd burst right out of my Mary Janes and my purple bell-bottom pants with pride.

Sunshine was not there to meet me at the end of our driveway with Grandma and, sometimes, Helen. Helen would often put two pencils behind her ears, or would bite into an apple and hold it in her mouth because she knew I was coming home from school. We would walk up the driveway, say hi to the horses and the sheep, pet any cats wandering around, and head back to the Schoolhouse House together.

I didn't see any of them, but I did see the lights flashing on the tops of the police cars.

Instantly panicked, I dropped the heart for Sunshine and my lunch box and ran as fast as I could to the house. I was so scared I remember wetting my pants as I ran. I was huffing a bit because I was already putting on weight, eating for comfort, eating to forget that my own mother had a Command Center, called Sunshine Trash Heap, and yesterday had fastened ropes around her head to make a hat.

I flew into the house and found the police, two paramedics, the local doctor, about ten of The Family and friends, and Grandma and Grandpa pleading with Helen, who was standing on a chair with her arms outstretched as if she'd been hung on a cross.

Helen was wearing my witch's hat from Halloween, which instantly made me feel sick. Helen had always said, "Witches are evil with sorcerers' powers. They're not allowed by Command Center. I don't listen to them because they do bad things and tell me to do bad things. Thormanntory or chitterbong."

"Helen," Dr. Mosher said. "Come on off the chair for a second, will you?"

"I can't. The spell master is starting soon."

"Helen, we need to know where Sunshine is," Grandpa said, his face gray.

"Tell us, Helen, my goodness, you have to tell us," Grandma begged. She was stark white, her hands knitting together, back and forth.

Helen took off her witch's hat, twirled it around, then put it back on her head. Then she opened up her trench coat. Underneath she was wearing pink pajamas with white rabbits. "Command Center said I had to do it. The witch said so, too. I had to do the first."

"Where is she?" Grandpa said, his voice snapping. "You drove her away in the car, Helen. Where is she?"

Helen drove the car? Helen was not supposed to drive the car. They hid the keys from her all the time. The last time she stole the car she put it in the fountain. Before that she drove it to the mountains, then danced on the hood in the rain.

"It's not here. It's resting. It's on a cliff."

Grandma burst into tears.

"Where's Sunshine?" I asked Grandma, already crying. "Where is she?"

Grandma shook her head, held me close.

Then Grandpa lost it and yelled at Helen, and she hissed, "I will not have you undermining Punk! He'll be meaner to me. Stop it! You pig! You overnoisy warlock!" She stuck her left hand out and shook it hard. "Get that off of me, get that off of me!"

"Helen!" Grandpa snapped. "Helen!"

"I said, off, off, it should be off!" She shook her left hand again.

I was sick of this. Sick of her, sick of her rantings and anger, sick of how sad and scared she made me feel, and I wanted Sunshine back. I wanted her back so bad. Sunshine, my little sister, my best friend.

I had no idea I was going to tackle Helen off that chair until I landed hard on top of her.

"You are a dumb mom!" Helen could make me feel like nothing because she never told me she loved me, and she could yell at voices and visions, and I could get by all that, but I could not get by her taking Sunshine from me.

"Where is she, you dumb Helen. Where is she?" I hit her in the nose as hard as I could, and I ignored her cry and the blood that spurted onto my charm bracelet.

Grandma tried to pull me off Helen, but Grandpa stopped her. Grandpa stopped them all. He barked out, "Let her be!" Of course, the man was desperate. He had been getting nowhere with his daughter, so perhaps her daughter could help get his granddaughter home.

"I hate you, Helen! I hate you!" I yelled at her, two inches from her face. "Give me back Sunshine right now! You better not have hurt her, you dumb Helen!"

I pulled her hair and she tried to get up, but I wouldn't let her and shoved my knees in her stomach. Later I heard the adults talking and found out that Grandpa was holding Helen's legs down in the back and Grandma was holding one arm, the doctor the other, but in my blind, red rage I couldn't see that.

"Where is Sunshine?"

Helen pulled her lips tight together. "It's hiding!"

"No, she's not!" And then I had an idea. "Where is *it*? Where is Trash Heap?"

"Command Center said I can't tell!" Helen said, rolling her lips together, the blood now in her mouth, but I saw something in her eyes breaking, something cracking.

I pulled her hair as hard as I could, my other hand on her neck. "Command Center is dumb! He doesn't know anything! He's a bad voice you hear in your head, and if you took your medicine, you stupid Helen, the voices would go away. Now, where is Sunshine?"

She started to cry but I didn't care at all, not one whit. I wanted my sister.

"Where is she!" I lifted her head with my hands and cracked it back down. I hated myself then. I couldn't believe I'd hit my own mother, couldn't believe I was so angry. I was an animal, a criminal, a horrible person.

"She's on the cliff by the stars." She breathed, then cried out, her eyes lost, pathetic. "I gave her away to the cliff so Command Center wouldn't get her."

"What cliff?"

She cringed, then tears rolled out of her eyes and they mixed with the blood, and I had her tears and blood on my hands. I slammed her head up and down again, hating myself to my deepest core.

Grandma, beside me, made a sobbing sound deep in her throat. I can't even imagine being in her position: allowing her granddaughter to hit her daughter so that the other granddaughter could be found.

"That cliff high in the sky near the stars." She relaxed underneath me, her eyes half shutting. "Now Command Center is going to kill me. He's going to cut me up with a sharp knife. Shut up, Punk! I hid Trash Heap from you. You can't get her now. Trash Heap is gone."

I froze. I remembered her painting with trees like jail bars and I knew what cliff Helen was talking about. It was hidden in the woods, off the trail that started in the state park. We had been there once before, when we all went on a hike and Helen had run off. We'd chased her to the cliff, an outgrowth of the mountain, shaped as a finger. We had found her lying on it, hugging it, the drop off that finger so far down I got dizzy staring at it. She'd called it the Star Cliff.

Helen stared right into my eyes, bringing me smack back to reality. "Now Command Center says he's going to kill you, too." Her eyes filled with huge tears, spilling out the corners of her eyes. "I'm sorry."

I couldn't move.

"I'm sorry, but Command Center says you have to die now."

"Oh, God," Grandma sobbed.

"That's enough, Helen," Grandpa shouted. "That's enough!"

Helen's eyes continued to flood with tears, rinsing the blood. "He says that's it," she whispered. "That's it for you and that's it for *it*." Her body trembled. "I'm so sorry."

She started singing "Amazing Grace," her voice scratchy and wobbly, and I thought she was begging God for help. I felt this cold shiver slither through me, but only briefly. I had what I wanted. I knew what I needed to know.

"Night night," Helen moaned. "Night night."

I got up and ran out the door, Grandpa, the police officers, and a bunch of The Family following me.

Sunshine was cowering on the finger of that cliff when we found her. Grandpa went out slowly, carefully and when he brought her back, Sunshine cried on my shoulder and wouldn't let go. "I knows you comes and gets me, Stevie, I knows it!"

I hugged her tight and rocked her back and forth, Grandpa's strong arms around the both of us.

That night Grandpa had a heart attack.

Grandma and a bunch of The Family went to the hospital with him.

A bunch of The Family came and stayed with me. Two of our cousins the size of oxen put chairs right outside of Helen's door so she couldn't escape.

It wasn't necessary. For the next three days, Helen went into a catatonic trance. The only time she spoke was when she whispered to me, "You're next, I'm so sorry." She wriggled her fingers at me, as in *good-bye*. "Night night."

* * *

Grandma and Grandpa were done. They were backed into a merciless, deadly corner and they had no choice.

Five days later, when Grandpa came home, and three relatives—two brothers and a sister—moved in to help, Grandma flew out to California to check out a mental health facility. She returned on Wednesday. I overheard Grandma and Grandpa's tearful conversation as they hugged each other close.

Basically it came down to this: save their daughter or save their granddaughters.

They decided to send Helen away permanently. That decision brought both of them to their knees. I saw them, arms around each other on the kitchen floor, foreheads together, the moon shining a light on their devastation.

Three days later, after three of the calmest, nicest days we've ever had with Helen, and a day before my grandparents were going to commit her, Helen picked Sunshine up and ran with her through the pouring rain to Grandma's gray car at 8:00 at night. The keys were always hidden from Helen, but I think one of our relatives accidentally left the extra set out. That's the only way she could have gotten the keys.

I ran after her, yelling for help. Helen threw Sunshine in the backseat, and I got in, too. I tried to get Sunshine and scramble back out of the car but I couldn't before Helen was slamming the door and speeding away, in her black dress and nylons, the lines completely straight, her best black heel pressed flat against the accelerator.

We were soon crisscrossing over the center yellow lines, her chants swirling all around, death following us through the slanted light of the moon.

29

Portland, Oregon

"You know I'm leaving for Venice soon," Jake said.
"I know."

"Stevie, I wouldn't go if I didn't have to. I signed this contract a year ago. I've been tied up since then, I've committed. . . ."

"I understand."

"I'll be gone for six weeks, at least."

I smiled, tried to be brave, tried not to carry on like a banshee stuck in menopause for ten years.

"Stevie, you could come with me."

"I could come with you, to Venice?"

"Yes, you'd love it. I'd have to work during the day, but we'd have nights and weekends."

"You have to be kidding."

"No, honey, I'm not. Come with me to Venice."

"Oh, I couldn't."

"Why? *Why not?*"

"Eileen," I said, surprised. I held the phone close to my ear, then decided to hang up. "I don't want to talk—"

"Don't hang up," she said. "Please. Please, Stevie."

I waited, struggling with myself.

I could hear her crying. "Stevie, I'm sorry."

I was silent.

"I am. I'm sorry. I know I embarrassed you in front of Jake."

"Well, thank you for apologizing." Even listening to her voice exhausted me.

"I was hurt because you don't spend time with me, you didn't tell me about Jake, you were being secretive, you didn't defend me at the teahouse, but still. That was wrong of me to make fun of you for being a chicken."

"And?"

"And making fun of your boobs and your operations, but you flaunt that you lost all that weight, and the way you dress now, so young. I'm worried about you. . . ."

I didn't say anything but, *my goodness,* as my grandma would say, all was clear: I didn't want to be friends with her anymore, and felt no more obligation to do so. "No, Eileen, you're not worried about me, and this isn't only about what you said last time, which was unbelievably hurtful and vindictive and immature. It's how you treat me altogether."

She sniffled. "I know. I know."

"Eileen, why do you treat me the way you do?"

She took a wobbly breath. "I know it's because I'm jealous of you. I know that."

"It's something else, though, too." I wasn't going to waste much time on this phone call. I needed all negative out of my life, and she was a negative.

"What?"

"Think. You're jealous of me, and I get that, I do. But there's something else, too. You're an angry person. You don't like yourself at all."

"I do. I make $250,000 a year. I'm a successful business person, I—"

"Are you?"

Silence. Deep, fraught silence.

"No, I'm not," she sobbed. "They all hate me. All of my dad's employees hate me. My stepmother hates me. Her kids and grandkids hate me. I don't have any friends except you."

"Have you asked yourself why?"

"Yes, I have."

"And what's your answer?"

"People don't like me because I'm fat."

"No, that isn't it."

"Yes, it is."

"No, it's not. It has nothing to do with it."

"I want to be friends with you, Stevie," she cried.

"Eileen, I'm sorry. I can't. This relationship has been toxic for me for way too long. Find another friend." I hung up.

Was I proud of that conversation? No. Was I glad that I was finally able to take a stand and remove myself from that situation? Yes.

You know how you houseclean to get rid of dust and dirt? Sometimes I think you have to people clean, too.

"I keep getting calls from this number, but no one says anything when I pick up. The name says Private Caller," Zena said, staring at her cell phone. She hadn't had to borrow any of my clothes for two weeks because, she said, "I'm totally sick of clubbing. Last night I drank lemonade with my neighbor. Tonight a group of us are playing Scrabble. You're welcome to come."

"I'm hoping that it's that guy from the party, but I don't think it is. . . ."

"Hmmm . . . let me see." I about choked on my epiglottis.

As soon as Zena left our cubicle area, I called Lance. "Quit prank calling Zena," I hissed.

He moaned. Groaned. "Honey, I'm not prank calling her. I call her and then I want to say hello and I can't, the word gets stuck and I feel so *scared,* and last time she said, 'Moron, you psychotic freak, whoever this is, quit calling me.' I'm so embarrassed. Dad was right. I will never make a good husband. . . . I'm huge, I'm clumsy, I'm not very bright. . . ."

I assured him he would make an outstanding husband. "You are huge. You are not clumsy. You are brilliant."

"I haven't had a real date in years. I can sniff out the women who are interested in me only because of my money, I'm not that dumb. But not Zena. She's strong willed and a fighter and funny and so sincere! So earthy and honest! But she scares me. My stomach bubbled all around at the Lance's Lucky Ladies party, my hands sweated, and my ankle's twitching! Hasn't stopped twitching. . . . I can barely walk, barely walk!"

"I'll figure this out, Lance. I will."

"You will?" Hope returned to his voice. Honestly, the man's a millionaire, and he's a baby.

"Yes, I will. Hang tight."

"Thank you," he breathed.

Should I tell Zena that he was my cousin? Not quite yet. Not quite.

I called Lance back. "This is what we're going to do. . . ."

The next afternoon the most exotic, tropical bouquet of flowers I have ever laid eyes on arrived for Zena. It was huge and flowing. Hawaii had arrived in our office. Lance had clearly overdone it. It was about four feet high and three feet wide, resembling something you would see in the entry of some fancy hotel. The attorneys and staff were oohing and aahing.

Zena, clad in her black knee-high boots, tights, and an African-style tunic, was utterly stunned as she stared at those flowers.

"I have never gotten flowers," she said, her voice small and young.

"Open the card," I urged her.

She did with shaking hands. There was the invitation for dinner the night after tomorrow. A yummy restaurant, intimate but not intimidating. He was friends with the owner. Lance had signed his first name and left his e-mail, as I instructed. Then he didn't have to talk on the phone before the date.

"Holy shit," Cherie said, grabbing the note. "Honey, if you don't go out with this guy, I will. In fact, how about if I take your place? I'll give you two pairs of my designer heels and you can be first out on the raceway in the race cars at the firm party in three months."

Another woman took the note. "Forget it, Cherie. Man, I might kill over this one. . . ."

Another woman. "Zena, he's not your type. He's my type."

My uncle called and left a message to call him back immediately.

I did not call.

Aunt Janet had called Cherie before she left, and Cherie talked to me about the divorce. I explained the situation, including the grand slam at the wedding, which she'd read about.

"He's a peach," she told me, biting into an apple.

"A true gentleman," I deadpanned.

"Don't worry, I'll decimate him." She took another bite of apple. "I love decimating assholes. It's my favorite hobby."

"Enjoy yourself."

"My pleasure."

Me and Zena saw Crystal.

She was working in her parents' Chinese food kiosk in Pioneer Courthouse Square.

We exchanged looks, then ordered lunch from her.

She was snobby, but I saw the tears, the embarrassment.

"Hi, Crystal," we said.

"Laugh your hearts out. I know that's what you want to do."

I shook my head. "I don't want to laugh."

"Me, neither," Zena said.

Crystal swallowed hard. "I know you don't like me."

"I didn't like you because you made me feel like ant drool," I said. "And you tried to annihilate the Athertons."

Crystal stared at the floor. "I did. I'm ashamed of myself. I really am."

And I could tell she was. She wiped the tears on both cheeks.

"She good girl," her mother said, hugging Crystal. "She learn humility now. Humility good. Pride, no good. We tell her, we tell her."

"Yes, we tell her," Crystal's father said. "You think you more than everybody else and you lose everything. Bad karma. God take it. But she not lose everything. She has us."

That was the truth. They loved their mean daughter.

"And our daughter, she try again. She go back to school. Be teacher. More nicer this time," her mother said. "Better. Good karma."

"Yes, she be teacher. She good teacher!" her father said, smiling.

I would rather have a barracuda for a teacher than Crystal, but I took my rice and shut up.

"You can do it, Lance," I said over the phone two days later. I stopped cutting the boards for the deck I was going to build under the arbor. Jake was right beside me. Now and then we had to stop and kiss over the sawdust.

"I'm hyperventilating. Me and Polly are the same," he said, panting. "I even have a bag."

"Lance, ask Zena questions about herself over dinner. . . ."

"I know, I will. I have a list."

"A list?"

"Yes, I've memorized the questions to ask and put a list in my pocket. For reassurance. I also put in my pocket a red ball of yarn from my knitting for reassurance, too." He breathed hard. "I need reassurance."

"Good idea. Stay calm. Think of it as a get-to-know-you session."

"Right. I also brought a tiny replica of a blow-up doll to put in my other pocket. You know, to remind me that I'm not a loser."

"You're not a loser."

"I can't get Dad's voice out of my head."

"You have to. You're a true man, Lance. You're a far better man than he can ever think of being. You're a successful businessman. Your employees love you. You work hard, and you're smart. You're kind and gentle and tough, too."

He sniffled. "I'm not tough."

"Lance?"

"Yeah, honey?"

"Try not to cry during dinner."

I could hear him trying to suck it up.

"I had dinner with your cousin last night, Stevie," Zena told me.

I about choked on my slice of apple. Two businessmen, up-tight and buttoned up, walked across Pioneer Courthouse Square, both on their cell phones ignoring life.

"Thanks for telling me about the relationship." She eyed me.

"I'm sorry. I wanted you to get to know him. I thought it might be weird for you. . . ." I ruffled my brown bag. Tried not to cringe. "How was it?"

She stared right at me with those huge eyes, her black wedge swinging around her face. "It was . . . interesting."

"Interesting?" I squeaked. I handed her some cheese slices.

"I don't need to tell you that your cousin is almost patholog-ically shy."

"Only around women."

She nodded. "That's not a bad trait, though, is it? I sure wouldn't want a boyfriend who wanted to flirt with anyone with a vagina." She handed me granola in a Baggie.

A boyfriend? I dared to hope.

"He asked me a lot of questions, and I had the feeling that he had thought about them, which is a miracle. Most men think of two things. Sex. Food. Sports. More sex."

"That's three things."

"Yeah, whatever. So he's in a suit. I think it's expensive but what do I know. I get almost all my clothes used. I'm in my sil-ver slinky shirt and a gold scarf and my jeans and my black heels with the rhinestones."

So. She was a gorgeous and sexy Tinkerbell. Lance would probably have choked on his own tongue.

"And I did most of the talking. . . . I tried to ask him ques-tions, but he kept turning it back to me, plus he *listened*. It was strange to have a man listen to me in that way. . . . He sweated some. . . . I think there was something wrong with his ankle. . . .

It seemed like he was having trouble breathing . . . put his hands in his pockets a lot. . . . He paid for the dinner . . . even bought me a takeout dinner for dinner tonight, which was odd but nice. . . . He's a mammoth-sized guy, isn't he, but . . ."

"But?" I squeaked.

"But I think . . ."

"Yes. . . ."

She smiled at me, her smile huge, taking up half her face. "I think I might like him."

I lay down on the steps of Pioneer Courthouse Square. This was a beautiful day.

I worked my chicken job that Friday night.

I danced and jigged. Two kids in a stroller watched me. One vomited.

Another teenager tried to take my head off. A woman asked me if I wanted a smoke, then stuck the cigarette in my beak.

In the middle of this carnage another chicken arrived. He was very tall with a brown chicken head and pointy yellow claws. He danced around with me for a while, then he pulled his head off.

It was Jake.

I pulled off my head and we kissed on the street corner. Cars tooted their horns.

My Jake, engineer and bridge builder, tall and strong, with soulful eyes I could swim in, was dancing on a corner with me, his chicken girlfriend.

Honestly, no one will ever do anything more romantic for me than that, I'm sure of it.

We went out for dinner later. "Stevie, I have never met a woman I admire as much as you." He leaned over the table and kissed me, right in front of everybody.

I tried not to cry into my spaghetti.

Later I saw in the newspaper that the Athertons were donating most of their settlement money to create a new organization that would help other families whose kids were dealing with serious injuries or illnesses.

"We don't want other parents to be as lost and frightened as we were," Mr. Atherton said. "Our insurance company kicked us out. The state wouldn't help. We were drowning in medical bills, and we were fighting a hospital that refused to take responsibility for what they did to our son."

"We will always miss Danny, but our gift to him will be the gift of help to others," Mrs. Atherton said.

Mr. Atherton was asked why they were doing it now, so close to the time of Danny's death. His response: "I have to have something to focus on that will help other families or I think my grief will kill me."

I thought of Grandma and Grandpa, how they had kept on keeping on even after losing their daughter and granddaughter.

The Athertons were having a kick-off spaghetti dinner and auction the following month at Danny's school and accepting items to sell for additional funds. A local band would play, as would the elementary school band, the middle school jazz band, and the high school marching and jazz bands. The choruses from all three schools would also sing. There would be four solos, and following that, a musical talent show.

It was called "Songs for Danny."

People who wanted to donate items could drop them off at the school.

That night I primed a chair in white. I asked it questions. How do you feel when you're alone? Do you like being alone? What do you like about yourself? What do you not like about yourself? Why aren't you braver?

The chair didn't answer.

How come you're silent? What do you hear in your head when you're silent? Does silence scare you?

I leaned back and sighed. All right, I said to that plain wood chair now all primed with white. A simple question: What's your name?

Loud and clear I heard it.

My name's Danny.

* * *

I asked Zena to come home with me after derby practice the next week to see the Danny Chair.

I'd landed a face-plant and come home with a bruise on my cheek, which went well with the bruises on my left arm from another practice.

I was so nervous as I unlocked the garage door I could barely push it up. The chair was in the middle of the floor, over plastic. The only people I ever let see my chairs were Polly and Lance, and they were wildly enthusiastic and loved them because they loved me.

Zena, dressed in a purple sheath with red knee-high go-go boots and beaded chains and bright red lipstick, had been telling a hilarious story about one of the attorneys at work who she'd seen at a party sporting a purple Mohawk and pink tights two months ago. He ended up wearing a martini glass upside down on his head.

As I pushed the garage door the rest of the way up, Zena dropped her red purse to the ground.

"Good God," she said. "Good God in heaven with all his flying, drunken angels, would you look at that!"

Me and Zena had to get the help of two neighbors to load the Danny Chair into The Mobster the evening of the Songs for Danny auction. It was good that Jake was out of town, in Seattle for work, so I didn't have to deal with hiding one more thing from him—my demented obsession with chairs.

Neither of the neighbors was helpful at first, because they wanted to walk around it, stare, and touch.

"It's incredible . . . magnificent. . . . You did this, Stevie? You did it? You're an artist. A talent . . . brilliant. . . . I had no idea! Are there more? There are? Can we see them? When? You do the sawing yourself? And the painting? Who taught you? How did you put this together?"

I blushed, I stuttered, I hemmed and hawed, but I was thrilled. They liked the Danny Chair! We loaded the chair up and the neighbors waved us off.

I felt bad I hadn't delivered the chair earlier, but with my regular job, my chicken job, visiting Polly, and the hours and hours I'd spent at roller derby practice getting me up to speed so I could "knock someone else's teeth out," as Zena said, and heart-throbbing Jake, I'd been busy.

Zena and I watched people walking in and out of the school with wicker baskets filled with treats and lotions. One guy hauled in a minibarbeque. Someone else had a girl's pink bike. Another person had a picnic basket with wine.

I was such an idiot. What was I thinking? *Why didn't I donate a basket of lotions?*

"Get out of The Mobster, Stevie," Zena said.

"I can't. I can't move." *Why didn't I donate a boom box?*

"Get out and help me move this magical thing into the gym."

"No. I've changed my mind. They're not going to want this. They can't. It's a monstrosity. A joke. It's insulting. Let's go home." *Why didn't I donate a skateboard?*

She groaned. "You're pathetic. It's not a monstrosity. It's art. They'll love it. Now, get out of the car and help me or I'll trip you during roller derby practice."

"You've already done that many times, you miniature maniac." I turned to her. "Can you do it? Please?" *Why didn't I donate some of my abundance of vegetables?*

"You have got to be kidding. I can't lift that thing myself."

It was true. We'd need help getting it out of The Mobster and we'd need help getting it back in the truck when the people in charge of the auction told us to get, get, *get out,* their faces appalled, offended.

Zena clambered out of the truck, her purple miniskirt coming to midthigh over her red tights. I lunged for her. She slithered through my hands.

"Hello there," she called to three football player–type men. "Could you give us a hand?"

They could. After they walked around the chair, stared, touched it, and asked me lots of questions. "I will never in my life see a chair that cool again," one said. "Darn, but that's way, way cool. Awesome."

The three football types carried the chair into the school and down the hallway and then put it in the center of the gym floor for the Songs for Danny auction. By then, they were being followed by at least a hundred people.

I tried to trail behind, but Zena dragged me with her.

I could hardly breathe. I had wanted to drop off the chair and leave. I had been hoping that I could slip in and out without the Athertons seeing me. I had worn a baseball cap with my curls piled up in it, a sweatshirt, and jeans. Maybe they wouldn't recognize me. It was the mean and nasty Crystal they'd focused on.

"Somebody go and get the Athertons, they have to see this."

"It should be in a craft museum."

"I have never seen anything like this in my entire life."

"That is beautiful. It's so beautiful I'm going to cry."

"I'm going to cry, too! It's the perfect testament to Danny, all his loves, in one chair."

"The Athertons are gonna love it. Here they come! Here they come! Look what someone built for your son!"

The jostling crowd pulled back, and there they were. Mr. and Mrs. Atherton, followed by the other three kids. They were grieving hard, I knew that, and there were more lines on their faces, but they were smiling until they saw the chair.

Both of their smiles dropped, their mouths gaping open in shock, as they stared up at it.

Mrs. Atherton put her hands to her face and cried.

I could tell Mr. Atherton was trying not to cry, his reddening face tight, his lips rolled in, a nerve thumping in his temple. But then their friends crowded around, thumped him on the back, kissed her on the cheek, and neither one held back anymore, the tears streaming down their cheeks, Mr. Atherton's shoulders shaking, Mrs. Atherton saying, "Oh, for heaven's sakes, oh, for heaven's sakes . . ."

"It's incredible," someone breathed. "It's incredible."

One of their boys stood right in front of it. "Hey!" he shouted, pointing. "It says, 'Danny's Chair.' Right there. See it? I can read that!"

They saw it. The three little brothers climbed up on the chair, sat down, grinned, and everybody clapped.

I shrunk back into the crowd, pulling at Zena. "We have to go," I whispered. "They might recognize me. Come on."

"Keep your booty on, your panties secure, your bra fastened," Zena said. "I wanna see what happens."

I turned to leave without the miniskirted wonder, but then people pointed at me, their smiles huge, excited, and I froze. The Athertons turned, and I was pinned to the gym floor by an enormous thunderbolt that God himself had thrown.

I saw the Athertons' faces freeze in shock as they recognized me. They gawked at the chair, then back at me, then at the chair.

Mrs. Atherton's expression changed from recognition, to shock, and finally understanding dawned. She fit together the pieces of a huge puzzle, a complex problem, a mystery. The mystery was the Dornshire letter, and it was now solved.

"It was you," she said, a stunned expression on her face. She wrapped me up in a huge hug, followed by her husband. "It was *you*, wasn't it?"

I whispered to her, "Let's keep it a girls' secret, shall we?"

"And Danny's Chair goes to Alexis Shelley, for $9,200. Alexis, come on up!"

The crowd cheered and whooped as Alexis hopped to the stage. She had dressed up as a fairy for the event and had sprinkled all with fairy dust. I learned later she was a renowned biologist and Mrs. Atherton's sister.

I was stunned by how many people were at the Songs for Danny auction. There were hundreds and hundreds of people all jammed together. The auction of my chair had been put off to the end, after the silent auction, the spaghetti dinner, and the music concerts.

I stood next to Mr. and Mrs. Atherton, who were grinning and cheering.

"I want the artist up here!" Alexis said. "Who wants the artist up here?" The crowd roared, and I was shoved up to the stage by Zena, the miniskirted wonder, who said, "Move your wiggly ass, girlfriend," and the Athertons.

"This is the best chair I have ever seen, or will ever see!" Alexis said.

More roaring.

I smiled at Danny's Chair. The chair that had told me he was Danny had ended up being a tiny rough draft of the one today.

I had built a seven-foot-tall green dragon chair. Danny loved reading about dragons, so I'd cut out huge wooden dragon wings for the back of the chair and painted them green and purple. They spread three feet out on either side of the chair. The back of the chair was a dragon neck and huge head. The dragon was smiling, big teeth, blue eyes. Across the dragon's neck I'd painted a purple sign. It said, DANNY'S CHAIR.

The arm rails were the dragon's arms. Instead of claws, though, I cut out a baseball and a catcher's mitt and attached them to the front. The legs of the chair were dragon legs. I cut out huge claws and attached them with nails and painted them black with purple toenails. I painted musical notes on the stomach and neck.

It was, I thought to myself, trying to be modest, quite a sight.

"Here she is, folks, Stevie Barrett! Artist extraordinaire!" The crowd roared, Zena hooted, Mr. and Mrs. Atherton cried.

I cried, too. I couldn't help it.

"But folks," the fairy said, throwing more gold fairy dust, "I got a little secret. I'm not keeping the chair. I'm giving it to my beautiful sister and her husband. They're going to put it in the entryway of 'Danny's House,' where we'll all work together to help families in need. Danny's Dragon Chair is going to be the first thing people see when they walk in." The fairy started to cry through her words. "It's gonna be magical! It's gonna be enchanting! It's the best damn chair ever, and Danny's House is gonna help one sick or hurt kid after another, yes, we are! Yes, we are!"

Deafening.

Absolutely deafening.

*   *   *

Zena took the e-mails and addresses of people who were interested in my chairs at the auction and promised I would get back to all of them.

I was soon deluged in orders for chairs.

Deluged.

Me.

Stevie Barrett.

Truly crazy person.

People wanted to buy my chairs.

I couldn't even believe it.

Zena picked me up on the way to derby practice. She insisted on seeing my chairs in my garage.

"You're going to have a Stevie's Chair Fest," she told me, tapping her foot.

"No way."

"Yep. Way." She shook her black wedge of hair. She was wearing jeans tucked into boots that went over her knees, two tanks, and silver chains. "Two weeks, Stevie. Hip, hop, get ready." She took out her cell phone camera and snapped pictures of my chairs, dragging them outside for the shots.

"No way."

"Yes. I'm going to e-mail the people from Lance's party and people at the office and the Athertons and the Break Your Neck Booties."

"No, those are my amateur chairs. They're a peek into a twirling, swirling, troubled mind—that would be my mind. They're kooky and hormone charged and troublesome . . ."

Then on Monday, a week later, Cherie dropped a newspaper on my keyboard. "There ya go, sweetie. Hope you're ready to roll."

My jaw dropped.

Zena smirked.

My chairs were in the newspaper. People were "respectfully invited" to my home *that Saturday* to come and buy them.

Cherie had paid for a colored ad. She hit me on the back. "Something tells me, Stevie, that you're going to want to get your ass home for the rest of the week and work your skinny tail off."

On the way home I called Mr. Pingle and told him why I needed to take the weekend off. "Those were your chairs in the newspaper? *Your* chairs! You're a genius! An artist! My! My! I'm coming, Stevie! I'm coming! Cluck cluck!"

"Cluck cluck!" I shouted back, knowing that would make him happy. "Cluck! Cluck!"

We gobbled off.

Jake came by my house after work.

I looked up from my band saw and felt this rush of pure joy at seeing him.

The other night we'd gone walking together in the forest in the hills above Portland, then we'd had a picnic. We didn't ever seem to stop talking.

"Jake, hi," I said. I stepped away from my saw. I was creating a tail for a lion chair. I walked over to give him a hug, but stopped when I saw his expression.

"Stevie." He held out the newspaper ad. "I'm learning more about you all the time."

"It was Zena. She came over and took photos of my chairs, and then my boss, Cherie, put an ad in the paper and now . . . I'm selling the chairs on Saturday."

He smiled at me, but he was holding back, I knew it. "You're incredibly talented. Can I see the chairs?"

"Yes, of course." I choked down my fear, and dared to dare. I showed him all the chairs, and he was profuse in his praise.

"You didn't tell me that you build and paint chairs."

"No, I didn't. I do it as a hobby, as a stress release. It's how I work out my issues, my problems, life. . . . I am not real stable, I've told you that, a bit crazed, fraught with numerous strange worries, definitely tilted off center. . . ."

"Why didn't you share this with me?"

"I'm sorry. I thought, until recently, that they were too odd, too amateurish, that I was too odd and amateurish. . . ."

"You're not odd or amateurish at all." He put his hand on a chair. "You're creative, you're funny, you're colorful, you think and reflect, you see things differently, Stevie, than the rest of us. You're insightful, smart, and I think you see a lot of good in the world. Your personality is reflected in your chairs."

"Thank you," I whispered. "Do you think so?"

"I know so," he said, linking an arm around my waist. "But I also know that I need you to at least *try* to trust me. Make an attempt, honey."

I leaned into him. "Okay. I will. Do you want to see the chair I made of Adam and Eve? I used real branches to form the apple tree...."

I worked until I couldn't see straight to make my chairs as perfect as I could make them. Jake brought me dinner at night, and he chuckled and kissed me and then hung around while I worked so we could chat, and laugh, and he told me about his day as if we were two old married people who had been telling each other about their days for five decades.

He knew his way around all the saws I had, and when I didn't need them, he used them. At the end of the week, he'd made me an arched bridge for my garden. *A bridge.*

Together we carried it out and placed it by the blueberry bushes.

"Thank you, Jake. It's . . . it's spectacular."

"Give me a kiss, that's all the thanks I need."

We took breaks, too, in the midst of all that work, and he kissed me in my kitchen once until my breathing was hard, but delicious, and he started to take off my shirt, and I held my shirt down tight and he stopped, his breathing labored like mine. "What is it?"

"I have a scar on my stomach. I have other scars, but the scar on my stomach is an anchor shape. It's not that old, it'll fade more, but it won't go away, and I . . . can we turn the lights off?"

He nodded, and I could see he was holding himself reined in

pretty tight, because we are so hot and heavy together. "We could, but we won't, because I want to see all of you. I know you have scars. They're part of who you are."

"But they're ugly."

"Nothing on you is ugly."

"It's a long scar, remember. I told you, it's an anchor."

"I like anchors; they keep you steady. I like boats; you can have adventures on them. Now take your shirt off before I rip it off." He smiled and kissed me and my anchor scar until I couldn't think, or worry, about my anchor scar at all.

Lance showed Polly the newspaper ad when we visited her.

"I can't say anything or I'll cry!" Polly wept. "I'll cry!" She patted her heart. "Thump for joy, heart, beat for joy for Stevie."

"I know, I know!" Lance said, howling. "Our Stevie! Our Stevie is an artist! Oh, Stevie!"

We got all emotional together. Lance had brought a doll named Jelly Jasper—big boobs, tiny waist, pink and purple bathing suit with jelly beans—and the four of us got a good, wet hug in.

There was no wet hug for Herbert.

"Stevie." Herbert's voice had crackled on my answering machine with annoyance and displeasure the night before. "I was by your house the other day and the day before. I came on the weekend, too, and was not able to reach you. You must contact me. If you don't, I'm afraid I'll have to go through our lawyer, and I don't want to do that."

What on earth was he talking about?

"I want to know if you have heard from your aunt Janet." There was a silence. "Call me directly."

I had heard from Aunt Janet. "You have got to see the sun in Africa, Stevie . . . but the poverty. I can't get by it. . . . I can't sleep because of it. So much need for the basics that we take for granted, for food and clean water and medication and the children. . . . Those eyes keep me up all night. I want to help, that's what I want to do. So does Virginia. It's our calling."

I knew Herbert was bluffing. There was nothing he could sue me for. I had no idea why he would need to call a lawyer about me.

I did not call him back.

When he pounded on my door I hid behind my garage and I ignored him till he scurried off. He is a cockroach.

30

Portland, Oregon

The morning of my Chair Fest, Zena, Cherie, Cherie's four foster kids, Lance, and Jake came early and helped me set up the chairs. We used my front yard and backyard, and we put out balloons to advertise, though I was pretty darn sure no one would show up. I was exhausted. I knew no one would buy my chairs. I knew I was ridiculous. It was pathetic. I was pathetic.

I had hardly known how to price them. Maybe $50 each? $20? But Lance had known exactly what to do and had put prices on each one. "Price them as art and they'll sell as art," he said.

Zena set up the payment table.

A half hour before we were supposed to open, we had a line outside the white picket fence of my little green house with the white trim and burgundy door.

We opened at nine o'clock and were soon mobbed, much to my raw shock. Lance was the "bouncer," he said. Zena and Cherie took the money. Her four smiling, shy foster kids acted as salespeople and loaded chairs.

In the middle of it, Mr. Pingle came up and gave me a hug. "Stevie," he said grandly, waving a hand at a woman in her sixties with upswept white hair, a kind face, and innocent blue eyes. "Please meet my mother, Rayelle. She owns Aunt Betta-dine's."

"How do you do?" she asked me.

"I do fine, fine, thank you," I stumbled out. "Fine." I hadn't known Mr. Pingle was the son of the owner. I'd had no clue. "And you?"

"You're a talent, young woman, a simply striking talent, and Aunt Bettadine's is honored to have you in our employ. My son has sung your praises many times, and we are most appreciative of your dedication to our company. We're family, you know, family!" She clasped my hands. "But, dear, I love these chairs. Love them. Especially the chicken chairs, no surprise there. I would love to commission you, Stevie. I want one giant chicken chair in each of our stores and in our executive offices. Could you build me twenty?"

I was speechless.

I opened my mouth but no words came out.

Mr. Pingle beamed and mimicked a chicken trying to fly. He was such a geek, and I loved that guy. "We're keeping it all in the family! All in Aunt Bettadine's family!"

His mother smiled, eager, earnest.

Since no words were forthcoming, all I could think to say was, "Cluck cluck! Cluck cluck!" I waved my chicken wings.

Oh, they were delighted.

They clucked and waved their chicken wings and I, Stevie Barrett, ex–extremely troubled person, was in business.

We were completely sold out by noon and closed up shop. Zena took personal orders from people for chairs. She had names and numbers and designs and down payments.

Cherie tallied up the money and said, "You're rich, girl-friend."

I took everyone who helped out to lunch for laughter. We went to an Italian café and ate pasta and drank wine. Zena and Lance sat next to each other, but I noticed they didn't say a word, not a word. Zena was unaccountably quiet. Lance was blushing.

There had been seventy chairs. They sold for an average of $300 each.

I was able to pay off most of my medical bills.

Now, that was a glorious day. Glorious.

The only inglorious thing was that I knew I would have to quit my chicken job and that would upset Mr. Pingle.

Cluck cluck. Sad cluck.

I had a chance to talk with Polly by phone later on that night. "I finally am not seeing food as the enemy. . . . I know I'm going to be dealing with this forever, I get it. . . . This time I'm going to get control and stay in control. . . . I do want to live. *I do*. And I'm learning to like myself. I didn't before. . . . I see Annie daily. . . . I like your garden, and being on the river in Lance's boat, and all the laughing we do, and I like when we dance in the rain and drink champagne and hug Lance's dolls and see your chairs. . . . I think I want to make a documentary film of what I've gone through and help other girls . . . and I'm sorry, Stevie, for hurting you with my problems . . . and I love you so much . . . and I'm finding that I do want to eat strawberries and ice cream and tacos. Want to come to my place soon for tacos?"

I did. I loved tacos!

I practiced over the next two weeks with the roller derby team. I was bruised and banged up. All the muscles in my body felt as if they'd been incinerated. My hair had been pulled, my left ear had been smashed with an elbow, my knees were swollen and purple, and my left buttock had a reddish, blackish bruise covering most of it. I could hardly walk.

I had never felt better.

"Ho ho," Zena said as we ate lunch in Pioneer Courthouse Square. "You've found your moxie, haven't you, Stevie? Where was it hiding? Your vagina?" She lifted up my skirt and tried to peer under it. I swatted her hand away.

"Yessiree, I think you found your moxie and it was between your legs."

I laughed. I handed her cucumber slices from my garden.

She handed me some peanuts in a Baggie.

That night I sat in a chair by the trellises and ate chicken that I'd cooked up with peppers and onions from my garden.

I kept eating food right out of my garden. Peas, leeks, beans, radishes, tomatoes . . . I put them in new recipes that I found. Sometimes I ate them plain, sometimes with salt, sometimes with dip. Earthy, raw, natural, yum.

I watched my sunflowers grow in the sunny patch. They're plant people. Any minute they could rip their own stalks from the ground, hop on over, and sit with you for tea at a table under a willow tree.

When I'd planted the seeds, I had done it halfheartedly. I had a vague image of sunshine, van Gogh, and my grandparents' fields. And now, I got it. I got why sunflowers are so . . . magical.

It's because they're plant miracles. Think about them. Flowers with a face that make food.

Maybe they're here to remind us to see them. *Really* see them. To take the time and stare at a sunflower. And be happy that you're alive, and well enough, to do so.

I ran a finger over a petal. I was happy to be alive, and well enough, to do so.

"I've been going out with your cousin a lot, Stevie," Zena said, scooting her swivel chair over to mine.

"Zena! Zena!" Schubert Nelson ran into our cubicle, puffing, red faced. "Did you remember to file the papers to the court about the water rights case in Washington? Oh, my God!"

She glared at him. "Yes, you river-dwelling, algae-sucking fish, I did. That'll be a $50 gift card."

He bent over, hands on knees, breathing heavily. "You're a fucking saint."

"Bad language," she said. "That's $75 now. Off you go. Ta-ta."

The lawyer went off, leaning against a wall for support. Later that day I saw the gift card. $75. She bought me coffee, as usual.

"So, your cousin."

"Yes?"

"Thank you for the advice."

I nodded. I had been very clever. I knew that knitting relaxed Lance, so I suggested to Zena that she ask him to help her start knitting.

"Knitting?" she'd said, derisive. "I'd rather poke my ass with the needles than knit."

"Lance knits," I said, watching her close.

She froze. "He does?" She blinked a few times. "Well, what idiot wants to poke their ass with needles anyhow?"

"Not me. Yarn is pretty, too."

She blinked again. "Yes, it is."

I patted her cheek and we went back to work.

"Your advice was good, Stevie," Zena said. "I invited him to my place last night and I told him I wanted to learn how to knit. I thought the man would die of ecstasy. He came to my house with half a store of stuff."

"Did you knit?"

"Oh, yeah, we knitted. He says I'm a natural. And while we knitted we talked. He finally talked. We were up until four in the morning. He slept on my couch."

"Did you have a good time?"

Zena smiled, huge. It took up half her face. "Oh, yeah. We did. He's beautiful, Stevie. Beautiful."

I nodded. I wanted to laugh. I wanted to dance. I reached over and hugged her at the exact moment a chair sailed through the glass of the conference room, glass shattering everywhere.

"Pig!" A woman's voice screamed. "You're a rutting *pig!*"

"Oh, my goodness," I said. Me and Zena both ran to help.

I got a call about ten o'clock a couple of nights later. I was designing all the chicken chairs I'd been hired to make for Aunt Bettadine's. They would be six feet tall, with huge wingspans, friendly chicken faces . . .

"Hello? Hello?"

Silence.

"Hello?"

"Stevie, honey . . ."

It was Lance. He was whimpering. I knew he was trying to pull himself together.

Finally, finally he said, "Honey, she's into knitting! She doesn't think I'm a geek. She doesn't think I'm strange, and I . . ."

"Yeeessss?" I drawled.

"I could talk to her. Same as I talk to you. Except—" He coughed. "Not exactly the same as I talk to you, because you know, well . . ."

"Because you don't want to kiss me?" I giggled.

"Right. But Zena . . ." He sighed.

"She's pretty kissable, isn't she?"

"She's so kissable. . . . But now, that makes me nervous and anxious, too . . . kissing her, I mean. How do I know *when* to kiss her? How do I know if she wants to be kissed? Do you think she'll think I'm being pushy? That all I want is . . . is . . . *you know* . . . which I don't. . . . Should I wait for her to tell me she wants a kiss? . . . Should I be a manly man . . . take charge. . . . What if she doesn't want to kiss me? My ankle won't stop twitching. . . ."

We were on the phone a long time.

All for kissing.

I had to quit my chicken job, that was a given. I was exhausted from those extra hours. I'd paid off most of my medical loan, and I was making chicken chairs.

"I'm sorry, Mr. Pingle," I said, taking off my chicken head for the last time.

He took the head, then bowed to me. "Stevie Barrett, you were the best chicken we've ever had. Anytime—" He paused, pinched the top of his nose. "Anytime." He stopped, cleared his throat. "Anytime." He stopped. "Cluck, cluck, chicken. You know what I want to say, don't you?"

"Yes, Mr. Pingle, I do." I gave him a hug, and we both cried a few tears. What can I say? The man had hired me. He had been honest from the start and treated me as someone with value. He had been kind. He had given me a raise.

He had brought his mother to my chair show, and she had hired me to make twenty chicken chairs.

"You're a good man, Mr. Pingle."

He stepped back and put both hands to his cheeks. "And you, Stevie, you are a woman to behold. A woman to behold."

I invited him to the Portland Roller Derby Championship on Sunday night. He clucked right up with a smile.

Me and Zena also invited everybody at the office to the Portland Roller Derby Championship. Polly and Lance and Jake came, too, and cheered the whole time.

My skate name was, get this, Hell Fire, and I dressed in the fishnets, short black skirt, and red satin shirt as the other Break Your Neck Booties. I wanted to put my hands in front of myself and hide, but I resisted. I did not start, obviously, as a new, beginning skater. But I skated some, and as one after another of our players got hurt badly (the defense attorney broke her arm, the minister broke two fingers, and one of the full-time moms knocked a tooth out), I skated more. In the last bit I was in the whole time.

The noise was deafening, on and off the track, even when I was tackled and smashed into the floor, even when I got that girl back and smashed her. Even when we were all breathing hard to get around another curve and all those screeching women were swearing and trying to elbow and push. Who knew women could be so violent?

And when they were violent with me? Well, I pushed back. No more Miss Nice Guy.

And guess what? We won. As soon as we won, one of the Slice, Dice, and Win Derby team members tripped me and I landed smack on my boobs. I sat up and grabbed them. Yep. Still there.

I struggled to my feet but was tackled back down by Zena, who was so happy she lay flat down on me and hooted in my face. We were joined by our team, two of whom were still bleeding.

"Yadaleehoo!" Zena cried. "We knocked them out, we spat them to the ground, we smashed them till they couldn't groove!"

And then, up on our feet, our trophy in hand, all our friends ran out to us. Mr. Pingle had worn my chicken head during most of the game "to show you my support!" The lawyers were positively giddy. This roller-skating violence was way out of their comfort zone. Cherie hugged me and Zena.

Jake kissed me, even though I was sweaty.

We won.

We had won.

And I, Stevie Barrett, had a dislocated shoulder to prove it.

Jake kissed it.

Afterward, I saw Lance and Zena together, on the way to Lance's car. Lance hadn't needed to worry about when or how to kiss Zena. Zena took things into her own hands. She leaned against his car, wrapped her arms around his neck, and pulled him down. Lance, thankfully, appeared to know what to do from that point on.

I saw his ankle twitching.

I talked to Aunt Janet. She had not changed her mind about divorcing Herbert. She loved Africa and had found her calling. "Sweetie, Virginia knew of a doctor from Portland who's out here at a medical clinic who needed volunteers at the desk, and to comfort the patients, do basic filing and organizing, and so on, so me and Virginia volunteered! We've been here for two weeks and it's already home. I love it. I have purpose to my day, I have a reason for being, and I love Dr. Dornshire! You will never find a more compassionate, competent doctor!"

Small world, folks.

"We're going to have to say good-bye, Stevie, in about five minutes."

It was raining and it was early morning.

Jake and I had been up all night talking, and now he had to scramble out of bed for a flight that would take him to Venice.

"Please come."

"I can't, Jake. What about my job? What about the orders for my chairs?"

"You have vacation time. Please, Stevie."

I saw a sheen of tears in his eyes, through the sheen on mine, the early morning shadows swinging between us.

"The real reason, Stevie, is because you can't commit to me, or to us."

"Jake, I'm trying here. There's a lot in my past I haven't worked through."

"Then work through it."

"Once you know about it, you probably won't want me anymore anyhow."

"I will want you. I do want you."

I swallowed hard, and it felt as if I were swallowing a dolphin. "First thing. I'm not having kids. I mean, I want kids but I'm not having them myself. I'm not going to get pregnant."

He seemed a little surprised, but then he nodded and said, "I've always wanted to adopt, anyhow. Lots of kids need homes. Especially the starving ones in other countries. What else?"

I felt my whole body tingle with relief. Had he said okay, had he said he would adopt?

"Come on, Stevie. What else?"

How do you break a silence, a secret that had lasted for decades, and tell someone your mother was schizophrenic, she killed your sister, tried to kill you, the grief killed your grandparents, you became hugely fat, married an abusive man, and lost two babies, without him thinking you were too much of a loon with way too much baggage to take on?

"Isn't that enough for now? It's raining." I had no idea why I threw the rain part in.

He stared at me pretty hard, then said, "I have no idea what rain has to do with it, but I want to give you something before I leave, and we're running out of time." He pulled out a small box. Inside there was a ring, diamonds surrounding a blue topaz. "Let me be a little old-fashioned with you, Stevie. It's a promise ring. I want you to promise me," he said, as he slipped it on my finger, "that you'll think about us when I'm gone. That's it. Think about us."

My grandpa would have gotten along with Jake, man to man, I knew that. He would have said that Jake was a man with integrity, who knew how to treat a lady.

And Grandma would have said, "Praise the Lord, let your heart sing with his and let your destiny be bound together from now till heaven."

And me? In my head, I said, *I love you, Jake.*

He kissed me long and warm and passionately, and I kissed him back; then he walked through the shadows swinging between us and left.

He left for Venice.

I was not with him.

I had said no.

I was unprepared for the stark, cold loneliness that struck after Jake left for Venice. It hit me like a steamroller. My whole life got . . . gray. I walked in the morning, but there was no one that I hoped to see. His house was empty. I went to work, knowing we would not go out in the evening. I had many chair orders, so I came home and worked on those each night, as our derby team was taking a break. I ate vegetables out of my garden, but they didn't taste good.

The pleasure, the joy, the golden light, so much of it was gone. I couldn't stop thinking about him. My hands started to shake, and my insomnia came back. I missed Jake so much, my whole body ached.

I started digging in the weedy corner of my garden, then pulled out a cylinder container I'd gotten at the nursery and sprinkled seeds all over.

Wildflowers. This would be my wildflower corner. Helen had loved wildflowers.

I studied my yard. I had grass to lie on and study the stars. I had tons of vegetables that I ate, and gave away to coworkers and neighbors. I had rose vines growing up three trellises, one for me, Grandma, and Grandpa. I had a circular patio with a mosaic design of china plates for Sunshine, blueberry bushes for Lance, camellias for Polly, pink and purple petunias in pots, daisies, marigolds, and sunflowers, because they're miracles. I would have wildflowers in memory of Helen, and I had a bridge for my future.

My corn was starting to grow.

I had made something out of nothing.

That night I went to the attic and opened my hope chest. Me and Lance and Polly had shoveled things in there as quick as we could the day of my grandparents' funeral while Herbert was downstairs yelling impatiently, "This is not a vacation, for God's sake. Hurry the hell up."

There were two quilts, both made by ancestors. There were the dollhouse figures that Sunshine and I had played with. Trinkets and Christmas ornaments and framed pictures of all of us and of the Schoolhouse House. There was artwork by me, Helen, Sunshine, and Grandma. There was little girl jewelry and books and a tea set and stuffed animals and two dolls, both Sunshine's, that I had given her. There were our collections of buttons and shells.

Each brought back a memory.

I was up all night.

And I knew the time had come.

31

Ashville, Oregon—2005

Ashville had changed in twenty-five years.

I know when you go home, after leaving as a child, that everything usually looks smaller—your home, your school, your neighborhood—than you remembered it.

That wasn't the way it was for me. Ashville had grown, in particular its main street, which was about three times as long as I remembered. There were art galleries, three ice-cream shops, restaurants with outdoor seating, coffee shops, bookstores, even a chocolate shop. On the hill the old outdoor theater had been torn down and a new one built, along with a new indoor theater for the plays the region was more and more famous for.

I walked to the park and sat on a bench in front of the fountain that my grandparents had paid for and Helen had smashed through. Off to the side, there was a statue of a woman, which I paid no attention to as I watched the water splash, the kids playing, people around me chatting. What caught my attention was a blue jay flying by, three feet from my face. It flew to the shoulder of the statue and cawed at me.

I blinked a couple of times.

Blinked again, and stood up.

It couldn't be. The statue was of a woman smiling, her arms

out, as if she wanted to hug you. She had long, curling hair and was wearing a dress and cowboy boots.

It was Grandma.

There was a statue of Grandma.

I am not impulsive, and I am not given to public displays of emotion, but I couldn't help myself.

I ran to the statue, my hand to my mouth. That was Grandma! There she was!

Grandma. A flood of memories came pouring in, all the love and kindness that that woman had given me. Her strength under unimaginable stress, her compassion for people, her leadership as mayor.

"Oh, Grandma." I sighed.

I am such a sap. And I am so ridiculous. I hugged that statue.

It was in the midst of my tears that I heard a few women whispering behind me. I didn't even care. That's how far gone I was, floating around in my own well of emotions, my own loss. What did I care what a bunch of people I would never see again thought of me?

And then I heard it. "Stevie, sugar . . . Stevie, honey, *is that you?*"

"You didn't know that the Schoolhouse House is yours?"

I shook my head, dumbfounded. "No. It can't be. He said he sold it."

"He lied. It wasn't his to sell. It was willed to you, not to Janet, *to you,* in your grandparents' will."

I closed my eyes against yet another onslaught of pain.

It had been Aunt Teresa and her daughters, all about my age, who had seen me hugging the statue of Grandma. Tay, the oldest of the three and a liberal hippie, insisted that we all hug together and hug Grandma at the same time. All of us cried.

Tay said, "Oh, my God."

Her sister Shar said, "She doesn't know."

The other sister, Clem, said, "How could she not know?"

"I'll bet no one told her. Chad died six months after your Grandpa, and then the jerk who bought his law office got dis-

barred and then he went to jail for embezzlement and drug dealing and shooting a cat. Maybe something got messed up then."

"It was that muskrat-faced uncle of hers. It was him. Vermin
man," Shar said.

Things in front of my eyes started to swim and I had to sit
down, right in the middle of the square in front of the statue of
Grandma with her arms spread out, smiling.

"She needs something to eat," Clem said, sitting down next
to me. She had one long brown braid down her back. She had a
horse farm outside of town. "If she eats she'll feel better. You
sure are a *skinny* thing, aren't you?"

"She looks so much like her mother, doesn't she?"

"Yes, she does. Not the hair, but the cheekbones."

"The mouth is Helen's, too, and that heart-shaped face of
hers."

"Your mother was the most beautiful girl in Ashville," Teresa
said with a sigh. "No one more beautiful, we all knew it, and
you're just as beautiful."

I felt my chest heave.

"Oh, no, oh, no," Clem said. "Why did you have to upset
her?"

"Me? You did it, too!" Tay cried.

"You're always blaming us, Clem," Shar said.

"I am not always blaming you, but you didn't need to go on
and on. We're seeing Stevie for the first time in decades—"

"But we were talking about love!"

"That's all you talk about, you romantic fool—"

"I do not. At least I don't go on and on about horses—"

"You're always talking about your weird collection of—"

"Girls!" Aunt Teresa snapped.

"It's okay, it's okay." And, it was okay, in a way. I was with
people who remembered my childhood here. They remembered
people I loved. I burst into tears again. Gall. When will I not be
a mess? Losing weight had released all my tears, I swear to you.

"I hate that rat Herbert. He ran your grandpa's company into
the ground. Our town almost went belly up," Aunt Teresa said.

"We should tar and feather him," Tay said.

"That's illegal," Shar said. "So we should get Cousin Robby to do it. He'll handle it and not get caught."

"Perfect idea, Shar," Clem said, in all seriousness. "You do always know how to commit criminal acts without enduring the consequences."

"I do my best," Shar said. "And Cousin Robby learned a lot in jail."

"Sure did," Tay agreed. She nodded at me. "We'll have Robby right things for you."

I assured them we did not need to do that. I remembered Robby. He was wearing diapers the last time I saw him.

"This is an event! A historical day!" Aunt Teresa declared. "This, truly, is one of the best days of my life. Wait till The Family hears!"

The girls hugged me and I hugged them back, then we hugged Grandma again.

Oh, how The Family heard.

The ladies took me up to the Schoolhouse House. I saw the bell tower in the distance, then our shiny red doors, newly painted, the front porch where Sunshine and I used to play, the stained glass windows, the back deck where we'd watch the sun go down.

Tay lifted a flowerpot on the deck for the key, then they all stood back as I walked through the doors. I did not bother to attempt to contain my emotions. There was our kitchen table where we baked gingerbread men, the coatrack with Grandpa's cowboy hats on it, my Grandma's rubber boots, Helen's red heart chair, two antique school desks, china plates hanging on the wall . . . and I swear it still smelled of chalk.

There wasn't a lot of time to reminisce, though, as we were mobbed by The Family and former friends. They came by the truckload, one long line, and out spilled old people, young people, and all ages in between. They all ran straight toward me, arms stretched out, laughing and crying and kissing me, and crying more.

They came with food, loads of it, piles of it, too.

It was an all-day party, and I cried my way through it. We laughed, too, and I saw scrapbooks The Family had, pictures of my extended family, pictures of Helen as a baby, a girl, a teen . . . all her photos when she was in the musicals at school. . . .

"Your mother, darlin'," my great-uncle Marv said to me. "She was so sick. So sick. Your grandparents did everything they could. They were heartbroken. But I know"—Marv wiped his eyes and thumped his cane—"I know Helen loved you. Beneath the sickness, sugar, she loved you more than anyone."

"That's the truth," Cousin Melody said. "She did. I knew your mother, Stevie, before and after she was ill, and I know she loved you."

The stories came: One girl had no friends, Helen was her friend. Helen smacked one boy for teasing another, he was no longer teased. Helen sang Happy Birthday to each kid, every year, in her class. One kid was sick on his birthday and so upset he missed his song that she went by after school to his home. She was kind. She volunteered to help with old people in high school and taught songs to kindergarteners. She played tennis and let the other girl win the state championship, they all believed, because the girl's father had recently died.

And, during it all, I sat on the same couch I sat on as a kid. My grandma's things and my grandpa's things around me. I had gone upstairs, but then had to come back down.

"Not ready yet, Stevie?" my cousin Shar said, so gentle. I shook my head.

This is small-town living, folks. The ladies and gentlemen of that town had taken turns. Once a month the house had been dusted and cleaned and aired out.

"The Schoolhouse House," my beloved great-aunt Dorothy told me, "has been waiting for you. It has been waiting and waiting and waiting. We thought you knew and chose not to come home, darling, because it was too painful." She kissed my forehead. "We have been waiting for you, too. Welcome home, Stevie." Her face got all scrunched up and her tears burst forth like the Rogue River. "Welcome home."

*   *   *

There were hard truths that night, too, as some people stayed until well past two in the morning to talk. They *had* written letters to me in Portland when I left, but they all went to Herbert's post office box, which is why I never received them. They *had* called. They *had* come by to visit at the mausoleum and at Herbert's office to plead with Herbert to let them take me home or at least to come for a visit. Herbert had refused to let them have contact with me. When he had finished grinding Grandpa's business into the ground, there was no further contact, even with him.

"He got control of the company, because your grandparents left it to Janet . . . but she wasn't up to running it. His fancy lawyers got the papers drawn up and signed in Portland, shoving out the employees your grandpa wanted running it. . . . Herbert overleveraged the company . . . tried to expand. . . . We warned him, told him it would ruin the company. . . . He got into shady deals. . . . He took on debt, your grandpa never did that. . . . He told us he knew more about running companies in his toe than we did in our whole body, then he fired a whole slew of people. Brought in his own guys. They proceeded to follow Herbert's insane business philosophy. Two of the guys Herbert brought in ran off with the money. They were caught. It was too late. It was all gone. The company buckled. . . . We just hate Herbert."

Fortunately, at rock-bottom prices, a whole bunch of employees bought the company back. It was employee owned. They hired the employees back who had been fired, and the company thrived. "Your grandparents' legacy still keeps giving back to the town of Ashville through the company. Did you see the statue of your grandpa?"

I shook my head. "Only Grandma."

"We got your grandpa, too. He's in the park with his cowboy hat and boots on."

I had to see Grandpa, too.

"We cried because you had to live with Herbert," Cousin Tore said, wiping off his glasses when they got fogged up with tears. "So many of The Family tried to get custody of you, sugar honey, or at least some court-ordered visitation, but your uncle put his foot down, asshole. Your uncle Marky, your great-aunt Lot, your older cousin Richard and his wife, Claude, your second cousin twice removed Court and his wife, Tok. No luck. You stayed with your aunt. Now, we love your aunt, sugar honey, but we didn't want you with Herbert. I just hate Herbert." He sighed.

"Your uncle tried to get a restraining order against The Family so we wouldn't contact you. . . . His lawyers all came down and read us the riot act, threatened to sue, came after us for stalking, yada yada. Grandpa Thomas shot at the ceiling of the town hall again . . . had to go to jail overnight. . . . A bunch of your hot-headed relatives got into a scuffle with those slick attorneys, and a whole slew of them ended up in jail, too."

And finally, they thought, maybe it was better. Better for me to have a new life, step away from that tragedy. Not to be reminded. But, oh, they hated Herbert.

But hell. They were "so damn glad to see you, let me give you another kiss and a hug, darlin'. . . . I cannot remember a better day. . . . You're staying, right? . . . We're having a dinner tomorrow night. . . . The tractor pull is this weekend . . . pancake fund-raiser for the school. . . ."

It did alleviate somewhat the bitterness that had started to swell in me over what Herbert had done.

Hate is not a good emotion to have, but I was teetering on it.

I eventually thought long and hard about my decision but did end up calling Cherie.

I decided to sue Herbert. Half of the company had been left to Janet, half to me. He had run my grandpa's company into the ground with appallingly poor business practices that a fifth grader would have avoided. He had sold off all the farm equipment, the trucks, and cars and kept the money.

What Herbert had done was unethical and criminal. I would not let him get away with this. I would not let him continue to abuse me now or the child I had been. I would not let him skate off into the sunset without any consequences.

I knew now why he was so frightened about me coming to Ashville. The man was even worse than I thought. He'd taken money from a vulnerable child who had lost everything and then he lied to the woman she had become about a home left to her by her grandparents.

"Hee haw," Cherie told me, when I told her the whole story. "That's a clear case of breach of fiduciary duties and unethical behavior. A judge will slice and dice him, and we will nail him to the wall. Leave it to me, Stevie, this'll be fun!"

He will have nothing left, *nothing,* when I am done.

I moved into the Schoolhouse House. I slept on the couch. I did not, at first, have the courage to go upstairs. I walked along our stream and through the fields and into the barn. I climbed up into the hayloft and lay there for hours remembering all the fun me and Sunshine had there. I remembered the horses, the chickens—especially the chicken that thought Grandpa was her father. I watched the sun go down on the deck. I put both hands out on either side, as if I were holding the hands of my grandparents.

I heard their voices, felt their smiles, their warmth.

And then I had a vision of Sunshine. She was running around in front of me, blowing bubbles, her golden hair flying out behind her.

In the distance I saw Helen, dressed in black, alone on a hill. I knew she was crying.

I scrunched my eyes shut tight.

My grandma left the answers I had hoped to find in her old, hand-carved hope chest that was rumored to have survived the Oregon Trail.

It was their bedroom I entered first. I opened the two windows, then lay down on the bed, which was still covered in the quilts Grandma had from her pioneering ancestors.

The letter and the photographs were in a manila envelope, as were the playbills and the newspaper articles. They were next to a stack of love letters my grandparents had exchanged starting when they were young and ending about a week before they died.

At the time of her total collapse from schizophrenia in her twenties, onstage, naked, Helen had been in love with an opera singer named Ricardo Cabrerra.

Ricardo had been called one of the greatest living opera singers on earth. He had obviously come out to the farm, because there were pictures of him with Grandma and Grandpa and Helen in front of the Schoolhouse House and the barn.

Twelve months after Helen left New York City in a strait-jacket, he was found in a back alley of New York, dead of alcohol poisoning. The article mentioned Helen as his "serious lady friend," and her schizophrenic break. "This is a terrible tragedy," the reporter wrote. "It is impossible to overstate the blow that the stage has endured with the tragic loss of these two immensely talented singers, one to mental illness, the other to grief. . . . Friends say that Ricardo was devastated, unable to recover, after losing the love of his life. . . ."

I stared at the pictures of Ricardo in the newspaper. They had included photos of him as a baby, a young boy, a teenager, an adult. I stared most closely at a picture of him as a baby. Then I picked up a picture of me as a baby, which was labeled with my name in the same envelope.

Me and my father had the same dimple in the left cheek, same hair and chin. We were twins, only separated by a generation, and he was a boy and I was a girl. I found his old records in the chest, and I put them on an old record player we had in the attic.

He was unquestionably brilliant, his voice a full orchestra, soaring and dipping, crescendoing, each note clear and breathtaking, like a teardrop and a rainbow in one.

I found Grandma's letter. "My dearest Stevie," she began. She told me that Helen and Ricardo had been in love for several years. They'd had a passionate romance, which produced me. It explained Helen's break with reality, how Ricardo had wanted to take care of her, but overnight Helen didn't want him and called him "a snake who sings who put a little snake in me. . . .

A loud man, he changes costumes, the voices don't like him." Ricardo came to see me many times. In the envelope I found photos.

In one photo, Ricardo was holding me in his arms, smiling, his face inches from mine, his black hair shining. Helen was staring blankly at the camera, about a foot away from him. She was wearing one of those pink pajama outfits with the zipper and the feet, a bandana made of foil, and a piece of lace that she tied in the front of her stomach in a bow.

The other photo was me and Ricardo on the porch swing, and I choked up, my chest hurting, because even I, damaged and hurting, could so clearly see the truth: My father loved me. It was in his smile, the delight and wonderment and awe on his face.

My grandma and grandpa had told me that my father had died in an accident. I had always assumed it was a car accident. I hadn't pressed for more details than that, simply because I'd had enough to deal with and saw Grandpa as my father. My guess is that my grandparents thought the truth would have been too hard for a young girl already dealing with a schizophrenic mother. As an adult, there was nothing to make me believe he hadn't died in a car accident, and that was that. I did not want to venture back into my painful past.

I stared at my father again, at his expression, the love that shone right off that photo.

"Never, ever doubt that both your mother and father loved you, Stevie," Grandma wrote. "They did. They always did."

The newspaper reporter was right. It was a terrible tragedy.

There were newspaper articles about the mental ward Helen had been in with Barry, where she'd been insistent that people were burned up and put in cans.

Grandpa and Grandma had taken care of part of the problem.

They had Chad, their attorney friend, investigate, and then they'd sued the mental ward. The press got involved, as did the state government.

The cans were discovered.

The mental ward was under the gun for answers to explain not only the cans but also its "treatment and rehabilitation" techniques for its patients.

Those answers were sadly, sickeningly lacking, and the mental ward was shut down.

Tonya had been found in a can in a dark room next to Andrew.

Barry went to prison.

Twenty-five years.

For rape and assault against numerous female and male patients.

In prison he was raped and killed.

Too bad for him.

I never thought I would return to the bridge that me and Sunshine were thrown from and Helen dove from headfirst, wearing her best black heels.

Of all the places in my life that I wanted to avoid, that was it.

Knowing I must be clearly of half a mind, I drove The Mobster to the bridge.

I didn't sway over the yellow lines, as Helen had done, and it was bright and sunny, not raining like the devil had opened up a bag of cannonballs and dumped it, but I could hear her voice, her chanting, in my head as if it were yesterday. I felt Sunshine clinging to me. I smelled her, the soap and the lemon shampoo, and the scent of an orange Popsicle.

The road curved before the bridge, and I parked alongside it. In my memory, it was a huge, arching, shadowy evil *thing,* an instrument of death that had helped Helen obliterate Sunshine, the river a black, frothing, rollicking killer.

I got out of the truck and headed toward the bridge, the sun warming my shoulders. I walked to the approximate place on the bridge where I had been thrown over, followed by Sunshine in her pink dress and Helen in her black cocktail dress, the black lines up her nylons perfectly straight.

Instead of the draconian bridge I remembered, it was a typical, one-lane country bridge, crossing a medium-sized river, flanked on either side by woods.

A peaceful, quiet place . . . a crime scene. One murder and one suicide and the attempted murder of another. I was the "another."

I leaned my elbows on the rail and bent over to watch the water flowing underneath it. I remember fighting to stay above the river's current, screaming for Sunshine, and then listening to that echoing silence, the silence of nothing, the silence of death, the silence of aloneness.

I had been hearing that silence my whole life.

It had deafened me.

The tears streamed out of my eyes, hard and fast, strangling me, my shoulders shaking, my elbows barely able to keep me propped up. Is there a certain amount of tears we have to shed for the horrendous times in our lives and if we don't shed those tears we can't move on? Why do the tears have to revisit us now and then? Why do we feel better after crying sometimes and other times more hopeless than ever? Why does life have to get so painful that we think we're going to choke to death on our own tears?

I don't know.

32

Ashville, Oregon—1980

My feet scraped against rocks and I struggled to shore in the pitch-black night. When the freezing water was still up to my waist, I screamed, raw and primal, into that wet, black night. I yelled for my Sunshine, again and again and again.

Silence.

I remember watching the sun come up over the river, twisting my charm bracelet, still calling out her name, but my voice was scratchy, my throat aching, my tears unceasing. I had no idea how much time had passed. I only remember that I could not close my eyes in case Sunshine floated by and waved at me.

Mrs. Zeebach found me. She hugged me close, and cried, rocking me back and forth, telling me she was so glad I was safe, that they all loved me and my grandma and grandpa would be so glad to see me. She blew a whistle and we were soon surrounded by people, and I was lifted up on a gurney and they tried to put me in an ambulance. I told them I didn't want to leave, that I was waiting for Sunshine, and she was coming by soon, I was sure of it—someone stay and wait for her—and they promised they would wait, and kissed my forehead, and only then did I let them put me in the ambulance.

When we got to the hospital Grandma and Grandpa stumbled in and held me close, not even trying to hold back their sobs.

"Do you have Sunshine?" I asked. "Do you know where she is?"

They cried harder and moaned, and The Family came and held them up so they would not collapse, and I knew. I knew.

I knew that my Sunshine, my sister and my best friend, was dead.

Helen was dead, too.

But I didn't care about that.

I was so angry I released an animalistic shriek. I shrieked so loud I'm sure each person in that hospital heard it, every sick person, every hurt person, every doctor and nurse and custodian, but I couldn't stop.

I did not rest until a nurse came, Mrs. Do, Phuc's mother, and gave me a shot.

Right before I slept I realized I did not have my charm bracelet. I tried to tell Mrs. Do, but I don't think she understood my words because I couldn't talk right. She brushed my hair back and told me to rest.

I dreamed.

In my dream I was in the water with Sunshine and we were holding hands. We were in a river, but this river was bluish green, the water clear, rainbow-colored fish forming a magical world of enchantment. We could breathe underwater, and we saw a smiling octopus wearing a top hat and a laughing jellyfish playing a guitar. A mermaid swam by and brought us flower leis and shell bracelets.

And then a shark came by and ate Sunshine piece by piece, and the river was filled with blood and I couldn't see, and I tried to grab Sunshine's hand, and soon the water was filling my lungs and I couldn't breathe.

The shark was Helen.

My own hysterical shrieking woke me up, and Mrs. Do came in again with the shot.

There was not enough room in our church for Sunshine and Helen's funeral, so we had it at Ashville High School, where

Helen had sung onstage and brought in enough money to fund most of the sports and activities.

As I was told later, there was not a person in town who did not come. Main Street literally shut down for the day. Grandpa came in a wheelchair, pushed by Lance, because he had had another heart attack two days after Helen's and Sunshine's deaths.

The crying in that church was awful. I can still hear it in my nightmares. It's a relentless, low-hummed cry of raw grief.

I sat by my aunt Janet, who sobbed uncontrollably into a white handkerchief, keening back and forth. Polly held my hand on my other side. Lance bent his big head and cried while Herbert put a heavy hand on my shoulder before the service and said, "I'm sorry about your mother and your sister." I saw something, maybe it was a sliver of heartbreak in his eyes, before they shut down and I was being pierced by the same tightly controlled, cold snake eyes I was familiar with.

I didn't hear what the minister said. I didn't hear what the eulogists said. I didn't hear what anyone said to me. I was in a miserable fog. My head was bandaged where I'd hit a rock. Both my arms were bandaged from scrapes. I had stitches on my leg in two places.

Grandma had to be wheeled out on a stretcher at the end of the service because she couldn't stand up, was dizzy, couldn't speak, and had a bad headache. Doctors in the service attended to her at the altar while the choir sang another two songs. She was rushed to the hospital because she'd had a stroke. Me and Grandpa stayed in the hospital with her. They brought in two more beds, and nurses watched both Grandma and Grandpa around the clock. The head of the hospital was Grandma's second cousin.

I was so scared, so petrified at the thought of losing both my grandma and grandpa, I could hardly move.

I could go on for many thousands of words to describe the grief that me and Grandma and Grandpa went through, but it isn't necessary. I will assume you have an understanding here.

They had lost their daughter and granddaughter. Their daughter had drowned their granddaughter, then killed herself. She had tried to kill me. I was deeply grieving and hardly speaking.

They had trouble getting out of bed in the morning and aged about ten years in ten hours. Losing Sunshine literally took the sunshine out of their lives, and losing Helen was crushing. All they saw was darkness. I know because I was in the same darkness with them. There were enough tears in that household, between the three of us and The Family and friends, to fill the town's swimming pool.

The Family brought food and I ate. I kept eating. Eating when I was sad, eating when I was lonely, scared, anxious, depressed, grieving, crying. I ate. People kept offering me food and I shoveled it down. My shorts got tight, my pants got tight, and Grandma's friends bought me new clothes.

I didn't wear them, though. I wore an old pair of purple flower sweatpants, Sunshine's favorite, and a sweatshirt of Sunshine's. It was big on her so it fit me right. There was a picture of a white, fluffy cat on it. I also wore Sunshine's jewelry, all the bracelets and necklaces that we'd made together, and I cried over losing the charm bracelet.

Mostly I sat in our room, though. I touched all her things, I hugged her stuffed animals for her, I played with her teacups and teapots, and her jeweled jewelry box, I tried on her hats, I stacked up her books perfectly straight after reading a few out loud to her, I and made sure her night-light was on when I went to bed in case she came back to visit. I figured God had made her an angel so she could do that.

I made sure that our room stayed clean and dusted, but I left out a couple of games we were playing. One of those games was Go Fish, with cards. She had laid her cards down flat, as I had, when we'd gone down to lunch that day she died. I didn't touch those. I didn't even peek at her cards.

She treasured her shell collection, and I spread all her shells out on her bedspread and stared at them. When I was done, I put them back in her jars neatly. I ran my finger over her drawings and paintings and put stars on each one because they all deserved a star.

I spent most of my time in our room with the door shut. Sometimes I'd wipe my face with my hands and I'd be surprised at how wet my cheeks were from my tears.

But if Sunshine wanted to come down from heaven and bring me back up with her, I wanted to be ready to go. So I hardly left our room.

Except to eat.

We functioned, that first year. We *functioned*. I went back to school. As for Helen's room, I never went in there. I never, ever wanted to. In fact, if that room burned down to a crisp, I would have been happy. The door was shut, and though I saw Grandma and Grandpa going in there now and then, I never followed.

Grandpa never regained his vigor, but he went to work. Grandma did not fully recover from her stroke, but she continued on as mayor. The left side of her mouth was permanently drawn down and she limped on her left side. I know Grandma and Grandpa were asked why they didn't retire, and Grandpa said, "Because if I don't work my grief will come and get me and kill me. I must stay alive for Glory and Stevie. Stevie is our gift." Cousin Nora Lee told me Grandpa said that.

Grandma said, "I have to keep moving. If I don't, I'll die. Albert needs me. So does Stevie. Praise the Lord for Stevie. We love that child." Second cousin twice removed Shenandoah Michael told me Grandma said that.

So, we functioned. Neighbors and friends came by. Chad, Grandpa's attorney, came several times with papers, and he and Grandpa and Grandma closed the door to the den as they talked.

Grandpa and Grandma and I hugged each other all the time. I saw Grandma sitting on Grandpa's lap. I saw Grandpa link an arm around Grandma's shoulders as they stood on the deck and stared at the stars, or danced, slow and sad, cowboy boot to cowboy boot. I saw them kiss, long, gently, their bodies close. I heard them say, "I love you, sweetie, you are my life," and "It has been a privilege to be with you all these years," and "I thank God for you every day," and "I miss Sunshine so much, and I miss Helen. I miss our daughter. . . ."

I didn't miss Helen. Only Sunshine.

She was a stupid, stupid mother.

One Sunday night, after church, they invited me into their room and we played cards on their bed.

"Stevie, never forget we love you," Grandma said. "You're our gift."

And Grandpa said, "God knew what he was doing, sugar, when we got you. You are a wonderful lady. A beautiful person. You're smart and responsible, Stevie, but more than that, more important than that, you're compassionate and generous and kind. You were kind to your mother and kind to Sunshine."

And Grandma said, "You've been through way too much, honey, but remember that grief and despair and tears make you stronger, even though they are so hard to bear. The Lord never told us life would be easy, but he did tell us he'd be with us."

"I'll remember." I remembered Sunshine, too. I tried to forget about Helen.

Grandma and Grandpa must have read my mind.

"You're going to have to forgive your mother, Stevie," Grandma said. "She was sick."

"She loved you, honey. I truly believe that when she threw you off that bridge, in her mind, she was trying to save you from Punk and Command Center," Grandpa said.

"I believe that, too. I believe she was also trying to save Sunshine," Grandma said. "She always said she didn't like Sunshine, but she threw you both off together, and I think she was trying to prevent Punk and Command Center from getting her, too. Had she been well, had she not had a sickness in her head, your mother would have been the best mother ever."

"She was terrible," I said, that anger that lived in my stomach like a rock liquefying and bubbling up. "She was the worst momma in the world. She was mean and awful."

Grandpa sighed. "She left something to be desired," he quipped.

"Yes," Grandma said. "The tin foil, the antennas, all the voices—that wasn't quite motherly, was it?"

I knew they were trying to make light of a hideous situation, but I couldn't laugh. I didn't know if I would laugh again in my whole life.

"Love makes the heart softer," Grandma said, holding my hands. "Love heals. Love will get you through life, honey. It will make life worth living. Be open, all the time, to love, even when it's hard. Even when it involves your mother."

I shook my head. I didn't want to talk about Helen. I hated Helen. They understood, they so got it, and we had a three-way hug.

"Stevie," Grandma said, tipping my head up and kissing my nose. "I want you to know, sugar, that you will always have a home here. You will always have the Schoolhouse House."

My grandpa ruffled my hair. "Yep. It's yours forever, sugar. Our gift to you, because you're a gift to us."

I didn't quite understand what they were talking about because I had stopped listening. I was too miserable.

We played Fish. Grandma won. "Praise the Lord, I'm a heckuva card player."

Because of my graphic night terrors after Helen tried to drown me, I slept on a bed they'd brought into their room the morning after I was released from the hospital. Piled up in the corner of their room were thirty new stuffed animals that The Family had brought me. I often went to sleep holding Grandpa's hand.

Three days later my grandpa's heart collapsed and he died, in bed, with Grandma. She woke up with his arms still around her. I woke up, saw that Grandpa was dead, saw Grandma's tears, and I ran. I ran and I ran. Two of my cousins saw me running down our country road and ran after me, and our neighbors ran to the house. When I could run no farther, my cousins hugged me close.

Two days later, as she was planning Grandpa's funeral,

Grandma died, too. She had a massive stroke. She was holding his old Bible in her hands and was sitting in his chair by the fire. I found her. She had a smile on her face.

So I was alone.

Horribly, rawly, grievously alone.

Alone.

That was me.

33

⌒

Ashville, Oregon—2005

Iremembered my grandparents' words that I would always have the Schoolhouse House as I stared out at that river from the spot where Helen had thrown me over.

You'll always have the Schoolhouse House, Stevie.

My grandparents, in their infinite love for me, had given me the house, and the land, so that I would have it forever. So that I would know and feel their love for me, throughout my entire life. It was a gift for forever.

I snuffled, I sniffled, and finally I laid my head down on the rail and cried my eyes out some more. Ingloriously, rawly, freely, brokenly, I made so much noise I could hear nothing but my own pain. My grandparents had provided for me even when they were gone.

My own noise blocked out the sound of footsteps.

I didn't hear him come up behind me until his hand was on my shoulder. I whipped around, panicked, breathless, and there he was.

Uncle Shane. One of grandpa's many cousins through his father. I'd been told to call him uncle because he was about thirty years older than me.

"Unc . . . Unc . . . ," I stuttered. "Unc . . ."

"There now, there now, don't say nothin'. I heard you were back, child. I heard." Grizzled Uncle Shane pulled me into his arms and held me tight while I cried and cried, all over his overalls, all over his flannel shirt, while he patted my back.

We watched the sun go down together, his arm around my shoulder. We didn't say anything else at all.

The next morning I took a deep breath and opened the door to my and Sunshine's room. It was another wave of grief, pure and piercing, and I had to lie down on my bed and stare up at the green, tulip-shaped light until I could function as a non-whacked-out human.

The Fish game was right where I'd left it. In my head I thanked the people of Ashville for knowing not to move that game.

For the first time I flipped over Sunshine's cards.

Not a bad hand.

I picked up my hand.

Yep. Sunshine probably would have won.

I touched the dollhouse Grandpa made us, then leaned back against the pink walls.

Yes, there was grief, but something else was sneaking up on me, too. Happy memories. Fun memories, here in the Schoolhouse House that still had that smell of chalk, gingerbread cookies, and fresh-baked bread. I remembered the dinners at the table, and painting with Helen on the deck. I remembered her songs and that beautiful voice, how she belted out "Superstar" or "Amazing Grace" in church, and her quiet times, when she would pat me on the head or hand. I remembered Grandma and Grandpa telling me good night and Grandma's "Praise God" talks.

I had, for sure, let the ending of my life here completely overshadow the good. Understandable. I got it, I'm not brainless, but here, in my and Sunshine's room, I started feeling the good, the happy, the love of my sister and grandparents. I didn't feel the love of Helen.

In the afternoon I went to a family potluck in my honor in the park near the statue of Grandma. We walked over to Grandpa's statue, too, and I am not embarrassed to say that I hugged him, too. There were only 250 people there. A small party with The Family.

The next night I went back to the bridge again. Same time. Same tears, same breakdown, same mix of hopelessness and loss, but this time, when I was in the middle of my breakdown, I thought of running through the woods with Sunshine. I thought of the white butterflies we'd chased. I thought of the candied apples we made with Grandma and the kite flying we'd done with Grandpa.

I heard his steps this time as he approached. He had brought his wife, my aunt Sallie, and their three kids, who were my age, and two other kids I used to play with, and they said they were so glad to see me—was I staying? Please stay. Please move home. I hugged all of them, and it was a mini-reunion. A reunion at a death scene, so to speak.

"Dear, oh, dear," Aunt Sallie squeaked. "I am so sorry, but I'm so happy to see you, my love, and I see your mother's face in you."

For the first time, I didn't cringe, I actually managed a smile. My mother had been beautiful, after all.

And then Uncle Shane told them to be quiet and said, "What are you, rabid, charging buffaloes? All this noise. Give the girl quiet," and I was glad of that quiet, and we watched the sun go down, me and my relatives and a couple of old friends, their arms around my waist, and I was not alone.

I was not alone.

This time, I opened the door and stepped into Helen's room.

Her room had been cleaned up. Perhaps the ladies couldn't bear to have me come home and see what Helen had done with it. When I lived there, Helen's room was *her,* disoriented, disorganized, chaotic. She had refused to let Grandma help her clean it and wouldn't allow me and Sunshine in there. Besides piles of stuff, there had been her collections of rocks (to throw at Punk), feathers (she would fly away one day), and chicken wire.

But they had cleaned it, ordered it, so it wouldn't bring back a wash of chilling memories. I flipped through the neatly hung prom and performance dresses from high school and her career onstage and wondered what might have been for her, and for my father, and me, if this illness had never existed in the first place.

I opened Helen's hand-carved hope chest.

There were the playbills from her singing days in New York. Photos of her and friends and family. High-heeled shoes. Dried corsages. Trinkets and boxes of jewelry a young girl would wear and jewelry that was clearly worth a ton, as the Tiffany boxes reflected.

And then there were the artists' portfolios.

I took them out, one by one, then climbed up on Helen's bed and opened them.

I was so shocked, I couldn't speak.

Pages and pages and pages.

More pages.

Hand drawn, with charcoal pencils and colored pencils and pastels. Painted in oils and watercolor.

Me alone.

Sunshine alone.

Me and Sunshine together.

Grandma and Grandpa.

On the deck, riding on horses, feeding the pigs, running through the cornstalks, dancing, playing dress up and checkers, baking sweet rolls and brownies with Grandma.

We were drawn and painted, normal, happy, cheerful. There was nothing skewed or twisted at all.

In fact, each picture radiated love. Warm, soft, yellow and pink and *motherly* love.

When, when would the tears stop?

At Sunday church I was welcomed with great applause, and I hung out with only twenty-two female relatives afterward. We went shopping for bras and got ice cream.

Later in the day, same time, though I told myself not to go, I had to—I was called to the bridge. Why do we have to go places that hurt us? Is it because if we don't we won't heal? Is it because our brains have to replay those tragedies until we can manage them, accept them, deal with them? Is it because we want to save our sanity?

I don't know that, either. I simply knew I had to go.

As I drove I remembered my poor mother, curled up in corners, crying, saying she was "just a Helen" and couldn't talk because the voices said, "Shut up, slut," and I felt sick for her, sick for the sickness that thrived within her mind. I remembered her crying that she was a "no love person," that she should die, she should be a squished bug, a dead dog, a dead kitty. I remembered her raging at the voices, her hopelessness and despair.

I heard a lot of footsteps as I stared down at the river. This time they were all there. The Family. Uncles, aunts, cousins, great-aunts and great-uncles, and friends from childhood and their families. Uncle Shane told them to be quiet, and said, "What are you, a stampeding bunch of hippos? All this noise. Give the girl quiet," and I was glad of the quiet.

I needed that quiet, for my soul, for my sanity, which seemed a little more firmly planted, and we stood on that bridge, a mob of family who is never quiet, and we were quiet for a long time. I heard people sniffling, and I heard the sighs and the soft moans, and I understood them, I did. I was not the only one devastated by what happened here, under an eerie red-gold haze surrounding the moon with frothing clouds.

A woman started singing "Amazing Grace," her voice rising and falling, full and soulful and ringing, it seemed, with the sound of every voice over all of time that had ever sung that song in pain, in desperation, in pleading, in grief.

Soon they all joined in, each note mixed with a tear, hands on my shoulders, pats on my back.

Twas grace that taught my heart to fear. And grace, my fears relieved. How precious did that grace appear the hour I first believed.

And on that jam-packed bridge, as I struggled with my memories, I felt my soul go soft, and then it was as if I was on the bridge, but not, and I was floating somewhere above it, and I saw Sunshine, and beside her I saw my grandparents. My grandparents had their arms out, and in my vision I ran to them and they hugged me tight, and I bent to hug Sunshine, but she had grown and now I was hugging a woman, the woman that my golden Sunshine would have been.

I saw my father, black hair and expressive eyes, and he was holding me as a baby, and he mouthed to me, I love you.

And finally I turned to Helen, who was wearing a blue dress with the collar up and smart red heels, her blond hair back in a ponytail, and she was smiling at me, as a normal mother would, with love and care and gentleness, and there was no madness in her eyes, there was no tin foil or floppy yellow hat, it was just her, as she had been, as she was meant to be, before the schizophrenia shredded her from the inside out and made her his.

She held out her arms and pulled me close and told me that she loved me, loved me, loved me—she was so sorry—and I pictured myself saying, "I love you, too, Momma. I always did, I always will."

She kissed me on my forehead and on my cheeks, and I closed my eyes tight so I could remember that love. I wanted to hold it, hold that feeling, so clear, as if it was really happening, so that on the rest of my journey, I'd have that love close by.

Because I knew, and I could *accept*, that my momma had loved me. She had always, always loved me.

Schizophrenia had simply been in the way.

I sang "Amazing Grace," not loud, not quiet, but I sang it. I sang it with The Family.

I had one final trip the next morning. I drove The Mobster down to the river, then walked down the hillside to the place, a sandy crescent of land near a big rock, where Mrs. Zeebach had found me in the early hours of the morning after I'd been tossed off the bridge. I waded into the water.

In the daylight, as a child, when I could think again, I'd recognized where I was. I was directly across from the swimming hole, which was backed into a bay, a rope hanging from a tree that I'd swung from with Grandma.

I had felt guilty my whole life for not saving Sunshine, but as I watched the water flow past, and noted how fast the current was, I knew that saving Sunshine would have been impossible, especially at the age of ten, injured, in the dark, in the rain, and stuck in two different currents.

Impossible.

I am not to blame for Sunshine's death. I had almost died trying to swim to her, to rescue her. I had stayed up all night, much of it standing in that freezing river, soaked, horrified, shaking, waiting for her.

Sunshine's death had not been my fault.

I can't say I was happy with this knowledge, but it did lift an enormous weight from me.

It was a stunning day, the sun bright, the sky cloudless, but soon my feet started to freeze and I headed back to the rock and sat down, idly running my hands through the dirt and sand, sifting it, feeling its warmth, the river rushing right on by.

I touched something, and it wasn't dirt, and I pulled on it, gave it a tug, and there it was, tarnished and chipped and worn, but still together, every charm still attached.

My hands trembled as I studied each little charm—the clover, the cross, the flower, the dog and the cat, the house and the heart—then I brought it to my lips, and I knew that the tears would probably never stop, and that that was okay, that was my life. I would never be whole, in the general, normal sense, I got that, but I could be *me,* and be stronger for it, and do a head-banging dance like a hard rocker and skate like a booty breaker and paint chairs that made people laugh and think.

I could do that.

I could be Stevie.

I put my charm bracelet on.

I sat on the deck outside the Schoolhouse House that night.

I had no idea what I would do with this property. I loved it. I could not see selling it. But could I live here? Could I live with the memories? Should I keep it as a vacation home, somewhere I would come, on the Fourth of July, for the parade, for the plays, for the long walks in the park that followed the stream that eventually met the river that flowed under the bridge?

Would I be fine with that?

More important, was I fine?

I thought about that, being "fine."

Who was *fine,* after all, all the time? I don't even think it's possible. We're the walking wounded, the walking hurt and betrayed and desperate and fearful.

And yet.

There's so much to live for, too. Daisies, for example. I love daisies, and sunsets when you're sitting by yourself on a hill are mighty spectacular. Gardens that grow and bloom and produce carrots and pumpkins, and paints of all colors that can transform a white canvas into a flowing picture of truth, are priceless. Brownies are delicious, as are Mt. Hood, Cannon Beach, white butterflies, Halloween, seashells, old books, and projects you do yourself. They're all worth living for.

And love.

Love is so worth living for.

34

Venice, Italy

When God made air, he made it sweeter in Italy.
The hills shine with a golden glow, the grapes crowd the vines, the water runs bluer, and the Alps peek into heaven.

When he was done with Italy, he must have sat back and said, "By damn, I'm good. *Damn good.*"

And then humans came in and built Venice, on the water, rising magically, a city formed by sound engineering, lady luck, and angelic blessings. Even the pigeons know they're special. From the winding alleys filled with flower boxes to the canals and gondolas and gondolier songs, to the history that hangs in the air, the memories of millions of people floating around, Venice is incredible.

It's enchanting and exciting and miraculous. The only sobering thought is that one day you will leave and Venice will go on without you, on a feather, in a dream, a vision you can't quite grasp again.

I thought I would surprise him, in this city built on water. I had located the apartment he was living in, down an alley, around another one, into a square, his shutters green, his windows overlooking the ocean.

I waited on a stone bench and admired a fountain, carved hundreds of years ago, with diligence and care, by an artist who had his own life, his own losses, despairs, loves, triumphs, and disasters. That's what we forget, I think, with art. Art does not simply appear. It came because someone dove into it, headfirst, with their imagination and their talent, envisioned what it was, what it could be, and how they could take it there.

I smiled at that fountain, awed, and suddenly he was there, with that long gait, those broad shoulders. He towered over all the other people in the square. He was carrying rolled-up plans and two notebooks.

Nothing had changed, I thought, as I watched the wind ruffle his hair, but as he got closer, I knew things had changed. He was exhausted, deep grooves down his cheeks. For a minute fear clutched my throat and I wondered if he was ill. I gripped the sides of the bench as the water from the fountain sprayed up. What a project that artist had tackled. Surely, if someone could sit and chip away at stone for years on end, I could get my butt off the bench and say hello. He was thirty feet away, and I didn't move. Then twenty. Then ten.

I stood up. The pigeons around me flew up into the air, and our eyes locked.

Right there, in Italy, in Venice, by a fountain that someone had envisioned in his imagination, with love and with talent.

I smiled. Then I cried.

Jake dropped his plans, dropped his notebooks, his arms pulling me close, our tears mixing together as we laughed, and cried, and kissed. Right there.

In Venice.

Later that night as the moon, white and bright, shone through the lines of the shutters, I lifted my hands up. They weren't shaking at all.

My name was Stevie Barrett.

Before that, before Herbert changed it, before I lost me from myself, before the darkness ate me, and I in turn ate everything in sight, I had another name.

It was Grandpa's and Grandma's last name, and my momma's last name, too. Sunshine had the same last name.

It is mine again.

I planted a garden and ate my own vegetables.

I planted corn, watched it grow, and I didn't fall apart.

I built, painted, and sold chairs with soul.

I skated in a derby competition, and I dislocated my shoulder. It was fun.

I fell in love.

I am on a journey.

The journey is sometimes pleasant, sometimes wondrous, sometimes tragic. The journey is not done.

I am excited about continuing the journey, but not now. Not today.

Today I am me, and I am with Jake, and we are in Venice, and we are watching the gondolas, happy to be healthy, happy to be alive, happy to have today.

Hello to happy.

My name is Stevie Rockwell.

I love Venice.

Even the pigeons think they're special.

SUCH A PRETTY FACE

Cathy Lamb

ABOUT THIS GUIDE

The suggested questions are included to enhance
your group's reading of Cathy Lamb's
Such a Pretty Face.

DISCUSSION QUESTIONS

1. Which character in the book do you relate to, or like, the most? Do you recognize any of your own personality characteristics in Stevie, Lance, Polly, Cherie, Herbert, Crystal, Aunt Janet, Glory, Albert, or Zena?

2. What are the differences in Stevie Barrett's life pre- and post-bariatric surgery? Would you want to be friends with her? Would you have been friends with her before the operation? If yes, why; and if no, what would have prevented that friendship?

3. Discuss Helen. Did she love both her children? What would it be like to be Helen? How did the author build sympathy for her, even though she threw both daughters over a bridge?

4. What in Stevie's past brought on her obsession with chairs? What do the chairs reflect about her state of mind? If you built and painted a chair that was a reflection of you, what would it look like? If you built and painted chairs for each other, what would they look like?

5. Stevie and Eileen's friendship ends by the end of the book. Should Stevie have ended the relationship or should she have been honest with Eileen about the relationship sooner so Eileen would have had the opportunity to change? Is Eileen capable of changing? Would it have been worth the emotional energy for Stevie to try to change this relationship? What do you think of Eileen? Do you sympathize with her at all?

6. Were Zena and Lance a good match? Would you rather date Lance or Jake? Both? Neither? Why?

7. Describe Aunt Janet and her development from the beginning of the book to the end. Do you respect her? Was she a pathetic figure or a strong one? Did she fail as a second mother to Stevie and as a mother to Lance and Polly by not leaving Herbert? Did she fail herself in staying? How so?

8. Stevie's Grandpa Albert says, "Hardship, honey, builds character. Having struggles in your life . . . will make you a stronger, more courageous adult. Learning how to find joy in the little things—the stream that runs through our property, the mountains, art, animals, the weather—this will set you up for a life of gratefulness and that will give you happiness. People who don't have to deal with heartache, or don't allow themselves to reach out to other people who are enduring heartbreak, end up being shallow, superficial, boring people, sweetie, they never truly live, they never get what life's about, they never become full, compassionate, caring people able to live with wisdom and grace." Is that true?

9. Stevie's relationship with Helen was fraught with pain, guilt, anger, blame, sorrow, embarrassment, shame, and hate, but she comes to a sort of peace with her mother by the end of the book. Was this realistic? Will Stevie ever "get over" her childhood?

10. Stevie's grandparents were in a romantic, enduring love affair with each other. How did this impact Stevie in her childhood and in her adult life? What did Stevie learn from them about life, leadership, love, compassion, heartbreak, and family?

11. Stevie asked one chair, "If you had to compare your life to a garden, what would you see in it? Dead trees and bushes, stuck in the middle of winter? Weedy? Swamped with too much water? Drought filled? Blooming with a pink dogwood tree, tulips, daffodils and gladiolas? What do you need to cut out of your garden to make it better? What do you need to add?" How would you answer these questions?

12. Were there any scenes in *Such a Pretty Face* that made you cry? Laugh? Reflect on your own life? What was your favorite scene?

13. There are many serious issues discussed in the book: obesity, anorexia, childhood abuse, gay marriage, divorce, self-esteem problems, death, grief, relationship issues, mental illness, and so on, but there are also humorous scenes. Did the author balance the two correctly?

14. What are the underlying themes in *Such a Pretty Face*?

15. What advice would you give Stevie for her future? What advice would she give you?

GREAT BOOKS,
GREAT SAVINGS!

When You Visit Our Website:
www.kensingtonbooks.com

You Can Save Money Off The Retail Price
Of Any Book You Purchase!

- **All Your Favorite Kensington Authors**
- **New Releases & Timeless Classics**
- **Overnight Shipping Available**
- **eBooks Available For Many Titles**
- **All Major Credit Cards Accepted**

Visit Us Today To Start Saving!
www.kensingtonbooks.com

All Orders Are Subject To Availability.
Shipping and Handling Charges Apply.
Offers and Prices Subject To Change Without Notice.